The divorcétante

HONEY BLOSSOM PRESS

The divorcétante

MIA HEINTZELMAN

Also By Mia Heintzelman

THE FORTEMANI FAMILY SERIES
The Accidental Crush
The Wedding Crush
Last Christmas Crush
One-Night Crush

LOVE & GAMES SERIES
Monopolove
Trivialized Pursuit
Clued in Christmas

TERMS & CONDITIONS SERIES
The Friendship Contract*

ALL MIXED UP SERIES
Mixed Signals*
Mixed Match*
Mixed Emotions*

WASTELANDS ACADEMY SERIES
Devastated

STANDALONES
Fake Around & Find Out*
Mingle All the Way*
Married & Bright*
Wrapped Up in Beau*
Cozy Little Christmas

Available in audiobook

Dedicated to anyone who's ever been
told it's too late to start again.

You're invited
to our
Wedding Day

Prologue

One Year Ago

Ebony

Ellswood, Georgia

I'M ALWAYS AMAZED HOW SMALL, seemingly insignificant moments can change the course of a life. Everyday choices and actions that feel inconsequential at the time can set off a chain of major, unpredictable events.

Switch coffee shops and strike up a conversation with a handsome stranger in line.

Take a new airport route, get stuck in traffic, miss the plane… *crash?*

Take the elevator instead of the stairs, get stuck for hours with the musky Old Spice IT guy who knows all the office gossip.

Send the text, and sexy gym guy responds immediately with, *What took you so* long?

Romance, great coffee, a near-miss brush with fate, and the inside scoop are all potentially life-changing outcomes. Plus or minus the potential survivor's guilt, but endless possibilities.

Consider the tale of the "picture-perfect" couple.

At sixteen years old, a West Coast swim sensation's father takes a high school principal position, relocating his family to Ellswood, Georgia. The transition is smooth for him and his elementary teacher wife, but the daughter's life irrevocably intersects with the small-*ish* town prince, *er*…captain of the football team.

Be still her teenage heart, because the boys back home were just all right…but *of course* this boy is *super* fine. Tall, muscular, golden-brown skin, nice lips. Not to mention wealthy, and the eldest son of Ellswood's beloved late mayor and the Zion & Zara chapter president.

It's a swoon-worthy new girl and small-town heartthrob meet-cute, practically perfect in every way.

Of course he's gorgeous.

Naturally, she's interested. In no time, she's taking the long way to class just to smile as they pass in the hallway. She's a sophomore, and he's a junior, but wouldn't it be perfect if he was into her, too? If, like in all those high school relationships in the movies, the universe conspired to make their worlds collide on this tiny pinprick on the map? I mean, she doodled her name with his last name, and *Lord*, if it didn't fit like a one-size-fits-one glass slipper.

That must mean something.

In her heart eyes, they just make sense. They'll date and hold hands. As with all the best romances, tradition dictates he'll give her jewelry or clothing, preferably a gold promise ring and his letterman jacket, which she'll flaunt in the halls. And if things *really* go to plan, they'll go to prom. Twice. His and hers. It would simply be magic at work…

More like a dream, she thinks.

So, imagine her surprise the following year, when the stars align at the hands of their own matchmaking mamas.

New Girl and Cute Guy start dating for real. *For real!*

If only she'd known his pompous, highfalutin mama was a full-fledged "I'm not one of your little friends" mama. That there is no way on Reverend Al Green's earth she'd leave the fate of her precious son's future and her family's prestigious name up to chance. After deeming New Girl worthy, she hand-grooms her to be a Zion & Zara, poised and polished debutante...and future wife.

Ah, nothing turns a daydream into a nightmare quite like an arranged marriage.

Or waltzing in a giant white ball gown while discussing which fork to use during the fish course. Or politely nodding while everyone asks when you're getting married.

The pair is living the picture-perfect fairytale, but the romantic spell is broken.

If only New Girl could go back and convince her father to turn down that promotion, she'd be home, swimming and doodling the names of forgettable boys.

But, alas, the fated house of cards falls.

After college, she and Cute Guy return to Ellswood. He's still charming and still gorgeous, though spineless when it comes to his mother. She'll make do. Two years later, their high-society engagement ends as they jump the diamond-encrusted broom, sweeping them into a lifetime of Lifestyles of the Elite and Loveless.

Now, he's the charming anchor for KTEG *News at Noon*, she's a premier event planner, and they're nearing their tenth anniversary—yet every day feels like déjà vu. She works days, he's gone most nights, and in between they smile for the cameras.

If the quiet walls of their six-bedroom estate could talk... *Thank God, they can't.*

Dad's seemingly insignificant choice to uproot our lives. That flimsy, fated house of cards. That's what's been running through my mind all morning. Another spade—or likely, a heart—feels like it's teetering.

My husband turned off his location on his phone.

It's a small, seemingly insignificant choice that could be for any number of reasons. Maybe I can't track his phone because it died. Or what if it was stolen? Maybe it's just a poor GPS signal. Our anniversary's in two weeks—he could be taking *extra* precautions to keep his gift a secret. I don't know.

But I can't ignore it.

It's just one of the many things that drive me up the wall, makes me do outrageous things I'd never usually do.

Which is why my mind's on the private investigator who's been tracking Julian when Azalea and Yvette, the co-hosts of Ellswood's nationally syndicated *The Morning Tea*, lean forward across from me—across from *us*. I'm with my client, Josephine Carter, promoting the charity gala I helped plan.

Josephine smiles, her expression screaming, *Welcome back to the present!*

Dang it. What did I miss?

The hosts lean in closer, giving off that casual, knowing air, as if it's just them and the audience, conveniently forgetting the millions watching from home.

Any loyal viewer—or slightly spaced-out guest—would clock the moment.

It's the switch-up.

I've seen a couple episodes. I get their format. The segment's ending soon. Tea must be spilled. Expeditiously.

Then again, that viewer—*or guest*—might also notice the poised elegance of the two Black women on the garish faux-fur guest sofa. Across from the matching pastel skirt suits and asymmetrical lace-front bob hosts, we're a stark contrast. Ankles crossed, angled just so, posture impeccable. The younger woman—*yours truly*—radiating quiet dignity in her tailored navy sheath dress, her flawless four-carat diamond ring gleaming under the studio lights.

But when Yvette looks at me, I can't shake the feeling. She sees an easy target.

"Ebony Grace Livingston…" She dips her buffed and over-contoured chin, her deep brown eyes narrowing under a dark umbrella of eyelashes. "Now, I know you're here, it's the end of April, you're helping Mrs. Carter promote the Mother II Mother charity next month, but *girrrrl…*" she says, far too familiar. "Can we get personal for a few seconds?"

Absolutely not.

"How personal?" I chuckle.

Azalea gives a quick nod to the production assistant behind the camera, who holds up the APPLAUD NOW cue card.

The audience erupts in cheers, and all I can do is smile.

I *knew*.

Somewhere deep in my gut, I *knew* there was zero chance these women would sacrifice ratings for respect. My boundaries will be steamrolled in two seconds.

Azalea and Yvette are known for trending gossip. Anything scandalous or salacious is right up their alley. Especially when it concerns Ellswood's elite. They built their fame on the back of *The Luxe Ladies of Ellswood* (seasons seven and ten, respectively), a reality-ish TV franchise showcasing the glamorous, drama-filled lives of the almost famous. They want exclusive, shock-value content that seeps onto social media like poison—and they want to use me as the needle to inject it straight into the bloodstream.

That's why I initially declined to appear with Josephine. Somehow, charity galas didn't seem exactly titillating enough for daytime TV.

But I run a premier event-planning company, specializing in high-end affairs with meticulous attention to detail. I offer elegance, sophistication, and effortless luxury to a discerning clientele. Whether it's a lavish wedding, an intimate gathering, or, in this case, a charity gala, I'm there to deliver. Even if that means accompanying my client onto a nationally syndicated "tea-spilling" morning show—broadcast by my *husband's* rival news station—I'm all in.

I also made it crystal clear to the producer that my personal life was off-limits.

Pause, peace, power.

I inhale deeply, then lock eyes with her.

"Now, Yvette…" *Girl, you know you're so wrong for this.* I flash a small smile, then glance at Josephine before pressing a steady hand over my dress hem. "We're here to celebrate an evening of elegance and lasting impact for South Georgia's youth ahead of Mother's Day next month…" *Uh…Mother II Mother. The gala is the reason we're here… Lord, do not let this woman come for me.*

It's most definitely a warning that I pray she heeds.

Except her full pink lips curl into a thin, placating smile. Then she shifts her gaze to the audience, her expression begging for sympathy. *I tried,* it says. *She's the one holding out on y'all…*

A collective sigh echoes through the studio, but I don't feel the least bit sorry. So, the poor, gossip-slinging daytime host won't get the scoop. *And?*

And scene.

That's where my mind goes, but Josephine naïvely eats it up.

"Oh, now, Ebony…" Her face softens, eyes pleading with that polite grandma *hush now* look. "We came all this way. We can take a minute if you want to share a little something with your fans."

All the way out here. Everything in this city is a twenty-minute drive, but okay.

"For the fans." Yvette smirks, and my blood boils something fierce.

Especially because Azalea leans forward, stretching her neck to the audience, her smile wide as the damn Cheshire cat's as she nudges Yvette's shoulder. "Yeah, Ebony, *girl*, it's just a couple questions…"

A couple loaded questions. Ugh, why did I agree to come on this show with these tired, low-class, shady…

Again, that restless, low murmur stirs through the studio, and I take a deep breath, which does zero to ease my nerves.

Pause. Peace. Lord, find your power, Ebony Grace Livingston.

"I guess I can answer one." I laugh, but inside I'm daring either of these women to try me and quickly find out.

"Fabulous!" Yvette claps and squeals. "Okay, we had so many questions come into the show when we announced that *the* Ebony Grace, half of the picture-perfect Livingston power couple, would be here…" Then her gaze drops to my stomach as she says, "Speaking of Mother's Day…?"

I don't need to hear the rest of her question—the audience is already a chaotic mess with applause.

Oh, no she didn't.

Fury flares in my gut.

The sheer audacity of this woman, this *TV host*—in her pastel-blue Easter suit with tasteless white stockings and black heels—insinuating that I'm pregnant.

Unless immaculate conceptions are a thing again, we'd have to be having sex for that to happen, I want to snap back.

But I can't.

I *won't.*

Do not let them drag you, willingly, into a public scandal.

Hand to heart, I summon every ounce of grace, forcing a smile for the audience. "Our family is looking forward to the holiday—"

You heard it here first, blazed in her murky brown eyes.

Whoops.

"By our family, I mean Julian and myself. Only." I toss a shaky laugh to the audience then pat my flat stomach as proof.

No matter how hard I work to dodge the questions about marriage and children, the rumors continue to circulate. Everyone's eager to know when they can expect a baby Livingston. My husband is Julian Livingston III, the charming anchor for KTEG *News at Noon* and Ellswood royalty. After ten "kid-free"—Julian's term, not mine—years of marriage, this town feels entitled to our life updates.

How dare I deny them access to my womb?

I'm just the upper echelon's favorite former debutante turned not-so-perfect wife who cooks, cleans, and tends to her husband's needs, however fleetingly these days. Who cares if my company is thriving and that I've planned dinners for actual royalty when I've produced no offspring?

Yvette doubles down, glancing pointedly at my stomach again before she goes for the gold on the untouchable Livingstons. "Got any news to share?"

I'm half expecting her to just blurt, *"Ebony, do you feel like you're married to a ghost with your husband always working late?"* so I can shatter this picture-perfect façade. *"Why, yes, I do. Since we're down to super-sexy 'Missionary Mondays,' I'm 99.9 percent sure the man is gaslighting me and is sowing his royal oats elsewhere—but I need proof first.*

At least honesty's got merit.

But the way these women go about spilling the tea…it's stale, dry, and leaves a bitter aftertaste, like last week's coffee.

Determined to regain control before I completely lose my mind, I twist dramatically on the over-the-top faux-fur sofa. "Josephine, shall we get the *morning tea* on this charity gala, benefiting the kids?" I clap, awkwardly at first, trying to summon some enthusiasm from the audience.

The production assistants, fashionably late, finally hold up the APPLAUD NOW cue cards.

With a cool blast, the air conditioning whirs to life, sending a chill crawling up my spine as time seems to stop.

Yvette and I are at an impasse, staring, waiting for the other to make a move.

"Josephine Carter and Ebony Grace Livingston, everyone!" Azalea says, and Yvette beams, laughing for the cameras like they've just won an award. "Thank you again for joining us today on *The Morning Tea...*"

Yes, Lord Jesus, please *let's wrap this up.*

"One more time, tell everyone about the event, and how they can show their support," Yvette prompts me.

Another chill skitters over my skin as I suck in a breath, my head scrambled. Except it isn't a chill. It's that shaky Ace of Diamonds—my watch vibrating with a text notification.

My pulse spikes as I steal a glance at the name on the screen.

All morning, these women have turned my life into their afternoon circus while a private investigator's gathering evidence of my husband's misdeeds, and now, there's an update I can't check until this circus is over. Just when I think it can't get worse...my diaphragm betrays me.

HICCUP!

Josephine laughs and rubs her warm, velvety hand along my arm, smiling as if to say, *No need to lie. This is happy news.* As if hiccups are a telltale sign.

I know that old wives' tale.

My own mother has accused me of hiding pregnancies when I've had hiccups and fish dreams, or if I slept too long. But this? This is nationally syndicated television. I'm angry. Some people cry; others lash out. I can't help it if untimely diaphragm spasms are my body's mode of choice for anger release.

Ugh—

HICCUP!

Stay calm. Rivers. Trickling streams. Rushing water. Waterfalls…

"I'll take this, Yvette." Josephine smiles, shifting into business mode and quickly giving the audience all the gala details, before she hands it back to Azalea.

"Thanks again to our guests…" Azalea, eyes fixed on the camera, fans out a hand at us. Her laughter slowly fades, and her voice smooths into a measured cadence. "Coming up at the top of the hour on KTLE's ten o'clock news, our own Nora Whitfield will be sharing the details on the upcoming Zion & Zara cotillion, and the city's plans to sell and restore Ellswood's famous downtown luxury venue Madison Manor to its former glory. After this!"

And that's it.

My heart is in my throat, and I'm free to go check my phone.

Breathe, Ebony—

HICCUP!

The audience applauds of their own volition, the producer wraps the show, and Josephine and I graciously hug our hosts before exiting stage left—with me barely holding on to the little dignity I have left.

I let out a small, stilted sigh as one of the assistants leads us to the green room where we stashed our purses.

But before we make it to the door, the wide-eyed, braided, and beautiful producer—Christina or Krystal, I can't recall—appears in front of the doorway. She's geared up in a headset, a clipboard under her arm, and a two-way radio squawking from her back pocket. She looks like she's about to make us an offer we can't refuse.

"Mrs. Livingston, Mrs. Carter…" She gasps, clutching her chest. "*Oof*, I'm so glad I caught you."

"Slow down, honey," Josephine says, warmly. "Take a breath then tell us what's on your mind, hmm? We're in no hurry."

Speak for yourself.

Christina—*or was it Krystal?*—grins. "I just didn't want to miss you before you left. I was hoping to get a little more, uh, footage."

Josephine and I exchange confused glances.

"No, not with Azalea and Yvette." She chuckles. "More behind-the-scenes optics to promote the gala. The two of you meeting mothers, shaking hands, extending personal invites while touring the station…"

My gaze drifts to the small group of women gathered at the far end of the hallway.

"Oh, *wow*. Okay, uh…" Another hiccup jolts out of me. "I really should take care of this. I'd love to, but—"

"Shucks, yes." She slaps a hand over her face, shaking her head. "Mrs. Livingston, I'm so sorry. This must put you in a tough spot with you husband working 'for the competition.'" She air quotes and shifts to the side, wincing and quietly chastising herself.

I nod.

Honestly, I'm relieved. Between the message waiting on my phone and the nagging feeling that just showing up here is a betrayal to Julian, I'm ready to get the hell out. I almost lean in to the traitor angle, but a man's voice crackles over her radio.

"Kristalina, we need Nora on set. I've got to brief her on Madison Manor. Looks like it's about to turn into a bidding war."

She silences the radio, her stare intense. "Y'all have got to meet her before she starts her segment. After you meet the mothers, of course," Kristalina insists. "If she hasn't gotten a ticket yet, she'll want to attend the gala. This will be amazing PR for everyone involved," she adds, clearly winning Josephine over.

Who in Ellswood wouldn't want to hobnob with Nora Whitfield, the most famous Luxe Lady turned news anchor? Not only is she drop-dead gorgeous, but the woman is also a verbal gymnast—hence, why she's everyone's favorite cast member.

It's not a tough sell.

I'm about to nod when I catch the red light on the camera aimed directly at me. I freeze.

Is she setting me up?

There is nothing this town—*the world*—would love more than a front seat to my cracking on live TV. What kind of tactless woman—plus invited guest and event planner—would say no to touring the station and shaking hands with mothers and fans? What kind of "soon-to-be mother," according to these damn hiccups? Furthermore, who would risk passing up a chance to meet *Nora* Whitfield?

My blood runs cold.

The way her *Luxe Ladies* fandom will fabricate a narrative and cancel me so fast, it would be an immediate fall from grace. They've done it to others before.

I bite the inside of my cheek, weighing my options for getting out of this without confessing that I hired a PI to track my elusive, location-less husband and I need to check in with him, stat.

Flipping my wrist, I see it's already a little after nine thirty. "I really do need to get going."

"It'll only take a few minutes," Kristalina insists.

Tension tightens my throat as I glance at the green room door, my mind fixated on the message waiting on my phone. It sucks to wait even one more second to uncover the truth about Julian, but I force a smile to mirror Kristalina's. "Sounds lovely."

Despite my initial reservations, the first stop on the tour isn't bad. The moms gathered at the end of the hallway are all kind and sweet, offering hugs, flowers, and gifts to Josephine and me. They're amazing, asking questions about the gala and donating. We stand to the side, quietly soaking it all in while KTLE's staff—who are practically glowing, possibly from meeting "the competition's" wife—scramble to find Nora Whitfield, who's notably absent from her dressing room.

As the scene plays out around me, I think of soothing water signs, and my body begins to relax. The tension drains from my muscles, my shoulders easing down from their uptight set. Even my diaphragm, which has been holding on to that weird, staccato rhythm of a potential hiccup fit, lets go. The rhythm breaks, the silence stretches, and a small sense of relief loosens the tension in my chest. The moment of uncertainty, the pressure to perform, fades away.

Kristalina snaps her fingers. "I've got it!"

Josephine and I share a quick laugh, already in sync after years of navigating these types of things. We've learned not to ask questions, just to follow Kristalina's lead. She guides us around the corner and down a quieter hall to a door labeled simply, *Guest suite.*

The door looks like it hasn't seen much action lately—scuff marks line the wood, and there's a faded nameplate that's been there so long it's lost its sheen. It's tucked away, almost as if it's forgotten. This room doesn't see much traffic.

"She comes in here sometimes to clear her head before going on," Kristalina explains, her fingers lightly grazing the door handle. She glances at the cameraman, signaling for him to get ready, then turns to us with a smile. "All right, ladies…"

It's all very much a showbiz countdown before she drags in a deep breath and fans the door open, and my stomach drops.

My jaw drops. "Julian—"

"Nora?" Kristalina inhales, sharply.

At the same time, Josephine gasps, and the cameraman's breath hitches behind us.

The room goes still, but I don't have to turn around to know the camera is on me.

In front of us, on a lumpy blue velvet couch, is Nora Whitfield, exactly where Kristalina knew she'd be, half dressed, on her back, beneath my husband.

I knew it.

In my gut, I *knew* I shouldn't have come here today. I knew Azalea and Yvette would bulldoze my boundaries, just like I know—without even checking—the text waiting on my phone holds the truth. I'm alone in this marriage.

The red camera light glares at me.

"Ebony, are you okay, honey?" Josephine cuts through the haze.

The world is waiting for me to react. But the words won't come.

Every fiber of my being screams at me to lash out, to charge at them for treating our lives like a cheap reality show. I want to scream at Julian—tell him I'm not surprised, just disgusted that he chose *this* moment, in front of the cameras, to humiliate me. *Humiliate us.* And Nora—how could she not see she's just a pawn, stepping into a life she's only seen on Instagram and PopShot, desperate to take my place, wear my clothes, hold my title?

But I don't say any of that.

Instead, I dig deep into my debutante arsenal and smile. "Thank you, Josephine, Kristalina. It was an honor to appear on *The Morning Tea.* I sure hope to see you at the gala…"

And just like that, I turn and walk out, not sure if I'm leaving my marriage or just running from the truth.

You're invited
to our
Wedding Day

You're invited
to our
Wedding Day

Chapter One

Déjà View

Ebony

"THIS IS ON *YOUR* TERMS, Ebony." My best friend Whitney plants her hands firmly on my stiff shoulders, leans in from behind me, and whispers in my ear, "We are not letting these bougie, low-vibrational folks define nor destroy your happiness for one more day."

A small laugh escapes me at her theatrics.

"But do you *hear* me?" she presses, her tone serious.

I nod, fidgeting with the hem of my blazer. "Yeah, you're right."

"Tell me something I *don't* know." She sucks her teeth, then guides me farther into the restaurant's main dining area with a flourish. "You look fine. LBD, blazer, neutral heels, hair laid—basically the recipe for *we out here*. Now stop worrying."

Meanwhile, she's in a deep V-neck black satin crepe blouse belted around a gold sequin column skirt that pops like pixie dust against her rich brown skin.

As we weave through Velvet Ember's pristine marble floor toward the bar, my eyes wander to the menagerie of glittering chandeliers, hanging over perfectly set tables like a five-star zoo exhibit. Then to the eerily familiar faces, scattered around. They've been watching me since the second I stepped through the door, the low hum of their whispers filling the smoky, savory air. Each one is disdainful, more superior, sharper than the last, cutting through me like a thousand silent judgments.

You don't belong here anymore, they say. *Crawl back into your hole.*

Never mind that *I* wasn't the one caught with my pants around my ankles on *The Morning Tea.* Somehow, though, in the court of public opinion—half of it, at least—I'm the viral villain. Julian's reputation has taken a hit, yes, but I'm the "bad guy" who wouldn't just forgive the poor, helpless, handsome "good man" who'd clearly wronged me. I'm the woman who dared hire a PI to confirm suspicions of my husband doing dirt.

How was I supposed to know he was doing it with *the* Luxe Lady?

The funny part about it is, I still don't blame Nora. I wasn't married to her. And yet I exposed the problematic Luxe Lady's deeds with a married man. So, naturally, I'm the one who gets publicly criticized and attacked by #TeamNora.

But that's what today is about.

I may have been down for the last year, licking my wounds, but it's time to put on my heels again and strut back out there. Tonight, my girls and I are out for Hillary's younger sister Hailey's engagement party. She's marrying Julian's younger brother, Donovan, so I know they'll be here. Right now, I'm finally going to face them—on my terms. All I've got to do is get through this evening without cracking. It's the ultimate test.

I pull in a long breath, letting it expand my lungs, before slowly exhaling.

You are Ebony Grace Livingston. You've got this.

My skin prickles with discomfort as I imagine their pitying smiles, and that familiar, dizzying fear crawls over me. *Damn, I don't got this.*

"Nope, I can't do this." My breaths grow fast and shallow. "I'm out."

I try to turn back toward the door, but Whitney steadies me.

"See Priscilla and Hillary, at the bar, wildly waving us over? It's just a regular Saturday night. You're here with your girls to celebrate Hailey and Donovan," she insists. "That's it. Neither Julian nor that trifling woman are going to matter, because this is your 'take back your life' moment, okay? Reclaim your identity."

My heart stalls.

Reclaim your identity.

For a beat, I let those words sink in. I block out all the faces, all the noise, and pull in a deep breath. Then I release it, along with all the tangled emotions around my divorce and the challenge of keeping my life—and my circle—close to my chest this past year.

Just me and my girls, I tell myself as I lift my hand into the air and repeat the mantra to myself. "No one else matters."

"Mm-hmm, *they* know, but do *you* know you're *that* girl?" Whitney, going above and beyond her best-friend duties, keeps lifting me up like it's her full-time job. "Don't go cowering, Miss Thang. *Command* their respect," she preaches, clearly channeling her inner Oprah as she stares a few bougie folks down on my behalf.

Admittedly, I feel a little more pep in my step.

"I know that's right. *Strut* for 'em, Ebony queen!" she hypes me up, snapping in time with my footsteps.

From the back, Priscilla—in an infinitely more couture LBD than me—chimes in, "*Yesss,* louder for the people in the back!"

By the time we get to the bar, it's Black Girl Magic in full force. It's all hugs and laughter with my girls, and I'm light as a rock.

At thirty-five, it feels so good to still be tight with the same crew I've had since I was sixteen, preparing for my grand social debut. As a little sister, Hailey's an honorary member, but, really, it's been the six of us—us four in town and two, Chanel and Tatiana, currently off globetrotting and scheming world domination. We jokingly call ourselves the Divatantes—the perfect mix of diva and debutante. Whether society is ready for us or not, we come in with equal parts high drama and old-school charm. Lord, if we don't wear our titles like sparkling tiaras…

"Hey, glad you made it." Hillary side-hugs me, sly smile in place as she tells me "everyone" is already here, then, with five simple words, answers my silent prayers: "We've got a private room."

"Hil…" I deflate against her tall, lean frame, relieved and laughing. I'm floating on Cloud 99 Problems but Public Humiliation Ain't One, and it feels *good*.

Hillary's smile is positively wicked. "Shall we?"

"Say less, friend." I tuck my clutch under my arm, straightening. "Where you go, I will follow."

She turns on her six-inch red-bottom black pumps and works the marble like a catwalk queen in her black cashmere midi-length dress. My posture is ramrod straight, shoulders back, chin high as I file in line with Priscilla and Whitney on my heel—gliding like a sexy royal processional past the bougie, low-vibrational set.

It feels amazing.

For the few seconds it takes for us to cross the dining room and turn the corner to the private party rooms, *I* feel amazing.

I'm with my girls, the great times are ready to be had, and for the first time in a year, I'm me again.

Then Hillary swings open the door.

It's not April Fool's Day, but we're barely ten days into May, and the spotlight is on me. All conversation dies in an instant. A dozen pairs of eyes snap to mine, and I freeze.

Then I see him.

The dark brown eyes attached to the man who shattered everything.

Julian Livingston III.

It's like a warped déjà vu.

All over again, it's the switch-up.

Fire ignites in my chest, searing through my veins, and for a moment I can't breathe. My stomach churns as I quickly shift my attention, searching the party for Nora's long, dark waves, her striking green eyes, and...

You've got to be kidding me.

Where is Nora?

I'm here on purpose, because my life coach said seeing Julian and Nora together, confronting the two people who bulldozed my life—on my terms, mind you—would work. It should've been simple. I face my demons, celebrate one of my best friend's little sister's happy news, then close this catastrophic chapter for good. But how am I supposed to do that?

There's only one demon here.

Dammit.

I scan the room again, my gaze drifting past Donovan, Nelly, and Cornelia—Julian's younger brothers and mother—then to the Winstons, Hailey and Hillary's parents, and a few women who I assume are her friends. But my focus snags on Hillary. She's settled in the chair beside Julian, sharing a quiet, but *heated*, exchange. Like, she is letting him *have* it. As in, the full riot act with her unblinking brown eyes locked on mine.

What are you doing, Hil?

I shake my head, a nervous laugh dissolving into a hiccup before I can stop it.

"Should we maybe regroup?" Whitney whispers in my ear, her voice a low warning. A *reminder*. "Let's make a quick restroom stop," she says, then plasters a smile on her face as she meets Hailey's concerned gaze. "Uh, we'll be right back. She saw someone in the same outfit. We may need a moment to recalibrate the whole vibe…"

She moves quickly, leading the way.

Priscilla falls into step behind us.

As soon as we're inside the decked-out restroom, Whit spins around, her stare immediately softening. "We're still here for Hailey and Donovan. Forget about Julian and—"

"Hold up." Priscilla grows still, as if she's listening for movement—presumably Nora's. She scans the stalls, nods when she's sure we're alone, and locks the door behind us. "All right, it appears she's not here, but it's not a big deal. Let's just have a few drinks, toast, and then I'll make up some excuse why we've got to leave."

I give a single nod.

The thing is, it's not that I *needed* to see Nora Whitfield, per se. I guess I just built it up in my head, what it would mean about *my* growth. If I could come face to face with them as a couple, and still be okay, I was healed—ready to start a new chapter.

More than anything, I'm disappointed she isn't present tonight.

Whitney starts pacing, flexing her fingers restlessly. "I know it's a letdown. I, myself, had a few *choice* words for that woman—"

"And what about Hillary?" I cut in, my head still scrambled. "I mean, I appreciate it, but she's got no shame at all. Did you see her all up in his ear, letting him have it? Why would she confront Julian with Cornelia right there?"

A small laugh rumbles over me.

My plan was all about killing them with kindness—look fierce, wordlessly show them they didn't win, and that I'm still standing. But calling him out in front of his mother? And at her sister's engagement party, no less? Even I'm not that ruthless. Hailey's the little sister I never had. I've always been there for her, selling

Summit Sisters cookies for that dumb doll Mrs. Winston wouldn't buy, driving her to school when Hillary had majorette practice. I love her like family. She doesn't need me stirring up messy post-divorce drama at her celebration.

"Honey, you already know Hil is a wild card." Whit dips her hand into her hair, zhuzhing up her curls and laughing.

"Mm-hmm." Priscilla shakes her head, her expression twisting. "Are you at all curious what she was saying? Because from where I was standing, she looked like she was putting that man to shame."

I scratch my temple, grinning.

A million and one scenarios run through my mind as I try to decipher how Hillary put Julian in his place.

"Hands down, she rubbed it in his face about the news station firing him." Whit laughs. "God don't like ugly, and KTLE sure doesn't like unprofessional conduct or a PR crisis that damages their reputation."

"And that's on period." Priscilla snaps her fingers and crosses the huge, ritzy restroom's black marble floor to us.

We all collapse into a fit of laughter.

The tension in my limbs loosens. If there's one thing my girls are going to do, it's aid and abet #TeamEbony. Their pettiness is giving *we ride at dawn*, and I'm all the way here for it.

We love to say that when people go low, we can always, *always* go lower.

"Okay, well, then…" Priscilla's lips twitch. "Should we go cheers Hailey, and add our two cents to Hil's?"

I'm still smiling, but I don't move.

"I know, girl." Whitney nods, sympathetically, like she senses I'm shifting my guards back into place.

The energy in the room begins to wane. They're waiting for me to decide what comes next, but honestly? I have no idea. Right now, I'm just numb. The hurt always overtakes the anger. This year, Julian and I have shared nothing more than awkward smiles and stilted phone calls—talking about trivial things like where to find stuff around the house, or the Wi-Fi password, or some client he referred because, of course, he still thinks we can be friends. But we haven't *really* interacted. That's been all on me.

I'm still trying to unravel myself from the Livingstons, trying to remember who I was before him—who I want to be now as Ebony Grace...

I stop pacing and stare at the textured beige wall, suddenly exhausted.

"All the work I've done this year?" I pause, still reflecting. "Like, just to survive this mess, I have a therapist and a life coach—"

"A damn good one, too," Whitney chimes in, nodding like a proud sister. "Savannah Sampson is no joke. I saw that star-studded special she did..."

"The one last year?" Priscilla dips her chin, immediately invested.

"Mm-hmm," Whit confirms. "Had me all up in my head, feeling some type of way—"

"Can we stay focused?" I cut them off, walking over to the sink and bracing myself against the smooth, cool surface. "I've still got to do this," I say, unsure if I'm speaking to them or to my own reflection at this point.

"You're right." Whitney gives a decisive nod. "So, how do you want to do this? Because I'm absolutely still *game* to march right back in there and throw hands in this vintage ensemble if that's what it takes."

Before I can even respond, a heavy knock on the door startles us, and we freeze in place.

"Guys, it's me," Hailey's high-pitched voice squeaks through the door, strained and panicked.

Priscilla and Whitney exchange a glance, both giving me the "your call" look, but I'm still not ready to face the symphony of awkwardness waiting for me on the other side.

"Who is me?" Whitney grins mischievously, buying me some time.

"It's Hailey! Can you please let me in?"

Sensing I'm still not ready, Priscilla jumps in. "What's the password?"

The three of us burst out laughing, the tension in the room finally breaking. After a beat, I finally—*begrudgingly*—unlock the door.

My girls fall into formation at my sides as the door swings open. Instead of entering, Hailey steps aside—and there's Julian Livingston III.

She hesitates like she's struggling to find the right words. "Okay, before you come for me, let me say that Hil and I *both* tried to talk him out of this."

"And by 'this,' you mean what?" Whit glares at Julian, too. "What could you possibly need to say to Ebony—on such a wonderfully festive occasion—to excuse your sorry self?"

Julian nods repeatedly. "You're right. I deserve that."

A collective "mm-hmm" echoes over us four women.

I love my friends.

Hailey takes a shaky breath, stepping farther into the restroom. "Ebony, I'm sorry. I didn't want to ambush you like this," she starts, her voice thick with guilt. "I know you're angry, and you have every right to be. But I *really* didn't want him begging or whatever he's hellbent on doing in front of the entire room. Even Cornelia told him to let the past go, but he when he saw you—"

"I knew this was my shot." Julian's deep, bass-filled voice reverberates around us as he inches toward the doorframe.

But Whit and Priscilla step in front of me like bombshell bodyguards.

"It absolutely is not," Priscilla snaps. "And you're good right where you are. We're listening."

My divas are seconds from choosing violence, and I'm tempted to let them.

But then Hailey gives me a pleading look.

"Ebs, if this were any other time, I wouldn't even entertain this fool. But it's Donovan's brother, and he wants him here—please, just give him two minutes so we can get back to my engagement party…" She trails off, guilt-tripping me with zero shame. "You know, the reason we're all here tonight to celebrate."

Then she steps back slightly, her face full of hope, yet giving me the space I need to make my decision. God, she looks so much like Hillary. Same petite, honey-toned skin, dark hair, and striking features.

There's a clear difference between the Winston sisters, though. Hillary's a loose cannon, a goal getter, while Hailey's empathetic, kindhearted, always thinking of others.

It makes me listen a little more closely.

The divas shoot me "say the word and I'll still throw hands right now" looks. When I glance back at Hailey, her expression is so raw and vulnerable.

I shake my head and let out a sigh.

"Fine." I step around my gorgeous shields, folding my arms across my chest, an impatient edge to my voice as I peer up at Julian. "Say whatever you've got to say."

"Thank you." He smiles, softly, all sparkly eyes and gleaming white teeth as he drags in a sharp breath. "Can we talk alone—"

We all shout in unison, "No!"

He chuckles sheepishly, then shifts nervously on his feet. "Okay, sorry, I had to try. I just… All I want to say is, please, let me *try* to win you back. I know I messed up, but I'm asking for a chance to make it right. I'm not asking for forgiveness yet, just time to show you I can be better, that I can be the person you fell in love with. *Please*, just give me this one shot." He swallows hard. "I swear, it was just the one time—"

A collective gasp falls over us.

Ta-da!

Wow, how lucky am I that he swears it was just the once? My heart is an angry mob of ventricles and nodes, contracting so fast, I feel like I might short-circuit.

"Are you serious right now?"

"Baby, I'm not with Nora anymore," he says with the full weight of his chest, as if it makes a lick of difference to me. "That's why she isn't here. I ended it. To be with you. I love you, Ebony Grace Livingston."

Fury flares in my gut, burning hotter with every passing second. How is this man love-bombing me like he valued anything we shared? The gaslighting is embarrassing. Does he really expect me to believe he's made this huge change? The sheer audacity eats at me, twisting my insides with the absurdity of it all. Even if I was stupid enough to believe him, it's exhausting and pointless. Once was all it ever needed to be.

"I don't want you back, Julian."

It's all I say.

If I had the good sense the Lord gave me, I'd congratulate Hailey and Donovan, down a glass of champagne, and be halfway to my divorce-decreed Lexus, burning rubber all the way to my waterfront townhouse (also decreed). I'd crash into bed and sleep like a baby knowing I'd faced at least one of my demons.

But apparently, I'm running on empty when it comes to common sense, because here I am—back in the "private room," standing against the wall, wineglass nowhere in sight to help me drown out my ex-husband's weak pleas for a second chance in my ear. No, because that would require logic, and as we've established, logic has left the building.

Beside me, Julian attempts to hold my hand, and I pull it out of reach.

"I won't give up," he whispers.

"Mm-hmm." I smile ahead, doing my best to look casual as I elbow him. Through gritted teeth, I urge him, "Please, give up and go sit down."

Donovan's chair screeches as he stands, grabs Hailey's hand, and turns to the table.

"I never thought I'd be standing here today, celebrating with you all, but here we are," he says. Hailey beams that infectious grin, going on about how incredibly lucky she is to have found someone who makes her laugh, supports her, and loves her. Then they toast to their engagement.

The room erupts with cheers and whistles.

"I'm about to marry the man of my dreams, and there's nothing more perfect than a fairytale wedding," Hailey gushes, her bright brown eyes locked on me. "One that only Ebony Grace can bring to life."

"Hear, hear!" Julian says, loudly drawing everyone's attention. "You're so fortunate to have found your perfect match." He takes a slow breath, his gaze flickering between Hailey and me. "Some people spend years figuring out what that really looks like. Others don't realize it until it's too late…"

His eyes briefly meet mine, the weight of his words hanging in the air.

What the hell?

The applause that follows is so loud it's almost a physical blow. My skin prickles. For a second, the air shifts. I try to tune it out, but my brain is fixated on the APPLAUD NOW cue cards. I can almost see them floating in front of me.

All over again, it's the robotic, foggy applause, hands suspended midair, faces contorted with amusement. I'm stuck in that never-ending loop, trapped in a spotlight moment. I can barely breathe.

They're all laughing.

Everyone knows what happened with Julian. They *saw* him humiliate me.

My throat tightens and my heart drums a solo against my ribs.

"I'd love nothing more than to plan your perfect day," I say to Hailey and Donovan, not even bothering to acknowledge Julian.

He doesn't get it. While I plan weddings, I'm not sure *I* even believe in happily ever after anymore. Not for me. So, yeah. I'm actually glad he cornered me by the restroom. He did me a favor. Now I *know* I don't miss him. I don't care whether he's with Nora or anyone else. That chapter is closed. All I want to do now is work on rebuilding my brand and putting my business back on the map.

A weight lifts off my shoulders.

But as Hailey starts walking toward me with her arms outstretched, I catch Cornelia's smile.

That smile.

It's not her usual *I've got the winning hand, and you're not invited to the game* smile, no. I know Cornelia's self-satisfied little grin when she's glowing with superiority. That same smile she had when she told me I'd never make it without her son.

This one's sinister, laden with warning. I saw it when the divorce was final. I got my car, money, priceless waterfall paintings, and a townhouse big enough to hide from her—*and* I got Ebony Grace Events. What really burned her up was knowing that Julian, despite her advice, gave me full control of my business. He relinquished his ownership. Without a second thought, I cut him loose, cut the Livingstons loose.

She was seething mad then, and now, not only has her son's reputation been dragged through the mud along with mine, but he's also lost his coveted job.

He's floundering without *me.*

Now, after his "perfect match" speech, Cornelia's smile is a warning. She doesn't want me anywhere near her precious son. She's got nothing to worry about there, but it couldn't hurt to let her believe she does, could it?

And now I'm smiling.

"Ebs, if anyone can make it happen, it's you." Hailey pulls me into a tight hug. "And you can bring a date, too—obviously, I want you to attend as a guest as well as plan things." She starts rambling about her vision board and a June—*maybe* a September—wedding, and I'm only half listening when she says, "Can you just imagine how elegant it'll be? Donovan and I, the first couple in ages to dance underneath the magical crystal chandelier...fall florals inside the grand ballroom at Madison Manor..."

My brain checks completely out.

Madison Manor.

An immediate jolt of tension rushes through me. It's slated to be restored and transformed into a luxury venue for public events. Formal gardens, extravagant rooms, an even grander ballroom—the whole nine. Last year, around the time my life got flipped-turned upside down, there was a whole bidding war to buy the historical mansion.

Cornelia won.

Oh, no.

I mean, somewhere in the back of my mind, I knew Hailey would ask me to plan her wedding. Actually, I was counting on it. A year's hiatus has been a death sentence to my bottom line. So, after sulking and therapizing my life's hangups, it's time. And how amazing to foray back into the event-planning scene for the powerful and privileged with a wedding in a legendary venue? Naturally, I knew that meant I'd be dealing with the mother of the groom. But it's only just now, in this very moment, it's hitting me that the "MOG" of the Winston Livingston wedding is Cornelia Livingston.

My ex-mother-in-law.

The recurring subject of many a therapy session, whom I've actively distanced myself from.

The spanking new owner of this premier venue.

She's the groom's mother.

And now I know what's behind that smile.

I close my eyes on a deep exhale, because *of course* this no-expense-spared dream wedding—that *will* put my business back on the map in a huge way—comes with a hefty price tag. Just to make things extra *fun* (because my life isn't complicated enough already), I'll have the dual honor of dealing with her as the mother of the groom and the venue owner.

Lovely.

"I can't wait to see what you dream up!" Hailey squeals.

Neither can I…right after I beg my life coach to work me in for an emergency session—because clearly, I'm about to need some serious therapy.

(410) 555-3269

Chapter Two

Decreed and Declared

Lincoln

"IT'S A TRUE PRIVILEGE TO stand before you today as we begin this monumental journey—one that will restore and preserve a vital part of our shared history…" I pause, golden ceremonial shovel resting in hand as I take in the late morning light cast over city officials and community members, and I smile at my family, friends, and crew.

Vincent, my interior design partner, already sensing I'm in my feelings and may get long-winded, groans comically loudly, adding some levity.

"*Aw*, now here we go…"

I bark out a laugh. "What? I can't celebrate this centuries-old building and rally community support?"

Put me in a room where people are debating politics, religion, or global issues, and I'm content to step back and listen. Sports, books, a compelling documentary, or even an eighties Black sitcom? Absolutely, I'm all in. But hand me a commemorative shovel, gather a small crowd around a dirt mound, and ask me to discuss architectural design—those grand staircases, the stained-glass windows, the crown molding that embodies the craftsmanship symbolic of our town's fabric—well, that's a conversation I'm always ready for.

Vincent waves me off, muttering under his breath. "It's way too hot for all this," he complains, shaking his head. "You should know better than to have everyone out here in this late-May humidity."

My guys, Josiah and Dom, are in the back, cracking up, probably wagering on the over-under of my speech time.

"You've got this, man!" they yell, still cackling.

"In all seriousness, though, I know it's humid, everyone's ready to get to the tour, and you don't want to listen to me rambling on." I straighten, pride swelling within me. "The long and short of it is, Madison Manor has long been a cornerstone of Ellswood's rich heritage and a beacon for our promising future…" Emotion lodges in my throat, stealing my words. I manage a small smile.

The crowd erupts in applause.

Half of me knows it's time to wrap up my speech, toss the ceremonial dirt, and get these folks out of this heat and onto the catered tour. But the other half is holding on to the hope that they understand the significance of this building and what restoring the foundational history means for our city.

It's about preserving integrity and reclaiming our roots.

We're a small, thriving community, predominantly Black, built by my mother's ancestors, the Ellswoods. For my company, Bridges Heritage Conservation, Inc., to have earned this contract? It's a full-circle moment.

I dig the soles of my work boots into the dirt. "Now, this building will likely host many art exhibits, teas, galas, and, uh…" I trail off mid-sentence, my focus snapping to Cornelia Livingston as she glides toward us, as if the very mention of elegant affairs summoned her. I swallow. "Milestone events," I continue, forcing a smile. "Birthdays, cotillions, and weddings."

Cornelia stops at the edge of the crowd, the picture of refinement, resilience, and timeless beauty. She's dressed in an elegant, tailored suit, and her silver-gray hair is swept back, framing the sharp, regal features of face. Her dark, deep-set eyes are locked on me, unwavering.

"At the end of the day, I want to celebrate the start of this exciting journey with you," I say, the lightness of earlier all but gone as I near the end of my speech.

I try to focus on the warm, familiar faces around me, but my attention keeps drifting back to Cornelia, a slight unease prickling at me.

Nothing about her presence should surprise me.

For all intents and purposes, Madison Manor is her territory, and not just because her name is on the deed. Once the interior restoration is complete, it's set to be a luxury venue, its grounds hosting lavish events likely curated—or endorsed—by her. Aside from the fact she has a penchant for stockpiling real estate, it makes sense that she was the winning bidder for the property. It's no secret she attempted to bring in her own design and construction team to restore the property to her exacting standard, only to be blocked by the city's priority to preservationists. Even after that, she interviewed my competitors.

So why, then, did we meet two weeks ago on the fifth? Why, after all that, did she ultimately contract Bridges Heritage for the job?

That's where I'm lost.

On the surface, Cornelia Livingston is as much a cornerstone of Ellswood as Madison Manor. A woman who, after the unimaginable loss of her husband and our mayor, Julian Livingston II, became a symbol of perseverance and hope. She remained a fixture here, this formidable leader of Ellswood's Zion & Zara chapter, guiding the youth, using her wealth, prosperity, and influence to reinvest in the town. I give her credit—she's reshaped this city, seamlessly blending modern luxury and cutting-edge innovation with our rich cultural history.

Cornelia is undeniably responsible for all of that.

But she's also the woman who has made no pretenses about her vendetta against my family.

I don't know what started it. I assume my mother still holds a grudge because, years ago, Cornelia rejected me as "not a good fit" for Z & Z membership, and old feuds die hard. But it goes deeper than that. She sought out other restoration companies for Madison Manor, blocked Mom's community initiatives, and actively sabotaged my last relationship by offering my ex a job with the condition that she cut ties with me. Fortunately, I never saw things progressing with her.

That diabolical grudge is alive and well, and it's personal.

So, again, why hire me?

This place has sat vacant for years, collecting cobwebs. There are other preservationists. What's her real agenda?

Josiah loudly clears his throat, snapping my focus back to reality. "Wrap-it-up." He masks his laugh with a robust cough, stringing the words together and sending laughter dancing over the crowd.

"Okay, okay. In *conclusion…*" I chuckle, pushing up my sleeves. "I hear you, the speech is finally over, but I want to assure you that I'll take my time with this incredible project—the legendary grand ballroom, library, gardens, conservatory, and rooms—so that the preservation lasts for many generations to come. Thank you."

"Now, work the shovel, so we can snap the photo and get to the tour," Dom chimes in.

After the Bridges Heritage plaque is unveiled and the pictures taken, I greet and shake hands with the community, thanking each person for coming out today. The entire time I'm sending them off for a light continental breakfast and mimosas, though, my attention is locked on Cornelia's whereabouts.

It's something about the way she moves, poised but deliberate, like she's always a step ahead, watching, weighing the moment before she strikes, that unsettles me.

Until she saunters in front of me in a cloud of rich, woodsy perfume.

"Congratulations, Mr. Bridges," she says, her soft voice calculated, rehearsed. Her dark, assessing gaze skitters over my skin, the taut corners of her mouth threatening a smile that never appears.

Oh, she wants me here about as much as she wants a tax audit.

The realization buoys within me, easing the tension inside.

"Thank you, Mrs. Livingston. I, uh, wasn't aware you'd be joining us today…" I grin, suppressing a laugh. *It is killing you to even look at me, isn't it?*

But then she lifts her sharp chin barely an inch, and there it is, a genuine smile from a woman who lives by a "never let 'em know your next move" mantra. Her obsidian eyes widen with false surprise, and the calm veneer cracks. Just that fast, the mask slips.

"Of course I'm here. It's my building…" She lets the rest of her thought dissolve on her tongue, and I've got no doubt it's a deliberate choice. The niceties and pleasantries are all but done. It's pomp and ceremony. A reminder of our roles. She's the owner; I'm merely the contracted hand here to do her labor. What's more, I'm sure she wants me to consider the possibilities of how she'll make my life hell for the next six to twelve months.

It's just bait, I tell myself.

Cornelia Livingston doesn't like being told no. Not by the city, and for damn sure, not by a Bridges. Every word, every gesture, is a test. She's waiting for me to slip, to reveal something she can use, something she can turn against me.

Widening my stance again, I shift on my feet, letting the dirt beneath my work boots anchor me.

"A pleasant surprise," I say, determined to remain professional. *This is about Madison Manor.* "I've got my team ready to start next week. I'm looking forward to getting this project underway."

Your move.

If I'd looked away for even a second, I might've missed her barely perceptible smile.

"Well, now, that's why I'm pleased we've got a moment to speak." The sunlight flits between the sharp angles of her face, illuminating her in just the right way to make her seem…predatory. "Since we finalized the contract, there's been a new development," she says, then tacks on, almost gleefully, "Of sorts…"

It's taunting. And yet I refuse to bite.

Instead, I nod, my eyebrows drawing together. Because "*She's fucking with me on day one?! You've got to be kidding me*" doesn't feel like the right response—at least not here. I settle on, "Interesting."

It's too hot for all this.

"Indeed, Mr. Bridges."

I shift on my feet, still unsure where this is headed, but secretly hoping this "new development" means less interference from her with the restoration. The last thing my team and I need is to be micromanaged.

Cornelia straightens, centering her gaze on me as she paints the picture for me in broad, vivid strokes. "Family and friends gathered the weekend before last to celebrate my son, Donovan's, engagement," she explains, her voice smooth but carrying an edge of something else. She goes on about the event at Velvet Ember, a sleek, high-end restaurant that's quickly becoming the center of Ellswood's social scene. Then she lists off the attendees like a roll call, including Donovan's *privileged* fiancée, Hailey Winston, whose dream wedding venue just so happens to be Madison Manor.

"Of course," Cornelia adds, the corners of her lips curling with satisfaction, "as the owner and an important member of this city's upper echelon, I thought it would be fitting for my son's wedding to be the first event on the property."

A nepo-christening.

Fun.

"Oh, a wedding. Okay, wow..." It's a little on the nose, if you ask me, but to each his own. "Congratulations. Yeah, the gardens would be great for the ceremony...and maybe then take the reception inside the grand ballroom once I'm finished—"

"By September, Mr. Bridges," she says, steady. Then, with cold precision, she throws down the gauntlet. "If we're going to host a Livingston wedding here, I need you to move up the timeline for the restoration. Bring in additional crew if you must—"

"Mrs. Livingston, we discussed anywhere from six months to a year." I scrape a hand over my mouth, dumbfounded by her audacity. "Memorial Day is next week. That's, what, four months, give or take?"

What the...?

"I've done most of the preliminary work," she insists, like fundraising and phone calls cover everything but logistics.

I suck in a lungful of air.

"Listen..." I even my tone, hoping this woman will hear reason, if not the risks involved when it comes to her precious son's physical safety. *Jesus.* "There are structural repairs required to preserve the historical integrity. I'm sourcing rare and custom materials to match the original construction. We're still waiting on some of the city permits. We can't just skip preservation guidelines because of a wedding."

Her smile is too perfect, the kind that doesn't quite reach her eyes when she speaks. "Mr. Bridges, I've interviewed countless preservationists, and you're the city's preferred vendor. I believe 'the expert' was the term I heard most often." She pulls in a short breath, smiling. "I have all the faith in the world that you'll get the job done."

Frustration flares in my gut. *What the hell is she thinking?* "It's not *realistic…*" I stress the word, mentally calculating how much more crew I'll need and which corners can be cut while still honoring the building's historical foundation.

This is bull.

"It'll have to be," she replies, seeming unfazed, her attention drifting to her phone. "The wedding's been set for Saturday, September twentieth, and I'm not asking you—I'm telling you. We'll need rehearsals the day before, and the vendors are going to require access well ahead of time to set up—florists, caterers, sound, lighting, the whole team. I expect you to coordinate with the wedding planner…" She breaks off, her focus trained on the phone.

Her thumb glides over the screen, her eyes briefly flickering at its content. Then, with a subtle shift, she lifts her gaze to mine, a glint of delight in her dark irises.

"You can't be serious—"

"The manor's going to be the backdrop for my son's wedding, Mr. Bridges," she cuts me off, leaning in slightly, a hint of iron in her voice. "I won't have anything less than perfection. Nor will Ebony. Do you understand?"

I want to say no. *I absolutely cannot comprehend a word of what you're saying because it's ludicrous. This timeline is not unrealistic—it's dangerous.*

But then my mind reels back, halting at the name.

"Uh, I'm sorry…" My throat dries up. "Wh-what did you say?"

Cornelia grins, that smug, knowing smile of hers. "I just got the email confirmation from the wedding planner. You remember Ebony, don't you?"

A jolt of fire surges through me, and my pulse quickens.

Ebony Grace Livingston. The name feels like a sucker punch. Cornelia's ex-daughter-in-law. My high school crush. My college one-night stand that lives rent-free in my mind. My former friend. The one who got away. *Because she was never mine to begin with.*

My head spins, her words scraping across the thinly dusted surface of my mind.

I never want to see you again, Lincoln Bridges. Stay away from me and stay away from my family.

I swallow as all the tension I buried comes rushing back. The thought of working with her churns in my gut, dredging up old regrets and unanswered questions. The thought of being in same room as her, the same space as *her*, unsettles me more than I care to admit. *Damn.*

"If I'm remembering correctly, you two have somewhat of a… shared history." Cornelia's high-pitched voice lifts with sinister joy. "She's also graciously agreed to take on the wedding, short notice. So, I guess this will be a reunion of sorts."

Yeah, of sorts.

I trace my tongue over my teeth, tension tightening the cords of my neck as I stare at this diabolical woman in utter disbelief. *What are you trying to do, Cornelia?*

This just keeps getting better and better.

First, she finalized the contract, shaving months off my timeline, and now she's thrown in a wedding that will require me to work with the one woman who loathes my existence. *Yeah…this is going to go sideways so fast.*

Cornelia straightens, practically glowing. "I'm going to rejoin the tour now, but I sent her your contact. Please take care to ensure everything's seamless."

Then she walks away, as if this journey isn't going to be monumental—or *complicated*—enough already.

I stand here, frozen for a moment, watching her enter Madison Manor, my mind racing.

Cornelia Livingston never approved of my friendship with Ebony, in high school or thereafter. Whether she knew Julian wasn't nearly good enough for Ebony or not, I've got to believe she was ecstatic when Ebony finally cut ties with me.

But what's in it for Cornelia with our working together?

As I stretch out the stiffness in my neck, my phone buzzes in my pocket. I pull it out, half expecting a permit email or update on the wood and stone I ordered. Instead, the screen lights up with a single message from an unnamed number.

+1 (470) 555-3269

Please let me know your availability to meet next week.

I don't need to look it up to know it's her. I've had the number memorized since I was eighteen.

You're invited
to our
Wedding Day

You're invited
to our
Wedding Day

Chapter Three

The Switch-Up

Ebony

MY PHONE TREMBLES AGAINST MY cluttered bathroom counter.

Giving myself a mental countdown, I meet my own lined and faux-lashed gaze in the mirror, taking in the warm brown angles of my half-contoured cheeks, then force myself to answer.

"Hey, Mom, I'm just about to head out the door. What's going on?"

Her excited squeal fills the line, and immediately I know. This isn't just her usual "maintain the façade of a perfect life" crusade. The Ellswood grapevine has twisted its way around her ear.

"Sweetheart, why am I just hearing your news? I about fainted." She heaves an exhilarated sigh. "And your first wedding back? Lord, won't he do it!"

Yes, it seems he will, given the opportunity, yoke my daydream to a nightmare. "It's really something," I say.

"Something glorious. Ebony, this is Hailey Winston and Donovan Livingston…" she states, as if I need the reminder that I just freed myself from the mother of the groom, and now I've gone and backtracked.

Right on cue, another text notification from Julian pops up at the top of my screen, which I promptly ignore, like all the others.

Pause, peace, power.

I'm gliding on the backing to my earring when she pauses, and I sense the other expensive shoe about to drop.

"Listen, I know you're still sour about the way things ended with Julian." *Why yes, I am, Mother.* "But there is a silver lining, sweetheart."

"Oh, there is?"

Her exhausted sigh echoes through the line. "Yes," she says, matter-of-fact. "It's no coincidence that we're here, a year later, and neither of you has been in any…noteworthy relationships."

I laugh, plucking lint from my cardigan. "*Wow.* Nicely done, Mom." *Let's just forget about infidelity and those pesky divorce papers. Who needs 'em, anyway?* "Eleanor King has her ear to the ground, ladies and gentlemen."

I suck in my cheeks one final time, assessing the results of my mediocre contour job in the mirror before I hurriedly tug on my cream-colored wide-leg knit pants.

"There's no need to get haughty with me. All I'm saying is, this wedding doesn't only have to be an opportunity for you career-wise. This could be the opportunity to get close to Julian, go to this year's cotillion together, and win him back from that…" *Hussy of a news anchor.* It's her usual preferred term for Nora Whitfield, but for some reason, Mom holds back. "My point is, people are talking—"

"Like I said, I really need to get going to my appointment. I've got, like, five minutes to zhuzh up the wrapped mane under this bonnet, throw on some heels, and grab my coat before I hop on the road, so…" The words are in the air all of two seconds.

"Ebony, he's a man, and they have needs—"

I cut her off as I grab my coat and keys, jingling them loudly. But something inside me snaps under the pressure of knowing how far she'll take her "good man who made a one-time mistake" crusade. "Besides, I haven't mentioned it, for obvious reasons, but I'm seeing someone, and, um…I might bring him to the wedding."

The lie catapults into the air, seemingly small and meaningless, but I can see the unsteady house of cards threatening in the distance.

Instant regret flares in my gut, and I brace myself for the flood of questions about the stock he comes from and his finances, wishing I could reel the lie back in.

But the toothpaste is out of the tube.

"Ebony, you didn't mention—"

And I'm not planning to.

"Gotta run. Talk later." I hang up and dash to my car.

I reach Sterling Plaza in exactly nine minutes. Breathless, I burst through Savannah's door, crisis mode ramping up thanks to my high-heeled sprint.

"Oh my God, hi!" I exhale a breathless sigh as I rush over to tufted cream-colored sofa across from hers. A wave of calm begins to wash over me.

Her office is spacious and serene, with elegant textured rugs in soft creams and beiges. Everywhere I look, bright hydrangeas sit in crystal vases, and vibrant floral-scented candles rest on warmer plates, soothing my senses. The place screams, "You're in the presence of a problem solver."

Lord, please let this woman have the answers.

"Take a minute and relax your nerves." Savannah flashes me a soft, endearing smile.

"Ooh, I can't thank you enough for seeing me. When I tell you I'm falling apart at the seams, and I need the *Lord*..." An exhausted laugh spills out of me. "You look amazing, by the way," I add, taking in how gorgeous she looks today.

She is the picture of blessed and unbothered in understated, white tailored trousers and a bold, flowy fuchsia blouse. She's in her early fifties, but between her flawless skincare routine—one I've tried to imitate, thanks to her social videos—and the way her rich melanin is hitting, she doesn't look a day over forty... Perfection.

Not to mention she's got the social calendar to match.

Savannah Sampson is as renowned as her elite clientele. She's got decades of experience in PR and talent management under her effortlessly chic belt. Almost single-handedly, she's crafted the careers of actors, athletes, musicians, and executives, so the seamless transition into life coaching just made sense. Her skill in helping her clients balance their personal and professional lives has made her one of the most sought-after coaches across multiple industries. But that high demand also means she's selective, and any new client better come prepared to be honest and vulnerable, ready to put in the work.

"Thank you. I feel good, too." She slides her notepad onto her lap, pen in hand, signaling I've got the floor. "Let's pivot a bit today, and dive into what's making you feel like your life is unraveling."

By the time I finish giving her the rundown on everything that's happened over the past three weeks—seeing Julian for the first time since the divorce, gearing up to plan an event that reconnects me to Cornelia, and now a love interest I've pulled out of thin air to throw off Mom—Savannah is nodding, her expression showing she gets why an emergency session was a must.

I don't even get to Lincoln Bridges or the fact that Hillary has ignored my last three calls and texts. At this point, it feels like overkill.

I'm fully expecting her to latch on to the low-hanging fruit, taking on a wedding after a year-long hiatus.

Except she throws me for a whole loop when she fixes me with a pensive stare and asks, "Do you want Julian back?"

Julian?

The crease between my eyebrows deepens, and I gasp. "What? No!"

She gives me that slow, deliberate nod—the kind that usually means she's weighing the truth in my words.

So, just to make it clear that hussy of a new anchor can have him, I repeat myself. "No. I absolutely do not want him back, under any circumstances."

Again, she nods her understanding.

But a flicker of disbelief flashes inside me. Out of everything I just unloaded, *Julian* is what she thinks I'm most hung up on? *How? Why?*

"Savannah, I've spent the last year finding my footing again," I say, the weight of this truth settling in my chest. "Yes, it was awkward and unnerving seeing him face to face, but trust me, I'm more certain than ever. I'm ready to embrace my independence, redefine my life on my own terms—without the social constraints set by my mother, the Livingstons, or any other highfalutin, entitled folks who think they get to dictate how I live my life."

"And you feel like you're ready to set goals and action steps toward that end?"

I pause, considering what she's really asking. I'm not even sure what life looked like before everyone started telling me what it should be. "Honestly?"

She nods, her pen poised above the page.

"I'm restless and unsure where to start, beyond planning this wedding." I laugh, feeling lighter. "Needless to say, after my marriage's downfall being broadcast for everyone to see, then my being villainized for it, I've got trust issues."

"That's fair." Savannah smiles, scribbling something down before meeting my eyes again. "But I also think it's important to remember that a lot of people are on your side. They've commended you for daring to leave a relationship that didn't work. For daring to be vulnerable and start over."

"Yeah," I say, solemnly.

"That takes courage, Ebony."

"And thick skin," I add, thinking about the weight of it all. The shame. The fear. The constant stream of vile comments—"You're giving up," "You drove him to cheat," "You refused to give him an heir"—as if he's some sort of prince instead of just another entitled Ellswood man, adored and revered by the title-seeking, money-hungry women who've put him on a pedestal.

Savannah folds her arms across her chest, her gaze sharpening with precision. "Tell me more about that. How does *thick skin* translate for you?"

I huff out a small, salty laugh. "Do you know how humiliating and wrong it feels to be married for almost ten years and then have to get checked for sexually transmitted diseases? To relive his betrayal every time I scroll through social media? The stares, the gossip, the quiet whispering in public?" My breath catches. "I'm mortified. I've built iron walls around my heart."

Savannah's expression softens, but she doesn't let up. "Those are two-way walls, though, Ebony. They keep your heart in, but they also keep love out."

A light bulb flicks on in my head.

She deepens her stare, asking without saying it, *Do you want to live a lonely, unromantic life relegated to planning others' happily-ever-afters, but never getting your own?*

A groan slips out of me, one of those frustrated, whiny ones that I know isn't going to make me feel better but somehow does anyway.

I sink back into the sofa, staring up at the gold-speckled ceiling. "Couldn't I just build a hidden door? With, like, a secret button or something, and only give out the password on a need-to-know basis?"

A knowing glint flashes in Savannah's eyes. "So romance is still on the table, then?"

Slouching deeper into the cushions—my mother would have a conniption if she saw my posture—I glance at Savannah, already sensing the action plan brewing in her deep-set brown eyes. She's too good at compartmentalizing my chaotic life into fun-sized chunks.

"It's on the kids' table," I squeak out with a shaky smile. "Right now, all I'm hoping for is a genuine connection. Whenever the good Lord sees fit."

In the way only Savannah can, she lays out my next steps with precision.

She sets me to the task of brainstorming solutions for each of my current struggles, breaking them into manageable, practical, actionable goals. One of my longest-standing best friends ghosts me? Write a letter in my journal, lending words to the hurt and sadness it's caused, then later call her when emotions aren't running so high. Create a "calming water sounds" playlist to release the anger. *No more hiccups.* Nervous about reentering the wedding circuit after a long absence and underhanded moves by Cornelia Livingston? Get your bag but go back to basics—meet with clients, consult with vendors, and pull out the trusty checklists. Take it one task at a time. And avoid the monster-in-law as often as possible. The ex-files? Show myself grace in a daily gratitude journal.

All of which feels reasonable.

But then she hits me with the kicker.

I jolt upright, eyes wide. "Homework? You mean, like, aside from the goals, you want me to turn in an assignment?"

Savannah's full pink lips curve up as she slides her notepad across the coffee table, then leans back against the sofa.

Reluctantly, I peer over the page, scanning her beautifully swirly penmanship. At the top, our next session date—Wednesday, June eighteenth—is underscored three times, which I'm guessing means that the slot is nonnegotiable. But then my attention shifts to the three bullet points listed on the first few lines—including *test the dating waters.*

My gaze snaps to hers.

"As in, sign up for a dating app or go *on* an actual date?" I ask, my heart skittering a bit at the prospect of opening myself up to the unhinged world of dating I've read horror stories about on social media. Coffee is one thing, but waking up to my living room covered in tarp because I accidentally invited Dexter into my home? Absolutely not.

Savannah shrugs, evidently amused by the sheer panic I'm sure is smeared all over my face. "Yes, you can explore dating apps, or take the organic routes—mixers, speed dating. I'll send you my dating concierge contact, if privacy is a concern," she says nonchalantly, as if it's the most natural thing in the world. "Perhaps you'll meet someone in passing or at the supermarket. Maybe you've got a friend who wants to introduce you to someone nice."

"Maybe not." I laugh. "But okay…" I trail off, considering the next bullet point.

Plan the Winston/Livingston wedding like it's the last you'll plan.

The corners of my mouth tug downward, my lower lip protruding slightly. Maybe thinking of it as just one wedding will make it feel more manageable. I can maximize my network of contacts and resources. If being a forever debutante and the Ellswood face of a divorcée has taught me anything, it's how to be graceful under pressure. I'm a lady first. One who doesn't air out her grievances publicly. One of composure, restraint, and elegance.

Not that my wardrobe has reflected as much lately.

"This one's fine," I say, reaching for the pen to add a "rebrand my image" bullet point at the bottom of the list, but my focus stutters on Savannah's third homework assignment, and I gasp. "Um, we are twinning, my friend. 'Brainstorm a personal project to channel your inner divatante—'"

"Or divorcétante?" Savannah dips her chin like she feels the synergy in the air.

I toss her a conspiratorial grin, because we are most definitely vibing on the same bandwidth.

"I *love* the sound of that." I scoot to the edge of the sofa, bubbling with excitement. "I was just thinking if I'm reentering the red-carpet world of illustrious events and whatnot, and I'm about to be out here hobnobbing with Ellswood's finest eligible bachelors, I might need to revamp my image. Reconsider what style guide embodies the true me. You know, the new, fabulous look for the new and improved Ebony Grace? But please, say more."

Her laugh is anything but delicate. "It'll be your grand reintroduction to society," she declares, theatrically fanning out her hands to frame her vision. "And this time, you get to make all the rules."

Over the session's final fifteen minutes—plus an extra half-hour because we agreed we didn't want to lose the momentum—we draw on the parallels between the modern debutante and divorcées, brainstorming not just fashion, but a project to really channel my divatante/divorcétante energy into a single source. Together, we come up with a singular outlet that combines my goals, homework, and reemergence onto social media all in one.

We'll call it *The Divorcétante Chronicles*.

Since the world is so invested in my life, I'm going to bring them along—on a newly branded social media series—as I date, plan the Winston-Livingston wedding, and throw spaghetti at the post-divorce wall to see what sticks. I'll talk about how my friendships have been affected, how I *really* feel about Nora Whitfield, and share entries from my gorgeous gratitude journal—which I've got to go buy posthaste—all while curating a new, charmed life.

Mostly, it'll just be me, embracing independence on my terms.

By the time I leave Savannah's office, I've got a little over twenty minutes until my appointment with Lincoln Bridges, and I'm doing the pee dance, trying to make to the restroom as I fire off a quick 911 text to the divatantes.

Fortunately, Linc's office is in the same building as Savannah's.

Unfortunately, the second my phone starts ringing with a call from my girls, I discover the restroom on Savannah's floor is closed for cleaning, and now I'm waddling to the elevator.

"Honey, in a world full of influencers, I'm about to burn up the headlines," I say, utterly geeked as I connect the call to a flood of excited squeals.

The doors glide open, and I enter, pushing the button for floor one.

Of course, Whitney is the first to ask what we're geeked up about. To which I simply say, "*The Divorcétante Chronicles*," before giving them my one-liner elevator pitch. "It's something like the pre-adventures of post-divorce Ebony. Fashion, freedom, friends—"

"And hopefully dating fine-ass men," Whitney quips, on brand.

Priscilla's high-pitched scream is perfectly timed with the dinging of the elevator as I reach the first floor. "Oh my *God*. I love it!"

"Me too!" I laugh. But not too hard, feeling the urgency intensify as I spot the restroom in the far-left corner near the directory panel. "*Chile*, can you imagine? Me, extroverting from the comfort of my own home? This is why Savannah is absolutely worth every dime I'm paying her."

In the background, Whit is laughing and singing the viral "Everything Is Content" audio sound, throwing in her own little remix.

"I cannot imagine anyone more perfect for this," Priscilla says, sweetly.

"Thank you."

"Sounds amazing. But can we revisit what coach said when you told her you going to be working with that fine-ass man?" Whitney's pursed-lip challenge crackles through the phone. "Planning this wedding or not, you know you want to see Lincoln—"

"For a logistics and planning meeting, on a Wednesday," I protest, weakly. "It's business."

"More like *unfinished* business…" Priscilla cackles.

I freeze just a few feet from the restrooms.

Unbidden, images of Lincoln Bridges and the last time I saw him trespass on my mind.

A few years ago, we bumped into each other at a church a couple towns over, where he was restoring windows. We grabbed lunch, and it felt like old times—joking and laughing about sports on the TV. But when the laughter faded, Lincoln looked at me tentatively with those soulful gray eyes, the way he did sometimes when I knew he was remembering that night in college when we blurred the lines…

I thought, *No, don't go there. For all that is good and holy,* please *leave our past buried safely in the past.*

But it turned out it wasn't our past that made him hesitate.

Throwing me for an entire loop, Lincoln asked how life as a Livingston was going. Then he dropped a bombshell so heavy it shook my entire existence.

Julian's with another woman.

It wasn't a question. By the somber look on his face, I knew he'd seen it firsthand, and while I'd suspected as much, I hadn't been ready to face the truth. I called Lincoln a liar and told him I never wanted to see him again—mainly because I couldn't bear that pity that I'd seen from others. But never from him.

This man, who knew how I'd been watered down yet still saw me clearly.

I couldn't stomach his pity then, and I'm not about to start now.

"Business my behind…" Whitney laughs. "You told me yourself you missed him."

"Past tense," I say, even though it's a fair point. Even though that picture of him in his work boots with his sleeves pushed up his forearms lives rent-free in my head.

Focus, Ebony.

Any other day, meeting up for business with a beautiful man—a friend who tried to protect me and whom I wrongly called a liar with my whole chest—would have me freaking out. But right now, I've got to get my game face on.

"And that's beside the point right now," I insist. "Cornelia didn't even mention Lincoln's company would be restoring Madison Manor until *after* I agreed to plan Hailey's wedding." Which I know was by her shady design. "I'm telling you, she's manipulative."

She knows exactly how vulnerable I am.

It's been a year since my last job. My clients have dried up, not just due to my depression, but also public opinion. #TeamNora didn't help, but Cornelia has slandered me, blaming me for the divorce and insisting women should "stay in their lanes."

Like, really? What year is this?

Maybe she should tell her son to stay out of the past lane, and stop texting me.

"Classic ex-monster-in-law behavior. Wouldn't expect anything less from her," Whit sums up, correctly. "However, in the words of the great Savannah Sampson, life coach to the *stars*…" She drags out the word dramatically.

"Um, crisis mode…"

My words go in one ear and out the other.

"If you're *unwilling* to tell the truth, to be *vulnerable* to those deep, heavy emotions," she continues, reciting her Savannah-ism à la the PopShot app, "then you're not ready to receive your blessings."

"Mm, mm, *mm*, mm, mm," Priscilla says, snapping her fingers like this woman has said a whole anointed word instead of a whole lot of nonsense that absolutely does not apply to anything concerning me and Lincoln Bridges.

This is what I get for activating the Divatante Bat-Signal, especially after I vented to them the entire Memorial Day weekend.

"First, there are no deep, heavy emotions. As far as I'm concerned, *his* involvement is a non-factor. Second, this is business."

"Try again. You said that already," Whit baits me, clearly ready for a debate I don't have time for.

I hesitate, though.

I'm not about to tell them that ever since I learned we'd be partnered, my mind keeps conjuring up glimpses of what might've been if I'd listened to Lincoln. I've been mentally replaying different versions of *The Morning Tea*—without the ambush—wondering if I would've been better off quietly divorcing Julian or staying unhappily married. I'm damn sure not admitting to imagining what would've happened if I'd listened when he warned me not to let tradition dictate my life, right before I moved back to Ellswood after college.

Nope, I need to be alert. Cover my bases.

"So that's your story? Business?" Priscilla laughs.

Breath traps in my throat, and all I want to do is end the call.

Except as I barge into the restroom, ready for relief, Whit loudly declares, "I would've paid good, hard-earned cash to hear the advice that woman gave when you told her y'all fell out because you were repressing your feelings for that fine-ass man," right as the universe pulls a swift Uno Reverse on me.

I don't have time to explain that I didn't discuss Lincoln with Savannah, or remind myself that he isn't supposed to matter, because standing at the sink, washing a pair of obscenely huge hands, is Lincoln Bridges.

Everything inside me stalls, my bathroom emergency all but forgotten because…

Respectfully, Lord have mercy.

It's the picture. The dusty work boots, Henley sleeves pulled up, soulful gray eyes on me. It's the blurred lines, threatening in the distance.

"Call you back," I mutter, humiliated but grateful Whit didn't say his name.

He shuts off the faucet. And… *Is he biting back a smirk?*

"*Ahh*, if it isn't Ebony Grace Livingston," Lincoln drawls, his voice so low, the texture so gritty, it sends a jolt straight through me.

I quirk a small, tentative smile. "Lincoln Bridges…in the ladies' room."

His eyebrows lift with amusement, and… *Oh, no.*

Oh, no, no, no, no, no.

The moment our eyes connect—*really* connect—I feel it. The warmth, that quiet pull I've tried so hard to ignore. His soft, familiar gray gaze, a striking contrast against all six foot, four inches of his sculpted frame drenched in rich, dark skin.

Shit.

We're standing a handful of feet apart now, and I'm acutely, biochemically aware of the fact that we're alone.

The attraction is still there.

Dammit. I feel it everywhere. Behind my ribs and in the weightless sensation of my left hand, my bare finger. And now I don't have the protective fence that shut out temptation in college, nor a marital shield. The undeniable connection between Lincoln and me hasn't faded.

And the timing couldn't be worse.

This isn't just another elite wedding to plan. This is *the* event that'll mark my reemergence back on the scene of premier event planning. Everyone who's anyone will be watching, and Cornelia—who is as genius as she is cunning—will be right there in her floral jacquard coatdress, ready to settle her vendetta. Every step of the way, judging, micromanaging, sabotaging me with outlandish wedding demands to get her licks back for my daring to leave her son and besmirching the Livingston name.

I absolutely cannot afford distractions, no matter how much my self-imposed celibate body craves this man.

Professional ruin is at stake.

Lincoln opens his mouth to speak, but I can't take the chance he'll say something cute. Or worse, sweet.

"So, do you always make a habit of loitering in here, or is it just my lucky day?" I interrupt him, my attention shamelessly locked on him drying those massive hands. *Jesus, were they always this big?*

Lincoln leans back, catching my stare. His gaze is steady, taking me in. "I guess I could ask you the same thing."

Straightening, I try to compose myself. My chin tilted up, I'm inching toward an open stall and clinging to self-restraint.

Then, like no one told him he woke up and chose violence, Lincoln gives me that signature smirk, dragging his tongue across his full lips as he tips his head to the side. "Just curious, you know, since this is, uh, the *men's* room."

Heat rushes my skin as my eyes lock on the unmistakable urinals—which I might've noticed sooner had I not been distracted by my divas and nature's call—and Lincoln Bridges's hands.

Oh my goodness.

He chuckles, and… *Why am I always so wrong around this man?*

Right then, two things hit me. I can't let Cornelia win, and sitting face to face with Lincoln for this planning meeting? It's about to take everything I've got.

You're invited
to our
Wedding Day

(410) 555-3269

Chapter Four

Masks and Models

Lincoln

"IT'S JUST AT THE END of the hall…" I say, my voice rough as I take long strides, hand shoved in my pocket to fish for my office key. I toss a glance over my shoulder at Ebony—still a few paces back—looking just as unsure about being crammed into another small space together as I feel.

The key ring's got two keys on it. And still, I almost drop the thing as I struggle to unlock the door, trying to keep my hands from shaking. Heaven forbid she stands anywhere near me for a few seconds longer.

Yeah, sure, we're supposed to be working together. That's fine. The attraction has always been there for me, simmering under the surface, but imagining if she'd walked into the bathroom two minutes sooner?

Jesus, that would've been *one* hell of an icebreaker.

"Here we go. Welcome." Finally, I swing the door open, stepping back to give her plenty of space as she steps inside.

Then she freezes in the middle of the room.

"Uh…where would you like me?" she asks, her voice soft, like she's already regretting this whole thing.

And that's when it hits me—I wasn't supposed to be showing her into the office. I was supposed to use the restroom, then rush back to clear the place before our appointment. Ten minutes, max.

But that was before the damn men's room run-in.

"Sorry, yeah, let me just…" I mutter, scrambling to clear the chairs in front of my desk, shoving papers, samples, and motivational self-help books out of the way like I can pretend this isn't the most awkward thing to happen since—well, since she walked in on me washing my hands downstairs.

When she remains standing, I follow her line of vision to her website portfolio gallery up on my computer screen.

"Okay, so we're just going to pretend that's not there. It's for my research." I chuckle, hoping she appreciates the levity. Especially since it's at my expense. But nope. Nothing but the steely façade. "Please, have a seat."

She hesitates, eyeing the chair like she's trying to pick which one is least likely to ruin her precious cashmere. Finally, she sits on the edge of the left one, as if she might need to make a run for it.

I take a few seconds to unload the junk in my arms onto the file cabinet in the back corner, but as I go to settle behind my desk, something else occurs to me.

Why the hell am *I* so jittery?

Yeah, it's been a while since Ebony and I last spoke, and we didn't exactly part on the best terms, but we've known each other forever. We met when she was sixteen; I was eighteen. I was her high school history tutor. Her college tour guide. Even after *that night*, we maintained loose ties.

We were friends, first and foremost.

This whole awkward exchange? Feels like we're doing too much.

I skip my chair entirely, plopping down beside Ebony with a grin that I hope comes off as casual. "So...how've you been?" I say, keeping my tone light, conversational.

Tight spaces make for creative solutions, right?

If we can just talk for a few minutes before we dive into the work, maybe this won't be so bad. Maybe we can get back to being Ebony and Linc?

But the way she looks just past me—her eyes wide, mouth hanging open like I've just asked her to bend over the desk and go at it right here—yeah, maybe I miscalculated.

"What?" I laugh, playing it off. "I'm just asking how life's been treating you. Are you excited to get back to planning events? What's new with you?"

She's silent for a moment, like she's still processing—or rethinking—this meeting, then clears her throat.

"All right, so, Madison Manor in September..." she starts, her voice clipped, all business as she dives into venue logistics for the wedding. In a single fluid movement, she pulls a sleek silver iPad from her purse, her fingers gliding over the screen as she swipes through tabs with methodical efficiency.

I watch her, only half listening, noting her intense expression as she skips my conversation starter and opens a checklist. The heading jumps out at me: *WINSTON LIVINGSTON.*

"Wait, you don't want to chat for a few minutes? Reconnect?" *Remove the stifling formality?*

"I want to discuss this wedding we've been hired to ensure goes off without a hitch in three months." Her response is so matter-of-fact. So definitive.

She doesn't even look at me when she says this.

And just like that, a light bulb goes off in my head, flickering to life with a sudden jolt of recognition.

This Ebony? The former Zion & Zara debutante, now the poised, polished anchorman's ex-wife with her sensible, elegant wardrobe and ice-cold smile? This Ebony, who doesn't laugh anymore, doesn't crack jokes? Who's all business, all the time? She's not encouraging this interaction. She doesn't want to relax and build rapport with humor and shared experiences. Honestly, I don't know if that's a relief or a damn shame.

This Ebony, I don't know her anymore. And she doesn't *want* to know me. Hell, *she* doesn't know *that* Ebony anymore.

"You're serious?" The words slip out of me, unbound, and she almost meets my stare. *Almost.*

"Uh, yes?" Her inflection rises in question, and I don't miss the amusement dancing in her bright brown eyes. "I mean, other than the gardens and the ballroom—with the restoration and everything, why wouldn't we also focus on the private spaces?" she asks, completely misunderstanding my confusion. "An affair of this size, we must ensure there's wedding party dressing areas, locations designated for photos, and a cocktail-hour spot. That's bare minimum."

I stare at her, completely dumbfounded.

It's like a weird game of Two Truths and a Lie, only I can't tell which version is the lie. Downstairs in the restroom, I thought her demeanor was playful sarcasm, but she's *serious* about this. No small talk. No catching up. Apparently, no eye contact. As far as she's concerned, we're not friends anymore—we're just two professionals in an office, ticking off boxes on a to-do list.

Admittedly, the fact that she's diving straight into wedding planning and logistics like we don't share a past...it stings. But what's even more frustrating is that it's clear she's got no intention of apologizing for calling me a liar when I tried to warn her about Julian.

It irks my nerves.

But yeah, okay, let's keep this to the business, because we *absolutely* don't know each other anymore.

"Sure, of course." I shake my head, forcing myself to focus on the iPad in her hands, pretending the sudden tightness in my chest isn't there. I'm struggling to catch my breath. A thousand questions are racing through my mind. Underneath the mask, how's she *really* doing? Is she okay with planning a wedding for Hillary's sister and her ex-brother-in-law? Does Cornelia have something on her, and that's why we're partnered? Does Ebony blame me for telling her about Julian?

Instead, I ask the one question burning a hole through me.

"Who are you?" The question slips out, jagged with disbelief, breaking the seal on the moment. An exhausted laugh claws past my lips. "Seriously, like…is the real Ebony in there somewhere? Should I flash my camera *Get Out*-style to jolt you from the Sunken Place?"

She straightens, her face unreadable, but I don't even care. I'm stunned.

"You seriously show up here after three years and act like this is just another vendor meeting? After all the bull that family put you through?" My eyebrows knit together as I glare at her. "No 'Hey, how've you been?' No 'Good to see you, Linc,' and definitely no 'Oops, my bad for ignoring your warning about my good-for-nothing, lying, cheating ass—'"

"That's enough, Mr. Bridges!" Ebony's glare hits me like a sledgehammer.

Mr. Bridges?

She's shaking, her entire body trembling with the anger that every debutante has been drilled to keep in check. For damn sure, every Livingston.

Self-consciously, she smooths a hand over her hair, like she's genuinely curious to know what's changed, and all the humor fades.

It's the first raw glimpse I've seen of Ebony King.

Forget the Two Truths and a Lie. Looking at her is more like analyzing one of those Find the Difference games in magazines with seemingly identical images presented side by side. At a closer glance, there are tiny, trivial changes. She's still Ebony, only they've altered the hairstyle and clothing, removed the wedding ring, and muted the vibrant color that was once there.

I only notice because I remember everything about her.

"We're not doing this," she says, her tone curt, steady.

"No, it's an honest question." I throw up my hands in surrender. "I get that we're here in a professional capacity, but you've got your hair back, pinned up in a sensible style. In this humid weather, you're bundled up in cream and cashmere, nothing too flashy, revealing, or colorful, of course. But then there's the fact that this is the first time you've looked me in the eye on purpose. That's not the Ebony I knew."

She blinks repeatedly. "Did it occur to you that I'm human?" she asks. "Maybe I was embarrassed that I walked into the men's restroom where I could've happened upon any number of…family jewels on display?"

I bark out a laugh straight from the gut. I'm breathless. "Family jewels? That's what you're going with?"

A red blush colors her cheeks, and I'm dying because this whole situation is laughable at best.

"You're being ridiculous." Ebony purses her lips. "And this outfit is appropriate for a semi-casual business meeting. Not that you would know."

"Ah, touched a nerve, huh?" I chew the inside of my cheek, smiling. "I mean, it's plain as day that I don't know you anymore, and that's fine. But do you?"

This earns me a small, shaky laugh.

Immediately, I know that's it. She's lost herself. In fact, I'd wager that she hasn't known the fun-loving, smart firefly of a woman who used to sing on a whim and dream about waterfalls and beaches for, oh, say, about ten years.

I reach across the other side of my desk, grabbing the giant conch shell she brought back for me from one of her vacations in college, holding it with both hands just to see if there's even a blip on her radar.

Ebony swallows hard, visibly pulling herself back together. She's rigid and determined to not react, and I admit, I sort of love the cracks in her steely demeanor.

"Just asking questions." I nod, chuckling to myself.

"I'm not going to stroke your ego, Mr. Bridges. I'm here to do a job. Nothing more," she snaps. "Is that going to be a problem for you?"

"Nah, I'm good." Except the ease of my tone seems to grate on her, and I sense the other shoe about to drop when she turns to me, gaze unwavering.

"Since you're so eager to stroll down Memory Lane, last I recall, Lincoln Bridges was a man fueled by integrity and reclaiming his family's Ellswood roots, right?" Her full, warm pink lips curve up with satisfaction. "I thought you were fighting to ensure the Livingstons don't rewrite history. Should we talk about why *you're* working for Cornelia, then?"

We stare at each other, at an impasse.

The air crackles with tension.

"No, it's fine," I say, straightening to focus on her checklist. "It's just business. Like you said, *we're here to do a job*, so let's."

And that's what we do for the next forty-five minutes. She outlines the restoration and wedding event timelines leading up to the September twentieth ceremony and reception. Together, we map out a rough schedule for her to bring around the couple and vendors to the space.

"I've created a visual render of the building," she says, tapping yet another app. But this time, it isn't a checklist or questionnaire. It's a bold red icon with *Mod3D* written in white block letters. After a few seconds, a 3D model of Madison Manor appears on the screen, complete with floor plans and layouts.

"This is based off a blueprint I found online," she continues, her eyes flicking between the model and her notes, "but I'll need the updated specifications to include any planned structural changes, if there are any. I sent you a collaborator invite earlier, so accept that when you get a chance."

As if she didn't already impress the hell out of me, she keeps going, offhandedly mentioning color schemes, expected guest count, and preferred rehearsal dates. We'll mostly correspond by email, she says, in person only when absolutely necessary.

I listen quietly as she asks to be CC'd on any restoration progress updates, but I'm not really hearing her anymore. I'm looking at her, at all the small, seemingly insignificant changes—her subtle shifts in posture, the way her fingers tap the screen, the way she avoids my gaze, as if she's hiding something. And I can't help but wonder about all this talking, the string of decisions masking her tiny, almost imperceptible sighs, they're just...what? Pieces of the mask? Me spotting the differences?

I don't know what I was expecting, though.

We haven't been close for years. We were never going to be best friends. There was never a clear path for what we became.

The room feels smaller, the air heavier. Everything's awkward, charged, uncertain, and none of it should matter, but it does in ways I can't explain.

She's just someone I used to know.

And maybe that's all she'll ever be. As much as I'm curious about the person she's become, if today is any indication, I don't want to find out.

You're invited
to our
Wedding Day

You're invited
to our
Wedding Day

Chapter Five

Night Terror

Ebony

I JOLT AWAKE WITH MY heart racing, Linc's voice from the dream still a burning whisper in my ear. *"Look at me, Ebony."*

(410) 555-3269

Chapter Six

Flip Side

Lincoln

"FIRST OF ALL, EBONY IS not thinking about your old, sorry, *tired* ass." Josiah hurls the basketball at me so fast, it knocks the wind out of me, causing me to stumble out of bounds.

For a beat, I stare at him. He mean-mugs me, breathing all hard.

Since he arrived at the court—*late*—with nothing more than "I got next" to say to us, Dom and I figured he was on one. But Josiah is one of those people you can't force to talk. He's got to come around when he's good and ready.

I guess that time is now. I think.

"You all right, bro?" I ask.

"Are you?" he snaps back, stretching his arms the full length of his massive wingspan. His thick, dark eyebrows braid together. "Thought you were supposed to be prime time…out here playing like this is a warm-up, as if we don't know what's up."

On the bench, Dom winces, covering his mouth with his hand, like he's secondhand embarrassed for me.

I scratch my temple, barely stifling my laugh as I chance a look at this gargantuan, six-feet-seven, sweaty Black hulk with his lumberjack beard and thick neck, out here throwing a temper tantrum. *In this heat?*

"Use your words," I tease.

"*Daaaaannnnnggggg!*" Dom, the master instigator that he is, falls out laughing on the bench.

Josiah waves us off, pacing the sideline.

The thing is, with my guys, we've got our roles in this friendship. By the sheer brute size of him, you'd think Josiah's that competitive athlete, always challenging someone, keeping score. But nah. This man is an introvert through and through. He's introspective as hell, listening more than he speaks. Whereas Dom lives for the drama. And the celebrity gossip blogs. I chalk it up to an occupational hazard with his sitting in front of screens all day, developing software. He's about as scandal-free as it gets. He's the wild card, bringing chaos via crazy dares or some last-minute "adventure trip" he swears will be fun, but never is.

And me? I'm just the loyal one, who's got their backs. I pay attention to the details, to what they say. In Siah's case, I also pay attention to what he doesn't say.

For damn sure, this isn't about Ebony.

Before his next pass crushes my ribcage, I tuck the ball under my arm. "Is it the long hauls you've been flying?" I ask, deciding to try a different tactic. "Everything's good with Jade?"

Work or a woman—which is it, my guy?

He shoots me a death glare. "Man, get the hell out of here with all that nonsense. Are we going to play or you going to just stand there, hogging the ball all damned night?"

"So it *is* about Jade," I say, knowing if I'm wrong, and he's frustrated about work, he'll correct me.

And three, two, one—

"And no, it's *not* about Jade, Mr. Know-It-All." He does a full about-face, his hard stare fixed on me. "If you really want to talk about something so bad, use *your* words, Linc. What's happening with Ebony *Livingston*?" He drags out every syllable of the last name, and while I know he's deflecting, that emphasis speaks volumes about what's been bothering me since she left my office last week.

She's one of them.

With or without the ring, not like us, he means.

Nothing has ever come easy to us. In this town, our names— Bridges Heritage Conservation, Carter Aviation, Owens Signature Software—stand for hard work and harder determination. It's not about clout and status. We've built from the ground up. Our family's histories have the deepest Ellswood roots, but somehow, the town's residents have slowly uprooted them. In its place, they're rewriting history. Erasing us.

It's why we can't let up.

"I'm listening," I say, meeting his stare.

The court floodlights flicker ominously as Josiah steps toward me slowly, sizing me up.

Even though every muscle in my body is tense, and my heart is racing, not knowing where his head is, I match his pace.

Is he really this mad? About what?

"Aw, hell." Dom pushes his tall, lanky frame upright, taking wide strides to reach the center of the blacktop before us. "Why don't y'all walk it off for a few minutes or—"

"Nah, I'm good," I say. "At this point, I'm genuinely curious what's got Josiah so bent out of shape." *Where's he going with this line of questioning?*

"Yeah, aight..." Dom scrapes his hand over his mouth, shaking his head. "Neither one of y'all is good, if you ask me."

I let out a quiet harumph.

"Unlike some folks, I don't have a problem being upfront about what's happening in my life. I'm an open book." I shrug like this is the easiest thing in the world for me. "What would you like to know?"

Josiah steadies his stance, drawing back his shoulders, chin up, throat bared. "That woman done married a whole other man, then ghosted you when you tried to warn her that he was in the streets. Yet you're still running behind her, settling for crumbs." He chuckles. "Pathetic."

"Oh, I'm pathetic now. Got it." I nod, the corners of my mouth tugging downward, lower lip protruding. "Did I know I'd be linked up with Ebony to plan a wedding when I signed on for the restoration of a building that's part of my family's legacy? Nope. Should I give up on the job just because you think—"

"No, I know," he says, matter-of-fact. "You *need* to give up on that uppity, money-motivated Zion & Zara she-bot. But we all know that's not how you're built." Josiah's tone drips with disgust. Then his expression softens as he adds, "It's time," and I know exactly what he means.

Way back when, I had a thing for Ebony King. She was vibrant and alive, with a laugh that I felt in my soul. We used to talk about everything under the sun, read books together, watch sports, and just find fun and joy in the mundane stuff. When she dreamed out loud about visiting waterfalls and beaches, getting back to swimming and collecting seashells and conch shells, I was with her. This woman listened without a hint of judgment as I shared my family's stories about Ellswood, and how they built this town from the barren ground up. So when we finally blurred the friendship line, I knew there was no going back. She was it for me.

I begged her not to let them water her down—to choose me.

At the end of the day, I wasn't her choice. I had to let go. No matter how hard it was.

And I did.

For almost ten years, I just settled for being friends to keep her in my life. Then I warned her about Julian, and she asked never to see me again. I respected that. I stayed away. Even when the news about Julian and Nora Whitfield broke, I found myself writing a bunch of texts and letters—maybe a dozen or so. I opened her contact a million times. I stalked her website and social media. But in the end, I didn't reach out. I stuck to my word, kept respecting her wishes, dated women here and there—nothing serious—and ended up married to the job instead.

I haven't had the time, or passion, for a woman…until now.

Damn.

"Yeah, you're right." I nod at Josiah, letting the tension drain from my shoulders. "It's long overdue."

Dom releases a relieved sigh. "Man, you all had me scared for a minute."

Josiah shakes his head, laughing. "Relax. We're boys. We can't be out here body-checking each other like this."

We don't sugarcoat or hold back with each other. It's raw, loud, and raucous, but when it's done, it's done.

"Nah, but for real, what are you going to do?" Dom asks. "The streets have been talking."

"And by that, you mean the blogs?" I chuckle.

He sucks his teeth. "Say what you want, but the blogs have been posting photos of your girl, so something's definitely brewing."

Josiah and I both burst out howling with laughter.

"My guy, you need better pastimes." Josiah claps a hand on Dom's shoulder. "Mind the business that pays you."

Dom ducks out of his grip, backing away. "That's how I stay in the know. You should be thanking me, Linc. And if you ask me, all that ultra-professional, keeping-her-distance-at-your-office role play… She's *clearly* hiding how much she wants you."

"That's what we're not going to do. We're not going to glorify this like some rom-com movie," Josiah says, attempting to nip that theory in the bud.

But it's too late.

"Remember that lawyer from Buckhead?" Dom lifts his eyebrows like that says it all. He groans when he's met with our blank stares. "Petite, thick, had that pet snake?"

"Is that a euphemism for—" Josiah starts, but Dom isn't having it.

He sighs loudly. "Whatever, man. My point is, she helped me review some of the legal stuff with that house I was renting out, and she was *into* me. It was obvious—body language, eye contact, everything. She wanted me but wouldn't cross that line." He dips his chin, clearly gearing up to make some elusive point, which I assume he'll deliver any second now. "A month after the business was done, she reached out. Full admission. She'd been fighting it the whole time."

Josiah and I nod, barely suppressing our laughs.

"Well, that's it, then." Sarcasm coats my tone.

But Dom continues, driving his point home. "Tell me Ebony's body language wasn't there. That in that restroom, she wasn't a deer in headlights, checking out your junk?"

"You mean his family jewels," Josiah corrects him, and it's the last straw. His smooth expression cracks.

These fools sprint a lap around the blacktop, howling and cackling, gasping for air at my expense.

"It's cool. Y'all got jokes." Shaking my head, I turn toward the bench, not about to stand here and watch.

Josiah runs me down, grabs his water bottle, and takes a long swig. "So, again. At the risk of harping on the same point, where's your head? What are you going to do?"

Dom walks over in time to catch the tail end of his sentence, so now the full collective weight of their stares is on me.

The thing is, seven days ago in my office, she set the tone. Logically, I know anything we shared was in the past. The problem is that there's also a stubborn part of me holding tight to something that felt so real.

"Honestly…no clue," I say. *I don't know this Ebony.* "I think I'm just going to play it by ear. Observe. See how she acts. Take my cues from her, and be professional. Live."

Dom's face is twisted into an emotional, pleading mess as he comes in for a bro hug with Josiah and me. "See, exactly. What we need is to take a guys' trip—"

We both duck out of his grip, in stitches.

"Get your friend." Josiah pokes the ball, freeing it from my arm, and shooting it toward the hoop. The ball soars through the air, descending with an audible swoosh. "*All* net!"

"Mm-hmm." I laugh. "When no one's guarding you."

Dom's undeterred in his mission to deliver us to the Temple of Doom, though. "Linc, when was the last time you used your money to travel, enjoy life, or buy some shoes that aren't beat-down work boots or dusty Dunks?"

Bunch of comedians tonight.

Josiah dribbles back over to us, steady bouncing with a huge smile on his face as he eyes me. "Your boy's not all wrong…"

"Meaning?" I prompt him.

"That it might also be time for you to stop holding your coins so close to your chest." Josiah's shoulders are up to his ears. "I'm saying, money-wise, you didn't *need* to take the job—"

I gasp. "Seriously?"

"*But*…I also know how important Madison Manor is to your family. So, yes, set your mind on finishing the restoration. Hire a backup team to expedite the job, if need be. Establish firm boundaries with Ebony. The less of her you see, the better."

I shift my attention to Dom, whose smirk is conceding Siah's point. "At least until the job is done," he echoes.

I nod a few times.

"So far, the communication has been minimal—texts, emails, plus we're using that new Mod3D app. Honestly, it's amazing." I pause, reading Dom's lopsided posture and how his mouth is open. "To answer your question, I haven't seen her since we met at the office last Wednesday, but I'm sensing there's more you haven't said yet?"

He chuckles. "You sensed correctly. When are you scheduled to see her again?"

I lean over my duffel sitting on the bench, pull out my phone, and bring up the shared calendar Ebony created.

"Looks like…" I keep scrolling. "Next week. Thursday, June twelfth, we're meeting with Cornelia and Hailey Winston at Madison."

Josiah tips his head to either side, weighing what I don't know.

"Not ideal," he says, tentatively. "But at least you won't be alone with her. What about the three of us head out this weekend? A short flight or road trip could be great to get you ready, mentally…"

Yeah, physically is another story.

For a beat, I observe my two friends, unwilling to commit just yet.

"I'll think about it, but, uh…was I right about Jade?" I reach for the ball, but he strong-arms me, holding it out of reach. "Did she finally kick your sorry butt to the curb?"

Josiah bounces the ball off me, laughing as he dribbles to the hoop. He dunks on me, hanging from the rim like he's Shaq in the Magic days about to tear down the backboard. "You can't see me!"

"I think everyone in a fifteen-mile radius can see and hear your loud ass." Dom laughs.

When Shaq 2.0 finally comes down, he's cheesing like a fool. "So, yeah, I might be kicking myself to the curb. Jade's hinting around for a ring, and—"

"*Ohhhhh*," Dom and I say at the same time.

Twenty minutes later, I'm home, drained, and struggling to find energy to hit the shower when my phone pings from the entry table. The moment I see the name lighting up the screen, I drag myself to the couch and plop down, bracing for battle.

Ebony

> Hey, when you get a chance, do me a favor and check your Mod3D messages. I reviewed the updated specifications with planned structural changes, and I sent a few requests for your consideration. Thanks.

For a moment, I stare at the message, reading and rereading, trying to decide what feels off. Each time, something else jumps out at me, before I realize it's because the tone is different. Nice. Every other text and email she's sent has been extremely formal. *Good morning, Mr. Bridges. Best regards.*

Suddenly we're on a "hey" basis? She wants me to do her a favor? For my consideration? Thanks, and not, thank you?

Oh, this ought to be interesting.

I feel the crease between my eyebrows deepening as I swipe over to the app, fueled purely by curiosity.

After a few minutes spent searching for messages within the app, I finally discover a tiny red dot under the ACCOUNT tab. When I tap it, a thread of five lengthy responses from Ebony Grace Events appears. Tentatively, I open the first one, and not even a full paragraph down, my focus snags on *…while beautiful, the layout isn't really practical for modern weddings.*

"Oh, because all centuries-old buildings should be gutted to accommodate a wedding guest list of people invited to stroke the mother of the groom's ego. Right."

I chuckle, continuing down the page to get a sense of the scale for the changes she's requesting.

And that's when my blood starts to boil.

"The hallways are too narrow?" I'm shaking my head, amazed by this woman's audacity. Cornelia already shaved the deadline, and I'm not about to cut corners. Ebony knows nothing about preserving historical integrity. All she cares about are aesthetics and modern amenities. It's not just the halls, either. According to Ebony Grace Events, the bathrooms are outdated, and the outlets are poorly placed. She wants more lighting, climate control, and a full audio/visual system.

My head spins.

And frankly, I'm too damn hot to respond in the app. Toggling back to messages, rapid-fire, I tap out a text.

Lincoln

> Lots of great suggestions, thank you. However, given the shortened timeline and the scale of the preservation, I think it's important that we avoid compromising the building's original character and charm. The history is what will attract clients, and we wouldn't want to jeopardize that.

"Shoot." I'm fuming. "*Telling me how to do my job…*"

Almost immediately, the phone pings again.

Ebony

> Of course not, but air conditioning and efficient electrical systems shouldn't affect the vintage appeal of Madison Manor.

Contrary to what she and Cornelia think, Madison Manor isn't just a wedding venue. It's got character and story. And yes, space and functionality are important, but I'm going to need her to realize the crown molding and stained-glass windows aren't just decoration.

Lincoln

Correct. That's why heating, cooling, electrical, and plumbing have already been approved. Have a nice night.

PING!

"Jesus, woman. Let it go. You're not going to win this one."

Ebony

The bathrooms are too small for the anticipated number of guests. Do you really expect us to bring in porta potties to accommodate everyone? Is that the image you want to portray at the manor's first event back?

Lincoln

Listen, we can't just gut the bathrooms, Ebony. We're preserving a building that'll serve more than just weddings.

Ebony

Why can't you compromise? Isn't there something we can do to keep the historical aesthetic intact while also allowing for modern amenities? Do you really think Cornelia isn't going to have a conniption if you don't try to make this work?

"There it is!" I push to my feet, fuming. "So, if you can't get your way, you resort to tattle-telling?"

For all of five seconds, I pace my living room before I respond… with necessary force.

Lincoln

Believe it or not, I'm not going to just flush the historical value of Madison Manor down the toilet because a Livingston decided to get married.

Ebony

Wow!

Lincoln

How about you let me take care of the restoration, and you handle the wedding planning? I've got a job to do. Is that going to be a problem for you?

The rest of the night, I check my messages again and again. I take a shower, eat, and turn down the bed, but Ebony still hasn't replied. She's left my message on read, and I should feel good—I made my point. I won. But as I lie in bed, I can't shake this uncertainty.

What did I really win, and at what cost?

You're invited
to our
Wedding Day

You're invited
to our
Wedding Day

Chapter Seven

Snapped

Ebony

"HI THERE, CAN I HELP you find anything?"

I look up from my phone, where I just sent another call from Mom to voicemail as a bright-eyed woman with long goddess braids and flawless brown skin weaves her way through the vibrant display tables of the boutique stationery store, heading straight for me.

I've been aimlessly browsing through a colorful sea of journals for the last half-hour, and spoiler alert, I still haven't picked one.

"Oh my goodness." I laugh nervously, suddenly feeling very self-aware. "You've probably been watching me this whole time, wondering if I'm really contemplating this deep or just dazed and confused."

To my relief, she waves off my comment, flashing me a reassuring smile. "Honey, I'm a planner girlie. I, for one, am not judging. Choosing the right journal—or planner, or shoot, even the right pen—is basically a life decision. It's as important as the words and plans that go in it."

We exchange a wide-eyed look of silent solidarity.

A relieved sigh seeps out of me. "Okay, good, because I was going to stay home and search online. But foolishly, I somehow thought coming here, getting up close, feeling the textures, and letting the colors fuel my inspiration would make all the difference." I smile, letting my nerves settle, like I've confessed some deep, vulnerable truth.

If she's secretly judging, thankfully, she doesn't let on. "You have definitely come to the right place," she says.

"Of course. This is absolutely a me problem. Recently, I've just been generally…indecisive? I don't know if that's the right word." I laugh. "But you get it." I gesture to the journal stacks, like they're the root cause of my woes when they're barely the tip of my emotional iceberg.

The thing is, I could've worked from home today. I could've torn a sheet of paper from an old notebook to get my Hillary homework done. I've also got updates from Cornelia on the guest list, plus a flood of emails I need to send to beg vendors to pull this wedding together on short notice. It's too late for save-the-dates, but Hailey needs to select invitations. Or, instead of staying home, I should head over to my office at Ellswood Mill, clean up the space, start sorting through my wedding arches and vases, and get everything looking presentable for client meetings—fingers crossed, those referrals come pouring in.

But how am I supposed to focus on checklists and an office moonlighting as a storage unit, or even my consultation next Friday with the dating concierge Savannah set me up with, when I can't stop fixating on that dream?

I drag the tip of my fingernail over the edge of my teeth, still daunted by the heady rush of Linc's throaty whisper. *Look at me, Ebony.*

Phew, Lord… It was so real.

The way my body prickled with awareness of his—

Too real.

See, this is why today, it's homework over working from home. I cannot afford to be distracted. I've got too much riding on this wedding.

But even Savannah's homework has been weighing on me. Not so much reaching out to Hillary or dating—more like, where do I start with *The Divorcétante Chronicles*? What's the logistics of building a social media series as an outlet? What's my real end goal with it? And, all things considered, am I ready to put myself out there to be judged even further?

After a beat, I realize I've been standing here, and the woman has been quietly watching me, lost in thought.

"Sorry." I laugh again. "My head has been all over the place. A gratitude journal was supposed to be my easy task."

Her expression is all determination as she pushes her sleeves up her forearms and plants herself across from me like an official guide to the world of journals. "Say less, sis. Let's check this one off your list."

I love this woman's take-charge energy.

She's still nodding as she gathers her wispy braids and twists them into a massive bun atop her head. After plucking a pencil from behind her ear, she fixes her hair in place, as if she needs more room to think. "I've only got a few more options to narrow it down."

Syd, I learn, is her name, and she turns out to be a godsend. After a thorough process of elimination—based on color, prefilled options, and inspirational highlights—I finally select a gorgeous lavender leather journal. The cover is engraved with the words *Reclaim Your Joy* in a shimmery gold metallic.

"It's perfect!" I squeal, genuinely happy.

She winks and dusts off her shoulder. "It really is, friend. *And* there's a buy-one-get-one-free sale right now. You're sure I can't get you a romance journal, in case you have a little summer fling going on?"

A full belly laugh rumbles out of me, and I can't fault the girl for trying. But also, why is she so hellbent on selling me a love journal? Is she…*flirting with me?*

I flash her a nervous smile. "Thank you, but I'm good."

Dipping her chin, she screws her deep burgundy lips to the side, reading my expression for truth. "I'm being so real. *The Story of Us. Love Letters to My Future Husband…*" She lifts the deep red one in her left hand and twists the pink one in her right. "You look like a woman who has a new boo in her life. Just out here on a Tuesday, glowing with all that melanin."

I'm holding my side, gasping for air and grateful I won't have to turn this sweet girl down. "You are too much!"

"And really great at reading folks." She tilts her head, fixing me with an intense gaze. "You're really telling me that's not 'new love' written all over your face? You weren't just over here daydreaming?" Syd deepens her stare like she will pry an answer out of me if she has to. "No lie, you've got this soft red aura."

"Yeah?"

Another customer enters the boutique, and I do my best to recompose myself, but I'm still breathless as I grab a project-based journal and follow Syd over to the counter to ring up my purchase. I feel giddy and accomplished, like I'm making real progress with Savannah's homework. But also, like a higher power ensured Syd's and my paths crossed today.

I needed her lightness.

"Ooh, *chile.*" I lean on the counter, my breathing finally starting to even out as I ignore the umpteenth call from Mom. She's eager to discuss my "new boo's" threat to a chance of my reuniting with Julian, no doubt. After his "I won't give up" spiel, I'm sure the whisper network has reached her.

Leave a message after the tone, please.

I'm all smiles, browsing small trinkets and magnetic bookmarks, thinking about what a great self-care decision it was coming here before my hair appointment and making my first journal entry at the salon a few blocks away. But then Syd moves in my periphery, stealing my attention.

What the…

A cold sensation washes over me as I lock eyes with her. She's still holding her phone.

"Did you…just take my picture?" My mouth falls open, confusion drawing my eyebrows together as I watch Syd—the same woman I was just so grateful to for helping me pick out a journal, for being so kind to me—freeze, guilty as all get-out.

And that's when I see it.

Nestled among the collage of stickers plastered inside her clear phone case, in the bottom-right corner, Pepto Bismol-pink and glittery, is #TeamNora.

You've got to be kidding me.

My heart *plummets* straight into my stomach.

"Sorry, I just…" She falters, perhaps realizing how stupid she sounds trying to deny it when I *watched* her, right here, focus, aim, and snap an unsolicited photo of me—pre-salon appointment, no less—that's probably going to end up on the gossip blogs, or worse, as some viral meme for Azalea and Yvette to dissect on *The Morning Tea.*

She shoves her phone into her pocket, rushes to the cash register, and scans the barcodes like she's praying I didn't just catch her in the act.

I track her every move as she bags the journals, silently daring her to forget my BOGO discount and find out.

"These are great choices." She tosses me an awkward smile. "I hope you really love them."

Oh, I'll bet you do.

The initial shock starts to wear off, giving way to a fiery heat creeping up my neck. I'm pissed now, standing here in disbelief. This woman—this undercover, low-class, trifling Internet troll—had the audacity to snap photos of me at her *place of employment?*

Nuh-uh.

"Oh, you're a bold one, huh—" Right on cue, an angry hiccup escapes me before I can stop it, and at this point, I couldn't care less how weak it makes me look.

"Listen…" Syd's eyes flutter-roll with visible annoyance. "Bruh, it was just one. Relax."

Relax? Bruh? Yeah, okay, sis.

"Wow!" Every inch of me boils with rage. "Listen, I'm gon' be good. But the next time you want to take my picture without asking, maybe ask yourself if you're ready for—" *HICCUP!*

And then she actually laughs.

"What you need to do is calm down before you give yourself palpitations." She tugs the pencil from her hair, letting her braids fall down her back. "What were you going to say? Am I ready for a lawsuit?" Then, almost as an afterthought, she mutters, "Should be thanking me for the free publicity."

For all of five seconds I consider going full reality-show meltdown, demanding to see the manager with a debutante smile and a gloved slap. But in a divine moment of clarity, I hear Whit's voice in my head. *We are not letting these bougie, low-vibrational folks define nor destroy your happiness one more day.*

Low vibrational, indeed.

Why would I voluntarily give the *Luxe Ladies* fandom ammunition? They're waiting for me to resurface on some blog so they can knock me back down.

"Cool." I nod and smile.

She giggles. "Cooler."

Lord, give me the strength.

I mentally brush it off. What did she even get out of this? One picture of me shopping for journals? Whoop-de-do. What are the blogs going to do with that?

As if she's reading my mind, Syd pulls out her phone again and starts scrolling, that smug smile front and center. She flips the screen toward me, showing a picture—this one from last week, taken as I was entering the Sterling building for my appointment with Savanah.

I shrug, not following. "What's this supposed to be?"

For a moment, I rack my brain, wondering why people are suddenly snapping photos of me again. Julian and I haven't been together in a year. The divorce is final, so he can screw around with every woman in Ellswood to his heart's delight. And I haven't been on a single real date, so...

"Everyone's saying you got a new man..." Syd trails off, her eyes flicking to my hands, and for a beat, I freeze.

And then it hits me.

The only person I've talked to about dating, aside from Savannah and the divas, is my loose-lipped mother. *When was it, last week?* I close my eyes against a long sigh, smiling to myself. If the blogs want to waste their time chasing down a nonexistent man, who am I to stop them?

"I'm telling you, I live rent-free in some of these folks' heads," I say, ready to let it go and give Mom an earful when I leave this place.

But then Syd looks me dead in the eye and says, "Can't be too serious with that chalk line around your finger." As if she knows I only recently took off my wedding ring, and how could I be serious about anyone new when the tan line proves I've been holding on to the old one? But she's wrong. I wasn't stuck on him—I was clinging to the old me.

Not like she deserves an explanation.

I'm stunned silent.

Then a shocked laugh escapes me, and I'm standing here, mouth open, utterly gobsmacked.

"You know what…" I unzip my purse, digging frantically around the bottom for my wallet, because this woman has outworn her welcome. "Let me hurry up and finish my purchase so I can move on with my day."

I'm muttering under my breath as I pull out my credit card and quickly tap to pay, fully intending to let her keep the receipt, since it'll be hell and high water before I set foot in this boutique again.

"Your ex is certainly moving on with his," she says, casually, like it's nothing.

With one simple sentence, she's shaken the ground beneath my feet.

Another hiccup bubbles up. It takes every ounce of dignity and grace left in my body not to snatch that phone from her hands to see what she's talking about. The only thing that stops me is knowing that's what she wants. It's what Nora and her whole fanbase want, and the unbothered woman I'm striving to be—the divorcétante—won't give them the satisfaction.

Instead, I say, "Have the day you deserve."

And I mean that with the utmost disrespect.

I manage to hold it together until I exit the shop and make my way a few stores down from the salon before I pull out my phone. My hands are trembling as I search for Julian's name, my heart stuttering as the headline knocks the wind out of me.

Luxe Lady Nora Whitfield Expecting—And Julian Livingston III Is the Father!

A tidal wave of emotions hits me all at once.

For a beat, I just stare at it, processing the words, the weight of the situation sinking in. My stomach twists with the bitter taste of betrayal. After all the gaslighting, about *let me try to win you back* and *I ended it to be with you,* he's back with her. *If* he ever cut things off. He isn't just building a life with the woman who tore ours apart. *They're having a baby.*

As a text notification from Julian pops up on my screen, everything clicks—this is why Syd took my photo. This is why people are snapping pictures of me walking into buildings. Why I've become a blog topic. They want my tearful reaction to Nora's pregnancy. They want the drama, the trending gossip, the exclusive, scandalous content. They want the shock value of seeing me broken.

Everything is content.

And boom, a quiet shift happens inside me.

Syd was absolutely right. Let them judge. Let them photograph me and fabricate their stories. They'll find something to write about. They always do.

But I'm going to tell my side, too.

As I open my Notes app and save the article link to my *Divorcétante Chronicles Ideas* folder, I realize—*maybe, just maybe—* that free publicity is perfectly timed.

(410) 555-3269

Chapter Eight

Crowned

Lincoln

I'VE GOT JUST OVER AN hour before I meet Cornelia, Hailey, and Ebony at Madison Manor to tour the wedding spaces. So I'm dressed and on the road, giving myself time to settle in before the crew arrives. With any luck, Ebony will show up early, too, so we can chat.

Of course, with all the potential for drama, I'm not surprised that five minutes into my drive, Dom calls in on Bluetooth.

I let out a quiet groan as I answer.

"Big Dom!" I put a little extra bass in my voice, bracing for his antics. Although mentally, I'm kicking myself for carelessly bringing up this meeting on the blacktop in front of him.

The man won't let up with his "body language doesn't lie" theory that Ebony's secretly into me. *Yeah, okay.*

"Figured you be up and racing to the site…" He snorts. "Cause, *boy*, when those nerves hit…" He releases an impressed whistle.

He's not wrong.

As much as I'm *thrilled* to hear Cornelia's latest to-do list, I'm hoping for a few minutes to pull Ebony to the side so I can smooth things over. After our last conversation, something didn't sit right with me. But that was over two weeks ago. All that awkwardness aside, I'm just wondering if she's okay—on a human level—because today, the "ear to the streets" guy that Dom is, he sends me a link saying Julian Livingston and Nora Whitfield are expecting, which, to say I'm astounded… The man is a straight clown.

Truly, it's embarrassing how this wannabe Casanova can't keep his dick in his pants—couldn't even when he was married. And now he's about to be someone's father?

He's a joke.

I lay on the gas, like if I just press harder, I'll make time move faster.

"Yeah, I'm on the way now. I want to get there and get settled," I say, sidestepping his comment. "Hopefully she'll have a minute to chat."

Dom hums his agreement. "Man, when I tell you they been *hounding* Ebony for her reaction. Coming at her sideways… It's just foul."

Fire blazes in my chest, and I scrape my hand over my beard scruff.

"*Pfft*. Mm-hmm." I nod, poking my tongue in my cheek and inhaling a long breath. "Least I can do is make sure she doesn't feel isolated if Cornelia tries to put her on the spot," I say, then I remember whom I'm talking to and clarify, "I don't need to be pursuing her romantically to show empathy."

He lets the silence linger for a beat. "All right, I'm not going to press you." *Yeah, you are.* "But you and I both know you're holding back like a *professional*."

There it is.

I bark out a laugh at the sheer level of his commitment. The lengths he'll go to in order to make his point is awe-inspiring.

"Go on. Get it out." I shake my head, smiling.

"Playing the long, *long* game, acting like you're on a high-speed chase away from your feelings," he continues. "The poster child for denial. Mind you, fooling absolutely no one—"

"Thank you so much for that riveting read. I'm so glad I answered this eight a.m. call." I'm still laughing as I pull into a parking space on the street, then tell Dom I'll hit him up later.

He's a fool, but I admit, I do feel lighter.

As planned, I'm the first to arrive, so I spend a few minutes inspecting the new shipments for the woodwork and paneling.

Yet I can't deny my disappointment when Hailey and Cornelia arrive.

"Good morning." I force myself to smile and greet them— really working that professional angle, as if I don't feel some kind of way about both of them for different reasons.

As Hailey leans in to hug me, over her shoulder, I catch sight of Ebony, and I'm completely caught off guard.

Damn.

Hailey pulls back, arching her dark, severe eyebrows in confusion as she meets my stare. *Did I just say that out loud?*

Apparently so.

That frown immediately turns upside down as she follows my line of vision. Not that I can blame her, because…*me too.*

"Hey, Ebs!" Hailey exclaims, twirling around in a heavy cloud of floral perfume, then rushing Ebony with a hug. "Oh my gosh. First of all, you look absolutely stunning. And second, can you freaking believe that I'm getting married at Madison Manor?" She unleashes an ear-piercing squeal, but I barely register it.

I feel the pull of gravity as if the ground itself is holding me in place, anchoring me to this spot.

The thing about Ebony Livingston is that she's always been undeniably beautiful. She's got this deep brown skin that shimmers with the subtle iridescence of Tahitian pearls, catching the last rays of daylight. Hypnotizing hazel eyes with olive-green undertones. And her lips…*Jesus.* Full, soft, begging to be kissed.

Even underneath, when she was the polished Christie doll on the arm of an undeserving anchorman, she carried herself in a way that commanded attention.

But this Ebony…she's unexpected.

Her long, dark brown waves, cascading down her back? Gone, replaced by a tapered pixie cut that frames her face in a way that, somehow, feels daring. Bold. And it's not just the haircut. The soft, debutante-approved pink lips are a velvet red. She's shed the usual chic-but-reserved clothing, too. The sleeveless corporate dresses and cashmere athleisure set have been swapped for an elegant, bold-print scarlet-red mini dress that barely reaches her smooth ebony thighs and fits like it was made to showcase every precision-cut line and breakneck curve of her body. Legs, collarbone—every exposed inch of her, every confident shift as she walks toward us, says she's unapologetically stepped into a new version of herself.

I'm not sure I've seen her this commanding or undeniably show-stopping since…well, since she was Ebony King.

All of me notices all of her, and I could easily lose myself again.

And, apparently, for too long, I do.

"Well…" Cornelia quietly clears her throat, then grins cheerfully. "It's lovely to see you two have picked up right where you left off. I just knew the, uh…synergy with this partnership would be off the charts."

Ebony manages a tight smile, and it's enough to remind me why I spent all morning preparing for this meeting.

I straighten, drawing myself up to my full height. "Oh, absolutely." I give a light chuckle. "Ebony is not just an outstanding event planner; she's been nothing short of extraordinary. Professional, dedicated, passionate—"

"Passionate?" Cornelia's eyebrows dip. She purses her sensible pink lips, like she wants to really explore the sentiment.

So, maybe I laid it on too thick.

But for the life of me, I can't figure why, of all the adjectives I just hurled at her, she latched on to that one. And I'm not about to try, either.

Instead, I simply nod and say, "Yes, in every sense of the word."

Evidently—by the fury blazing in Ebony's eyes—that was the wrong response.

She immediately interjects, "What I think he means is I've made it abundantly clear that not only will we meet your expectation of the job..." She pauses, and they're stuck at some sort of an impasse. A subliminal challenge waged right before our eyes. Then she continues, sharply, "...we'll exceed it. We'll restore the beautiful heritage of this historic manor, on schedule, for a timeless wedding." She turns away from Cornelia with a downright sinister smile on her face as she shifts her focus to Hailey. "Trust me, it's going to be breathtaking."

Well, hell. I guess she didn't need me to have her back.

"I do," I reply. "Implicitly."

Ebony flashes me an intense stare, watching me curiously. Which, considering our texts last week, and now my overselling of her qualities to her ex-mother-in-law, I get.

A few seconds later, she enters Madison Manor with Cornelia trailing on her heels, leaving Hailey and I knee-deep in their wreckage.

"Damn," she and I say in unison.

She offers me a warm smile, lingering for just a beat longer than necessary. "*Ugh.* That was probably about Julian," she says, and even if it's an act, she's got the decency to look contrite on behalf of her soon-to-be brother-in-law.

It makes me pay attention.

Half of me unsympathetically feels she should've anticipated the War of the Livingstons when she asked Ebony to plan this wedding—fresh off a divorce due to the "irreconcilable difference" of public infidelity. But the other part of me? I'm looking at Hailey's pained expression and the way her shoulders are pulled low.

Sometimes, you can't control whom you fall for. Other times, that person isn't the one you're supposed to be with, and you deal with it.

A soft sigh spills out of me.

"Listen, Hailey, you're probably right. Those two have been battling long before today. So how about for now we focus on you, hmm?" I playfully nudge her shoulder with mine, waiting until she meets my stare. "And congratulations again."

"Thanks." Hailey's lips curve up slightly. "I'm so in love with that man, I don't what to do with myself."

Again, I study her, dissecting her tone, the inflection in her voice, now paying way too much attention to body language, thanks to Dom. Surprisingly, though—despite my inherent biases, knowing the stock she comes from—I don't get the "Land a Livingston" craze from her. She didn't thrust her hand out to wiggle her ring finger in my face like a gemstone trophy to gloat over.

This feels genuine.

Families are made up of individuals, I remind myself, considering maybe I've misjudged her.

"Probably a good thing." I smile at her. "It's going to be an exciting chapter." *And a wedding that's going to be one for the books.*

When we rejoin the others inside, Ebony wastes no time getting down to business.

"Firstly, I'd like to thank you for being here today. In the essence of time, I thought it would be the best way to ensure we're all on the same page logistically before I continue confirming with the vendors." She pauses, making individual eye contact for our buy-in. "Fantastic!" She perks up, smiling at me. "Now—"

"Wait, I really want to echo that sentiment. Thank you, from Donovan and I, too." Hailey beams at us, her eyes brimming with tears. "Truly, for making this dream into a reality." Her lower lip quivers.

Fortunately, Cornelia's here to hand her a balled-up pocket tissue and a cool *there, there* pat on the shoulder.

Lord.

Ebony softens, meeting Hailey's watery gaze. "We are just as lucky. We can't wait to transform this…romantically illustrious, historic venue for this monumental occasion. It's going to be stunning," she says, and then proceeds to make us believe it.

She ushers us out of the bright foyer, guiding us into the center of the reception hall, where she paints a vivid picture with carefully curated buzzwords. She calls it a five-star luxury manor that channels romance, history, and style. A worldly escape of the highest caliber, and even higher style.

My mouth is on the ground.

To hear her talk about how it will be "quintessentially Ellswood," and watch Cornelia and Hailey eat it up—it's an acutely skilled talent. I can just imagine these two going back, gabbing to their so-called elite friends about the dedicated catering staff. The six elegantly designed suites to accommodate wedding guests. The way Ebony sells it, space isn't the issue because it's "an intimate yet worldly escape."

She makes it look so easy.

A small, proud laugh bubbles in the back of my throat.

To be fair, though, we haven't moved more than twenty feet, and I'm leaned against the wall, listening, and feeling transported too.

She's amazing.

"We'll be buying out the property for the entirety of the weekend," she says, gaining agreement from Cornelia, before she briefly checks in with Hailey whether she'd like to take advantage of the space to host a bachelorette party or bridal shower here. Of course, it's a prime location for a bride-to-be to "indulge in the ultimate comfort."

Wow.

I see why Hailey insisted that no other wedding planner would suffice.

Five minutes pass with them confirming the wedding party (five bridesmaids and groomsmen, respectively) and the event weekend, which will begin Friday, September nineteenth, for the rehearsal, followed by a serene dinner in the indoor garden—my eyebrows shoot up, because I guess that's how we're now referring to the conservatory—with the ceremony and reception, Saturday the twentieth, culminating on Sunday with a morning-after brunch on the terrace lawn.

Jotting down a few notes on my iPad, I listen as she points out the striking white marble floors and alcoves set to be restored to showcase flower arrangements, as this is where guests will gather for cocktail hour before they're granted access to the grand ballroom.

I follow closely, listening to them *ooh* and *ahh* as we tour the library, conservatory, and drawing room—a great location for engagement photos, according to this renowned event planner.

Ebony reaches for the door to the billiard room, but before she opens it, I rest my hand on the small of her back, giving a small, wide-eyed head shake, wordlessly warning her that it's under construction and likely not the best area to show Cornelia our progress so far.

"U-uh," she stammers, her smile faltering for a moment as our eyes connect. "Let's, uh, keep going…toward my favorite space." She forces the words out, improvising as if she too felt the electric jolt between us.

Whoa.

It was only an instant, but my pulse is racing.

Ebony stalls outside the double doors of the ballroom. It's barely noticeable, but her hand trembles as she presses it to her chest, as if she's trying to catch her breath. But like a pro, she snaps back, using that adrenaline to impress Cornelia and Hailey.

"We're here," she says, beaming.

Hailey's eyes light up. "I'm so ready!" She squeals and bounces like she's on springs.

I'm guessing it's just the reaction Ebony was hoping for, because she clears her throat, her entire body snapping to attention as she smooths her expression. "The legend of the manor's grand ballroom promises that if a couple shares their first dance beneath its crystal chandelier, their love will last forever." She pauses, letting that tidbit hang in the air. "Before the building was condemned, many had come to test it, but none have disproven the magic."

The bouncy squeals return in full force.

Hailey—and Ebony, it seems—are clearly believers.

"Now, please keep in mind," Ebony continues, "we don't have a ton of time until September twentieth—exactly one hundred days from today, according to my calendar countdown." When she says this, her eyes sparkle and the inflection in her voice rises just so. It's really thoughtful how she makes even a random Thursday in June feel like a milestone. "And Mr. Bridges and his team are in the midst of preserving some of the structural integrity of the space, but..."

Then she opens the doors, and...I cringe.

It looks like a giant monster swallowed a lumberyard then decided to cough up a DIY project.

Honestly, it's an embarrassing letdown, seeing the space in this state after all the buildup. The wooden floors are in need of sanding, restaining, and lacquering, so there are stacks of reclaimed wood strewn everywhere. The gold leaf on the gilded wall panels is peeling, the ornate plasterwork needs work, and the color of the stained-glass windows has faded with time. All of it's in progress, but about the only saving grace *is* the nineteenth-century chandelier.

Naturally, Cornelia ignores Ebony's forewarning. She's got all the questions. What's our construction timeline? Do I have an updated layout or rendering of how it'll look once it's finished? Will the bathroom facilities be fully operational? Is my team available to answer these questions?

Yes, where is my crew?

Ebony must not see the worry on my face.

"Uh, Linc?" She defers to me, like handling Cornelia is the simplest thing.

Oh, and what happened to Mr. Bridges?

Technically, this is where everything could've gone wrong.

But leave it to Ebony Grace, planner extraordinaire, to help Cornelia see the jewel amongst the junk.

"Yes, it's hard to imagine now. But do me a favor. Close your eyes and picture this." Then she inhales and smiles. "It's dusk on a warm September day. A soft breeze carries the sweet, floral scent of magnolia blossoms."

"Mmm..." Hailey inhales—probably centuries-old sawdust, but that won't make a lick of difference. "Go on."

Ebony seems all too happy to oblige. "We've just come indoors after an intimate courtyard ceremony where you and Donovan exchanged vows on a beautifully manicured lawn." *Genius.* "You've captured the sunset photos to prove it, and now, with cocktail hour wrapped, your loved ones are eagerly awaiting a phenomenal culinary experience."

Hailey swoons, and I have to bite my tongue to hold back a laugh.

"They walk into a majestic ballroom where a few dozen white-clothed ten-seater tables are scattered around the gleaming wooden dance floor. At the heart of each table, towering vases overflow with white roses and rich red zinnias. Or maybe dahlias." She flashes a conflicted smile, like she's still debating. "The Baccarat crystal chandelier, timeless furnishings, an air of natural elegance—"

PING!

My phone yanks us out of the vision.

"Ugh, sorry. I need to take this. Please continue." I slip my hand in my pocket and hurry out the door to the terrace, praying it's my project manager, Manny, or one of my guys calling to explain why the entire crew is still MIA. Or even Vincent, who was supposed to be here with the interior design plans.

When I make it out to the hearth room patio, I check my screen and let out a heavy sigh.

The message isn't from them.

Dom

Your girl...

Website: The Divorcétante Chronicles on PopShot: "High society to high jinks—Pre-Adventures of a Post-Divorce Diva. #TheNextChapter

The next chapter?

Confused, I tap on the text. The message opens to a preview link with a full image of Ebony's face. Sporting the new pixie cut, red-lipped Ebony is... *Sitting in her car? Is this today?* But again, the handle isn't Ebony Grace Livingston; it's *The Divorcétante Chronicles*…

"What in the hell is a divorcétante?"

I lower my volume, letting my finger hover over the link, unsure what to expect once the PopShot app opens.

Then I tap it.

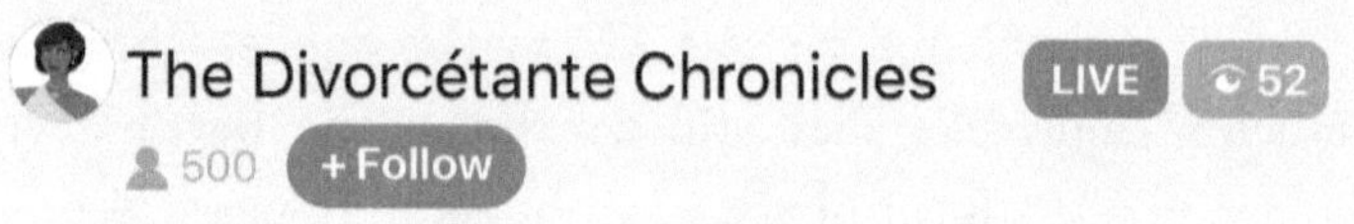

"Hey, and welcome! It's your girl Ebony. Some of you might know me from my event-planning company, Ebony Grace Events, where I curate premier weddings and celebrations. Others might recognize me as a member of Ellswood's Zion & Zara chapter. And then there are those who know me from that viral episode of *The Morning Tea*. Yeah, the one where my ex-husband ended up in a, let's say…compromising situation."

She laughs.

"Whether you know it or not, you're here for part one of my new series that I'm calling…"

She pauses, briefly reaching out of shot before returning with a sparkly tiara in hand. Then she looks directly at us.

"…*The Divorcétante Chronicles*. And what's that, you ask? It's me—part debutante, part divorcée, all hiccups. All real. All the pomp and ceremony as I tell my side of the story. I'm living the married-single life, and yes, I'm even being villainized as a cheating victim. Because, let's face it, you've already heard the version from the 'Luxe' team."

Ebony throws up air quotes, and it doesn't take a mind reader to know she's referring to the hashtag #TeamNora.

"The reason I know that's why you're here is because some of you have taken my picture as I enter office buildings for business and personal appointments. One such person was so bold, she snapped a photo dead in my face. Shoutout to Syd, the multitasker, who somehow managed to violate my privacy *and* help me pick out an amazing gratitude journal.

"You want my reaction so bad.

"You want the scandal.

"You want the shock value, the trending, viral smear-campaign drama.

"And guess what?

"I'm going to give it to you, because I'm still here. They thought I was down for good, but I'm reclaiming Ebony Grace, daring to reinvent myself outside of my ex's family dynasty.

"As a divorcée—just like I trained as a debutante—this will be my reintroduction into society, but on my terms this time.

"I'm about to tell you how I really feel about those news anchors procreating—by the way, congratulations and good luck with that. Plus, you'll get an all-access pass to my newfound freedom and fashion as I find myself, and, yes, as one of my divas likes to say, as I find the fine-ass men.

"Y'all, it's true. I'm on the market again! And no, you won't catch him by stalking my every move. But don't worry—I'll share all the salacious details. Like the fact that I've created a starter profile with a dating concierge and I've got my first consultation tomorrow!"

She crosses her fingers.

"Wish me luck. And let's just hope my days of Missionary Mondays are soon to be a thing of the distant past.

"I'll take you along with me as I plan the wedding of the century at the architecturally stunning Madison Manor, currently being restored by Bridges Heritage Conservation. Congratulations to Hailey Winston and Donovan Livingston on your engagement. So stay tuned."

Fittingly, she steadies the crown atop her head.

"For now, pause, peace, power. Signing off, the Divorcétante."

The video starts to replay, and I close out of the app, feeling… restless? Inspired?

I'm not sure, but I feel like I've just watched one of those underdog sports movies when the tables turn, and I'm left with this overwhelming sense of pride for her.

I'm still reeling as I duck back inside to rejoin the group as Ebony walks Cornelia and Hailey through the wedding night sparkler send-off.

She's beaming and beautiful, and I'm blown away by the prospect of Ebony King's return.

Glancing at my phone, I silence it and hit play on the video again, watching her light up the screen as she speaks her truth. Without a second thought, I follow her account.

You're invited
to our
Wedding Day

You're invited
to our
Wedding Day

Chapter Nine

Outmaneuvered

Ebony

THE SECOND THE MANOR'S DOOR shuts behind Hailey and Cornelia, it's like a confetti cannon goes off in my chest.

"*Cele-bra-tion time, come on.*" I moonwalk through the foyer, singing Kool & the Gang's "Celebration" at the top of my lungs. Digging deep, I then drop my voice for the low notes.

My skin buzzes with excitement as I make my way to the library, prepared to lock up, say a quick goodbye to Lincoln, and sprint to my car. I feel like I'm in a parkour video as I quickly, but carefully, run down the hall toward the grand ballroom, switching off lights and vaulting over debris and cords, still bustling with energy.

A scream leaps from my gut into my throat as I turn and spot Lincoln's interior designer, Vincent. Even on a Thursday, he's dressed to kill—kelly-green button-down, perfectly tailored khaki slacks, and a dark brown leather belt that matches his loafers—and he's grinning and doing some ridiculous conga line dance behind me.

"*Ooh*, shit. You scared me." I close my eyes, smiling, and clutch my chest.

"My bad."

I raise my free hand, thumb and forefinger nearly pinched together. "Just a small heart attack. No big deal."

He lifts a shoulder and lets it drop with a small laugh. "Hey, I was just taking my cue from you, ma'am." Vincent does a full-body shimmy, then spins around while continuing the lyrics, eighties heartthrob-style. "I mean, with the sheer creativity behind those enthusiastic lyrics, I'm guessing you and Linc crushed it with Cornelia and Hailey."

My smile stretches across my face. "Your guess would be correct, sir."

"Oh, do tell." He chuckles.

A few minutes pass as I lock up the terrace and patio doors while bringing Vincent up to speed on the tour—and the magical vision of Madison Manor I painted in their minds. When I'm done, he gazes around the grand ballroom the same way I did opening those doors this morning. He's in awe. Not of the room, of course. The room looks like crap. But of my ability to win my clients over without their seeing it first.

"I can't believe it either." I shrug, looking around. "I basically had to hypnotize them to see my vision, but we made it through."

Vincent dips his chin, a challenge flickering in his soft brown eyes.

I shrug, laughing. "Obviously, this was Cornelia, so it goes without saying she threw in a few savage one-liners." I roll my eyes, then mimic her snooty tone. "'Ebony, the restrooms are outdated. Mr. Bridges, the outlets are poorly placed.' Both of which, mind you, I already warned him about."

"Oh, trust me. I said the same thing." Vincent nods, and his eyebrows climb up to his tapered hairline. "But let me guess—did Cornelia take one look at this place and frown? I can just imagine her tone, cold and resigned as ever. Her stony façade in place as she cleared her throat. 'There's nothing grand about the state of this ballroom.'"

I gasp for air, pointing at him. "Verbatim!"

We both dissolve into giggles.

"That woman is ruthless." Vincent cackles, clutching his middle. "Subtlety is *not* her thing. But being unnecessarily mean, brutal, and just straight-up abrasive? Oh yeah, that's her default setting."

"Mm-hmm. I took it in stride, but she was definitely on brand."

"A bad and bougie brand," Vincent adds, fueling our laughter all over again.

By the time I catch my breath, my happiness meter is off the charts. "Listen, any day that Lincoln Bridges and I can actually manage to pull off our first wedding client meeting is a good day. Trust me. And if a few nitpicky comments are all that woman's got…" *Maybe I've blown the whole sabotage thing out of proportion. Maybe, with my resources, my network of contacts, and Lincoln's drive to keep Ellswood's history alive, we've really got this.*

I exhale, sinking into the eerily quiet worksite, breathing a little easier.

Maybe a little distraction won't hurt.

"So, all in all, it's been a good day, then?" Vincent asks, cutting into my thoughts. He walks away, his attention zeroed in on the peeling wall panels.

"Can't complain."

He nods as he glides his manicured fingers over the threadbare gold-leaf texture. "Good, good…" But then his hand halts, like he's still turning something over in his head. Finally, he tosses me a pensive look and asks, "And you've been here *all* morning?"

I don't know whether to focus on the way his voice rises at the end or the question itself—why is he asking? It's barely a quarter after eleven. The day is just getting started. Where else would I be for the tour?

What isn't he saying?

"Yeah." I give a noncommittal nod, slightly weirded out.

Again, he nods himself, like my story tracks with whatever's going on in his head. "Did you know Cornelia gave the entire crew the day off while y'all were touring the manor?"

That, I didn't know.

"Uh, no." Curiosity twists my stomach, leaving me slightly uneasy. "That makes no sense. Why would she do that when we're going to need every day to get this place in shape before Hailey's wedding? But also, you're telling me that she had all these questions for the crew, asking about their whereabouts, when she gave them the day off?"

"Yes."

I frown. "See, she's definitely up to something."

Vincent inhales, sharply, like he's about to drop a bomb, then plants himself back in front of me. "All right, I'm just going to say this real quick. While you were over here painting visions for her and Hailey, and Linc was busy following you—"

"Wait, what?"

I freeze.

"Oh, you didn't see the news?" Vincent says, vague as hell.

The world just stops cold. Clearly, there's more coming, but this right here? I can't just let it slide. I tilt my head toward him when I ask, "Linc followed me where, exactly?" I glance over my shoulder, still trying to figure out where that man vanished to.

"Ooh, okay, I see you're one of those post-and-ghost folks." Vincent continues with his cryptic commentary. He shakes his head and exhales like he's been holding in a secret way too long. "See, me? I'm messy *and* petty, honey. I stay on PopShot. So, as soon as you said 'divorcétante,' I followed you. Then I practically broke an ankle running to your comments, and whose name do you think popped up?"

"*Nooooo.*" My jaw practically hits the floor.

"Yes, honey."

I'm stunned. Like, genuinely shocked, already unlocking my phone. I glance at the screen, and it's lighting up with… "Over a thousand notifications? *Shit.*" I scroll through a deluge of comments, utterly dumbfounded.

In all the fuss trying to impress Cornelia, I forgot I posted the first video for *The Divorcétante Chronicles*. But why the hell is Lincoln Bridges following me now? Is he actually interested in my posts? I did *not* take him for the messy-blog, piping-hot-tea type. Does he think I'll follow him back? Is this going to make things even more awkward than they already are? And how the hell did he even know I posted? Does he think I'm desperate now that I'm divorced, like we can just pick up where we left off?

Does he want that? Do *I?*

Again, I glance toward the ballroom doors, just in case Linc materializes.

"*Pause, peace, power,* diva!" Vincent snaps twice, pulling my attention back. "I ran into Linc headed out on my way in. He went to pick up more hardwood for the billiard room. He said he'd be back soon." He says it like he's trying to calm me down, but the softness in his voice only makes me feel like I'm about to combust over a new follower.

Ugh, what does that mean?

With the phone burning a hole in my hand, I blink repeatedly. "Okay, so Lincoln Bridges followed me? Why? I'm genuinely so confused."

"Don't be." Vincent holds up a hand. "That man doesn't even know how to use PopShot. And now that I'm thinking about it, it was actually Bridges Heritage Conservation that followed you. So he probably won't even comment. The business account is used mostly for portfolio pics. That's it."

I nod and let out a shaky laugh.

"Yeah, you're probably right…" But just as the calm loosens the knots in my stomach, my thoughts screech to a halt. "Wait, so Linc's business following me is newsworthy, somehow?"

"To the invested interwebs, absolutely. But also, let's reel it way back, because things are clearly getting jumbled." Vincent slices his soft-looking hands through the air, starting over. "We've got to keep our timeline in order, so I'll go slow. Now, again, you were schmoozing and cruising these halls—"

A laugh bubbles up in my throat, and he pauses, clearly annoyed with my interruptions.

"No, I'm with you. Please continue." I wave him off, my lips still twitching because this man has never met a catchphrase pairing he didn't like.

Vincent purses his glossy lips and swallows. "It's fine. I've got a quick question, anyway. Now, I know you took some time off from event planning, which, absolutely, understandable." He gives me a wide-eyed stare, like he knows exactly how hard I fell, both personally and professionally, post-divorce. "But I'm just curious— are you still renting that office at the old Ellswood Mill?"

Immediately, I cringe. "Uh, long story short, yes…" I trail off, weighing how to actually trim the details and get to the point. "I haven't really been using it for business, per se. Up until recently, it's mostly been a storage spot for all my oversized event props—floral arrangements, chairs, cake stands, various linens, photobooth stuff, you name it."

"Oh, I didn't realize you owned all that."

"Not everything." I shrug, still swiping through comments. "But keeping some stuff on hand helps with flexibility. Especially when I plan multiple events, or have shorter timeframes."

He chuckles. "Like this one?"

"Exactly like this one." I smile, smoothing my hand over my short hair. "I love being able to add personalized touches, here and there, for my clients. They're trusting me with their milestone events. The least I can do is make it magical, you know? My props are invaluable."

"Yeah…" Vincent lets out another heavy sigh, and I swear he curses under his breath. "I'm sorry, Ebony. It's gone."

I laugh, raising an eyebrow. "What's gone?"

"I'm guessing you haven't seen the news today."

A wave of worry hits me, sharp and fast, as I swipe out of the PopShot app and open my web browser. "Vincent, I don't have news apps on my phone. I don't need that negativity. Just tell me what happened already."

"The Ellswood Mill burned down."

All the air seems to drain out of my lungs. "Burned? Like someone set it on fire?"

"The news said it was an electrical fire sometime after nine thirty this morning." And that's about all I catch before my mind starts swimming in a soupy mix of fear, anger, and utter disbelief. An electrical fire? What the hell were people plugging in? Who doesn't use surge protectors? Was there no one around with a fire extinguisher?

I shake my head, squeezing my eyes closed.

"The whole building?" I drag in deep breaths, willing myself to calm down. "I was about to stop by after I locked up here."

Vincent's posture softens, his voice turning solemn. "Ebony, I'm so sorry. Hopefully replacing your props won't be too hard. You said it was mostly the big stuff, and most of the smaller things are at home—"

"No, they're not." I close my eyes and shake my head as the reality of losing all of my physical assets hits me. "Vincent, I moved my entire planning inventory there last week. And now it's all just… ashes. *What the hell am I supposed to do?*"

I start pacing the room, kneading my temples as the floorboards creak beneath each leaden step.

"And we're already in mid-June." I huff out a sigh. "There's no way I can replace everything by September. I don't have that kind of money right now."

"What about the insurance?"

My heart skips to an up-tempo beat.

"Oh, thank God I paid that premium last year. Yes!" Hope starts to bloom inside me, just a little. "I'll call when I get home. They'll need to assess the damages and all that, but I can't see it taking longer than a month to approve the claim."

"Yup, and in the meantime, just work from home." Vincent looks around, then gestures to the pile of sawdust. "Or you could always work here at the manor. You've got to be in the space anyway, right? The billiard room's almost done, and the library's got a desk. Or there's the six rooms upstairs. It wouldn't be too much trouble. I'm sure Linc wouldn't mind you being on-site too."

Too.

"He's working out of Madison Manor?"

"Well, yeah." Vincent shrugs like it's a given. "With Cornelia cutting down our time, he'll basically be living here to get it done. The man's all about the details. I wouldn't be surprised if we're down to the eleventh hour before the wedding."

"But I thought the permits were good, and he'd already sourced most of the materials…" The corners of my mouth tug down, my lower lip protruding as Vincent shrugs again.

"Give or take a few rooms. But he really wants to do a great job. His family's name is on that placard outside."

I nod, because that tracks. The Lincoln Bridges I knew was never one to cut corners because he could. If he was interested, he put in the time, effort, and care, knowing that anything meaningful required more than just a quick fix. His work—and relationships—deserved nothing less than his best.

That's what worries me.

The next day, despite the ominous glare of "FRIDAY THE 13TH" staring at me from my wall calendar, I take Vincent's advice. With the last dregs of night smudged across the sky and only my iPad and laptop in tow, I settle into the dusty library at Madison Manor, thankfully equipped with an old oak writing desk and a chair. *Uh, win.* Now, granted, the library isn't my bright, beautiful townhouse with endless snacks and the TV on for white noise, nor is it the office space that—as of last night—I've confirmed has now been reduced to a soot-filled carcass, but it's also not Crystal Lake, with camp counselors meeting their grisly fate, so I guess it'll work.

Since I've got the entire building to myself, I blast some happy music. A little Michael Jackson—minus "Thriller," because…read the haunted-looking room. I spend the few minutes singing and coughing up dust as I sweep the floor, sort through weathered book spines, and set up my devices to start my workday. But as I moonwalk myself over to my chair and settle in—and because I'm still alone with my overactive brain—I try calling Hillary again.

As the line rings once, then twice, I hold my breath, hoping in my gut that since Hailey didn't mention any emergencies when we met yesterday, her sister's okay. Then the third ring comes.

No surprise, I get her voicemail.

"Hey, Hil…" I pause, evening out my tone, not wanting to sound too eager or angry. "It's me again, just checking in. I'd love to know what's going on. I hope you're okay. Please know that whatever it is, I'm your friend, and I'm here for you if you just want to vent or you need advice… Give me a call when you can. Love you."

That familiar, uneasy sensation trembles over my skin. I wish she'd just talk to me. I know we can work through it.

I pull in a deep breath, hold it for a few seconds, then slowly release it through my nose. Then I move on to greener pastures. Rather, slightly less yellow pastures. Emails, wedding announcement cold calls, and the insurance claim. But fifteen minutes into my call with the insurance company to file my claim, voices pick up outside the library door, and I go full deer-in-headlights. My attention is laser-focused on the loud, thudding footsteps and shadows passing beneath the jamb.

"Please, hurry up," I whisper to myself. "Keep going—"

"Yes, ma'am," the claims representative's voice blares in my ear, giving me a full-body jump scare. "I've only got a few more questions for you."

"Oh, no, I didn't mean you," I say apologetically. "There was, uh…a bug coming dangerously close to me, and I wanted it to hurry up and go away."

She laughs. "Of course, I completely understand."

After we spend an inordinate amount of time exchanging insect trauma stories to the soundtrack of MJ and power tools roaring to life throughout the manor, finally, she tells me my claim has been filed. It's now pending a supervisor review, since she's new to the job, but I've got nothing to worry about and should expect a callback within the week. It feels like the best-case scenario.

Especially since I want to be in the right headspace as I switch gears. My virtual consultation with the dating concierge Savannah set me up with—the one my followers can't stop talking about—is in two minutes.

I flip open my laptop and toggle to the camera to check my makeup, and as soon as it opens on me, I twist around, scrunching my face. My backdrop options consist of dilapidated and ugly bookshelves—no thank you—and a discolored fireplace that probably hasn't worked in decades.

"Not ideal." Tilting my head and squinting, I sing along with "Smooth Criminal" as I frame the mantel with my hands. "Maybe with a little pop of color…"

Dashing out the door, I round the hall, cut through the foyer, and into the front garden, where I quickly grab a bunch of vibrant yellow tulips and loose foliage. As I'm rushing back to the library, Linc's thunderous laughter echoes through the manor.

"Annie, are you okay?" he teases, making an adorably horrible attempt at Mike's gravity-defying forty-five-degree tilt. "I'm a smooth law-abiding citizen…"

He's all full-teeth smiles and lighthearted banter. I'm assuming his easygoing demeanor's got everything to do with my following him back on PopShot yesterday and now working on-site. Our past is water under the bridge. We're now free to share cute jokes and expose our extremely toned forearms. *Yay, me.*

Admittedly, I preferred the stilted interactions.

For professional reasons, of course.

Lucky for me, I don't have time to stop and chat. Not that I'd want to. I've been actively avoiding him all day, locking myself in the library. Again, Cornelia cannot win. On principle. I'm chasing life on *my* terms. He's presumably still on a mission to reclaim his family's roots, one Ellswood landmark at a time. So, no room for distractions.

Letting the door drift closed behind me, I toss the flowers on the mantel, angling them just so, and plop into the chair.

"Breathe, Ebony." I inhale, deeply, then click the Virtucon notification link, waiting for the app to load.

My picture flashes onto the screen, right next to a black square labeled *Leslie Browne* in the corner.

I've never actually met the person I'm about to meet with. Up until now, all I've done is create a "starter profile." Today's the day that Leslie, I guess, will help me navigate online dating apps and revamp my profile. She'll suggest the best photos, figure out my preferences and dealbreakers, and they've got professional matchmakers on standby. Easy-peasy.

Except, as my attention flits between the black square and the time glaring at me from the top-right corner of my screen, I wonder if she's really late. The camera's off; the mic's muted. She could be sitting there, silently watching, analyzing my every move like a two-way mirror situation.

Why do I suddenly feel…paranoid?

Be normal.

I force a tight smile, just in case Leslie can somehow tune into the movie reel of Linc glitching in my head.

Stop thinking about MJ 2.0. and his forearms right now.

Of course, Julian sends another *I haven't given up* text now. "Not today, sir." I quickly swipe it away, smiling at my reflection on the screen.

Thankfully, the mic clicks on, followed by the camera after a couple of seconds. I'm not certain whom I was expecting by that name, but it absolutely wasn't a gorgeous white guy in a gray tweed snap-front newsie hat wearing an *I got six and a possible* T-shirt. I mean, yeah, he's wearing a wedding ring, but my *gawwwd*!

"Sorry about that. A meeting with another client ran over just a bit. But, uh, hello. How are you?" *Jesus, the smolder.*

"Hi!" I smile way too hard, my voice shooting up to glass-break pitch, and naturally, the rest of the meeting goes just as smoothly.

He broods. I blink. Somewhere in between, he gently informs me that my profile "needs some work." Which, *understatement.* After hearing about all the effort that goes into a successful first impression, I can't help but think, yup, that's about right.

Leslie, my very own dating concierge, has challenged me to take some "casual, bright photos." Nothing too staged. Meanwhile, he'll work his magic on my profile, adding my dealbreakers. No addictions, no narcissistic, ambition-less incel types, no men with questionable hygiene (or cologne abuse), no cheapskates, no love bombers. And, of course, no Livingstons. *Luxe Ladies*-watching cheaters are just *implied* on the list.

It's a little lengthy, but let's be real: a woman knows exactly what she doesn't want.

As for what I *do* want…

Not as simple.

"For sure, I need someone committed, consistent…and cute doesn't hurt." A self-conscious laugh squeaks out of me.

"Don't be ashamed," Leslie reassures me. "That's a great place to start."

Really digging deep, I add, "Maybe someone handy—not handsy. At least, not right off the bat. He's got to have life goals, strong values…" I trail off, and he nods repeatedly, urging the rest out of me. "He's thoughtful, can actually laugh at a bad joke, dances on beat, knows how to play Spades—I don't know."

Leslie barks out a laugh. "Jotting that down and underlining it three times. How about physically?"

"It's been a while, but kisses me tenderly until my toes curl, using his magic fingers to make me—"

"Uh, sorry, I meant his physical description."

My face bursts into flames. "Oh." I cringe, giggling. "In that case, I'd love it if he was tall, athletic, with deep brown skin. Ooh, gray

eyes? Well, that would be nice, but I'm not making it a dealbreaker…
yet."

"Okay, great. For now," Leslie says, his fingers moving rapid-fire over the keys, "based on all that good stuff—and the gray-eyed Spades champ with the magic fingers, of course—I'll work with our executive matchmakers to schedule you for one of our private mixers and send you on a couple blind dates—"

I miss the rest of his sentence when the library door creaks, and suddenly, I'm acutely aware of two fundamental truths. I never fully closed the door, and I have no idea how long Lincoln Bridges has been standing in the doorway.

Oh, God.

The way his eyes flicker to my screen tells me he's heard enough.

"Oh, uh…Leslie, one sec." Panic streaks through me as I jab the mute button and jolt off my chair to talk to Linc. "Hey, what's up?"

Who knows? Maybe he didn't hear everything. Maybe he only needs my input on Vincent's interior designs.

"No, I was just going to go grab lunch for my guys," he says, his voice a little more strained than usual. "Thought I'd ask if you wanted any tacos—"

"Tacos?" I perk up.

His smile's tight, like he's trying to maintain his usual easygoing demeanor, but it doesn't reach his eyes. His steely-gray eyes linger on me, like he's holding something back.

My chest tightens.

Why did he have to show up right now?

"Uh, yeah. Nothing too fancy." He shrugs. "There's this food truck a few blocks from here that sells them, street-style. The guys love it. But I didn't want to interrupt you if you're, um, busy."

Again, Linc's gaze darts past me to my laptop, where Leslie's still waiting for me to come back to the screen, and I know.

Linc's heard everything.

And he'll keep hearing it, too. He's following *The Divorcétante Chronicles*. He's going to know all about my dates—the good, the bad, the ugly, and possibly the ones that end with *good morning*.

I force a smile, resting my hand lightly on his forearm. "Say less, sir. My answer will always be yes to tacos." I laugh, but it's a hollow sound, trying to ease the discomfort radiating off him.

I hate how wrong this feels. How wrong *I* feel. *Say something.*

"Well then, ma'am…" He grins, slipping his phone from his back pocket and unlocking it to a note cutely entitled *Lunch Orders*. "May I take your order?"

I glance at the screen, where there's a running list with all the crew members' names.

"Do they have a shredded chicken one?" I ask, biting back a laugh at how cutely he's taking notes.

As he continues, adding my cilantro, lime, and feta cheese, then teasing when I ask for a side of tomatillo sauce, not "green sauce," I'm completely fixated on his face. His piercing gray eyes. Smooth, intricate shadows and lines drenched in rich, dark brown skin. The light dusting of salt-and-pepper beard scruff, catching the light spilling in from the windows. Full, soft-looking pink lips.

My heart rams my ribs.

His smile snaps me out of my thoughts, and I've got no idea how long I've been standing here just staring at him.

"Pause, peace, power, right?" he says, cutely.

Inside, I'm melting. Like, I'm just a jumbled mess of bones and nerve endings because… Why is this the worst situation ever? Why can't he just be bitter and ugly? Why is his V-neck…showing so much neck?

"Uh…oops, shoot. Please, don't forget my tomatillo sauce." I smile awkwardly, rushing over to grab my purse, but Linc waves me off, telling me it's his treat. Because of course he does.

He lingers, and for a moment, it's just us, and everything we've left unsaid.

The awkwardness presses down on my chest like a weight I can't lift. The tension is so thick I could cut it with a rusty butter knife.

"Linc—"

"Ebony, are you still there?"

Shoot, Leslie.

The universe saves me from myself. I toss a glance over my shoulder, torn between making Leslie wait and finishing my thought. But really, there are two doors I can choose from: keep chasing the illusion of some perfect man who might love and cherish me or face the one standing right in front of me. I'm learning it's rarely ever a simple choice.

Except I don't get to choose.

Leslie's voice muffles as he starts talking to someone off-screen. "She said she'd be right back. I want to make sure we schedule two dates and the private mixer for her…"

Linc smiles. "I guess I'd better let you go."

And everything inside me fights the truth of his words, even though I hate that he's right.

You're invited
to our
Wedding Day

(410) 555-3269

Chapter Ten

Collateral Damage

Lincoln

MONDAY MORNING, I'M DRAGGING. MANNY, the crew, and I stayed at Madison all through the weekend, and I slept like shit. So on the way in today, I dip into Bean & Gone for a nitro cold brew, hoping a highly concentrated caffeine boost will give me the energy to get through another day knowing Ebony's on the other side of the wall, thinking about men making her toes curl.

Jesus.

"Which reminds me…" I move up in the line, tapping out a quick text to Josiah and Dom.

Lincoln

> What time are we meeting up this Saturday?

Siah's response appears almost immediately.

Josiah

> That depends. Bones, Spades, or gym?

I chuckle, ready to opt for the last when Dom, who isn't great at either game, replies.

Dom

I'm open for anything after noon. Got a brunch date.

Neither Josiah nor I respond. He'll probably send me a separate text. It's well established that whoever answers Dom first will end up being his Spades partner.

"That's all you, Siah," I mutter, laughing to myself and already figuring how I'm going to convince them to hit up the gym.

I lift my head at the two girls standing side by side in front of me, watching a phone on full volume. Yesterday's date scrolls across the bottom of the image next to the KTEG *News at Noon* logo. The screen is split. On the right side, none other than Ellswood's golden prince, Julian, is tuned in live—on the station that fired him—from his house as a guest. On the left, his red-haired former co-anchor. They're both smiling and chatting, and he's wearing—

I lean in, straining to make out the... *Is that a giant blue gift bow on his head?*

What in the world? Why would he subject himself to this torture? They're not going to rehire him.

Jesus.

"...Well, we want to say a big congratulations to our old friend, Julian Livingston—"

"The third," a male voice off-camera adds, chuckling. "Julian Livingston III. Can't forget that third, Parker."

She straightens, her smile gleaming as she taps the edge of her paper stack on the desk. "Yes, let's say a huge congratulations to Julian Livingston *III*, on becoming a father-to-be!" The entire news station erupts in congratulatory applause and whistles. "This is a day I don't think *any* of us ever saw coming, including you," Parker roasts him.

The girls in front of me about fall out laughing, and I have to bite my tongue to keep from joining them.

"Honey, the way Julian Livingston becomes a daddy was not on my bingo card..." the one on the left says, her textured dark curls and blazer-clad shoulders trembling as she's gasping for breath.

Her friend throws her head back, nearly whipping me with a massive ponytail of purple and black braids swinging wildly. "*Phew*, Lord! The shade Parker be throwing is *wild*!"

They lean on each other to keep themselves upright, and her finger must hit the volume by mistake because the entire coffee shop is plugged in full surround sound when Parker asks Julian, "What do you think, Daddy? Any comment on the divorcétante casting her dating net for the plenty of fish in the sea? Your mother sure had a lot to say about..."

A collective gasp echoes around the shop, and by the grace of God, through the tiny gap between the girls, I get a glimpse of the phone.

Never in my life have I been so excited to see Julian Livingston III's pretty-boy face. His emotions flash across the phone in 3D Technicolor—resentment, anger, embarrassment, guilt, regret, shock, and powerlessness all wrapped up under that dumbass royal-blue bow on his head.

Now *I'm* the one holding my heart and gasping for air, barely able to stand upright.

It's a gift to my soul, and I can't contain my laughter as an *Ellswood Times* headline scrolls across the bottom of the screen.

Esteemed Matriarch Cornelia Livingston on The Divorcétante: "From Debutante to Divorcée: A Masterclass in Rebranding Desperation"

Oh, shit.

Except when my attention drifts up from the phone, my eyes lock on a fuming Hillary Winston ahead of the girls.

Her long, dark hair is swept behind her slender shoulders, and she's draped in all black from her sleek dress to her oversized designer shades, like she's in mourning.

My, my, my… Karma's in motion.

"Chile, pure, unfiltered comedy, this early in this glorious a.m. Am I right?" The girl with the braids twists around, steadying her appraising gaze on me.

"No truer words." I flash her a small smile, breaking the starting contest with Hillary to up the ante with my new friend. "Think he's going to congratulate the divorcétante?"

She sucks her teeth, tucking a loose braid behind her ear. "Sir, be serious. That man still wants Ebony, but now he done messed around and got Nora knocked up. We all know Mama Livingston will make him marry Nora, and that's the end of it. Can't have him sullying the family name."

At this, I finally turn away from Hillary. "Nah, definitely can't have that."

"Cold brew for Parker!" the barista calls out, stirring the coffee shop into another bout of laughter at the sheer comedic timing.

Thankfully, the line moves, and Hillary turns back toward the front, inching forward.

Soon, she orders her coffee, then the girls in front of me move to the register. I'm next to pay for my nitro cold brew, the hum of undecipherable chatter returns to Bean & Gone, and I figure, that's it. We've never shared a friendship, and we're not about to conjure one up out of the thick, French-roasted air. We've got nothing to discuss.

At least, I've got nothing to say to her.

But a few moments later, she's still here.

Why hasn't she left? What's she waiting for?

"Hey there, what can I make for you this morning?" the perky barista asks.

I make quick work placing my order and stepping out of line to wait for my drink. I'm careful to avoid Hillary, who's standing near the side window, away from the pickup line. Even after my name is called, we still don't exchange words.

It's not until a few moments later, when I weave past the line to the condiment station in the corner for sugar packets, that she moves too, settling at my side.

I glance at her, restless and breathing heavy like she wants me to speak first. And so I do.

"What do you think, Hillary?" I clamp the sugar packets between my thumb and forefinger, shaking vigorously before I rip the corners and pour the contents into my cup. "Mama Livingston's going to make Julian lock it down with Nora for good, or nah?"

"Why are you asking me?"

After a quick stir, I cap my cup and take a long sip. Then I meet Hillary's gaze.

"I suspect for the same reason you came over here to talk to me." I shrug, purposely blasé. "Thought you, of all people, would know."

She gasps, mouth agape as she stares at me, horrified. "What?"

Oh.

Back there in the line, her glare wasn't just a dominance play, like I thought. No, that direct eye contact was a warning—protective behavior. She was on defense.

She didn't think I knew about her and Julian. Three years ago, they didn't see me, but I saw them kissing in a darkened parking lot.

They thought they'd been careful, discreet.

"Are you ever planning to tell your 'friend'?" I toss up the best air quotes I can manage with my coffee in hand, then I turn toward the exit.

Naturally, she's on my heels, stalking after me.

As I reach the door, I grab the handle and step back to hold it open for her, but she stops me cold in my tracks.

"I'm not sure what you *think* you know—"

"No, I'm certain." I chuckle.

Fire blazes in her eyes, but after a beat, realization snuffs it out, leaving only devastation in its wake.

"More than anyone else, I thought *you* would understand." She watches me, her lips quivering. "Everyone knows you've wanted Ebony Livingston forever, and if she'd given you the chance to be with her, I *know* you would've—"

"No." I shake my head. "I wouldn't have. We're not the same, Hillary. *I* would never take part in ruining her marriage. *I'd* never betray my best friend."

She swallows, blinking back tears. "Yeah, keep telling yourself that."

I shrug, releasing the door and stepping out onto the pavement as she turns and walks away. Hillary makes it maybe ten feet away before she comes back, hopping mad.

"It's funny. Ebony told us that after college, before she came back to Ellswood, you asked her to choose you." She smiles, smugly. "She didn't want you then, and guess what? She's divorced, single, with no husband in the way, and still not rushing into your arms. Nothing's changed."

I nod, speechless, giving her the space to take her frustration out on me.

But then she shifts her weight. "So, you can stand there on your little soapbox, judging me, if you want. But if you think I'm the only one who'll be burned by the Livingstons…" She snickers. "Well, you've got another thing coming, Lincoln Bridges. Watch your back."

With that, she stalks off, leaving nothing but curses in the air and a thousand unanswered questions.

By the time I get to Madison Manor, the nitro cold brew is buzzing on my tongue, the caffeine jolt enough to jump-start the work in the grand ballroom. I dive into the restoration, my hands moving over the plans and tools with a frantic energy that I can't quite shake. Brushstrokes, sanding, and the hum of power tools blur the hours and lines. I can't tell if it's the coffee firing through my veins, the realization we've got just three months to finish the manor, Ebony's quiet presence in the library, or Hillary's words echoing in my head that keep me focused.

"What are you running from, Linc?"

For a split second, I freeze, my heart racing as I stare at the freshly smoothed plasterwork, wondering if the old legends are true and that these walls can magically talk.

Maybe next time, I'll skip the nitro.

But then I hear the tapping of a pair of patent leather loafers and groan. "Vincent."

"The one and only," he says, his tone taking on an impatient lilt. "Now, if you're ready to collaborate with your professional partners today, that would be great, because I've got sketches, swatches, and color schemes galore, and they need your approval."

I huff out a sigh. "Can you come back in an hour?"

"Well, since you said that an hour ago, and the hour before that, no."

Vincent Baker doesn't waste time waiting for me to descend a ladder, set down my spackling knife and putty, and give him my undivided attention. That would be too sensible an ask. Instead, he takes even strides across the ballroom, plants his sharp, structured plum-purple suit against my wall, and wields his judgy expression into my line of vision.

"For the last time, I'm going to ask: what's bothering you?" he says.

"Is that a promise?" I scoff.

His precision-arched eyebrows shoot up to the edges of his tapered fade.

"Oh, so you got jokes?" He releases a downright sinister chuckle. "So, this isn't about Ebony Grace Livingston—"

"*Shh.*" I practically glide down the ladder rungs to whisper-yell at him. "Are you crazy? She could hear you."

Vincent's glossy lips screw up to the side. "Mm-hmm. That's what I thought."

I reach back, kneading my neck to loosen the tension.

Meanwhile, Vincent is all smiles now. "To confirm, then, this Energizer Bunny routine *is* about She Who Shall Remain Unnamed?"

"A little," I admit, before he grabs a foghorn and announces it to everyone in Ellswood.

He nods. "Fine. At least we're getting somewhere now," he says. Then, abruptly, he snaps his fingers and gestures for me to follow him outside to the terrace, where the landscapers are mowing down weeds and planting sod, trees, and flowers for the gardens set to flank the courtyard.

"It's too loud," I yell over the roar of a leaf blower.

But Vincent is undeterred in his mission, leading me to the far end of the property, where the noise is just muffled enough for him to interrogate me in peace.

"Whatever's bothering you, I need to know now," he says, dead serious. "Because your body has been in that ballroom all day, but I think we both know damn well your head's been in the library. So, spill."

Frustration sags through my limbs.

Ever since he and the crew didn't show up for that initial tour with Cornelia and Hailey, and I later learned that Cornelia purposely misinformed them about a delayed starting time, something hasn't sat right with me. Her motives don't make sense. But listening to Hillary's warnings earlier at Bean & Gone, and overhearing Ebony make plans with a freaking dating concierge, nothing feels cut and dried anymore.

You're still running behind her, settling for crumbs.

Maybe Josiah was right. Maybe I *am* pathetic.

"Aloud, please…" Vincent prompts me.

Because maybe I might need a little help sorting out my thoughts, and this caffeine buzz doesn't seem to be fading anytime soon, I tell him everything.

Over the next twenty minutes, I bring Vincent up to speed on all the highlights of Ebony's and my history. I start in high school as her tutor, skipping to the night we blurred the friendship line in college, and continue to that lunch we shared three years ago.

"Wait…" Vincent's eyes are saucer wide. "No."

I nod. "Mm-hmm."

He averts his gaze, still shaking his head, his manicured hand clutched to his invisible pearls. "So…" He blinks, repeatedly. "That sleazy, slimy, no-good man was cheating on our girl"—Ebony's *our girl* now—"with not only Nora Whitfield, but Hillary Winston, too?"

"Yeah, and that's why I was trying to warn her."

"Nuh-uh." Vincent gives me a slow, disapproving head shake, narrowing his dark eyes like he's seeing red. Then he holds up a hand. "Wait, isn't she the bride's sister *and* one of Ebony's best friends?"

I give a single nod.

"Damn, these hoes ain't loyal."

A laugh rises from deep in my chest, rolling over me. "All right, with that little nugget of info, let's go back three spaces," I say, piecing it all together. Cornelia hiring Ebony and me separately, then this new "professional" version of Ebony that's been emerging, not to mention the glimpses I've caught in her *Divorcétante Chronicles* posts, and now, us working on-site together. Vincent—and the entire crew—already heard about the dating concierge. "So, while Hillary said to me earlier that, given the opportunity, I'd have broken up their marriage, that's not what worries me."

"Oh, shoot." Vincent braces himself, seeming fully invested. "I can't wait to hear this."

"It's more that she's not married anymore, and she still doesn't want me."

It feels like a *drop the hammer* moment.

A huge, light-bulb epiphany.

But Vincent simply straightens, his expression a mess of pensive contortions.

For a second, I think, *Hmm, maybe he didn't hear me.* So I say, again, "We're both single, and she's not jumping at the chance to be with me." I throw my hands up.

It's not like I expected her to be sitting around thinking about one stupid night we shared over ten years ago, before she was married. That would be ridiculous. But still, if there's even the slightest chance we could get close again—maybe even more—I'm in.

Vincent lets out a sharp sigh.

"No, no, I heard you. I'm just thinking," he says, and I actually believe him, the way he tosses a slightly dismissive hand at me.

This goes on for another excruciating two minutes until I lose my patience. "Okay, I'm going back inside, where—"

He claps his hands—*finally*—looking at me with solution-shaped stars in his eyes, and I'm here for it.

But then he says, "I'm going to help you."

It's my turn to be confused. "With what, exactly?"

"I'll be *your* dating coach. For free," he clarifies, since my "love life" and my "brooding era" are apparently messing up this project that he really wants to include in his portfolio.

The funny thing is, he's absolutely serious. In a matter of seconds, he's on his phone, pulling up the calendar app, skipping past June and calculating that Ebony and I have ninety-six more days working together—so, roughly, three more months—until the wedding. Or, as he calls it, D-Day—the D standing for divorcétante.

"So, what's the plan, coach?" I laugh.

Vincent fishes a pen out of his interior coat pocket and positions it behind his ear, getting into character, and the curiosity is killing me. Mostly because I've seen the sheer number of men falling all over themselves for Vincent. He must have a secret strategy.

"Step one. You're going to *be* there for her," he says, cryptically.

At this point, I'm hoping the B stands for something else, like *blow jobs*—anything besides merely existing.

I open my mouth to protest, then immediately close it again.

"Don't give me that confused, deer-in-headlights look. I said what I said." Vincent clears his throat. "We all overheard her dealbreakers, her preferences. I looked him up, by the way. Leslie Brown is *fine as hell*. Married, though, so you don't have to worry. But my point is, he just hand-delivered the ultimate cheat sheet. Not that I think you should use it like a checklist."

I tip my head to either side. "Okay, I'm listening…"

"I mean, you already know the things that she wants that you've already got: you're a clean, decent-smelling, gray-eyed, Spades… novice, at best—"

"Now, wait a minute." I laugh, personally affronted. "I may not be the champ, but I've always got books."

Vincent rolls his eyes, fluttering his long eyelashes. "Save it for the divorcétante. Barking up the wrong tree here, hon."

I flex my restless fingers, still wrapping my mind around everything.

"Remember, she's about to go on dates, but she'll learn really fast that most of these men can't tell their mate from their mama." Vincent snaps twice, like I need to clock it. "All you can do is *show* her that you're the best man for her. There is no alternative."

"Absolutely." I nod a few times, mentally pumping myself up as we start walking back toward the terrace.

"Learn what's important to her."

Inwardly, I'm listing all the things that I know matter to her, like her family and her girls, her business, and now her new series. I've watched every video, and it's clear how much it means to her. I know she's rediscovering herself.

"This really helps," I say, and I'll admit, I'm feeling lighter somehow. "Thanks, man."

"Nuh-uh, don't thank me just yet. Work on being cute, consistent, and committed." Vincent dips his chin as we reach the steps. "And hone those magic fingers of yours."

I start to respond and nearly choke when I see the long, smooth brown legs at the top of the stairs. Her musical laugh echoes as she walks toward the hearth room, then she follows Manny and a few of the landscapers until she's out of sight.

I all but move on autopilot into the ballroom, the words *nothing's changed* repeating in my head while the rest of me pulses with the desperate urge to hone my magic fingers and show her just how much I'm the best man for the job, seven days a week—not just on Missionary Mondays.

Damn.

You're invited
to our
Wedding Day

You're invited
to our
Wedding Day

Chapter Eleven

Exes Mark the Spot

Ebony

"REMEMBER, THIS IS FOR YOU, not for her." Savannah nods, softly. Her voice takes on an urgent intensity, encouraging me to unlock my phone. "When we make the decision to move on, it needs to be with conviction and action. No lingering regrets."

Right, no regrets.

I take a deep breath as I sit opposite Savannah on her cream-colored sofa, staring down at Hillary's contact.

The petty queen who lives inside me feels like, *Hey, let bygones be bygones and get on. I'm not the one who's in the wrong, here.* So I'll have no problem "in real life" muting and blocking. Because I've called her more than once. I wrote a sentence in my journal. Albeit, it was last night, and I knew Savannah would ask me about my homework progress today. But also, it's what, the eighteenth of June? That's more than a month since we've spoken, and the phone works both ways. If she values this friendship, if it's worth salvaging, why hasn't she reached out to me?

Again, this isn't for her, though.

"Here I go…" I tap Hillary's name, fueled by Savannah's authoritative yet approving smile. The line rings once before—

"Hey, you've reached Hillary…"

Disconnecting the call—*I will die a slow, soulless death before I leave a message*—I set my phone in my lap, speechless. A humorless laugh huffs out of me. "Wow…"

Savannah uncrosses and recrosses her bare legs, the skirt of her sleek, cerulean-blue mock-neck midi dress flouncing into the air. "Would you like to share what happened?"

"Uh, this woman sent me to voicemail, that's what." I shake my head, still lost in my thoughts, a mix of powerlessness and curiosity swirling in my gut. This is so much deeper than ghosting me since Hailey's engagement. This is something else entirely.

But what?

Frustrated, I lean forward, reaching for my coffee, and take a small sip.

To her credit, Savannah doesn't rush me. She lets me feel every emotion coursing through me before she stands, rounds the table, and settles on the sofa beside me. "Would you like to share your journal entry?"

The letter that I tried—and never got more than a sentence through—to write to Hillary, she means.

She smiles one of those *I'm reading between the lines* smiles. "You didn't write it."

It's not a question.

"No," I admit, sheepishly.

"And that's okay." She rests her warm hand on mine. "This is a journey. Remember when I said, 'Take it one task at a time'? I wasn't only referring to dealing with your ex-mother-in-law or event planning. I really want you to work on showing yourself the grace you deserve."

I lower my gaze to our hands, nodding. I don't think I realized how much I needed to hear this today.

"And I don't know when you would've had time anyway. I see this new hair, the face," she adds. "Okay, lips!"

A full-chested laugh tumbles out of me, loosening the tension. "It's my new signature." I pucker and pose, giving her Black-girl glam. "Red Dahlia from Diva Dolls, who may or may not have sent me a DM this morning offering a massive brand deal to the divorcétante."

Savannah cranes her neck back, her appraising expression screaming, *You ate and left zero crumbs!*

"Speaking of…" She cocks her head, and I just know that whatever comes next is going to leave me giddy. "Shall we discuss the date that Leslie's lined up for tonight?"

We might as well be preteens hollering about the school dance, the way we squeal.

"Oh my *God*, Savannah!" I deflate into the cushions, then immediately jolt right back up, ready to unload. "Honey, the way I don't know what to do with myself. What the hell is a Wednesday date night? I feel like I *should* ask Leslie more questions or make up a pre-date ritual. Maybe do some emergency Google searches, preview the menu, or test out pheromone-enhancing perfumes, or something."

She snort-laughs.

"I know *nothing* about this man." An equally unladylike laugh sputters out of me. "This is a true blind date. I'm completely trusting Leslie to deliver, because the last time I went on a *date* date…"

Savannah doesn't miss a beat. "Uh-uh!" She wags her elegant pink nail at me. "Nope, what was that?"

I open my mouth to speak, but I choke on the words before they can leave. It's not just the words—it's *everything* else. The weight of it. The ache.

God, the ache.

I saw that intensity in Linc's eyes last week in the library, the way he looked at me before he let me go. And then without my consent, the memory slips so seamlessly into another. One that's so vivid it burns the surface of my mind. Linc and I, crammed into the corner of that dingy college bar. The air thick with the sour stench of spilled beer and too much Axe, mingled with dramatic sports commentary and brokenhearted emo songs. The indistinct chatter, all blending together like radio static. It was chaotic and messy, but somehow…it felt like home.

We were there, lost in the middle of it. We sat on those torn-up stools, laughing at the stupidest things like we didn't have a care in the world, like we weren't slowly losing the battle with temptation.

That's the feeling I want back. That time when everything was easy. Just dreaming—no consequences, no pressure.

How do I put that on my dating profile?

Savannah closes her mouth, silently observing me. Graciously, she doesn't intrude on the moment.

"There was someone," I say, hesitating, choosing my words carefully. "A guy I think I would've chosen for myself, if Mom and Cornelia hadn't been so set on their own plans back then."

She nods, slowly. "I see. And where is he now?"

"He's still around," I say, but it's Linc's face that morning, a million years ago, when I woke up in his arms, that flashes across my mind.

Savannah's question—and those memories—echo in my mind as I leave my appointment. They gnaw at me, replaying over and over all afternoon as I try to stay out of the way back at Madison Manor.

But…*Linc.*

He's *always* here.

I swallow, twisting the clip of my pen between my teeth, my attention drifting to him.

He's in every inch of Madison Manor, moving like a force of nature—sweat dripping from his brow, his thin gray T-shirt sticking and pulling tight across his shoulders and chest. And he doesn't stop. He just keeps going with a relentless drive as he unloads wood stacks from the trucks. His muscles, draped in rich, dark brown skin, flex and stretch with every movement, each turn of his body taunting me—

"Did you need anything, Ebony?" Vincent catches me staring at Linc, and I almost choke on my pen. I quickly look away, but his cackles erupt into the air as I stumble over electrical cables, rushing back inside to the library, where it's safe.

Ugh.

"Ebony, get a grip," I chastise myself. "You cannot be the one who doesn't pull her weight. *Do* something!"

And for a solid twenty-five minutes, I do a dozen somethings.

Turns out, repressing emotions is excellent for productivity. I double down with the phone to my ear and fingers flying over the keyboard. I follow up on my insurance claim, which is…*drum roll…* further delayed because the adjuster needs to reach out to Cornelia as the CFO for JDC Livingston Inc., the family's umbrella company, and the named insured on the policy. *Boo to the Gramm-Leach-Bliley blah blah blah Act.* The great news is that Hailey's inbox is on fire.

The dress and tuxedo fittings are scheduled. The guest list is still an ugly battle, but I get it narrowed to a nice, round three hundred, and almost finalized. And, because distraction is apparently grade-A jet fuel, I'm in rare form, chopping it up with Syd's manager down at that cute little stationery boutique—who, as it turns out, is a fan of the divorcétante.

Won't he do it!

So, those elegant rose-gold invitations with the sweeping, foil-lined garden crest flourishes that Hailey wanted but thought it might be too late to get? Not only does my new bestie pull a few strings, but they are approved, ordered, and expedited, along with the matching enclosure cards.

At this rate, she might hand-deliver them if I promise to take a selfie with her.

Hailey, your girl is on fire.

No linens, wedding arch, or gorgeous ornate vases yet, because I refuse to replace them before I know I'm being reimbursed by insurance—and *four* of my rental supply contacts are booked up on September twentieth—but there's still time. We do, however, get dahlias *and* zinnias for the floral arrangements, alcoves, and bouquets. Along with the officiant, I've lined up a makeup artist, a photographer, and a string quartet.

Winning is an extremely exhilarating high.

Except the instant I slow down, thinking about my re-debut date and what I'm going to wear for this mystery man, again, I hear Linc's voice. He's in the ballroom, organizing the crew, calling out orders, racing from room to room and fixing everything in sight like some hard-wired machine, and it feels strangely symbolic.

I'm supposed to be dating, reinventing myself, starting anew. Yet with every step, Lincoln Bridges reminds me he's a perfectly viable option. He's always been right here.

He'll always be here…anytime I want to take my eyes off my business long enough to let Cornelia Livingston sabotage me.

I stare at the door, my mind drifting back to the conversation with Savannah earlier. To the silence that lingered.

Where is he now?

I drag in a deep breath, still unsure how I should've answered.

Of course, I've been avoiding him, scheduling my hours not to overlap his. I can't look at him, especially if there's the slightest chance that he might look at me like he still wants me too. Every time I see him, my emotions fight against logic.

The irony of it all? Lately, Linc's been giving me more space.

After that first lunch order—since he overheard my dating concierge consultation with Leslie—he's kept his distance.

But somehow, he's still always here.

I'm talking to the caterer, and I hear him barking orders to his crew. I'm discussing dress alterations, and I catch him walking through the hallway, seeming completely oblivious to me, focused entirely on the task at hand.

I bite my lip, lost in the memory of Linc and me.

What would Savannah have said if I told her Linc's not just "around"? That he's in the same building, mere feet away from me, in the legendary grand ballroom that's witnessed countless love stories? What advice would she have given if I confessed that we're working side by side to ensure this wedding goes off without a hitch?

PING!

My phone cuts through the silence, snapping me out of my thoughts.

When I look at the screen, my heart stalls.

Hillary Winston

I'm sorry. I'm not ready to explain yet, but I will soon.

I stare at the message, every inch of me screaming, *That's it? Just a half-assed apology and an open-ended date when we'll meet?*

Fire surges through my veins, my body vibrating with the urge to lash out. But I won't give it any more energy. Not today.

The day isn't over, but it might as well be. I stand, smoothing the puff sleeves of my cosmo-flower blouse, and grab my things. Hillary, *Linc*, all the emotions feel too tangled and messy.

Tonight, I'm taking Savannah's advice and giving myself grace. I just want to focus on something uncomplicated. Something good.

My date.

I glance at my desk. On a deep breath, I walk out of the office, past Linc, leaving the weight of the day behind.

Two hours later, it's just me, my Red Dahlia lipstick, and my divas helping me choose a date-night dress for my first *Divorcétante Chronicles* live Get Ready with Me video.

"Okay, are y'all ready?" I ask.

Whitney and Priscilla are stretched out on my bed, phones in hand, not paying me a lick of attention, so I finish setting up my ring-light stand and angle my phone toward the hall closet between my bedroom and en suite bathroom.

"Ebony, have you been reading the comments?" Whit asks, her thumb steadily gliding up the screen.

"Only a handful here and there," I explain. "Too many *Luxe Ladies* trolls."

She hums her agreement. "No, I get it, but…there are some great ones here." Her smile widens as she listens to my first video on replay. "'I'm seated with my mug awaiting the freshly brewed tea,' 'We need the skincare routine,' 'Out here defying gravity.' These folks are hilarious."

"Oh, no, that's not even my favorite," Priscilla says, seeming fully invested. "For me, it's a toss-up between 'Pause, peace, power. I'm stealing that,' 'That face card,' and 'Standing on principle. That's that 92 percent energy!'" She's breathless, and her shoulders tremble. "She's really over here, building a fandom out the thin air like it's no big deal."

I deflate into an amused sigh. "I love the ones that are like, 'I broke my neck running to the comment section.'"

"*Lissstennnn.*" Whit sits upright. "This mystery man is about to be on a date with a bona fide celebrity and doesn't even know it."

A laugh tumbles out of me. "I don't know *him*. Which is why I need to hurry up and get this video started."

Priscilla pops up too, giving me her full attention.

I position myself in front of my phone, open the PopShot app, and take a deep breath before I press the live button.

A three-second countdown starts, and then it's just me…plus a thousand people, and counting.

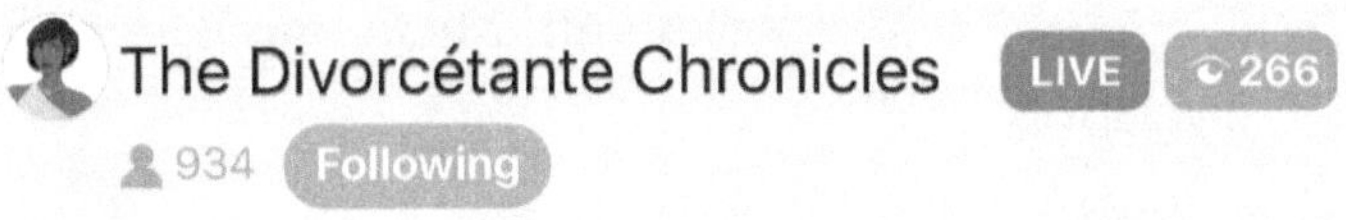

"Hey, divas, the divorcétante is here! Tonight, I'm live-streaming for the first time…with great reason!"

Tiny bursts of animated hearts, flowers, and coins rain down on the screen as the comments climb like vines.

"We love the drama. Nothing like some exclusive, scandalous content."

I look into the camera, curving my red lips teasingly.

"But what if tonight is about something better? What if it's the moment we've all been waiting for?"

We're over ten thousand viewers on a Wednesday night in less than a minute, and the comments are a scrolling blur of excitement, flying up the page.

"It's our date night! I announce, twirling in my lavender satin robe. Y'all, I'm so excited to meet this guy. Excited to put myself out there again. Pumped to see if there's any chemistry, am I right?

"So, the reservation is at seven thirty, and no, I'm not telling you where. But I've got the address, and three hours to get ready and meet him there."

Hearts explode, as glorious and triumphant as I feel.

Whitney and Priscilla are cackling and carrying on as they join the live—for moral support—along with our other two divas, Tatiana and Chanel, joining in the comment section, adding their tiny animated flowers to the fray. Plus, they add a few *I love Black women* comments, to keep the general merriment going.

"Now, you might've heard a bunch of giggling and keekee-ing in the background. That's because my divas are here with me tonight to help us out. See, I was hoping, since we're live, I might do a Help Me Decide spin on the Get Ready with Me for this date night. So, are y'all staying with me?"

The viewer count continues to grow.

Right on cue, Whit turns a Black Girl R&B playlist on low— *For ambiance*, she mouths—and I'm absolutely here for it.

"Okay, so far, we're going with the new hair. I'm loving my new cut. For the makeup, this is the beat. I went with a soft, glowy complexion, amping up the sultry look with a smoky eye and winged liner for the drama. Always bring the drama." I laugh. "And, of course, my Red Dahlia lip. Done and done.

"Now, this is where you come in. I've got three outfit options. Classy chic diva, spicy vixen, and dazzling, grown, and sexy. So, let's choose an outfit."

I dash out of view to where I've set aside each look, and I quickly shimmy into a simple pleated and belted black minidress.

"Okay, let's get into this classy chic diva, I say, posing and playing up my angles. Easy, elegant, sexy, no fuss. I'll pair it with diamond studs, black strappy heels, a statement clutch…"

I lean in to see what the consensus is, and the comments do not disappoint.

A full-body laugh washes over me as I take in the onslaught of "no"s, thumbs-down emojis, and the glaring *Is sexy in the room with us?*

"Um, so I'm just going to go, and, uh…tear this off my body."

Unfortunately, I barely make it into shot in the sleeveless bronze sequin scoop-neck midi dress that I picked for the "dazzling, grown, and sexy" option before it's shot down, too. Not that I didn't switch up the order on purpose, secretly hoping they'd go for the spicy vixen because, frankly, even keel isn't going to cut it tonight.

I need high romance. Elegant, but summery. Flirty.

"Yes, I know what time it is. It's six thirty-two, so y'all better love this last one, because we are fresh out of options."

When I step out in the black bustier wrap Bodycon minidress that's molded to my curves, I feel all twenty-five thousand pairs of eyes trailing from the thin spaghetti straps to the sweetheart neckline, inching lower to the sheer lace bodice.

Heat singes my skin as I sway to the smooth, soulful music.

"Is this too much? Because I think this is the one."

"It's giving icon, legend, the whole moment," Whit says, passing me a champagne flute.

Priscilla clinks my glass with hers, then Whit's, before she takes a long pull of the effervescent amber liquid. "It'll be perfect with the strappy stilettos and diamond-drop earrings…"

I smile at the screen. "Not going to lie, y'all. I'm feeling this outfit."

Before I end the live, I scan the incoming comments to answer a few questions.

"Let's see… Yes, I'll give you all a little update after the date. The lipstick is Red Dahlia by Diva Dolls. And yes, I'll be including all the links in my shop by tomorrow."

I keep scanning, thanking everyone for all the love, and skipping past the *Luxe Ladies* questions because there's zero chance that I'm letting them ruin my night.

I'm just about to thank my viewers for getting ready with me tonight and remind them about the private mixer Leslie scheduled for me in August when my finger hovers over the most recent comment…from Bridges Heritage Conservation.

Breathtaking.

You good? Whit mouths from my periphery.

I jerk back, forcing an unnaturally wide smile. "Mm-hmm, yup, yeah… So, that's it. Thanks for getting ready with me."

Except maybe I should've asked them to wish me luck, because at exactly seven thirty p.m., I walk into the Golden Olive with my heart in my stomach. The hostess escorts me to the table, and either my mind is playing tricks on me, or my date—I can't be sure yet, since I haven't counted his fingers—looks like a disturbingly asymmetrical, AI-generated version of Lincoln Bridges.

It's a disaster.

You're invited
to our
Wedding Day

(410) 555-3269

Chapter Twelve

Old Flames, New Sparks

Lincoln

I'VE BEEN ON THE LAT pull-down machine for the last ten minutes, earbuds in, game face on, really concentrating on isolating my muscles and releasing the tension with each chest press. Or, at least, I'm trying to.

It's a bit difficult to manage a solid, closed-grip lift when my guys are on either side of me, and Dom can't seem to talk about anything other than the divorcétante.

"Seriously, I'm trying to focus here." On the last set, I felt the stress in my rotator cuff. It's getting dangerous.

"All I'm saying is—"

"Please, I'm begging you…" I tilt my head, stretching my neck as I try to stay centered. "Say less. She's dating, planning events, dealing with the Livingstons of the world. Believe me, I see her daily, so I'm aware." *More than I'd like to be.*

Josiah tosses us an exasperated look from his machine, mid-set on a behind-the-neck pull-down. I think we're both tired of replaying this same episode.

"And before you say anything else, Dominic Owens…" I shoot him a pointed stare. "She hasn't been 'fighting it the whole time.' I *know* for a fact because I've been playing it by ear—observing, waiting to see how she acts. And if I'm taking my cues from her, it couldn't be clearer that I need to finally move on."

"Finally," Josiah grunts, straining to pull down the bar.

"*Ahhhhh…*" Dom points and gawks. Honestly, if he didn't have at least two chaotic rebuttals lined up, I'd be worried about him.

Josiah and I chuckle, both of us waiting to see what's inspired this outburst.

And then Dom steals the air from my chest.

"You watched her date night Get Ready with Me video." His face is a mask of pure, smug exuberance. "And don't think I didn't see Bridges Heritage's comment."

Damn.

At that, Josiah releases his grip on the bar, letting the weights drop with a thunderous crash. "He commented?"

"Mm-hmm." Dom grins from ear to ear, turning to Siah. He lowers his voice dramatically, purring, "*Breathtaking.*"

I knew I shouldn't have commented.

I let out a long sigh, dragging a hand over my beard. "It was a simple compliment."

Josiah nods, slow and deliberate. I already sense where this is headed in a hurry. "That's some word choice. Not 'You look pretty' or 'Nice dress,' or 'Love your hair.' No, not from Lincoln Bridges…"

Ignoring them, I widen my grip on the bar and start another set. But my frustration builds with each rep. I drop the bar and swivel to face Josiah. I expected the usual fandom-chasing chaos from Dom, but not from him.

"Correct me if I'm wrong, but wasn't it *you* who was so eager to know what I was going to do? Didn't you tell me, the pathetic crumb chaser, to give up on her? Shoot, what were the exact words you used?" I snap my fingers a few times, pulling the memory into focus. It's on the tip of my tongue for a split second before it hits me. "That's right. The 'uppity, money-motivated Zion & Zara she-bot.' *Wow*, what a way with words. What a choice."

A manic energy floods me as I glance back and forth between them, waiting, looking for their validation.

But it doesn't come.

My guys just stare, concern etched into the shadows and lines of their faces. They pity me. And as far as I'm concerned, that's about as low as it gets.

"So move on," Josiah says, quietly. "If you're serious, one of our avionics techs just started dating again. It's been a few years since her divorce. She's nice, good-looking, kind—also a Zion & Zara girl— *but* not into Livingstons or *The Luxe Ladies of Ellswood*."

You date her, then.

We sit here, the silence thickening, ten seconds stretching into forever.

Yeah, I know it's time to take an honest look at the things I need to change in my life. I *know* my solo status is self-imposed. For my own peace of mind, though, I should ask Ebony outright what's wrong, why it's never our turn.

But deep down, I know I won't be able to stomach her answer. I can't volunteer for her to reject me again.

So, yeah, I've only gotten as far as moving on from Ebony, not yet to what—or who—is next.

"Good looking out, man." I nod, my brow trenched as I turn back to my machine. "I think I'm going to hold off for a bit, but...I really appreciate it."

"No sweat." Josiah stands and walks over to the treadmills.

"*Damn*." I exhale sharply.

I watch him for a beat until he disappears into the locker room. I'm debating whether to follow him and hash this out when Dom turns to me, his eyes wide as saucers.

Letting my shoulders slump, I flash him an exhausted stare. I really don't have the patience to pry whatever's on his mind out of him. "Just say it."

"She just dropped the date night update."

This is the part where a better man would remember the sermon that he just preached to his friends about moving on and actually take his own advice. He'd think long and deep about the emotional torture of being repeatedly rejected by this woman and promptly get himself a life.

What he *wouldn't* do is follow one of those friends to an empty SoulSync classroom to watch *The Divorcétante Chronicles*—where, just minutes ago, Ebony gave a detailed account of the date she had with a man who isn't me.

Nope.

And under no circumstances would he stand there, fully aware of where she is at work—in Madison's library—and revel in the fact that the date was a bust.

And yet, here we are.

"I feel so bad because he was such a nice guy, y'all. Like, opening doors, asking questions about me, saying all the right things…" Ebony sighs, smiling somberly at the camera. "Have you ever met someone who, on paper, is everything you said you wanted and more, but there's just…nada? No spark. No fire in your belly because you can't wait to see him again. Just nothing to write home about."

Dom and I are ravenous, scouring the comments section, for…I don't know what. A clue? A sign? What exactly was wrong with this guy? What do women even do when this happens? More importantly, how do I lock down the spark?

But there's nothing. Only people empathizing and telling her the next one will be better. Or that dating is a game of numbers—none of which sits right with my gut, but I'm glad it seems to soothe her.

Ebony looks at the camera, her stare far away as she asks, "Have you ever thought about the small, seemingly insignificant choices we make? I always wonder how my life would be different if I'd listened to my heart and not our, *er…* my mother."

My heart races, something like hope quickening my pulse.

"What would you risk for a second chance at love, hmm? Your personal and professional reputation? His?"

Speculation dominates the comments. *I told you she has a man, The one that got away, It's never too late,* and my favorite, *Risk it all!*

On the screen, she softly shakes her head, a warm smile coloring her cheeks, and all over again, I'm mesmerized.

"That was just food for thought." She shakes her thoughts loose. "But no worries, I've got another date soon, and a mixer—"

Dom locks his phone, ending the video, like he senses my mind warring. Like he knows I'm replaying Vincent's words in my head, trying to decide my next move.

When the opportunity presents itself, be there for her.

Except I don't want to wait anymore. I *can't* wait any longer.

"I'm good," I say, and for the first time in a long time, it's not a lie.

I've felt stuck, trapped in this endless loop with no way out. But watching her in her element—surrounded by friends and followers, excitedly getting ready for a date, and even after a setback, knowing she's still looking ahead—something's clicked. It's having an eye-opening effect on me. The blindfold is off, and now I need to decide what I'm willing to change to move on, too.

And I am. It's time for me to stop reliving an ancient fling and get a damn life.

"You're sure?" Dom asks. "Because—"

I rest my hand on his shoulder. "Let's get back to Siah. He's probably looking for us."

We move through the foot traffic path back to the lat pull-down machines, spotting all six-foot-hulk of him in the middle of a set. Dom quickly claims the machine to his right, and I hang back, then work into the rotation. When Josiah stands to switch out with me, I nudge his shoulder with mine and quietly say, "Send me Alexis's phone number."

On the way home, I'm on top of the world. Even with the thick Ellswood humidity, the windows are down, and nineties hip-hop is blasting into the warm summer air. It's Saturday night, and I'm not ready to call it a day, so I swing by Madison Manor to check on the landscaping progress and secure the building. But when I pull around the back, I notice the late crew have left some of the lights on, so I figure, two birds, one stone.

A Tribe Called Quest's "Scenario" is buzzing in my head as I park, and I walk around back.

"Whoa!" I slow my pace, unsure where to look. They've done a stellar job.

A couple of days ago, there was patchwork sod and flags marking the areas for plants and trees. Now, the courtyard leading up to the terrace is a lush, fragrant, green sanctuary with towering, spotlit magnolia trees casting warm, dappled shadows over the sprawling lawn. Bougainvillea and wisteria vines are draped elegantly over wrought-iron trellises, showcasing their violet and pink blooms. Path lights lead up to the pristine gardens, overflowing with a variety of gardenias, azaleas, and hydrangeas, adding more vibrant bursts of color. And even on the terrace, tall boxwoods and sculpted topiaries lend a sense of refined luxury to polish off this worldly escape.

"*Phew*, they've outdone themselves," I muse, climbing the steps to the ballroom entrance. After fishing out my keys, I unlock the door and enter.

Tools are all over the place, and I briefly consider tidying up for safety reasons. Instead, though, I leave them so on Monday the guys can pick up where they left off.

It's a decision I immediately regret after I shut down the ballroom lights and stumble over an extension cord, sending me tumbling to the ground in cloud of curses.

And that's when I hear the footsteps.

Rather, fast-clicking heels on the move.

"Ebony?" I call out, concerned.

Except since I'm grumbling from the pain, it comes out a husky, gritty, barely decipherable growl with more bass.

The comedy of it all is that from my vantage point on the ballroom floor, I get to witness Ebony in the hallway—with zero grace, purse and jingling keys in clenched hands—hauling it toward the front door before she meets a similar, floor-eating fate as I have.

Fortunately—or, unfortunately, I'm not sure—I'm able to peel myself off the ground and lunge out of the shadows in time to experience the visible terror on her beautiful face as she crawls and unleashes an ear-piercing scream into the air. It's still pinballing around the alcoves of the foyer as she slowly faces me, then deflates with relief.

"What the hell? Linc, you scared the crap out of me." Terror and levity twist the soft lines of her face. "And what are you doing here on a Saturday night, anyway?"

"Oh my goodness…" I'm bent over in stitches, mentally replaying that military crawl. "It would be *so* over for you if this was a horror movie."

Her eyes narrow with indignation, but there's a smirk tugging at the corner of her lips. "I thought for sure I'd be a final girl. I can't believe I'm a faller."

We both erupt into laughter this time.

Ebony sits up, shaking her head, I'm guessing at her abysmal survival skills.

"Yeah, sorry to be the bearer of bad news, but you, Ebony Grace Livingston, would not make the final-girl cut," I say, still chuckling as I take her hands, prepared to pull her to her feet when I notice that not only is one of the heels on her black pumps broken, but her leg is bleeding. "You're hurt." The words come out barely above a whisper.

"No, I'm fine…" Ebony looks down at her leg, her face contorting in surprise as she sees the blood.

It's a thin gash running down the side of her calf. Basically, an oversized paper cut. Had it been any of my crew, I'd have thrown them a Band-Aid and kept moving. But this isn't one of my bulletproof guys, or a scratch. This is Ebony.

Urgency crashes through me, this unwavering need to make sure she's okay.

Before she can protest, I lift her up in my arms and rush over to the steps, where I gingerly set her down. "All right, sit tight. I've got a first-aid kit in the kitchen."

I'm gone just long enough to grab the kit and an ice pack. When I return, she's wincing and trying to stand, clearly not thrilled to be wounded.

"Okay, you've got a flair for the dramatic, I see, but you really don't want to bleed out over a busted heel," I say, taking her arm and helping her settle back on the step. "Besides, this is what happens to folks who don't make it to the end of the movie."

"Ha, ha. I could've sworn I saw someone outside, but…" She lets out a breath, amusement coloring her cheeks as I gather the supplies to tend to her wound. "I get it. I'm a mess. I might not be final-girl material, but hey, you heard me hollering. I'd make a killing as a scream queen."

She gives me a mock-terrified look, like she's ready for her close-up, but then cringes slightly as the pain in her leg catches up with her.

"It's just a little peroxide to prevent infection," I tell her, gently dabbing at her cut. "And to answer your question, I wasn't planning on being here. It was such a nice night, I didn't want to head home yet, so I was just going to drive by, check on the landscaping, and make sure the crew locked up, when I saw the lights on."

"Yeah, I've noticed you working longer hours. The clock's ticking louder for me, too." She gives me a small smile. "I was going to work for an hour, but then I got an email about the insurance claim for my office at Ellswood Mill."

I wince. "Vincent told me about the fire. Sorry about your props."

"My desktop and printer, too." Ebony sighs, somberly. "Pretty much all my business's fixed assets. Gone."

"Well, that's what insurance is for," I say, tossing aside the cotton pad. "Next, I'll add antibiotic ointment, bandage you up, and put the ice pack on for a few minutes. You'll be good as new. Is that okay?"

Ebony nods. "Unfortunately, my claim was denied."

"Why?"

"That's the complicated, enraging part about it." She begins explaining why she doesn't have a policy for Ebony Grace Events. Instead, all the Livingston businesses were covered by an umbrella policy under JDC Livingston, Inc.—named after Cornelia's sons, Julian, Donovan, and Cornelius. With the corporation as the named insured, even though Ebony paid for her business's coverage, she can't file a claim. As CFO of the corporation, only Cornelia can.

I tear open the antibiotic packet. "Oh no."

"Right. But at the end of the day, the claim is basically a moot point now." She lets her head fall back on her shoulders with a sigh then meets my gaze again. "As part of the divorce settlement, Julian relinquished his rights to Ebony Grace Events, *but*, and this is the infuriating part I learned tonight," she says, shaking her head, "three days after I sent Cornelia my annual payment, JDC removed Ebony Grace Events from its policy. Which means, rather than inform me about the cancellation, that vindictive woman—who I *knew* was trying to sabotage me—will be laughing all the way to the bank with any fire-related payments going to JDC. Meanwhile, I'm uninsured and shit out of luck."

"I'm sorry, Ebony."

"Well, I've got a new policy," she says, "though it doesn't do much for the props I've lost."

Her face betrays every frustrated and overwhelming emotion she's feeling. And I can't ignore how much it means that she trusts me enough to share this with me.

The silence thickens as she watches me take care of her wound. And there's a moment, a tiny shift in her posture, the brief staccato of her breath, the weight of her stare. I sense she wants to say something. We both do. But I don't want to be the first, and I guess she doesn't either.

And then I'm finished, and like I've had to do for the past week of our working together in the manor, I remind myself that nothing's changed.

"All better, scream queen." I force a smile, pressing the ice pack over the bandage before I sit back on my heels.

But she doesn't move, so I don't either.

"I hate this," she says finally, and it might be the moonlight glinting through the window, but her eyes are glassy. It makes me pay attention. "I'm so sorry I didn't believe you when you tried to warn me before."

I drag in a small breath, my heart racing.

How many times have I imagined us having this conversation? *Are* we finally having this conversation?

"Thanks for saying that." I laugh. "I was trying to be a good friend, but maybe I shouldn't have sprung it on you like that."

Ebony's expression is a watercolor blur of remorse and resentment, but I don't rush her. "I knew he'd been with someone else," she admits, and for a split second, I think that's it, that's the end of it. We've apologized, and we can move on. But then our eyes meet. "Everyone was looking at me like I was this pitiful pearl, and I just couldn't stand the thought of you looking at me like that, too. And now look at us…"

Taking her hands in mine, I search her eyes. "I've never pitied you. I was furious, outraged with Julian, and…" I pause, almost blurting out the truth about Hillary. *Almost*. But this moment is too important. Too fragile. I don't want to ruin it. "I just wanted you be able to make an informed decision. That's all."

Ebony leans forward, her eyes bright with renewed determination.

"I regret not giving you that chance." She exhales a relieved sigh. "And that's why I wanted you to know what I'm up against with Cornelia. She's been biding her time, waiting for the perfect opportunity to sabotage Ebony Grace Events. Rather, punish me for tarnishing the Livingston name. She blames me for Julian losing his job."

"What? How does that work?"

"Right?" She shrugs. "Get this, at Hailey and Donovan's engagement? In front of the entire party? That's when Julian thought it was a *great* time to plead for another chance. He acted like he was addressing his brother and Hailey, but he looked at me as he spoke, insinuating that I was his perfect match. He'd just realized it too late, which is just wild!" Her face scrunches with disbelief. "I wish you could've seen the sinister smile Cornelia shot me, like she was daring me to come close to her son and step into her booby trap."

I raise my eyebrows. "I'll bet. Not her precious Julian…"

"You have no idea. The whole dynamic is a weird, if-I-can't-have-you-no-one-can situation. Except with her son. Our marriage is over, and he ruined his own reputation and family name, but my business and I must now be destroyed." Ebony shakes her head, her expression turning dire. "I've got a gut feeling she's about to take me out."

My mouth is on the floor. "Like, send you on a permanent vacation?" I bark out a laugh.

Ebony falls back on the step, cackling. Then quickly shoots back up again. "Who knows, though? Maybe. Fire…" She giggles and taps her finger to her temple. "At the very least, out of the equation. Linc, when was the last time Cornelia Livingston did anything to help anyone out of the goodness of her heart? Down to her bones, she's a self-serving woman. Ask yourself, what's in this situation for her?"

It's a fair point. I tip my head to either side, considering this.

Even Hillary warned me to watch my back, saying she wasn't the only one who'd likely get burned.

She said a *lot* of things I can't ignore.

"Okay, let's say you're not completely off base." I screw my mouth to the side, still chewing on this theory. "Aside from the shady business with the insurance, why else would she do anything to sabotage you when you're planning her son's wedding?"

Ebony shoots me an exasperated look. "Come on, it's ninety-one days away. I've got an event countdown going—don't laugh." Then she laughs at herself. "The wedding will be over before we know it. She's all about long-game revenge. Do you know how pissed she was when Julian relinquished his rights to Ebony Grace Events? Were you listening about the insurance? Three days. She canceled my coverage three days after my divorce. Be so for real with me right now."

I try, and fail, to stifle a grin. "Fine, okay, yes."

"And what about the *Ellswood Times* article with her talking about *The Divorcétante Chronicles*? 'Rebranding desperation'?" Ebony narrows her eyes. "That woman is calculating to the nth degree."

"Uh, yeah. It would seem that way." I wince.

"She's absolutely coming for my business, but for her to really relish in my demise, she's got to ensure it's of my own doing. She can't reason with her son, so she's going to take down the business she believes is rightfully theirs. Or at least half his. She's got me right where she wants me, close enough to track my every move and worm her way back into my day-to-day. She hates that Julian gave up his stake in my business. *Hates* it."

I'm nodding, piecing it all together in my head. "And you really think she'd go to these lengths to take you down?"

"Yes," she answers with not a hint of hesitation. "That uppity heifer is running her mouth, shading *The Divorcétante Chronicles*. She can't stand the idea of me building, thriving without them. She's bragging about the Livingston *Luxe Ladies* baby to any and everyone in the Ellswood elite at charity galas, Zion & Zara meetings—you name it. She talks to anyone who'll listen because she thought she'd already taken me down. But the audacity of me, out here living my life…" She taps her fingers to her temple, then explodes them outward, smiling ear to ear. And for a fleeting moment, I think, *Finally, this is us. The way we used to be.*

But slowly, her smile fades. "This is why I can't let her win," she says, and all I hear is the unspoken part. The reasons why nothing's changed. Why we need to professional.

I clear my throat. "Of course."

She exhales a deep breath. "Like I said, I hate this."

Me too.

"This should be good now." I remove the ice pack, ready to get us both out of here now that we know the plan.

"It's been so hard, being here and not being close to you. I'm glad we finally got a chance to talk, Linc." Ebony quietly helps me repack the first-aid kit. "Then when I saw your name on my live… Your comment was so sweet."

I swallow, shielding myself against the weight of her words. "I was just telling the truth."

"I didn't even know you watched my videos," she says a little self-consciously, and I hate the tiny glimmer of hope that sends my pulse racing. "I don't know what I'm doing. I haven't dated in…forever."

Every inch of me wants to ask if she regrets choosing Julian, but there's an undertone of hurt and longing in her voice. I can't help but notice it. That's the thing with us—I'm attuned to all her little nuances, the way even the slightest subtext rises to the surface without her seeming to realize it.

But if anything, listening to her theory about Cornelia's diabolical plan, all the reasons why she can't let her win, why business comes first—that only underscores everything I felt earlier at the gym chatting with my guys.

I've got to move on. It's as simple as that.

"Well, let me know if you need any advice for your next date. Believe it or not, I've got one lined up myself."

"Wow." But then she swallows, nodding repeatedly like she's processing what I've just said. "Yeah? I'm sure she's probably amazing."

Is she jealous?

No, I tell myself. *Definitely not.* It's got to be all in my head, right?

Except Ebony's eyebrows lift, and she releases that same impressed smile she gives Cornelia when really, she'd rather throat-punch her.

It tickles me, watching her hide in plain sight.

"How about we test this out?" I stand, offering her my hands. But as she rises, caught in the middle of everything we've said, we both forget about her broken heel. She stumbles toward me, and I catch her, the soft curves of her body flush against mine. Our faces are inches apart, our breaths mingling, eyes locked, and for a heartbeat, we just stare at each other.

And then she kisses me.

You're invited
to our
Wedding Day

Chapter Thirteen

Running Into You Again

Ebony

I'M SPIRALING.

Today, I'm supposed to go on a date with this guy that Leslie swears has "real long-term potential." *Whatever the hell that means.* Meanwhile, I don't know how I'll get through the first five minutes when my mind keeps replaying my kissing Lincoln Bridges. Repeatedly, like an idiot. And with tongue. Like, did I not just outline Exhibits A through Infinity why we damn well shouldn't let the ex-monster-in-law win?

And yet I did it anyway.

How could I not?

How could I not tell him about Cornelia's revenge plot after he rescued me? Well, he scared the hell out of me first. But then, like it was nothing, he swept me off my feet and cradled me in his strong, capable arms. How could I *not* feel like I was precious to him?

Right then, I knew I was losing my will. And I thought maybe this was just leftover embers still glowing.

But no. This was so much more, explosively new. Somehow familiar and fantastical, watching this rough-and-tumble man so tenderly, so *sweetly*, bandage up my leg. It would've been criminal *not* to kiss him.

And so I did.

With my heart thrashing behind my ribcage, I succumbed to temptation like I *knew* I would. I let him drag his tongue over my lips, teasing and tasting. I sank into the warmth and wetness of his mouth, loving the way his eyes softly glazed over with lust, and the tiny growl that seeped out of him. His needy hands set free on my skin, coaxing horny little moans from me, and my entire body vibrated against the thrum of his heart. All the while, my mind filled in the glorious blanks of what would inevitably come next.

I was at a point of no return—stop, or end up ravaged on the steps of Madison Manor, unable to move again, and be exposed to his entire crew within the next twenty-four hours.

Somehow, my mouth formed the words "We can't."

I broke the kiss.

We'd just established we'd *both* planned dates with other people, so what the hell was I doing?

I take several deep breaths, realizing we've been working at the manor together for twenty-three days. Twenty-three long, torturous days of fighting the good fight that…I don't know, just doesn't feel that *good* anymore.

Why can't I stop thinking about the kiss?

"Pause, peace, power," I whisper into the air, hoping today it'll work like a giant sage bundle, clearing my karma and banishing all the bad spirits. I grab my keys, lock my front door, and drag in a deep breath. Hopefully, along with the thick humidity, I'll catch a strong whiff of the gumption I need to meet up with another guy who isn't Linc, and somehow be witty and charismatic…in two different shoes and no earrings.

Lord.

"Okay, see? No." I turn right back around, letting myself inside, then lean the full weight of my body against the door. "Snap out of it! It was just a kiss."

So why can't I think of anything other than doing it again?

Determined to get my act together and show up for Mr. Long-Term—gracious, elegant, and appreciative of his time—I march into my closet, find a matching pair of heels, swipe on my trusty Red Dahlia lipstick, and I'm ready to go.

For good measure, I grab my empty gratitude journal, determined to get right with the universe, and jot down a single sentence: *Today, I'm grateful for self-control.*

I slip it into my purse, hoping manifesting really works.

Except when I swing open the front door again, Mom is standing, stone-faced, on the other side like a surprise test. "*Ugh*, why are you here? I'm on my way out." I pout, impishly. "Seriously, I don't have time for this."

Her sensibly pink lips purse judgmentally as she steps past me, saying, *Make time*, without using the words.

With my hand still on the door handle, I let out a huge sigh, already pre-annoyed.

"I understand that you're busy, what with the wedding, and your new beaux…" *There it is.* She blinks repeatedly, summoning all the melodrama. "However, Ebony Grace, it's vitally important that you answer when I reach out to you. Anything could've happened to you—"

"Oh my God, Mom, stop!" I release the door, letting it slam closed, and stomp back into the living room, where she's already made herself at home on the sofa and is reaching for the remote, no doubt to turn on some reality TV show.

Anything could've happened.

Ugh.

In other words, he—as in the fake beau that I've told her nothing about because he doesn't exist—could've hurt me. I could have been "lying in a gutter somewhere," as she loves to say.

I'd love to know why this mysterious gutter is always her go-to final resting place for me.

"Yes, I've been ignoring your calls for precisely this reason." I throw up my hands and let them drop limply at my sides. "You never know when to quit. Why should I talk to you when I already know what you're going to say?"

Mom raises a thick, penciled-in eyebrow, giving me a glassy stare. "I highly doubt you know what I'm going to—"

I clear my throat, interrupting her to get into character. "'Ebony, tell me about your new fella.' 'How's everything with Cornelia…and Julian?' 'I know you said you didn't plan on attending the cotillion, but…'" My smile slips. "Fill in any number of reasons you've come up with as to why I need to be there."

"Well, it's a time-honored tradition," she reasons.

Proving my point.

Snapping my fingers, I flash her my *but wait, there's more* stare. "Still a hard no on the cotillion, but…we can't forget my personal favorite Mom-ism, the one you were likely planning to throw in a the end—like that wasn't the entire reason you called. *Wait for it…*" I dig deep, twisting my face into a mask of shame and hopelessness. I definitely get this from her. "'Did you hear that Julian and that hussy are expecting?'" A smile stretches across my face as I curtsy like a good little debutante.

In classic Eleanor King form, Mom's brown eyes snag on my not-so-sensible red lips and bright yellow sundress. On the thin straps and the deep neckline exposing as much of my gold-glitter-dusted cleavage as I can get away with at brunch. A sneaky bout of joy nestles in my chest as her expression tightens, her laser vision measuring the inches between my hem, barely brushing my thighs, and my knees.

Oh, she's itching to pick apart every detail of my look, but she hits me with the deadpan, supposedly unimpressed "I resent that."

"So do I." I laugh.

For all of five seconds, she sits there, beautifully fuming in opulent jewels and a pristine pink Cornelia-esque jacquard dress like it's not a gazillion degrees outside, before she proves me right. "Well, are you going to tell me about your young man, or not?"

Or not would be so amazing right now.

The last thing I want to do after posting about dating online is fess up to fabricating a pretend suitor, then be forced into a deep dive on the seriousness of lying to a loved one.

No thanks.

Plus, it'll only prolong the inevitable questions about my dates. I've already seen—and memorized—her dummy alphanumeric PopShot handle. *Who else is out there with a faceless account, faithfully posting old debutante photos of me, Mom? Try harder.*

"It didn't work out," I say simply, casually. Just one of your run-of-the-mill, surface-level situationships.

Thankfully, she doesn't press the issue.

Then again, Eleanor King has never been direct about her disappointment. So, naturally, instead of asking about Julian and Nora, she again reaches for the TV controller on my coffee table, aims it at the television, and, after it turns on, says into the remote, clearly enunciating, "*Luxe Ladies of Ellswood.*"

There is no way…

On the screen, the first season's promotional photo pops up, featuring seven glamorously styled and profiled cast members dressed in varying shades of rose-gold and posed against a lush, opulent wall of deep ruby and blush-colored roses. At the center of the women is Nora Whitfield at her peak.

America's favorite hussy of a news anchor.

I'm speechless. Did Mom really come into my house and turn this on?

"Well, it's a shame it didn't work out with him," she says, and part of me wants to believe we're still talking about Faux Beau or AI Linc. But deep down, I know we're always talking about Julian Livingston III. "There's still a handsome, wealthy, eligible bachelor with your name on him."

She whips around, and I'll admit, I resent the gleeful twitch of her lips. My mother's never subtle. Everything she says, and doesn't say, has meaning. Nora may be having his baby, but I've still got his last name. Despite everything—infidelity, public shame, the divorcétante, Cornelia—he still wants me.

It's what everyone's saying.

I've seen the million-view PopShot videos of him on the news when his co-anchor asked what he thought about my dating again. Commenters dissect the emotions that played on his face, weighing in on every minute detail. There are Julian-and-Ebony stan accounts popping up everywhere.

"Ebony Grace." Mom deepens her stare, without words telling me that all I have to do is…say the word? Pretend he wasn't unfaithful? Forget about his unborn child? Forget about the pieces of me I'm only just rediscovering?

Live my life on their terms.

She doesn't say that, but it's what I'd need to do. Forget about the loss of love, the emotional turmoil and resentment, my low self-esteem, and the fact that I'd never be able to really trust him. All I have to do is put on my crown and smile for the people.

I won't do it.

"No." My face contorts with annoyance. "Just any random handsome, wealthy, eligible bachelor, huh?"

Something about hearing those words aloud irks me. That's always been it, hasn't it? Looks and money. Easy enough for Julian to check both boxes. But no, my mother isn't concerned with shared values, intelligence, capability, tenderness, or loyalty.

Just cute and able to provide.

What a fairytale…

I shake my head, and a humorless laugh slips out me because everything about her archaic standard is Ellswood.

Cornelia Livingston's Ellswood.

The thing is, Mom is not Cornelia. But I won't say she's nothing like her. In a dozen given ways, at the core they come from the same old-school, high-saddity, holier-than-thou place of Black excellence. Women are supposed to respect their elders, do as we're told, and stay in line. Any deviation is considered defiant. They're appalled by my audacity to not be their puppet.

Indignation boils in the back of my throat, and I can't help but laugh. "You know what, Mom? You need to stop worrying about my love life, okay? I don't want your help, nor your input. When it comes to the person I'll end up with, *if* I ever find him…he'll be my choice."

"Ebony Grace, what has gotten into you?"

"I suspect something akin to courage," I say with every ounce of conviction that I feel. "Courage to be unapologetically me. I'm *so* done being your little debutante doll. Now…" I take the remote from her hand, turn off the television, and fan out my arm toward the door. "I've got a date, so you've got to go."

She blanches, her mouth slackening, perhaps in disbelief.

I'm surprised, too. But for completely different reasons. I never talk to my mother this way. Every inch of my skin tingles, though in the best way. Something has changed inside, and it feels damn good to stand up for myself for once.

Whisk & Whistle probably wasn't the best restaurant choice for a first date. On the surface, it seemed like a win-win. With Fourth of July falling on Friday and Saturday reserved for hangovers, Sunday brunch *could've* been the perfect option. Fried green tomatoes with a side of remoulade for Zeek—that's his name. Bright, sunny, highly visible, upscale brunch spot for me.

Everyone makes it home safe.

But I forgot about the New Eateries segment on *The Morning Tea*. This place has been *perceived* by the Ellswood elite. Everyone who's anyone *needs* to make an appearance this week. So the venue's loud and overcrowded, and the wait time to be seated is more than an hour.

I'm praying the line for the women's restroom is shorter.

Weaving through the sea of people holding wait-list buzzers, I make my way to the hostess station. "Hi, excuse me, uh, you wouldn't happen to have someone on the list named…Zeek? We're supposed to meet here at eleven." I feel like an idiot, not knowing his last name.

The hostess glances up, and I see that slight hint of recognition on her face. I'm sure she's fighting the urge to yank out her phone and blast me to the trolls. Thankfully, though, she just smiles and scrolls down her screen.

"Oh, yes, actually. Looks like he's already seated." She walks from behind the counter and gestures for me to follow her. But as we turn a corner near the booths, she slows down and tosses me a little wink. "Good luck, divorcétante!"

Okay, fans…

I mouth my thanks just as she stops in front of a man who isn't another AI Linc so much as a classically corporate Black guy. He's got the rich brown skin and the towering height, but he's skipped the gray eyes, and his idea of athleticism seems a little more akin to that of a sedentary retired basketball player.

"Ah, you made it? It's Zaire, but my friends call me Zeek." He stands, stepping his long legs out of the booth to hug me. "*Wow*, you're even more beautiful in person."

And that's ten points for starting out the gate right.

"Thank you." I smile, sliding in on the left side. "My friends call me all kinds of inappropriate things, but you can call me Ebony."

We both laugh, and already, my nerves start to subside.

See? This isn't so bad.

We quickly fall into an easy conversation about Leslie. It's both of our first times using a dating concierge, so we swap stories about our most recent relationships—my marriage, his series of almosts. It feels like a small red flag. Why didn't *any* of them turn into more?

But I brush it off because I'm enjoying the conversation.

When our server arrives with warm banana bread and whipped honey butter, we place our orders. Fried green tomatoes to start, and a plate of shrimp and grits each, paired with bottomless peach mimosas.

"So, what do you think makes your profile stick out?" Zeek asks as soon the server leaves.

For a beat, I'm confused. Did he even look at my profile before he agreed to join me on this date?

191

"I guess that I'm an event planner." I laugh self-consciously. "I don't know, and also maybe it stands out because Leslie asked about my love of waterfalls and swimming. I collect conch shells because I love the sound of the ocean. How about you?"

"Travel." He nods a few times. "Definitely my love of travel," he says, and ain't that about a B? I went into great detail, providing multiple tidbits about myself, and he's tossed out a vague answer. Travel to where? What places *geographically*? And what kind of first-date question is that anyway?

Grabbing my appetizer plate, I load it up with a slice of banana bread, then evenly spread on honey butter and try not to judge this guy too harshly.

When I lift my eyes, though, my attentions drifts past Zeek to a table directly in my line of vision where Lincoln Bridges—with a fresh tapered haircut, wearing jeans with a casual white button-down—is pulling out a chair for *her*.

Now, I've got no right to feel anything. We shared a kiss. Singular. Then I told him it couldn't happen again. But as I look at this woman, I'm silently praying, *Please be ugly. Please be ugly.*

I hold my breath as she turns slightly.

Dammit. Even her profile is gorgeous. Deep brown skin, long, textured dark curls, cheekbones to die for, and full, wine-stained lips. She's got a cute boho chic vibe about her. It only stands to reason, by the adorably boyish smile teetering on Linc's dangerous lips, that there's a strong chance he's noticed too.

Shoot.

"Is everything okay?" Zeek draws my attention back to him. "I lost you there for a second."

"Sorry. I was just trying to remember if I, um, left my iron on." *Smooth, Ebony.*

He chuckles, nodding, and I breathe a sigh of relief because that was a close call.

But as my attention drifts slightly past his ear again, Zeek shifts gears, taking this conversation from easy coast to interrogation overdrive. "High-pressure situations," he says, straightening as if he's really about to discover what makes me tick. "How would you say you handle conflict and confrontation? Relationship-wise," he adds in what feels like more of an afterthought than a getting-to-know-me query.

The red flags are soaring. *What is happening?*

I look away for a few seconds, and suddenly, we're planning for our first fight? I don't even know this guy's last name, let alone his middle. Or how he takes his eggs and coffee. What size shoes are those clodhoppers? Where's his family from? What are we talking, hygiene-wise? Let's start there.

And it doesn't stop.

In a matter of minutes, I learn exactly why he's got a deck of *almosts* up his sleeves. How would my friends and family describe me in three words? When was the last time I did something completely out of character? Would I consider myself a girl's girl? Like, what in the actual hell?

How about. Not. The. One?

I figured this date couldn't be worse than dating AI Linc, and yet here I am, being interrogated by Ellswood's weirdest, and the real Lincoln Bridges is sitting there with another woman he's clearly into when my lips are still raw from our kiss.

"Okay, last one," Zeek says, and I'd scream if I weren't so curious which whopper he's saved for his finale.

I nod, barely holding it together.

"Do you watch any reality TV shows like *Surreal Life*, *Home Innovations*, or, say, *Luxe Ladies*?"

And that does it.

As I grab my purse off the booth seat, about to stand, Zeek reaches for my hand, his dark eyes pleading.

"Ebony, give me two minutes to explain." The urgency in his voice is so alarming that it stalls me.

All I can think is, *Why is he trying so hard to keep me here?* We've been in this restaurant for less than half an hour, and the spark is not in the room with us. We're clearly not a match. So what could he possibly need to explain that he thinks will make a lick of a difference?

Maybe it's the old me—not the one who puts her mother in her place, but the one hoping he'll say anything that'll help me understand what Leslie was thinking when he matched us. But I listen.

Then immediately wish I hadn't.

The reason this date feels like a strange interview is because, well, it is. In a plot twist I never in a million years would've seen coming, Zeek—or Zaire Harrison—is the casting director for *Luxe Ladies of Ellswood.* He knows exactly who I am and is prepared to offer me an obscene amount of money to join the show.

With my highly publicized divorce, and now my reentry into society as the divorcétante, apparently I'll be "perfect" for the cast. I've got the profile that fits the "tone and dynamic" the producers want to create.

By *dynamic,* he means messy drama, built-in storylines, and audience appeal. Perfect, considering not only have they already signed Nora Whitfield for the next season, but they're bringing back Sherry Easton—a.k.a. the wife of software mogul Warner Easton and the infamous hair-dryer-hurling baddie who hurt Nora, got kicked off the show, and was harassed so bad by #TeamNora that she had to go into hiding.

Jesus, that top-tier Luxe Ladies *money must be good.*

"So, would you like to be our newest cast member?"

It just feels like it would be passing the puppet strings from Cornelia and Mom, this entire society, over to them. All I'd have to do is say the word. Downplay Julian's disloyalty and play nice for ratings. Meet his unborn child. Throw hands at Nora over dinner during some tropical vacation with the cast under the guise of "bonding." Just forget about the pieces of me I'm only just rediscovering.

Again, live my life on their terms.

I won't do it.

That courage I felt earlier to choose myself? It stretches my lips into an easy smile. "No thank you."

Shock twists the lines of Zeek's face. "Are you serious? Do you know what kind of ratings we'd get if you were both on the show? What it would do for *The Divorcétante Chronicles?*"

Again, because *no* is a complete sentence and I've reached my time capacity on this fake date, I repeat myself, then push to my feet.

Somehow, he translates that simple answer as a need to speak louder. "Ebony, you don't understand, this is going to be huge. There's talk of Warner Easton relocating his entire hub to Ellswood," he adds, as if the prospect of a huge software company moving in—likely boosting jobs and population—should somehow convince me. As if a spotlight on our little pinprick on a town is incentive.

Still no.

Wildly, the man follows me to the doors and grabs my arm to stop me from exiting. But he quickly releases me as I fix him with an unyielding stare.

"*Never* touch me," I say.

Zeek, clearly realizing his mistake, throws up his hands and takes a step back, smiling like I've just proven why I'd be perfect for the rough-and-tumble cast. "Sorry, I'm just surprised, is all."

He pauses, tugging at the lapels of his blazer. His movements are frantic, like mentally he's still grasping at straws. "Well, what about your friends, the rest of the divas? We could take them too to make things easier for you. Whitney is definitely queen bee material or an instigator; Priscilla's the sweetheart; and, uh, the newcomer for Chanel—"

"What don't you understand about *no*? Leave me and my friends alone," I snap, my voice cutting through the restaurant chatter. I inhale deeply, finally noticing all the phones aimed at me—and the familiar faces.

A few feet behind him, Linc is staring at me, as if he's waiting for the signal to destroy Zeek.

I swallow, forcing a smile. "Please pardon my interruption," I say to the people gathered, then turn and head for the exit, stepping into the warm breeze, feeling like I might explode.

"What was that?" I murmur to myself.

I've started walking toward my car, debating whether to cancel the mixer Leslie scheduled for me next month on the first, when someone calls my name. I toss a glance over my shoulder and find Linc running toward me.

"Hey, are you all right?"

"Well, I *thought* I had a date." I laugh, keeping it light, even though my mind is spiraling. Especially since I'm pretty sure one of those familiar faces I spotted in the restaurant was the PI I hired to follow Julian. Lord only knows what case he's working now.

"So, it wasn't a date?" Linc scratches his temple, like, *Please, make it make sense.*

A small giggle rumbles over my shoulders. "Turns out he just wanted to offer me a job…as a *Luxe Ladies* cast member."

Linc presses a fist to his mouth, clearly trying to mask a laugh. "Hey, look at it this way—I hear they make bank."

Playfully, I swat at him. But he catches my hand, holding on a little too long to be casual. We're lingering in each other's space a little too long for it to be meaningless.

His intense gray eyes flicker in the vibrant sunlight, and I see the moment when the words *we can't* iron out the lines of his handsome face.

And he's right.

We've got all the reasons to keep our distance. To be professional. To stymie Cornelia. To respect his stunning date, who's presumably still inside Whisk & Whistle. And still, as he releases my hand, I can't help but wish we could disregard all of them.

(470) 555-3269

Chapter Fourteen

Crystal Clear

Lincoln

EBONY WANTED TO KISS ME again.

I saw it burning in her bright hazel eyes. Right out in the open, in the middle of that parking lot where anyone and everyone could see, she looked at me like she needed me to be the one to step up this time, and I *really* wanted to.

Jesus, for all that is good and holy in this world, the urge to tug her flush to my body and feel her soft skin, her tender lips moving greedily against mine—it was there. In spades.

But I just kept asking myself, *What are you going to do about it, Linc?*

And the answer wasn't, *Fuck it! Just kiss her until she's teetering on the edge of release. Take her, out here, so all of Ellswood can see I'm damn good enough for her.*

No. *Nah.*

Instead, a highlight reel flashed behind my eyelids, burning into my skull. I could see it—that look Ebony gave me when she saw me standing there in the crowd at Whisk & Whistle. Her eyes seared me, full of hurt and humiliation. She didn't need to say a word.

I already knew.

And then the fury that followed—molten rage clenched my fists, made my knuckles ache as I watched that bastard's hand on her. Every muscle in my body screamed at me to lunge at him. But I just stood there like I had nowhere else to be, no one else to be with.

Alexis's disappointment felt like a physical weight pressing down on me as I muttered some hollow excuse as to why I needed to step away. I was supposed to be over Ebony. I promised myself I would be. But here I am, still torn between loyalty and that damn ache in my chest that refuses to die.

Whatever happens next between Ebony Grace Livingston and me, it's got to be her move.

I won't be her fallback. My intentions have always been plain. I've made my moves. The next has to be hers.

So, for the last week, I've been giving her space—as much as I can with us both at the manor. In the meantime, working on the finishing touches for the wedding party suites with the crew is helping me keep my distance.

"Wallpaper is going to make all the difference." Vincent takes wide strides across the room, his hands framing the visual he's painting for Manny and me. "Think about taking that unfortunate rosebud motif and magnifying it so it gives us a bold, original pattern. That way, it makes the space feel cozier, warmer. Still historically accurate, but surprisingly contemporary."

Neither of us says a word.

My budget is tight enough as it is. Exorbitantly priced wall rosebuds? When I'm already cutting corners to update restrooms, relocate poorly placed outlets, and add more lighting? Yeah, that's not in cards.

Vincent sucks in a deep breath and holds it, visibly incensed. "Listen, I'm going to need verbal feedback here, and now. It's already mid-July, honey. We've got a couple months left, and I don't do half-assed, so…" He drags in a deep breath. "Let's just say, with your input, I'd like to finalize this as *soon* as possible."

Okaaay.

"Well, are there cheaper—"

He tilts his head, impatience smoothing his expression. "Bridges, honey, we've got to be decisive, and beautiful things cost money. Right now, we've got botanicals, but if that's not budget-friendly, say that. I've got less elaborate wall coverings, from damasks to large-scale murals, medallions, and paints. Don't even get me started on fabrics, baby, because silk is just the beginning of the textiles I can—"

CRASH!

The commotion came from downstairs, but Manny, Vincent, and I freeze, listening for movement to pinpoint which room the sound originated in.

At first, the entire manor seems still. Then a stampede of footsteps and voices groan through the floorboards.

The three of us dash into the hall and quickly descend the stairs, following the jumble of chatter until we enter the grand ballroom, and my heart stalls at the double doors.

"Mr. Bridges, we don't know what happened. They just fell," one of the guys says.

"We can fix it, no?" asks another.

I walk slowly to the center of the room and crouch down, mentally scouring my contacts to determine where I can, first, find a skilled artisan from whom I can source a half-dozen matching nineteenth-century hand-cut chandelier crystals that'll preserve the original craftsmanship and historical accuracy of this piece. But then this savior's got to fit us in—and complete the work—in less than eight weeks.

Give me a break.

"Can someone get me a drop cloth?" I groan.

A horrified gasp sounds behind me, and all I can do is close my eyes.

"*Oh* my goodness!" Ebony scurries into the ballroom and drops to her knees at the perimeter of the broken glass. "The legend—"

"Is still intact. I'm sure of it," I say, with more confidence than I actually feel, taking the cloth from Manny and gently gathering the fragments. "It's lasted a few centuries. We'll replace these crystals and preserve the authenticity, just the same as the wood and plasterwork throughout the manor."

Ebony looks at me, her eyes pleading, as if she's asking if I'm certain.

"I've got an entire list of trade craftsmen." I give her a reassuring nod, smiling. "I promise, I'm going to reach out to them right now." *And pray someone can work magic.*

Relief sags her shoulders. "Thank you. It'll really mean a lot to Hailey."

"And Ellswood's history," I add, softly. "I want to preserve the legend as much as you do."

For a beat, she stares at me, as if she's reading the truth in my words. She knows what it's been like for me—constantly relegated by the likes of the Livingstons to the outskirts of this community my ancestors built. Always fighting against the grain to preserve our history, reclaim my identity before they erase us completely.

"I know how important this is to you." Ebony gives me a small smile.

She walks back to the billiard room with me, where I've been working lately. And, of course, my desk is buried underneath blueprints and piles of textiles that Vincent's forcing me to wade through to "feel the richness" of the fabric.

Ebony laughs. "You can take the mess out of the office, but, uh…"

"Hey, I know it looks like chaos, but it's organized." I chuckle, scrambling to remove the clutter on top of my laptop, shoving fabric, tassels, and motivational paint swatches out of the way like I can pretend this isn't the most usual state of my desk since—well, since she walked into my office in the Sterling building.

Once I've cleared the surface, Ebony settles on the edge, crossing her legs and giving me a glimpse of her smooth bronze thighs.

"…hard."

My attention snaps up, guiltily. I gulp. "Wh-what did you say?"

"Working *hard*," she repeats, giggling, absolutely at my expense. "I mean, aside from the fact that a centuries-old legend might be in jeopardy, the whole place is really looking great, Linc."

She knows what she does to me.

"Thanks." I laugh. "Always working hard. But, uh, let me see who I can reach about the chandelier…"

Grateful for the distraction, I flip open my laptop, quickly scanning my glazier contacts who've worked on glass repairs for me in the past.

In the first five minutes, my go-to lady asks for a picture, which Ebony eagerly supplies, along with a snapshot of the carnage inside the drop cloth. My lady takes one look, then immediately wishes me luck because, apparently, I'm going to need it.

I didn't know how right she was.

The second person at least gives me a name for it—nineteenth-century Georgian-style cut-crystal chandelier, handcrafted in England somewhere between 1860 and 1880—which would have been super helpful, if he wasn't set on buying it from me instead of selling me replacement crystals. By the sixth artisan—a referral from the third craftsperson—I've got two more offers, a handful of best wishes, and it's feeling like I'll be stepping out on a wish and prayer. Until the sixth artisan says she *knows a guy.*

Don't we all.

Except I look him up, and lo and behold, the guy is legit. Bonus, he's a specialized artisan who both understands and values historical integrity. And double bonus, he lives in Dawsonville—that's roughly a ninety-minute drive from Atlanta. So easily less than two hours from Ellswood. Most importantly, he schedules me for a same-day service appointment in two weeks, on Saturday, August second.

That leaves over a month before the wedding, just in case anything comes up and we need to make other arrangements—so what if my budget is busted?

"Sounds like you're headed on a road trip!" Ebony hops off the desk, rounds the corner, and leaps into my arms, and I don't even care because it feels like a win.

The legend of the chandelier lives!

But as I set her back on her feet, the air crackles with electricity.

I settle on the edge of the desk, my heart crashing like cymbals against my ribcage.

And then she steps between my thighs, clasping her hands behind my neck, searching my eyes. "You know, I've been thinking a lot about dating." She pauses, and her gaze briefly slips to my lips before she meets my eyes again. "The first one was…not it. Let's put it that way." She laughs. "The next one wanted to hire me, and I'm starting to wonder if *The Divorcétante Chronicles* is bringing all the weirdos out of the woodwork."

I swallow, unsure where she's going with this, or if she's even aware how wrong it feels to talk about other men with her face only inches from mine.

Either way, I just go with it.

"Could be." I shrug.

"At this point, I think I'm out of practice." She eases closer still until her warm, sultry scent leaves me dizzy. "How would I even know if a man is really into me?"

"He'd have to be a fool not to be."

Ebony erases the distance between us until the swells of her breasts are pressed flush against the ridges of my chest, and I feel the rhythm of her heart pounding, her breaths growing shallow.

"What should I do?" She tucks her lower lip between her teeth, and suddenly, I understand. She's not asking about these other dudes. She's asking me how to start again—to pick up where we left off.

At least, that's what I *think* is happening.

"Well, let's take the guy from date one, for example," I say. "What was so wrong with him?"

Tenderly, she drags the pads of her fingers along the back of my head, tracing along the nape of my neck, and it's clear she's stalling. But why?

"So far, I've heard you say he's 'not it.'" I chuckle. "On your post, you said no sparks, nothing to write home about, *nada…*"

A small sigh escapes her, and fire ignites in her eyes, turning them a vivid shade of whiskey.

"You really want to know?" Ebony asks, softly.

I nod, genuinely curious. What could be so bad that she can't even lend a name to it?

"He looked like you," she blurts out, cringing as she adds, "in a way…"

"Like me?"

Ebony squeezes her eyes closed, letting her chin drop to her chest. "Description-wise, twins!" She lifts her head with tears of laughter in her eyes.

"Oh, this ought to be good." I tip her chin up to read her expression. "Don't hold out now. I'm dying to know why I have—"

"An AI twin?" She stumbles back, almost losing her footing, but I grip her hips, steadying her.

Of course, I know this. I've got the gray-eyed Spades champ with the magic fingers cheat sheet, as Vincent put it. But I love hearing the words from her beautiful mouth as she tells me that she wants me.

"*Ugh.* This is so embarrassing, but…I sort of told my dating concierge that I wanted a man who was tall and athletic, with deep brown skin, and that gray eyes wouldn't hurt, and, well—"

"So, you described me?"

A blush spreads on Ebony's cheeks. She opens her mouth, but nothing comes out.

"Ebony Grace King Livingston, I see the way you look at me." I smile, unable to take my eyes off her. "Have you been fantasizing about me?"

Then, suddenly, her bright hazel eyes focus on mine, her lips twitching guiltily before she deflates into me, and I'm only human.

I don't have the resolve to resist.

Not now. Not when she's put in an exact order for me with her dating concierge. Not when I can still feel her lips on mine from the last time we kissed.

I catch her mouth with mine, dragging my tongue over her lower lip then softly biting the fullness. "When did you start thinking about me? Since the kiss?"

Ebony's breathless as she admits, "I haven't been sleeping well…"

"And why not?" I ask. Her soft moan drives me crazy. "Why haven't you been sleeping well?"

"Because thinking about you is keeping me awake."

Jesus.

My heart stutters in my chest as I study her expression, looking for the lie. But it isn't there. There's nothing I love more than knowing she's been in bed and turned on with me on her mind.

It drives me crazy.

"Tell me you want me. I need to know I'm who you want, Ebony." I kiss her slow, gentle, savoring the sweet remnants of coffee on her tongue. "Or tell me to stop, and I'll forget this happened. I'll come to work every day and be the professional. Nothing has to change."

Tell me I'm who you want.

"What if I don't know? We're both dating, figuring out what we want."

I lift a hand to her cheek, grazing the delicate skin with my fingertips as I correct her, "*You're* figuring out what you want. I've always known since you showed up in the library with your history book."

She kisses me.

A full-body, hands-on-my-face, whimpering kiss, like she's done enough sampling and needs more.

"Can we just, like"—she peppers more kisses, licking and tasting, her heart drumming against my chest—"enjoy each other for now? It's sort of hard to think straight with your lips…and you just smell so good."

I laugh into the kiss then pull back slightly, nudging her chin higher to look her in the eye. "So, in other words, just shut up and kiss you, then?" I chuckle, squeezing her waist.

"Mm-hmm," she moans, ghosting her lips along the column of my neck. Her warm breaths are like feathers, ever so lightly stirring me from the inside out as she guides my hands to her ass, granting me permission, possession. "I just need to feel your hands on me."

Every muscle in my body hardens.

But then Ebony presses her pelvis into my aching hard-on. Arousal courses through me, and I lose the battle. I have no choice but to oblige, tugging her into my lap, her dress hem gliding up her smooth thighs until she's straddling me with only the delicate fabric of her panties as a barrier.

My dick is painfully hard.

And as her mouth travels back to my lips, I tug her closer, loving her gasp as she no doubt feels what she's doing to me. My body moves in muscle memory. My hips pulse, and I'm grinding in a heady fog of euphoric lust. Our mouths tangle in soft moans and hungry whimpers, and I'm barely resisting the urge to remove every last barrier between us and bury myself deep inside her until the truth unravels on her parted lips.

Or until someone clears their throat behind us.

Vincent doesn't even try to make an exit. No, he stands there, ramrod straight, the smug bastard. "I didn't mean to interrupt..."

Yeah, you did.

Ebony slides off me and stumbles backward, her chest rising and falling, doing nothing to convince anyone that we weren't just going at it in this billiard room with the door wide open and the walls paper thin.

"I was, uh…just checking on the progress with the chandelier crystals." She nods—too many times, unnaturally—as she turns to me. "There's a guy in Dawsonville, right, Linc?" She gives me a wide-eyed, pleading look.

"Right, yeah." I start to stand, then settle back on the desk, dropping my hands into my lap. "I've got a same-day service appointment to repair the chandelier, the weekend of the second," I say, my voice rough and gravelly to my own ears. "He's supposedly an incredible artisan. Came highly recommended."

This is embarrassing.

"My, that sounds *expensive*…" Vincent gives a single, deliberate nod, clearly enjoying our discomfort, while reminding me *beautiful things cost money.* "Maybe you can go with him, Ebony. We need that precious chandelier to be perfect for the reception, and someone should take care of that beauty while he drives," he says, looking unmistakably at me.

Nice one, coach.

She swallows hard, her hands restless. "Uh, yeah, I'll think about it." And then she turns on her heel.

The moment she leaves, Vincent flashes me a downright sinister grin. "You're welcome."

You're invited
to our
Wedding Day

Chapter Fifteen

Mixed Up

Ebony

I'M ADDICTED TO KISSING LINCOLN Bridges.

There, I said it. Because…

Lord, help me!

We've been sneaking into every room of Madison Manor for the last three weeks, finding little corners to steal moments in the shadows, a mess of lips and tongues and hands, like teenagers. I can't explain it, except to say it's a relentless pull. Just this overwhelming force that draws me to him.

Let's say the florist I wanted was booked, but after some calls and scouring the interwebs, I find a website with tiered cakes, lush flower arrangements, and charming sunset wedding photos—and the owner is available. Or I learn my favorite bakery shut down six months ago, but after chatting with the owner on a divorcétante post, she's now working exclusively with me. In my mind, I deserve a little reward, right? Next thing I know, I'm slipping into the billiard room, closing the door behind me, and suddenly Linc and I are lost in each other, lip-locked, inching toward more.

So far, it's just been kissing and a little—okay, a *lot*—of recreational dry humping.

But the desire to take things further? It's there, constant, like a little red devil tapping me on the shoulder, telling me how good it feels. *Take what you want,* it says. *Be bad. Everybody's doing it…*

Ugh.

And that's the cycle—bursts of productivity followed by mind-numbing kisses, leaving me wanting more. But there's no lasting peace because I'm already thinking about the next one.

Just shameless.

Today, Linc finished up the stained-glass window repairs and needed to make an "important phone call" outside in one of the gardens—of course, due to the noise levels. Couldn't have been because he knew, thirty seconds later, we'd be dipped behind a hydrangea bush, sucking face and avoiding bee stings.

Nope.

Regardless, Linc's still heavy on my mind as I leave work early, battling traffic and drizzle to get home and change for tonight's mixer. It feels strange, spending the afternoon making out and climbing Mount Bridges in the billiard room, then somehow planning to walk into a room full of suitors like I'm ready to give them any sort of real shot. But there's no time to overthink. This is my last scheduled event with Leslie, and maybe I'll cancel the concierge service after this. Maybe.

But right now, I've got to send Hailey and Donovan a quick progress update and a to-do list, and shower, within the next ninety minutes.

"Serena, turn on my Melanin Magic playlist."

A smooth neo-soul rhythm fills the air as I kick off my heels and settle at the dining table, quickly pulling out my laptop from my tote. I check a few emails from Mom about the cotillion that will not go away, and one from Savannah, rescheduling our next appointment, before drafting a new message to Hailey and Donovan. My fingers move rapid-fire over the keys, first providing the probate court hours to submit documentation and the fee for the marriage license. Then I update the seating chart—Hailey's bougie, drama-magnet friend Renee *has* to be moved away from her ex-husband and closer to Nora Whitfield. *Shocker.* Next, I report that all vendor selections are finalized and attach the signed agreements, relieved this email is moving faster than expected. Finally, I'm sharing vow-writing ideas and gift suggestions for the couple, plus thank-yous to the wedding party, when my phone buzzes across the glass surface of the table.

I glance at the screen. I'm jarred.

"Julian?"

My first instinct is to let him go to voicemail, because why is he calling me, interrupting my peace? But overwhelmingly, I'm shocked, a little surprised, and filled with dread. Curiosity and anxiety tangle in my chest because I've left a dozen texts unanswered, but he never *calls*. We don't call each other anymore. Ever.

What does he want?

My mind immediately nose-dives into bad-news territory. Is someone hurt? One of his brothers, Hailey, or even Cornelia? Worse, has his man-radar gone off and he somehow know about Linc and me? *Is* there a me and Linc? *Lord, Ebony…*

Reluctantly, I tap to answer.

"Yes, what's up?" There's silence, and at first, I wonder if maybe he's butt-dialed me, so I check the screen again. "Julian?"

"Oh, I didn't actually think you'd answer," he says, and annoyance creeps over my skin.

I sigh. "Well, I did. So, again, is there something you needed? I've got things to do."

He stalls, and I'm halfway expecting him to tell me something messy, like he's disputing Nora's pregnancy and waiting for the results of a paternity test. Or worse, to apologize and beg me to come back to him. Again.

But then he says, "You know those undershirts you used to buy for me? Where'd you get them? I can't find them anywhere."

The rage that boils inside me is lethal.

I'm so amazed by the sheer audacity of this man, who has already asked for *my* mom's spaghetti sauce recipe, the Wi-Fi password, and which detergent I use because his clothes don't smell like they used to. And now this…this overgrown clown who never appreciated all the things I did for him dares fix his lips to ask where to buy his favorite undershirts?

"Disrespectfully, Julian…screw all the way off, and figure it out like I had to do for over a decade. While you're at it, lose my number. I'll never want you back."

I stab my finger on the widget, disconnecting the call, my good mood gone. I'm restless, and angry, just staring at the phone like it's at fault, when my attention shifts to the time.

I've still got ten more minutes before I *need* to shower and get dressed to leave.

Quickly grabbing my ring light, I affix my phone to it, open the PopShot app, and press the 'live' button.

"Hey there, friends. I wasn't planning to post yet, but I just got a call from my ex-husband."

It's so messy, and I would log off right now if I had any sense. I'm the divorcétante. I'm supposed to be this put-together example of a woman flourishing post-divorce. I've got new clothes and a fierce new haircut. I'm a lipstick brand ambassador. I've filed a trademark on the phrase "pause, peace, power" because it's now part of the global lexicon. I should be the bigger person…

"Remember that first video, when I promised I'd give you the scandal? The shock-value, trending, viral, smear-campaign drama that you want?

"Well, I feel like I've short-changed you on that a bit. I jumped straight into reinventing myself outside of that family's dynasty and the fandoms. I put decorum and etiquette first. I was so eager to prove I'd moved beyond anger and pettiness.

"But today, that man called my phone to ask me where I used to buy his undershirts, y'all. His damned undershirts!"

The viewer count and comments start zipping up the screen.

"And you know what? I think that act of violence affords me the right to tell you that I'm pissed, no, *furious* that I wasted almost ten years of my life on a man who begged for my time, then wasted it.

"Am I angry about the infidelity and the divorce? Hell yes. But also, I feel like you should know that the affair with that woman was just the final straw."

The comments section is on fire.

Glad you left his ass.

Decenter men!

Not the undershirts being the last straw.

We love you, Divorcétante!

Honey, congratulations on your prison release.

I laugh, shaking my head.

"And I love you back. I'm so grateful. Thank you, truly, for holding space for me.

"For so long, this man made me feel invisible. He overlooked a million tiny labors I did to keep him happy and our house feeling like a home.

"That single call reminded me he doesn't miss me as a person—he misses the perks of being married to me. Magically, the dishes were always clean and the microwave was spotless—am I right, friends? The towels washed themselves, and there was never any dust.

"Well, you know what? All you folks out there who feel 'blindsided' when she asks for a divorce? She's been making all the magic happen. All the invisible labor. She's the house cleaner, short-order cook, personal admin, and laundry maiden. She's been doing it all, unappreciated."

Magically walked out that door, too.

Left mine after twenty-five years. Never looked back. Best decision I ever made.

Baybee, he didn't know his mate from his mom.

Men know what they're doing. Weaponized incompetence!

The gaslighting…

My face when I got the word my divorce was finalized 😬

And yet he's baffled.

"Yes! Hello, the divorce didn't come from out of nowhere. He had almost ten years to change and didn't.

"Y'all, I couldn't see it back then, but I was slowly disappearing with every unnoticed act. Now, I couldn't be happier to be a walkaway wife. In fact, I *wish* I'd left sooner. Phew!"

A huge weight lifts off me, and I feel like I'm breathing easier.

"Anyway, I've got to go, but I'll leave you with this. Exit immediately if you're unhappy, and if you choose to find someone else, make sure that person is willing to give the help, support, and love you need.

"For me? I want someone who'll show up, you know? He's got to meet me halfway and keep the romance alive."

I sing that last part, shimmying my shoulders for the divas.

"That's all for now. As always, pause, peace, power."

An hour, two dress changes, one very apt "grateful for my Calming Water Sounds playlist" journal entry, and three almost-called-Linc moments later, I'm at the mixer. It's in a private room at a swanky downtown hotel, and I'm rubbing elbows with Ellswood's crème de la crème, chatting and looking fierce in a tailored black velvet gown with a plunging neckline and a thigh-high slit, cinched unbreathably tight with a diamond-encrusted belt.

Also, I'm bored out of my mind.

It's not that there aren't any decent-looking guys in attendance. No, I've talked to a few who actually have potential—CEOs, pilots, construction directors—all great conversationalists, above average height, and physically fit-*ish*. Thankfully, no AI Lincs or undercover casting directors.

That I know of.

Honestly, Idris Elba, Aaron Pierre, and Morris Chestnut could be begging me for a date and dessert, and I wouldn't even blink right now. Unloading on Julian left me feeling lighter, bolder. But all I want to do is leave, find Linc, and let go.

"Ebony?"

I turn to see Nelly—or rather, Cornelius, Julian and Donovan's youngest brother—standing behind me. Compared to Julian's razor-sharp confidence, Nelly's got this laidback energy with an easy grin and relaxed posture, like he's always a few steps ahead of the crowd without trying. His towering height and playboy aesthetic don't hurt either. Still, my stomach drops.

Panic shoots through me, and I wonder if he's seen today's *Divorcétante Chronicles*, or if he's just living under a gold-plated rock.

"Hi," I say sheepishly, my focus darting past him to a man in the distance, phone aimed in our direction… *Is that the PI again? Who is he following?*

I quickly scan the crowd, hoping to spot a familiar face from Whisk & Whistle, but really, it could be anyone.

Nelly clears his throat. "Listen, Ebony, I just want you to know I don't agree with how my brother treated you."

Wait, what?

His words hit me like a gust of wind, stealing my breath.

"You don't?" My voice trembles in surprise, and I must look at him like he's sprouted a second forehead, because he barks out a deep, guttural laugh that's strangely comforting.

"No, I don't. I still think of you like a sister, E-boogie." He nudges me with his elbow, taking in my appearance, from the strappy silver heels to the bold red lips, lingering on my short hair. "I like the new look. It suits you." His smile softens, then fades into something more wistful. "I've been listening to your videos, and, uh, knowing Jules didn't value you like he should have…" He shakes his head. "If he wasn't my brother, I would've kicked his ass."

We both laugh, and I love him even more for saying that.

The fact that I can be angry with his brother and still care so deeply for him is a reminder that, even while I'm reinventing myself, I don't want to lose my core values. I never want to hide behind a hard shell, distancing myself from the people who make me feel like the best version of me.

"Thank you for saying that, Nelly Belly."

He pulls me into a smothering big-little-brother hug, assuring me he'll always be there for me.

"Nelly?"

We both glance just off his shoulder toward a stunning Black woman with rich, radiant dark skin in a flowing gown. Her seductive eyes, framed by thick lashes, are locked on him, and we both know I should probably leave because I'm—

"Yeah, you're cock-blocking, E," Nelly whispers out the side of his mouth.

Exactly.

"Oh, well, it was so good seeing you. Take care." I wave awkwardly at the woman, then hurry out of the private area toward the restroom.

Except, when I step back out, makeup refreshed and ready to jump into the mix before the event wraps up, I can't make myself move past the bar. My feet root to the ground as I spot Lincoln Bridges sitting on a center stool, legs stretched out, work boots planted on the floor, and sleeves rolled up, showing off his tattooed forearms.

Dear, sweet Jesus.

A beguiling smile curves his full lips as he watches me.

Immediately, I can't tell if I should be glad or mad at myself for choosing this dress, because I'm going into withdrawals. Even thinking of his mouth on me feels like a gateway drug, and I'm heading down a dangerous, addictive path. Every time I see him, all I can think of is how I want more—harder, faster—hits of him.

"Any luck?" he asks, casually, across the bar.

"What?" At first, I have no idea what he's talking about until he tips his head toward the private room. "Oh, no." I chuckle, finally regaining feeling in my feet long enough to walk slowly over to him and settle on the stool by his side. "Were you in there, too?"

Linc softly shakes his head, letting his gaze drift, agonizingly slow, over my exposed thigh peeking through the slit.

"You look stunning," he says, his words landing like a match striking low and tight in my belly.

"Thank you." I avert my gaze, focusing on the fresh glass of honey-amber liquid in front of him. "Early nightcap before your road trip tomorrow?"

"Ah, no. Just buying myself some time before I head over for dinner with my mom and dad."

I smile. "Oh, wow. You all still do weekly dinners?"

"Mm-hmm," he replies, grinning.

But then our eyes meet, and I'm not sure if he's testing my memory, recalling all the times he cut our tutoring sessions short to make it to family dinner night.

We both say, almost at the same time, "The best flowers come from the roots you nurture."

In a glimmer of a moment, I forget all about the understated luxury of my dress and my Chanel clutch.

We laugh, obnoxiously loud and unhinged.

It feels so damn good.

How many times did he repeat Grandma Bridges's motto to me? How many times did we say those words, mimicking the warm, gravelly croak of her voice? We always recognized the wisdom behind her words, but *Lord*, when we were younger, she said it every. Single. Time.

We'd roll our eyes, like, *we get it.*

But now, I guess we finally *do* get it. The importance of investing in the people and values you care about in order to flourish. We do need to tend to our foundational relationships. More than ever, I see that now.

Linc smiles at me, and in the mix of nostalgia and the loose threads between us, I sense that he gets it too.

"I'm glad I ran into you," I say.

"Yeah?" He lifts his chin, the cords of his neck growing taut as he deepens his stare. Then the edge of his lip curls, and something hits me.

"Wait, did you *know* I was going to be here tonight?" I narrow my eyes, studying his expression. *Nope, I never said where I was going on my live.* "You checked my calendar, didn't you?"

He laughs, a guilty laugh. "What?"

"And here I was thinking, wow, he's so sweet. It must be the stars aligning that he's here tonight, looking like a snack. And lo and behold—"

Linc tugs me between his legs, still laughing. "Wait, so you think I look like a snack?"

He's all mesmerizing gray eyes and lopsided smile, the scruff of his dark beard lightly dusted with gray.

I squirm, trying to pull away, but in the middle of messing around with this man, I somehow forgot this dress is backless, requiring certain undergarment, um…*choices*. His massive hands are flat against the small of my back, his long fingers inching lower. But the way his grip is firm, possessive, just the way I like…

"Correct me if I'm wrong." Linc tilts his head, amusement dancing in his sparkly gaze. "Didn't you say you wanted a man who'll show up? I think the exact words were 'meet me halfway.'" He pauses. "'Keep the romance alive.'"

I don't know whether to be flattered that he watches *The Divorcétante Chronicles* or semi-annoyed that he's using my own words against me.

"And this was how you translated that, huh?" I nod a good dozen times, utterly tickled—and completely turned on.

He shrugs, adorably. "What's more romantic than walking a woman to her car to make sure she gets home safely?"

I'm parked in valet, but I don't have it in me to steal his thunder.

Then I glance at the fresh drink, the half-melted ice bobbing at the surface, the glass sweating with condensation.

He hasn't touched it.

Lincoln Bridges may wear rough work boots and roll his sleeves up the second there's work to do, but he's not the kind of man who drinks and drives. A chasm opens in my chest. He's been sitting here, patiently waiting for my event to end, just to make sure I'm safe.

And that is…*incredibly* sexy.

"Yes," I say softly, needing to see him when I say the rest. I need to read the invitation in his whisper-gray eyes, that silent plea telling me to choose him, to forget about the other dates and whomever I met at the mixer. "Remember when you asked if I'd been fantasizing about you? My answer is yes, and I want you, Lincoln Bridges."

And just like that, he stands and searches my eyes, looking sheepish. "Are you ready?"

It feels like a loaded question. Ready for him to walk me to the valet? To kiss me silly? To swipe away every drink on this bar and take me right here? I don't know. Do I want none of that or all of the above? My answer is still a resounding yes to anything he has in mind, because I've decided. Right now, with him breathless and still searching for adequate words, I'm ready to try again with Lincoln Bridges.

I have to squeeze my thighs together just to get the word out. "Yes."

You're invited
to our
Wedding Day

(470) 555-3269

Chapter Sixteen

Chasing Waterfalls

Lincoln

I SKIP THE LIQUID COURAGE, rushing to pay my tab before I take Ebony's hand, guiding us away from the valet toward an emergency exit, which, at the moment, feels appropriate. Hand in hand, we spill out into a darkened side street, sirens blaring in my head, pulse racing, the rain coming down in thick sideways sheets. But I stop, muscles locked up as the deluge cascades down the side of the building.

A waterfall.

In the middle of the city, there's a waterfall, like the scene's been set for us. It's perfect. *She's* perfect.

When did I get this romantic?

Slowly walking Ebony toward valet, I ask, "You okay with getting a little wet?" *Jesus, that sounded better in my head.* "I meant to kiss—"

"Yes," she says again, surprising me.

And now, suddenly, I'm overthinking everything. Did I mean the rain, or our makeshift waterfall? Yeah. But would I absolutely be on board with any activity in which my participation involved making her wet? Hell yes.

But what did *she* think I meant?

She glances down the street, looking both ways like she's making sure it's safe to cross this line before she finishes what I started, stepping backward until she's against the wall, water streaming over her like she's my personal wet dream.

"Jesus, Ebony."

In a single stride, I erase the distance between us, flattening one palm on the side of her face and brushing the pad of my thumb over her lower lip with the other. "All day, I've been thinking about these lips."

She sets her hands free on my stomach, then weaves them to my back, tugging me closer. "So, kiss me already," she purrs.

I lean in and drag my lips over hers, curling my fingers into the fabric of her dress. I sink into the sensation of us, drenched in uncensored desire.

There's no one out here. Nothing stopping us this time. The thought alone makes my dick hard. Ebony deserves to be kissed properly, as long and hard as she wants.

I thrust my hips, using my weight to pin her against the wall, sucking along her neck and behind her ears until she's breathless and panting.

Her hands are on my back, her nails digging into my skin. Her chest swells, and *Jesus…* She kicks her leg through that damn slit, hooking it over my hip, and I don't know whether to freeze or fuck her raw as she writhes against me in—

I gasp as my hand glides up her thigh, then I pull back to meet her gaze.

"Ebony, where is your underwear?"

Those bruised lips part. "Baby, you can't wear a dress like this and have panty lines. It's like serving a five-star meal on a paper plate."

Suddenly, I can't breathe.

Or move.

Not only is she soaking wet in a dress that's hanging on by a thread, but her leg is wrapped around my hip, my hand is mere inches from heaven, and I've got no condoms.

I'm only supposed to be kissing her.

I close my eyes, uncertain of my next move and mortified even as the words slip out. "We can't." My voice comes out strained, understandably. "Anyone could see us here."

She leans forward until our noses touch and looks me dead in the eye as she says, "Right now, I'm so horny, I don't give a damn who sees us. It's been over a year." Then she runs her tongue along the tip of my nose and slowly traces it down to my lower lip before she gives a soft bite.

I almost come.

By some otherworldly miracle, my brain remembers it controls my motor skills. Through sheer adrenaline and determination not to fumble ten years of riding the bench, I step back.

"Ebony, you can't say things like that to me. I'm telling you… I've wanted this too long. We can't even mess around because I don't have a condom. I *won't* be able to stop—"

"*I* don't care," she counters, yanking me back to her, kissing me breathless.

It's like a green light shining, but my instincts are wildly waving red flags. Then an idea floats to the surface of my mind.

Just in case, I scan the street and realize we're in a service alley. Dark, wet—as established—and completely deserted. What kind of man would I be if I didn't offer a little…*service?*

"Why are you smiling?" Ebony laughs, but it's obvious she doesn't get it.

She starts to catch on, though, when I kiss along her collarbone, gliding her dress strap away and sucking on the swells of her small, round breasts. Her tiny whimpers swirl into the moist air as I drag her nipple into my mouth, teasing it with my tongue.

"You asked me to kiss you already…" I dip my hand into the dress slit, finding her slick and ready. *Jesus, so wet.* As I slip two digits inside, lengthening each stroke until she syncs to my rhythm, I whisper softly, "What do you think? Are my fingers magical enough?"

She moans, the picture of uninhibited perfection.

Gliding in a third finger, I quicken the pace, scattering more kisses between her breasts until she shivers and convulses around me tightly.

As I remove my hand, I lower to my knees to kiss her sweet, hot pussy. She absolutely gets what I'm smiling about now. When I open my mouth over her soft, sensitive flesh, darting my tongue in deep, long strokes, laving and lapping at her five-star meal, I have no doubt she's tuned in to the fact that this, right now, prioritizing her pleasure—that's only the teaser of the man I want to be for her. And as an orgasm vibrates through her, she gasps for air, writhing against my hand flattened over her stomach to hold her upright. I'm certain we're, line for line, on the same page about exploring this unwavering flame between us.

When I stand, she collapses into me.

"What about you?" she asks, her voice soft. "Let me take care of you." She breathes the words like they're a promise.

I have to admit, looking at her breathless and spent does wonders for my ego. But as perfect as she is, as perfect as this oasis waterfall is, she said it's been over a year. The last time she had sex, she was still married.

If we take this further—*when* we take this further—it won't be on a whim in a dark alley. She means too much to me.

"Baby, I'm satisfied when you are," I say, then brush a chaste kiss over her lips. "We'd better get going, though. We definitely don't want me to be late."

Half an hour later, I'm sitting in my car outside my parents' house, changing into my gym shirt and scrolling through Ebony's latest PopShot videos, still trying to shake off my smile. Part of me wants to skip this dinner and call Ebony to see if she wants company, to pick up where we left off. The other part, though, still can't believe what just happened behind that hotel.

It feels too raw.

After cutting the engine, I exit the car and head up the path to the front door. I bypass the doorbell, instead playing a drum solo on the wooden panels with my palms until the door swings open.

Mom is standing on the other side, her dark hair lined with grays and pulled back into a loose bun. She's wearing a soft, earth-toned blouse and black pants. Nothing too flashy, but everything about her, the way she carries herself, has always shown class and a quiet elegance.

"Ooh, Lord, anyone would think you were raised by heathens." She wipes her hands on a dishcloth, fixing me with a chastising look that quickly morphs into a soft smile. "Now, give me some sugar, then get on in here and wash your hands before your daddy eats up all the gumbo." She shakes her head, giggling.

Yes, washing my hands would be awesome.

"Yes, ma'am!" I do as I'm told, planting a big, hard kiss on her soft, velvety cheek, skipping the usual bear hug. I'm at the kitchen sink not even twenty seconds before she sidles up beside me while I'm lathering my hands.

She fixes me with her *Mama knows* stare, taking stock of my clothes, shoes, posture, everything.

"Yes?" I chuckle.

"No, I'm just looking. Seems someone's in a good mood…" she says, clearly fishing.

But I'm wise to her tactics. "Always, when I get to catch up with my folks and eat some good food." I drag in a deep inhale, savoring the robust, smoky scent of her famous—in our house—chicken and andouille sausage gumbo simmering on the stovetop.

Her lips purse, tellingly. "*Mm-hmm*. Dare I ask who *she* is?"

"She?" I scrunch up my face, cutting off the faucet and drying my hands on the dishtowel draped over the cabinet door. I'm borderline offended she can read me so easily. "Oh, you must be referring to Carlotta Ellswood Bridges, mother of the century and my own personal hero. I don't have the faintest idea who else you could be talking about, ma'am."

"Oh, hush." Mom waves me off, but a glimmer of determination swirls in her steely, dark eyes.

Before she can dig any deeper, with my fresh hands, I finally sweep her up into that bear hug, spinning her around.

She fusses, but the smile on her face is a mile wide when I set her back down. "You and Daddy come now and make your bowls so I can have a good sit-down and hear what's been going on with my handsome son."

I let out a sharp laugh. "You mean pry."

Dad, who's been "taste-testing" straight from the pot, barely manages to hand me a bowl with his broad shoulders shaking with laughter.

"Yeah, laugh it up, old man." I grab the wooden spoon, stirring the rich, flavorful roux loaded with big chunks of meat, okra, bright green bell peppers, onions, and celery. "We both know she'll turn on you in a second."

"And *you're* well aware your mother has a sixth sense about these things." He grins, plucking a sizzling piece of chicken straight from the pot, blowing on it, then popping it into his mouth. "Resistance is futile."

I nudge his shoulder with mine, chuckling as I scoop rice into my bowl. He's not wrong.

Looking at my mother, most people would see an elegant, beautiful, eloquent Black woman with neatly coiffed curls. They'd see the light makeup, deep dimples, and approachable smile, and easily match her elementary school teacher job with the quiet simplicity of a doting wife—Theodore "Teddy" Bridges's high school sweetheart. Nowhere in that soft smile would you see glimpses of the Bridges household disciplinarian. Yes, she's modest and classy in every respect. But if there's one thing about Carlotta Ellswood Bridges, it's that she's not to be tested.

Period.

So when she tells Dad and I to settle down or she'll make us, we quickly hurry to take our seats at the dining table.

"Got you drinks, silverware, napkins…" Mom scans the kitchen, mentally crossing her Ts and dotting her Is before she plops down on her chair at Dad's right, facing me.

The three of us link hands, and Dad leads us in grace. "God is good. God is great. Let us thank him for our food, and everything—"

Mom swats him playfully, cackling. "Now, Teddy, there won't be no playing with the Lord's blessings." She's still chuckling as she forces us to bow our heads again while she properly shows her respect and appreciation for this meal.

Then we dig in.

Five minutes pass with us shoveling gumbo-drizzled rice into our mouths before Mom, over a mouthful, points her fork at me. "Now, this good mood you're in," she starts, unable to leave well enough alone. "It wouldn't have anything to do with your working at Madison Manor with Ebony King—"

"Livingston, you mean," I correct her. "Her name is still Ebony Livingston. And no." I laugh, completely telling on myself. "It doesn't have anything to do with her."

"*Ahh*, so you're lying to your mother now."

Here we go.

"Thank you *so much*, really, for noticing my good mood. But can't I just generally be happy? Does it have to be about a woman?"

The look she gives me—a *please, I wasn't born yesterday* look—has the three of us bursting into laughter. We all know I'm lying and deflecting. I've always kept my feelings for Ebony under wraps. And yet, somehow, Mom has always been able to suss them out anyway.

After a minute, when Dad is still breathless and gasping for air, we just stare at him.

"*Ooh*, Lottie…" He slaps the table, leaning his large frame over to lay a quick kiss on Mom's lips. "Lord, the kid has no idea. I was just like him."

Okaaay…was it that *funny?*

"Uh, you want to let me in on whatever's got you so tickled?" I shake his forearm, teetering on that fine line of smiling at and cringing over seeing my parents still so affectionate after all these years.

I'm always amazed by the attentiveness that they show each other. It takes effort, care. And day after day, they choose each other.

It's aspirational, for sure. I can only hope that one day I'll be so in love, so blessed to share my life with someone who loves me so deeply.

My thoughts drift back to that afternoon in the billiard room with Ebony, her embarrassed and tongue-tied, trying to form coherent sentences. Then tonight, a complete three-sixty, calling me a snack and telling me she fantasizes about me—that she doesn't "give a good goddamn who sees us."

Damn.

A small laugh escapes me.

"Uh-huh. Not about a woman, my tail," Mom says, reading between the lines to the blaring subtext. But then her expression smooths, hardens. "Now, don't you go getting your heart involved again, you hear?"

Her warning is loud, but half of me is still focused on Dad. Where Mom can be an eagle heart and stone-faced—nothing's getting by her—he's an open book. Whether he's happy, excited, upset, or hiding, his emotions tell on him. It's a gift and a curse. It keeps him honest. Sometimes, too much so.

"What did you mean when you said I have no idea? That I'm just like you?" I ask.

Again, Mom purses her lips, and it's a telltale sign I'm barking up the right tree.

"Come on, Dad. What aren't you saying?"

"Teddy…" Mom warns, and it feels sort of hypocritical. She can read our every emotion, body language, dissect my good mood, and I can't ask Dad for clarification when he's the one who had a slip of the tongue?

"Seriously, Mom? Let the man talk."

She sucks her teeth, incensed, shooting daggers at poor Dad.

"He's working with the woman, Teddy." Her eyes darken, and I swear there are red flames in their depths. "Don't."

As soon as she says the word, though, Mom knows she's made a mistake. The man respects his wife, but they never tell each other what they "can't" do.

Dad exhales a deep sigh. "It's not as dramatic as your mother's making it seem," he says, but everything about his stiff posture says otherwise. Whatever he's about to say, Theodore Bridges is actively downplaying it.

"Oh, hell, Teddy. You really burn me up." Mom turns her back to him and folds her arms across her chest, fuming.

"What your mother and I share—it's not a love you let go of easily, son. You fight for it," he starts, then proceeds to tell me that not only was he the escort for Cornelia Livingston—formerly Sterling, and yes, of *that* Sterling real estate conglomerate—but their cotillion arrangement left their parents wanting more for such a perfect pair. The wealthy debutante princess and the straitlaced but strong-willed football phenom. They got to the point where their parents were discussing marriage. There was just one minor hiccup: he was already in love with the Ellswood girl.

"Wait, wait, wait, wait, *wait!*" My heart is beating a million miles a minute, and I'm still grasping for straws because… "Are you telling me Mom stole her man?"

Mom jolts, indignation billowing off her. "First off, we were spending time together *before* Cornelia beat me to the chase and asked him to be her escort. So, *no!* I absolutely did not *steal* your father!"

I rest my elbows on the table and drop my head into my hands, still wrapping my mind around this bomb they just dropped.

"You knew y'all's parents were talking about freaking *marriage*, and you did what? Go behind her back with Mom? Help me understand, because none of this is making sense."

They share a loaded glance, Mom's expression screaming a *you did this* accusation, and I'm guessing she's hanging him out to dry, because she goes tight-lipped.

"Listen," Dad says, "this was a long time ago. Back then, parents were always making plans and arrangements for us while leaving us in the dark." The crease between his thick eyebrows deepens. "I wanted to be your mother's escort, but all the women in the family said it was too late because Cornelia had already asked, and I said yes. So I was going to take her—*as a friend*. When it was over, I was always going to choose my Lottie."

I nod, still processing. "And you didn't know about the marriage?"

"No." He shakes his head, but his gaze is faraway in time.

Suddenly, I am too, shifting so many missing pieces from my past into place. I know why Cornelia hates my family. Why she rejected me from Zion & Zara. Why she went out of her way to ensure I never felt remotely good enough. Why, now, Ebony's theory about sabotaging her business may *not* be just about her.

Everything makes so much more sense.

The same way Cornelia claims Ebony's business should rightfully belong to a true Livingston, she believes the Bridges stole the life that was meant for her.

I'm the collateral damage of a betrayal that happened long before I was even born. And now, I've got to consider that her revenge plan is either two-fold, or may not even be about Ebony at all.

Slipping my phone from my pocket, I tap out a quick message to Ebony.

Lincoln

> Hey, can't stop thinking about you. I know you told Vincent you'd think it over, but are you actually considering coming with me to Dawsonville this weekend? I'd love to spend some real time with you. Also, got some new stuff to share about your Cornelia theory. Let me know. Talk soon.

You're invited
to our
Wedding Day

Chapter Seventeen

The L Word

Ebony

I GLANCE AT MY PHONE, where the divatantes—minus Hillary, of course—are still double-checking their calendars for Hailey's bridal show next weekend. Relief floods through me at the thought that we'll finally be in the same space and able to get to the bottom of whatever's going on with her. *Temporary* relief. Because then, on the screen, Tatiana pulls her hair into a giant, messy bun atop her head and asks, "Can we please get back to Lincoln Bridges saying he'd love to spend time with you?"

And just like that, I start freaking out again.

The texts.

I let out a full-chested sigh. "Yeah, so, then he says, *Let's make a day of it...*" I shrug, fresh panic surging through my veins. "We're supposed to be sourcing replacement crystals for the grand ballroom chandelier. Like, sir, why do I need hiking boots and a swimsuit? I'm just along for the ride, not to scale a mountain or dive into the deep end."

That's what I say out loud.

Inwardly, though, I'm still thinking about how close I came to my first post-divorce sexual encounter—right in an alley. Now, hours alone with Linc? It feels almost guaranteed that the sex is going to happen, which… *Yes, please!* But also, what if I don't live up to the hype Linc's built in his head over the years? Or worse, what if I *do?* What if it makes me want more?

Shit.

"Shoot, you could scale him and let him dive into your deep end…" Whit sucks her teeth, clearly still teasing me about the hiking boots and swimsuit.

Exactly.

I roll my eyes, but Priscilla, Tatiana, and Chanel are outright cackling, as if a two-hour road-trip with a man who freely gifts waterfall orgasms on a whim and sexts with those magic fingers isn't cause to panic.

Lord, that man's definitely got magic fingers—

PING!

I nearly drop the phone when a text notification drops from the top of my screen because, *of course*, Linc's already asking for my coffee order. *Perfect. Just perfect.* Meanwhile, half my makeup is laid out on the counter and my tote looks like it was packed by an angry two-year-old with a vendetta.

With any luck, the coffee shop will be busy and give me an extra few minutes. There's always a line on Saturdays, right?

Ugh, why am I so nervous? I'm a grown-ass woman. If I choose to partake in consensual, mind-blowing sex with a gorgeous, giving man, then that's what I'm damn well going to do, because I deserve good things.

Pause. Peace. Power.

Our plan is simple: drop off the chandelier and crystals for repair, take a quick hike on the Lake Lanier Trail, maybe, *finally*, let him lay me down in a sunny field of flowers, then swim at Veterans Memorial Park pool (no way I'm touching that haunted lake). Afterward, we pick up the chandelier, have a quickie in the backseat, and head home. Done.

Shouldn't be a big deal.

Shouldn't…

Again, I look at my half-empty tote, frazzled.

Snapping my fingers in front of the camera to focus their attention, I blurt out, "Linc just texted, and he's on his way. Quick, what else do I need?" But as the words leave my mouth, an intrusive thought nags at me—what if we're rushing this and I'm playing into Cornelia's hands? What if this road trip is me handing over the strings, just like the puppet she thinks I am?

"Snacks!" Chanel and Tatiana say at the same time, cutting into my downward spiral, then they start cracking up.

Focus.

"Got you!" I say, pushing all thoughts of Cornelia to the back of my mind and trying to perk up. "Watermelon Sour Patch Kids and Boom Chicka Pop. Check and check!"

"I've got a short list," Priscilla says, because whose ultimate safety-first girl doesn't? All she thinks about are worst-case scenarios, so naturally, her suggestions include a printed map (in case the GPS goes out), an upbeat playlist full of songs we *both* love (music is universal), sharing my locations with them (you never know), SPF 50+ sunscreen (the Veterans Memorial Park pool is outdoors), and, finally, condoms. Because, apparently, now we're all fixated on what happened with Linc in that alley after the mixer.

"You know, just in case," she adds, a giddy smile stretched across her face.

The divatantes are living for my hot-girl summer day trip.

All of us.

I glance at the industrial-sized box of condoms on my bed, the one I bought the day before my first meeting with Leslie, wondering how last night might've gone if I'd had one with me. If he said he didn't care either.

My entire body shivers at the memory of Linc on his knees, his tight grip on my hips, his slick tongue sucking and stroking—

"Ebs?" Whit snaps her fingers, jolting me out of the highlights reel.

"Yup, check!" I'm alert.

But leave it to Whitney to cut straight to the chase. "Yes, all of that, but also, what y'all did on the side of that building…*chiiiile*, that tells me you need to pack the essentials."

"Aside from condoms?" I ask.

She flashes me a *be serious* look through the screen before she vaguely says, "The Four Ls," like somehow that's clearer. Like this is child's play, and I *should* know these things. Then she huffs out a sigh—you know, humoring me because we're friends. *Noblesse oblige.*

"Lipstick," she starts, lifting a finger, like she's about to tick them off, but she's generously leaving room for the class to chime in.

"Red Dahlia locked and loaded. Check!"

Immediately catching on, Chanel adds, "An LBD?"

"Yes!" Whit blusters with pride, lifting another triumphant finger. Then she pauses, her long fringe of eyelashes fluttering as she deepens her stare, subliminally willing us to say the last two Ls.

Tatiana, only half listening, doesn't even bother looking up from her romance book while Chanel looks at Priscilla and me, seemingly content with her contribution.

"Louboutins?" Priscilla's expression twists hopefully.

The disappointment on Whit's face is palpable.

"While a great addition, they're not essential…" She sighs and glares at us. "However, please tell me, what is a 'road trip rendezvous' without *lingerie* and *lube*?"

A collective groan falls over the four of us—mine, disrespectfully, louder than the rest.

"*Ugh*, come on, Whit. I'm being serious."

"So am I." Her perfectly micro-bladed and arched eyebrows scale her forehead. "Diva, you are a Southern debutante reinventing yourself post-divorce, daring to find love again—"

Love?

"Uh, okay, relax," I interrupt, since clearly there's been some confusion about what's happening here. "No one said anything about love. Strong…like? Yes. Lust, absolutely." *There are some L-words for you.*

Even though it feels completely wrong—crystal hunting and condoms don't really pass the vibe check—I make a dramatic display of grabbing the bulk box and eyeing my divas as I shove it into my bag.

They're hemming and hawing about love and "that's how you prepare for a day trip, diva," but I need them to focus.

"Lust," I repeat, my voice booming with indignation.

The gesture lands about as hard as a feather. My divas don't even hesitate to put me into my place.

"*Baybee*…" Chanel laughs, leaning into the camera. "I'm pretty sure *lusting* over the same man since you were sixteen, decade detour or not—and spare us the denial—qualifies as something much deeper."

"Again, strong *like*. I just enjoy being with him." *And kissing him, and his magic fingers and tongue…*

Jesus, help me.

They all hum their agreement, cosigning this damn ambush before Whit primps and postures, clearly preparing to deliver today's sermon.

"And if what y'all share isn't love…honey, I don't want to know what is. So, to finish my *sentence*…" She pauses, reloading her rant. "I was going to say that you're *daring* to find love again."

Again, that woman and her puppet strings veer into the forefront of my mind, taunting me. *Walk into my trap…*

My heart kicks into overdrive.

But also, would we say I'm finding love? Is *this* love? How could it be?

I'm barely dipping my toes back in the dating waters. Trying to reclaim my identity, bringing the old me back to the forefront, rediscovering the person I want to be—yes. And Cornelia *is* as diabolical as an antagonist gets. So are the Ellswood elite, the blogs, and all the bougie people who want a say in my life, though. Why does a road trip have to *mean* something so significant? Can't Linc and I just enjoy each other's company? And maybe take advantage of my condom surplus *without* it turning into a quest for true love?

Ugh. Enough with the L-words.

"Um, okay." I meet their stares, going for clearheaded and sound of mind, even though, right now, I feel anything but. "So, first off, *Whit*, how do you go from hiking boots to happily ever after? I'm just curious…"

She glares at me through the screen.

"No, thanks. You, diva, can keep your two cents to yourself, because I'm not collecting change at the moment," I snap, then smile. "And second, this goes for the rest of you—this is a *road trip*, okay? If all goes well, there'll be amazing, *pull over now because I can't drive another mile* backseat sex. I'm not about to make it out to be more than it is."

They go quiet, but make no mistake, their silence isn't agreement.

Of course, with all the judgment they're not saying aloud, we end the call a moment later, and lipstick is the only thing I'm sure about packing.

I manage to finish my makeup and throw on a cute lavender sundress and espadrilles. Along with my hiking boots and swimsuit, I add a change of clothes and a blow-dryer to my tote bag. But when Linc's horn beeps outside, I panic. At the last moment, I yank a cute black minidress off the hanger, then toss in lube and a sexy little black lace negligée.

You know, *just in case.*

Ten minutes after, Linc casually kisses me hello and takes my bags. It should be no big deal. He's a gentleman who hasn't lost the ideals of chivalry. To him, it's old hat. Easy. Comfortable. But as he stows our stuff on the backseat and pulls away from the curb, I get the same déjà vu, as if we've done this a million times over a million lifetimes. We're just being together like there's *always* been an us.

I guess the best way to explain this feeling is like it's a favorite movie. Except our story's been paused for ten years, and now we've pressed play again.

He's got nineties hip-hop bumping, our coffees nestled in the cupholders like adorable his-and-hers caffeine receptacles, cool air blowing through the vents, his clean, warm scent whirring through the car, and we've not exchanged a single word.

It's off-putting. Everything with Linc just feels so normal. Easy. It's the most I've felt myself since the divorce. In maybe a decade.

Naturally, I freeze up, eager to get back to the flirty, sexy version of us that doesn't involve my heart scratching a broken record.

Daring to find love again…

I glance over my shoulder at the backseat where our bags are, since the chandelier's in the trunk.

"So, what'd you pack?" I put a little extra cheer in my voice although, mentally, I'm kicking myself for carelessly opening myself up to a conversation that could easily, prematurely slide into condoms and the godforsaken four Ls.

Thankfully, the man is a saint.

"Let's see, the crystals and chandelier, of course. My laptop, boots, trunks, towels, blankets." He glances down at the center console, where his phone and keys are tucked under a thin paper packet. "A printed map—"

A laugh spills out of me. "Oh my goodness. You and Priscilla. She's all about safety first. *What if there's a dead spot?*" I fake a look of fear.

"Exactly." He grins, eyes softening as he reaches over and intertwines our fingers, then brings our joined hands to his lips in a gentle kiss. "Can't be too careful. I've got precious cargo to protect."

See?

The divas would quickly twist his words into some sappy romantic breadcrumb. Not me. My heart holds up a tiny APPLAUSE NOW cue card. Instantly, I feel vindicated. Who wouldn't want to unleash all kinds of lust on a man who calls you *precious cargo?* That's basically code for, *Let's pull over now and rip open that box in your tote.*

I reach for my coffee and take a long, satisfying sip. "Anything else?"

He twists his lips to the side, his eyes trained on the highway. "Oh, yeah, I brought some cards, too." Casually, he reaches forward, tapping around his dashboard to change the music to a Smooth Grooves playlist, and suddenly, Maxwell's "Ascension" is seducing me as Linc adds, "Figured while we wait for the glazier to work on the crystals we go on a short hike, maybe rest for lunch, and work in a few hands of Spades. *If* you're up for it."

If I'm up *to it?*

I swallow, squeezing my thighs together.

Now, roadside quickie, sexy waterfall fellatio, that's lust. But casually turning on classic foreplay jams and adding in Spades… You don't just play Spades with any old body. That's strategic teamwork, whether four players or two. It requires trust and reading each other's rhythm and intentions. It's flirty foreplay with repetitious mini battles and outsmarting each other with a smile. Hell, I might as well give him the key to my heart now. What's the use? *Shit, apparently, he knows where I hide the spare anyway.*

Oh, I'm onto you, Lincoln Bridges.

He shoots me a hungry stare, easing off the gas like he wants to milk every minute we're together, simultaneously tugging at my heartstrings and libido, and it's way, *way* too much to handle.

"*Pfft…*" I nod, poking my tongue in my cheek, taking a deep breath. "Mm-hmm. Should be fun." Inside, though, I'm scrambling for a way to change the subject. With a snap, I untangle my hand from his, whip out my iPad from my purse, and say, "Since we've got the time, I brought my checklist for Madison Manor."

And that's how we spend the first hour of the drive—caffeine-fueled, with the suburban Ellswood skyline fading as we head north on through stop-and-go traffic, all while going over restoration progress updates to mask how utterly turned on I am. Once the chandelier repairs are done, the grand ballroom will only need a few final touches. The reception hall and alcoves are finished with stunning white marble. All six suites? Pretty much done—duh, because Vincent, while theatrical, is efficient as hell with his design process. The terrace lawn, courtyard, and hearth room have been finished for weeks. In fact, ever since Manny and the crew kicked me out of the library to start renovations, they're some of my go-to spots for "working." Now that the guys have started the billiard and drawing rooms, and the indoor garden leading into the conservatory, Linc and I have been "running into each other" a lot.

Soon, the tree-lined roads weave into a blur of the densely forested landscape as we approach the foothills.

"Do you think the conservatory is missing something?" I twist in my seat to face Linc, studying the shadows and lines of his beautifully familiar face, his long eyelashes and the fullness of his mouth. The striking gray eyes against rich bronze skin. The light dusting of silver sparkling over his jaw, catching the sunlight.

Ugh, I've got it bad.

He tosses me a warm smile as he lowers the music and sips from his travel mug. "Like what?"

"I don't know, but it feels like there's too much empty space. No texture." I shrug. "Not enough sensory cues, I guess."

Linc nods thoughtfully, as if he's considering what I've said. "Let me think on it. I'll talk with Manny and Vincent and see what options they present."

The conversation lulls, and I scramble for something else to say, but soon we fall into that easy rhythm, snacking on popcorn and Sour Patch Kids. We talk about sports, books, documentaries, eighties Black sitcoms, swimming, beaches and waterfalls—you name it. But we carefully steer clear of anything wedding or Ellswood related.

It's just the two of us, comfortably lost in each other's company, the road stretching out before us, my house of cards quietly restacking.

And then a sea of red taillights flares in front of us.

"Accident reported ahead," the GPS chimes, piercing through the calm. *"Rerouting due to traffic. Follow the new path—"*

"Nope." I jolt upright, eyes wide, as Linc slows to a stop. I glance out the window at the thick, dark woods around us. "Absolutely not. This is how it happens."

Linc drops his head back against the seat with a heavy sigh. The car goes still for a beat, the only sound the hum of the engine.

Then he bursts out laughing—genuinely, uncontrollably loud and hysterical. Most likely, because he's been tossing back Sour Patch Kids for the past hour, and now it's like the sugar rush just hit him. "How *what* happens?"

"You seriously don't see this?" My voice wavers slightly, and my heart thuds in my chest. "We're stuck out here, in the middle of nowhere, for who knows how long, with nothing but trees for miles, and now your British GPS is trying to send us down some random dirt road? This is *exactly* how every horror movie starts."

"Oh, God, you're killing me." He laughs even harder, gasping for air. "But I'm *definitely* not driving down some random road."

I narrow my eyes at him. "You think I'm overreacting, but I'm telling you, this is *exactly* how it goes." I throw my hands up. "A fun little road trip gets detoured, then we're hacked to pieces by some creepy guy with a chainsaw."

Linc's laugh reaches a whole new decibel level. "But you're the final girl, the scream queen! You make it out alive."

I turn away, folding my arms, adrenaline pumping through me. My eyes are on the trees, though. Just in case.

Linc leans closer, his voice softening as he pries my hand free, intertwining our fingers, gently lifting them to his lips. "Ebony," he murmurs, his lips brushing my skin, "you really think I've waited this long to be with you, and I'm going to let some creepy woods or a serial killer stop me from…this?"

I glance at him, my lips twitching despite myself. The absurdity of the moment—the sincerity in his eyes and the vulnerability in his voice—hits me all at once, and my heart aches. The world outside the car disappears for a second, and it's just us.

The air between us crackles.

"All jokes aside—and hopefully, whatever's going on up ahead, everyone's okay—I'm glad that we're stuck here," he says softly, almost too quiet. "That I get more time with you. It feels like…"

"Like what?" I ask, suddenly desperate to know this rush of longing isn't one-sided.

My heart thunders in my chest. No detail is too small or insignificant.

I need this to be real.

He takes a breath, tightening his fingers around mine, and presses our clasped hands to his chest like he's grounding himself in the moment. "Okay, I think it's safe to assume we both love movies, right? But what if this isn't one of those final-girl stories? What if this is the other version of us, the one where we made different choices, and now we're seeing what might happen if we choose each other?"

I stare at him, heart in my throat, trying to wrap my mind around dual timelines and parallel universes. Two divergent paths but one moment—one choice—changes everything.

What if we were supposed to be here all along? What if this is the version of our lives that was meant to be?

"You're saying…we're like the alternate timeline of our lives?" I ask.

He exhales deeply, like the weight of everything he's been holding in is finally released. "Exactly. I know what my life was like without you in it. And now I'm excited to find out what it's like with you in it."

For a moment, everything else fades. The trees, the detour, even the absurdity of our being stuck in the middle of nowhere— it all slips away. All I can feel is the truth in his words, the quiet intensity behind them.

"Okay," I whisper, my voice barely above a breath, "let's see what happens."

Before long, the traffic ahead starts to move, and Linc eases off the gas, proceeding to the route. But as the forest clears, the rolling hills sweep across the horizon, and our easy silence returns, Linc's GPS isn't done with us yet.

"Incoming text message from Dominic Owens. 'So, this is what it is, huh? I say take a short flight or road trip with your guys, you say you'll think about it, and now you're out there slipping and falling in love—'"

Linc jabs a finger at the screen, switching to music. *Loud* music.

He glances at me, blushing cutely. "Sorry about that."

I bite back a laugh, loving every second of embarrassed Lincoln Bridges crushing on me. And there's that word again. *Love.*

It feels like the elephant in the car, squished between us, and weirdly, I don't mind the idea of us in love, seeing where this could go.

"It's fine. My divas are calling me out, too." I smile nervously. "So, I'm guessing right about now you'd love to change the subject to anything else."

"Great guess."

"Should we maybe talk about that theory you wanted to tell me about?" I trace the edge of my fingernail between my teeth, still studying him.

Linc glances at me, self-conscious and clearly uneasy under the weight of my stare.

I see the way you look at me.

Damn right.

"Yeah, about that…" He swallows. "Are you ready to have your mind blown?"

Among other things.

He pauses, then dives in, telling me about family dinner night, and I learn that his mom swooped in and took his dad from Cornelia. I'm already speechless. But the kicker? Not only has Linc bought into my theory about Cornelia setting me up for a downfall, but he also believes *he* might be her second target.

My mind is officially boggled.

"It's crazy, right?" he says.

The silence lingers, though, because how do I respond to that? She's made us both her enemies. She wants to take us both down. So, what's she waiting for?

I'm still considering what this means when we reach the glazier's small shop in Dawsonville. I haven't said so much as two words to Linc as the guy sorts and examines the broken crystals, carefully determining the extent of the damage. But I feel Linc's eyes on me, stealing glances, as if he's guessing whether he should've told me.

I'm too in my head to comfort him, though. I can't. Not when I'm still mentally reorganizing a puzzle where the pieces were closely shaped but shoved into the wrong places. So as the glazier separates a half-dozen salvageable crystals and begins discussing the replacements needed with Linc, I step outside to catch my bearings.

A few minutes later, he joins me.

"Okay, so he said there's about seven crystals he's got to precision cut and shape to fit the exact specifications of the original design, *but*…he won't have them finished until the morning." Linc winces. "This was supposed to be a day trip, but what do you think about booking a hotel room for the night? We can leave first thing tomorrow," he rushes to add.

"Sure, okay. I don't mind."

Linc takes my hands, his eyes searching mine. "Are you still thinking about what I said about Cornelia and my parents?"

Reluctantly, I nod. "I knew she was holding a grudge, but…"

"Listen, I honestly don't care about that woman or what vendettas she's harboring. My mom used to say, if you're doing anything meaningful, people are going to come for you," he says, inching closer. "It's just what happens when you threaten the way things are."

And I don't know if it's the somber tone of his voice or the fresh air after inhaling his pheromones for the last couple hours, or even all the alternate-timeline talk. But in this moment, everything starts to click.

All this time, I thought that I was the target, that I didn't need anyone distracting me. But no. It's so much worse than that. This is about her—restoring the Livingston name, yes, but also wiping out anyone who stands in her, or Julian's, way. Me, the woman who dared to divorce her son. And Linc, the son of the woman who took everything she wanted.

We're not just obstacles. We're her whole damn plan.

No.

A dogged determination creeps up my spine, hot and urgent. Because screw Cornelia and her manipulation.

My heart swells as I press a soft kiss to Linc's lips because I damn well want to. "I don't want to hold back out of fear anymore." I tip up his chin to meet his devastating gray eyes. "She can smear my name, destroy my business, try to blame the divorce on me—I don't give a damn. We can't let her win. We get to choose this version of us. So, if you really want to try this—"

"Ebony, I'm yours if you want me." He punctuates his beautiful words with a kiss, so slow, so intoxicating, that the world around us fades away. It's urgent, hungry, every brush of his tongue sparking against mine and tracing the outline of a story that's been brewing for ten years in the back of my mind. In the ache of my fingers. Nestled in that hollow whisper just behind my ribs.

I don't know if this is love.

For damn sure it's more than lust, though.

My whole body is a heartbeat, throbbing, pulsing at the feel of his hands cradling my face like he's afraid to let go.

And I feel it, too. It's like something powerful is drawing us closer, something beyond our control. A gravitational pull, every second pulling us farther from everyone, everything we know.

I'm weightless, suspended in air.

Every inch of my skin tingles with the heat rising between us. The warmth of our breaths mingling. Our lips brushing like tinder, setting me aflame.

"You're my choice, Lincoln Bridges. I only want you," I say into the kiss, my heart, mind, and every inch of my body bypassing the hike and swim and going straight for the unwritten quickie stop on the agenda. "I need to feel you right now."

Apparently, that makes two of us.

Linc stalls for a moment before he tears away from me, leaving nothing but the lingering ache for him—an echo of a force I can't ignore. He doesn't hesitate another second, roughly grabbing my hand, moving with urgency toward the car parked along the curb.

We drive for five excruciating, high-speed minutes. Then Linc skids to a stop in front of the first chain hotel he sees. He exits the driver's side and opens my door to help me out, then snatches up our bags from the backseat, tanking my delusion of us old-school pretzeling our bodies in the backseat, just wildly going at it and fogging up the windows.

But not Lincoln Bridges.

Not my man.

"One sec," he says, his voice as tormented as I feel. He dashes inside to the registration desk and returns a moment later with a key, breathing hard, and I can tell he's barely holding it together, which only turns me on more.

We barely make it into the simple, no-frills room before he drops our bags and starts kissing me again, hard and messy. We're a jumble of hands in hair and on skin, our breaths ragged as we tug at each other's clothes until I'm in my underwear—an obstacle he doesn't seem to appreciate as much today as he did last night.

Then he's standing in front of me bare-chested, tattooed, and chiseled from the gods' personal Pinterest board. Half naked. Hard. Beautiful.

Good Lord.

"Well…" I toss up my hands, surrendering, needing more than a minute. "That's a funny way to propose, but sure, I guess I'll marry you." I giggle.

Linc snorts, barely containing his laughter. "Yeah?"

"I'll just be over here, casually drooling." I take a deep breath in, then release it slowly through my nose.

"Hey, you should see *my* view."

"No, seriously," I say, because he's not understanding that it's been over a year—closer to two, not counting Missionary Mondays—since I had sex, and I'm starving. "I guess I assumed, you know, with the job, you'd sort of need be fit. But my *God…*"

Linc licks his lips, slowly, torturously, unzipping his jeans. He strokes his tremendous dick through his black boxer briefs. If he wasn't before, I'm sure he's well aware now, and absolutely enjoying what he's doing to me.

"I'm glad you like what you see," he rasps, his voice gruff, gravelly in my ears, watching me as he works himself to the shaft, hardening in his hand, and all I have to say is… *Baybee…Julian Livingston III could never. AI Linc 2.0 and casting director Zeek could absolutely N-E-V-E-R.*

I shake my head, correcting him. "*Love* what I see."

When I think he couldn't possibly get better, with his free hand, Linc slips his hand in his back pocket, fishing out a condom, and I burst out laughing.

One *condom?*

"Baby, I can do you one better." I hold up a finger, then rummage around my tote, a second later revealing "the box" in all its supersized glory. "Plus…" I grab the lube, lingerie, and LBD for good measure, like, *Tell me what you need.*

Linc snorts a laugh. "Oh, *wow.* All the above, please. Woman, you came prepared, huh?"

"Hey, safety first."

Like a savage, I rip open the box, then tear the foil wrapper with my teeth. I lean in again, skating my fingers over his tapestry of tattoos, down the smooth ridges of his abdomen, gliding my hand lower to wrap my hand around his enormous dick and circling the head with my thumb.

A soft gasp escapes his lips when I roll it down his shaft.

And that's it.

Linc lowers me onto the bed.

"Spread your legs for me." He puts lube in his hands, rubbing them together before he drags his hand over my pussy, massaging and slipping his fingers inside until I'm aching for more. Then, when I can't take it a second longer, he hovers deliciously above me, centering himself between my trembling thighs, his mouth inches from mine. We breathe into each other's mouths as he stretches, fitting himself inside me, and I feel like if I died right now, it would be with a permanent smile.

Then he pumps.

Slow and steady at first, until I take every inch of him. He groans, quickening the pace, deep and hard, hands gripping my hips, in a dizzying frenzy until the sensation is so slippery, so heady, there's only a symphony of shallow breaths and skin kissing skin.

I throw my head back, arching into his strokes, feeling all his roughness, seeing an entire constellation of stars just for us. I lose sense of time and space because there's only us, like this, climbing together.

"Baby, I can barely breathe. Come for me." He grunts, desperate and needy, opening his mouth and torching the skin of my neck and collarbone, then licking my breasts and dragging his fingers between my thighs as he continues driving inside me. "Hurry, I want you to come first."

Every nerve ending in my body ignites, a slow burn that builds until the fuse finally snaps, and the aftershocks linger, pulsing through me. The delicious tightening in my belly, the electric shiver crawling over my skin, the blissful, toe-curling current that radiates from deep—they all combine, leaving me heady with bliss, and my heartbeat syncs with Linc's.

It's overwhelming, all-consuming.

Then Linc lets go too, abs flexed and shaking in a series of spasms. He collapses at my side with a rough groan, tugging me into him.

He's still struggling to breathe, eyes hazy, voice hoarse. "Ebony Grace…"

"Hmm?" I moan, molding my body to his as he buries his face in my neck, his warm breaths evening out as if he's drifting to the edge of sleep. I'm euphoric in a way that leaves me breathless, suspended in warmth, my heart still playing the broken record.

Daring to find—

"I've never stopped loving you," Linc says, and it scares the hell out of me.

I know I feel the same, and that makes me…vulnerable. I'm just starting to rediscover who I am, and already, I'm losing myself in him. And while once upon a time I loved my ex-husband, walking into a trap or not, in my heart I think I've *always* been in love with Lincoln Bridges.

So I remind myself that I deserve good things, even if they terrify me, then push the fear aside and say it anyway.

"I love you too."

Saying it feels huge, like everything's shifted, because loving this man? Nothing about this choice feels small or insignificant.

It's going to change everything.

(470) 555-3269

Chapter Eighteen

Breaking Spades

Lincoln

I WAKE TO EBONY TWISTING in my arms, her fingers gently tracing patterns on my chest like she's trying to map out the world's worst hidden treasure, and I can't stop smiling.

I groan, thrusting my hard-on against her stomach. "A little lower, please."

She laughs softly, but it's the kind of laugh that doesn't pass her lips. Her heartbeat pulses against my skin, steady, but somehow…off.

Worry jolts through me, and I scoot down to search her eyes, my chest tightening with all the familiar insecurities. Did I misjudge the situation, move too fast? Did she wake up and realize I'm not worth the hassle, not good enough?

"Hey, what's going on? Talk to me."

A small smile curves her lips, but again, it doesn't reach the rest of her face. She stays silent, her attention flickering somewhere just beyond my shoulder.

All at once, my ribcage feels like it's been wrapped in a vise, squeezing tighter with every breath. I shift, turning onto my side so

I can really see her—scrutinizing the soft curve of her cheek, the tiny furrow of her brow. "Is it the, um…love stuff? Because I meant every word. But we can go as fast or slow as you want."

Ebony closes her eyes, and it's like the air thickens, making it harder to breathe. I'm waiting for something. Anything.

Please don't take it back.

"Do you regret it? This? Us?" *Say I'm enough.*

"I'm just happy," she whispers, and suddenly, the grip on my chest loosens just enough for me to take a real breath. "Being here with you… For the first time in a long time, I slept so comfortably."

I tug her on top of me, needing the closeness as much as I need her to understand. "Look at me for a second, baby," I say, my voice still a little raw. "That's because we *belong* together, you know that? It was always supposed to be us."

Ebony nods, her bright hazel eyes brimming with tears.

I lift my hand to her cheek, gently brushing them away. Slowly, I lean in, my mouth soft against her lips as her knees spill over my thighs. She rocks over me, her hips rotating and grinding, her body telling me what she needs. That she needs *me*.

"Let me grab a condom," I say, but she halts my hand, keeping me from moving. She can't seem to be apart from me for even a second. So, with her insistence that it's "just this once," I lift her slightly. Raw and aching, I glide inside her. "*Fuck…*"

Dear *Lord*, she takes every inch of me so well, I'm nearly undone before we've even started. I have to take my time. I could be like this with her forever. I've always known I loved Ebony. But to this extent?

I'm wrecked.

I'm utterly spoiled, because we're connected, heart to heart, flesh to flesh, with no barriers between us. We kiss like this, no rush, just the quiet rhythm of our breaths as I move inside her with purpose. My arms are wrapped around her, holding her close so she feels nothing but safe and loved. And still, I feel the urge to ask if she's happy. To squeeze her tighter, because…how can I be going through withdrawals, needing her nearer, when I'm still inside her?

As her orgasm swells, I sink into the warmth of her soft breaths on my neck, her hands on my skin like a balm to my heart. I tell her, "I love you." Then I tell her over and over until we're kissing and trembling together because she's a woman who should be told as much and as often as possible, and by me.

Then we sleep again.

And when we rouse to refuel on order-in pizza, as we fall into an amazing *eat-sex-repeat* cycle for most of the night, I've never been happier. Every few hours, one of us kisses the other awake, starving and desperate for more as we rapidly go through her big box of condoms until the sun is high in the sky again, and we're forced to get up before checkout.

We shower—gloriously, together—then throw on plain clothes and hiking boots, our swimwear tucked underneath. I make a quick call to the shop to check on the ETA of the chandelier crystals. It'll be a few more hours, so I grab some waters and replenish our snacks, then we head out for a hot August morning on the trail.

A mix of nerves and excitement stirs in my stomach, and I hope she loves it.

As we drive up to the trail, Ebony gasps. "Amicalola Falls State Park," she says, her eyes lighting up. "As in *water*falls?"

My heart lurches. I love that my surprise is exactly what she needs. "I know how much you love them."

She still looks at me, a bit puzzled. "Wait, what happened to the Lake Lanier Trail? The pool?"

I shrug, a grin spreading across my face. "It's a little shorter than we planned, but there's still a mile hike to the waterfall. Then we'll drive over to the Amicalola River Trail to swim. *If* you want…"

Without warning, she lunges over the console, squealing and wrapping her arms around me. "This. Is. Why. I. Love. You," she says, punctuating each word with a kiss, and I know this is why I'm whipped.

It's almost embarrassing how in love I am with this woman. There's nothing I wouldn't do to make her smile.

Thirty minutes—spent nearly sprinting—later, we snap cutesy couple pictures together in front of the Amicalola Falls State Park sign, carve our initials into a tree, share a stolen kiss under its branches, and barely dodge a run-in with some curious wildlife. Then, finally, we reach the observation bridge.

For a moment, we stand here, mesmerized by the sight of this magnificent seven-hundred-foot wonder of nature. Glittering water cascades down layered drops, shrouded in trees and wildflowers in full bloom.

"It's beautiful," Ebony whispers.

"It sure is."

She turns to me, catching me watching her with a soft smile, her eyes sparkling with love. She clasps her hands behind my neck, pulling me close. "Thank you for this. For just…being you. I love it. I *love* you."

I lean in, slanting my mouth over hers. The kiss is soft, tender, every brush of our lips a quiet promise that I would do anything for her.

We lazily walk back to the car before we drive to the river trail to swim. For hours we luxuriate in the water, splashing, playing, then wading aimlessly together, every second falling deeper. All I can think about is how I'd wait another ten years if it meant I could feel this way forever.

I watch her until the sunlight starts to wane, at home in the water—with me.

But a knot forms in my stomach.

These two days with Ebony, these perfect, carefree days, feel like a dream I never want to end. But is it all just for the weekend?

When we get back to Ellswood, will we still be like this? Will the distance, the routine, and the real world creep in and pull us apart?

I want to believe it won't. That what we've found again will last beyond these couple days. But part of me is afraid to lose this.

"I'm turning into a prune." She laughs, and I shove my thoughts aside.

The sun's dying down, casting that warm glow over us as we dry off, wrapping ourselves in towels. Since we haven't heard from the shop yet, I find an empty park bench, figuring now is as good a time as any.

I whip out my fresh deck of Bicycle playing cards.

"All right, Miss Ebony Grace…" I scoot back, leaving space between us to play the game. It's not a kitchen table, but it's the best we've got out here in the wilderness. "Let's see who's going first."

I hold out the deck for her to pick a card.

Naturally, she picks an ace of spades like she's come to destroy my entire existence. I raise an eyebrow and pull a two of spades.

"So, am I going first, or how do you want to play this game?" I ask, throwing out the options, hoping we'll quickly knock out the house hierarchy. "Joker, joker, deuce, ace, or joker, joker, ace…"

She sits up straighter, the drama loading. "First off, sir…" She's got that sinister smile, like she's secretly plotting my downfall. "Spades isn't a game. We're not playing that Google trick-taking recreational activity, okay? We're playing Black Spades, which means I'm here to take books and names."

I swallow hard, trying to hide my grin. "Okay, so, ace high, deuce low, or…"

The smirk on her face is comical. "Joker, joker, ace. Obviously."

Obviously.

I nod, trying and failing horribly at tamping down the urge to kiss her. "Cool, cool. So, you're going first, and I'm just going to shuffle." I chuckle, giving the deck a quick mix.

Naturally, she laughs in my face. "Oh, Lincoln Bridges, sir. If you play Spades like you shuffle, you're about to get whipped," she says, coming hot out the gate with the trash talking.

I scrub a hand over my face, already knowing this is about to be a mess.

"Ma'am, just cut the cards, so I can deal." I shake my head, still laughing. "We're playing to five hundred. When the glazier calls, we stop. Highest score wins."

Ebony's still giggling as she cuts the deck. While I'm dealing thirteen cards to us, she's over there, digging in her tote. I'm thinking she must be looking for paper to keep score. Nope, she pulls out a long convenience store receipt, a pen, a half-empty bag of Sour Patch Kids, her phone, and AirPods.

She pops one into my ear for us to listen together, and her Domination playlist starts bumping, setting the tone. According to Ebony's "house" rules, playing Spades requires snacks and music.

"Oh, you broke out the old-school jams," I say as Tupac's "2 of Amerikaz Most Wanted" fills my ears.

"Mm-hmm. You're about to learn what happens when the beat drops and you get played." She grins, innocently. "Now, let's get to business."

We review our cards and start bidding—five for me, two for Ebony.

And somebody's sandbagging books…

For a good forty-five minutes, it's nothing but back-and-forth on sandbagging, weak trash talk, and what constitutes the "big" joker. It's to the point where we're forced to defer to the president of the National Association of Spades Activities (Dad, apparently), before we settle on hand-writing "big" on one Joker.

"Man, I didn't peg you for a cheater." I shake my head, letting her have the book, but I'm still up one-fifty to ninety.

I figure we've got time for one more hand anyway. The chandelier pick-up call should be coming any minute, daylight is waning, and you won't catch me in a forest at night. We won't make it to five hundred, but I'll make this last one count.

On the next hand, we're still playing it semi-civil, just tossing out diamonds, hearts, and clubs. Then I drop a four of hearts, and she stands up like she's about to deliver a sermon, slamming down a three of spades with her whole chest, her voice booming. "This is not the cookout, baby, but you're *cooked*!"

A woman climbs out of the water, ready to towel off, and glances over at us, startled.

I almost choke on my laughter, watching these poor folks around us innocently trying to enjoy nature.

"Oh, you ain't said nothing but a word. You're playing with the right one, today!" I chuckle, tossing a king of clubs and taking the next book. And the one after that with a nine of diamonds. "Talk all you want to, but at the end of the day, you're going to have to play those cards!"

But then the unthinkable happens.

I throw down a jack of hearts, and Ebony has the nerve, the *audacity* with all that trash talking, to slam down a queen of hearts.

"You have nothing!" She laughs like she just knows she's got this game in the bag when I'm already off the bench, running and cackling like a fool, waving my towel like a goddamn checkered flag.

"Tell me you didn't just renege?" I'm breathless and bent over in stitches. "I must be seeing things."

Ebony just stares at me, beautifully waterlogged and utterly wrong, as she swears, "I have *never* reneged a day in my life!"

But as we go through her *six* books, the evidence doesn't lie. My four of hearts that she took with a three of spades—caught in the act.

"Trash." I shake my head, narrowing my eyes playfully at her. "I'm sorry to be the one to tell you, but your Spades *game* is utter garbage, Ebony Grace—"

And just as I'm about to finish this victory…my phone trembles across the bench.

"It's him." I answer the call to confirm the chandelier pickup. "Yup, we'll be there shortly. Thanks."

When I get off the phone, Ebony and I slip into our dry clothes and pack our belongings. And even though she's a sore loser and clearly still salty about the beatdown, we both fall in step, walking back to the car hand in hand.

The chandelier pickup is smooth, and the repairs are flawless— every crystal a perfect match and all affixed to the chandelier. So we're on the road home in no time, the windows cracked just enough to let the warm breeze inside, music playing softly, settling us into the rhythm of the drive.

Not even half an hour in, though, I glance over at Ebony. Her head's resting against the window, and she's blissfully asleep.

But the closer we get to Ellswood, I envy her as that knot in my stomach returns with a vengeance. It grows tighter, feeding my dread that everything we've shared this weekend will change the second we cross the city line.

I nudge her gently, waking her as we near her place. "Hey there, sleepyhead. Almost home."

She blinks, her eyes still heavy with sleep. "I don't want to leave you," she whispers, and without a second thought, I change course, headed for my house, knowing Ebony's not worried at all. She's happy being with me. I'm enough.

At least for now.

You're invited
to our
Wedding Day

(470) 555-3269

Chapter Nineteen

Sucker Punch

Ebony

THE NEXT MORNING, AS MUCH as I'd love to stay in bed with Linc and pretend it's still the weekend, it's Monday, and the cruelty of adulting calls. Plus, there's no way I'm walking into Madison Manor holding hands with him and grinning like I've spent the last two days getting properly laid. Even if it's true, I'm not doing it in hiking boots and a swimsuit, with my hair looking like a bird's nest after a windstorm.

"I can wait," Linc says from the driver's seat. "I don't mind."

I lean across the console, brushing my lips softly over his, lingering. "Thank you. But I'm fine. I won't be long." *I hope.* Lord knows, I need to do more than shower, considering the state of this hair. I spare him the manual-labor details of washing, conditioning, blow-drying, and flat-ironing. "Get that chandelier back and installed before the universe releases the Kraken on us."

After he drives off, I rush to my door and unlock it only to discover my mother has shoved an envelope with my name—

267

embossed, letter-pressed, and practically screaming pre-DC (*Divorcétante Chronicles*) Ebony—underneath.

"Ugh, Mother!" I groan, tossing it on the kitchen island. "How many times do I have to tell you that I'm not going?"

I stand here, tucking my nose under the collar of Linc's T-shirt that I slept in, inhaling his scent. I'm in complete disbelief that this weekend wasn't a dream. *Ah*, love.

And it's not just about the love itself. It's the fact that I'm *in* love with a man with whom I share a deep connection rooted in compassion, values, and ridiculously amazing sex. He's so tender with me. So sweet. So…*fine*.

Plus, it doesn't hurt that we've got a common enemy.

Again, I glance at the cotillion invitation, but this time, adrenaline and annoyance flare in my gut as I think about how long I've let Mom and Cornelia pull those strings.

"Nope. Not anymore." I grab it off the counter and slide my finger underneath the flap to slice it open. And sure enough, inside with the invitation is the RSVP card. Rummaging through my junk drawer, I fish out a pen and practically carve a huge X on the "declines with regret" line. "Unfortunately—*for you*—I'll be unable to attend because I'll be too busy having marathon sex with the man who is cute and can take care of me. Are you happy, *Mother*?" I yell into the open air of my townhouse.

Extremely satisfied with myself, I march off to the bathroom.

Half an hour later, I've showered, my hair is wrapped in a towel, my Calming Water Sounds playlist is humming through my phone, and I've been standing in front of my closet for the last ten minutes. My business mode is loading, my game face on, and I'm really concentrating on what to wear that says, *I'm not the one, Cornelia Eunice Livingston, so keep it pushing.* Or maybe something that says, *Professional on the outside. On the inside, not so much.*

After pulling out my red elbow-sleeve sheath dress, I pair it with my leather red-sole ankle-strap stiletto sandals, which isn't exactly a great choice for an active construction site, but they make my legs look fabulous. And maybe they'll inspire Linc to sneak away into one of the suites with me for a few minutes.

"Oh my Lord!" An exhausted sigh plumes out of me. "Jesus, why am I so horny? Get a hold of yourself!"

I drag in a deep breath, willing my libido to calm its happy little self down so I can get focused.

The thing is, work-wise, I've got a ton to do. All week I've got wedding consultations for new clients. For Hailey and Donovan's, the vendors need to be reconfirmed, RSVPs reviewed, and the ceremony programs inspected before our final planning meeting. There's no time to be ducking and diving around Madison Manor for quickies, no matter how sexy it would be.

After tossing the dress and heels on the bed, I hurry and blow-dry my hair. But as my flat iron heats up, I can't stop my mind from reeling.

It's a bit difficult to think about being productive today when my mind is torn between the joy of being in love with a man who makes me feel…everything, and the anxiety of my ex-mother-in-law—and current employer—actively trying to sabotage us.

Before I can second-guess it, I turn off the calming sounds of water rushing and swipe over to phone.

After two rings, Savannah picks up.

"Hi, it's Ebony. Have you got a few minutes?"

Surprisingly, that's all it takes to bring her up to speed on my Cornelia theory and how things have progressed with Linc despite it. As I flat-iron my hair, bumping the ends into curls, I tell her I'm going to thank Leslie for his services and hold off on dating to give things with Linc a real shot—*and* let the divas say they told me so *later*—but that I need advice on how to proceed with Cornelia.

"What's the worst she could do?" Savannah asks, and I don't really know how to put in words that I don't actually have any proof that sabotage is in fact Cornelia's motive.

Yes, she's responsible for hiring Bridges Heritage Conservation and Ebony Grace Events. And she did cancel my insurance, leaving me to scramble for wedding props. But what else has she really done?

Linc is the best at what he does, and Hailey chose me.

I tilt my head, stretching my neck as I try to stay centered.

"The thing is…I don't know," I say, slightly defeated.

Did I make all of this up? Is it all an elaborate, unfounded theory? Is this all some weird, extreme stress reaction about Julian and Nora? What am I so *paranoid* about?

I set the flat iron down and stare at my reflection—without the makeup, the jewels, expensive clothes, and long hair running down my back.

"I don't know." It comes out barely above a whisper. "And now I'm starting to wonder if I'm overreacting, and what that means?" Am I just afraid of being happy with Linc?

"Okay, you're right." Savannah's tone softens. "We don't know what she's capable of, or that she'd want to hurt you or Lincoln…" Pressure builds in her pause. "But we also don't know that you're wrong. God gave us instincts, gut feelings, for a reason. I'm not going to be the one to tell you not to trust them."

I'll admit that I'm fully vindicated that she doesn't dismiss me completely. No, actually, quite the opposite.

"Let's talk about some tools to keep handy, starting with setting boundaries and prioritizing joy," she starts before outlining ways to protect my peace. I'm to limit all interactions with Cornelia to email, and only when necessary—for professional reasons—hold in-person meetings with others around. "You don't owe her anything and shouldn't give her power to define your worth or impact your happiness."

"With Linc, you mean?"

"*Especially* with him," she says. "Ebony, you're a single woman, and while Cornelia and Julian were once part of your life—and we always wish them the best—they don't get to say when or whom you get to love. If Lincoln Bridges is making you happy"—her smile vibrates in her voice—"and I suspect he is, judging by the fact that you're even considering any of this. I want you to love on him and let him do the same without putting limits on it."

I could cry, I'm so happy.

And suddenly, I'm glad I decided to do my makeup last, because tears singe the corners of my eyes. I smile, blinking them back, eager to wrap up this call and get to him.

"Thank you, Savannah." Emotion thickens my voice as I open my makeup drawer and pull out my primer.

"You're absolutely welcome, honey." She blows out a long breath. "And remember to keep living authentically and truthfully, even if your theory turns out to be right. Don't get caught up in people's toxic stories or let their narratives overshadow yours. Stay tight with your family and your divatantes. Even your *Divorcétante* followers can help protect your reputation, integrity, and professionalism."

"You're right. Ahh, you're so right." I smile, feeling lighter.

The sound of paper rustling in the background grows closer. "And if things go sideways, there's always legal action. But we're not there yet, so enjoy every minute of this man who's helped you believe in love again."

And that's exactly what I plan to do.

After finishing my makeup, I slip into my dress and send Linc a quick text with a picture of our initials carved into our tree. I tell him I love him and will see him soon.

Then I'm out the door.

The drive to Madison Manor is smooth, with the morning rush long gone. The sun seems like it's shining brighter, the sky a perfect, clear blue. And then I find a parking space right away, too. Suddenly, it feels like talking to Savannah was exactly what I needed to slow down and enjoy every minute of loving Lincoln Bridges.

Maybe one day, it'll be us dancing under the grand ballroom's magical crystal chandelier.

When I walk into Madison Manor, though, I don't hear the busy chatter of voices or loud power tools humming. No hammers tapping. Not even the soft whoosh of sweeping and painting. No, it's dead silent.

My heart jackhammers against my ribs.

Slowly, I step inside, standing still, ears straining to hear anything. This scream queen will *definitely* not call out, "Is anyone there?"

"Yeah, well, I don't see how that's any of your business, so you can see yourself out."

Oh, shit.

Linc.

I inch farther inside through the foyer into the reception hall, my ears perked toward his voice in the study. But who's he talking to?

A thunderous laugh rips through the hall, stealing the air from my chest.

"How many women do you think are lined up at my fucking door because they want to be the next Mrs. Julian Livingston III?" *Oh, screw you, Julian.* "Do you actually think Ebony would've given you a second glance if I hadn't fucked up—"

"But you did." Linc's voice is tight, controlled, like he's one wrong word from laying Julian out. "And for what? Some random ass?" He snickers.

That's right, baby. Tell him.

There are a few slow, hard footsteps, but I'm too scared to move and make a noise to get closer to see what's happening.

272

"You're right." There's a coolness to Julian's tone, like he's trying to maintain his composure. "I'll admit, it sort of took me off guard, hearing about you two."

Hearing about us? How?

"Yeah, I'll bet."

"*Mm-hmm...* I mean, I'd heard about y'all back when she was at State. Had yourself a little fling, ended up begging on your hands and knees for her to choose you..." Julian huffs out a small, humorless laugh. "Couldn't be me. But, uh, I'm just curious—did you think she was *actually* going to choose you when she had me?"

This mother—

"Fuck you!" Linc takes the words right out of my mouth, making me proud. "What, you scared that she was with you all those years, wishing she was with me?"

Julian barks out a raucous laugh and starts to say something, but I miss it when something moves behind me, and I almost jump out of my skin.

Luckily, it's only Vincent.

"Hey, Linc is in there with Julian," I explain sheepishly, still clutching my chest. Then I giggle. "I'm eavesdropping."

We all are, he mouths, circling his finger in the air.

A laugh bubbles in the back of my throat as I imagine the entire crew scattered about the manor with their ears pressed to walls and doors, working hard to get the scoop.

Vincent inches forward, and that's when I notice his leather loafers are off and he's tiptoeing barefoot toward the study. I can't tell whether his motive is simply to hear better or to be ready in case Linc needs backup, but I bend down and unbuckle my heels too.

"For ten years?" Julian sucks his teeth loudly. "Nah. She could've left any time she wanted to."

I grab my heels, holding them by the straps, and tiptoe closer too, trying to catch up to Vincent, who's got his ear pressed to the door.

"Who, the divorcétante? I'm pretty sure she said you made her feel invisible and underappreciated. *Yikes!*" Linc laughs, and I couldn't love him more. "'Couldn't be happier to be a walkaway wife,' I think she said. 'I *wish* I'd left sooner.'"

The tension is thick, and my heart is pounding *so* fast.

I just know this isn't going to end well.

"Damn, Julian. The woman had to go and reinvent herself because you made her feel like she was disappearing in your marriage."

I adore Linc for watching *The Divorcétante Chronicles*.

But then he hammers the nails into the coffin. "Rest assured, though, Jules, I see her, and my plan is to spend every day and night for the rest of my life appreciating the hell out of her perks—"

"You sorry motherfucker, that's my *wife* you're talking about…" Julian's grunt is followed by furniture scraping against the floor, then shuffling footsteps. There's scuffling, stumbling, and heavy breathing as he continues cursing Linc.

PUNCH!

Someone groans, crashing into furniture.

In the hall, I'm on pins and needles, debating whether to enter the room.

"Ex-wife, you mean!" Linc corrects him, feet still moving. "Because you couldn't keep your dick in your pants. Didn't anyone ever tell you about the eighty/twenty rule? You had a hundred at home."

PUNCH!

Again, one of them coughs and groans, sounding like he's taking an absolute beatdown, but he's too stubborn to know when to step back.

"See how I extended my arm while rotating to make sure my fist lands with my knuckles?" Linc chuckles like he's unfazed. "I hope you're taking notes there, buddy, because that was a weak-ass punch you threw.

"That's for Ebony." *PUNCH! PUNCH!* "And that's for making her sit back and deal with your sorry ass while you were fucking around with Hillary Winston and Nora Whitfield. And whoever the hell else."

I gasp, my heartbeat thumping in my ears.

Suddenly, the dull thud of a fist connecting with flesh and bone cracks the air, and then a body hits the ground with a thunderous crash.

"*Oof!*" Julian groans. "Fuck you, Linc. You're going to hear from my lawyer."

"And say what? That you threw the first punch?" Linc counters.

On autopilot, I turn the doorknob and swing the door open. I don't have the energy to assess the damage to the room or my disgusting ex-husband laid out on the floor, choking and coughing. I don't care about him.

My attention is fixed on Lincoln looking unruffled and directly at me.

"You said Hillary." The words squeak out of me, weak, even to my own ears.

Linc takes wide strides, rushing to my side, his expression urgent and panicked. "Baby, that's what I tried to tell you that night at the bar. I saw Julian with Hillary, and I was going to tell you."

A sharp pain tightens my chest.

That was three years ago.

My mind winds back to all the dinners and events where Hillary would laugh and joke with Julian, their conversations always so effortless and comfortable. I remember thinking, *How lucky am I that my friends love my husband so much?* They always seemed so at ease with each other. But now, I guess I know why.

My heart stalls all over again as I think about the half-assed apology she texted back when I called her.

I'm sorry. I'm not ready to explain yet, but I will soon.

This time, though, fire doesn't surge through my veins. I don't have the urge to lash out.

Instead, I close my eyes, lowering my head, vacillating between disbelief, hurt, and disappointment in myself that, again, I've trusted the wrong person.

The wrong people.

Julian's wheezing laughs pollute the air. He's enjoying every minute of Linc's discomfort.

"Baby, are you mad at me?" Linc cradles my face in his hands, frantically searching my eyes. "Talk to me."

"No, I just… I think I'm going to work on client calls from home today. I need some time to process all of this. I'll…I'll see you later," I say. But as I turn toward the door where Vincent is standing, eyes wide, staring at his phone, his phone pings.

Then Linc's and Julian's, do too.

"Vincent?"

His gaze snaps to mine, horror glazing over his over-steeped brown eyes. "Ebony…" He flips the screen to me, and there it is. Proof that my intuition is firing on all cylinders. That my theory wasn't unfounded.

Ellswood Prince Breaks Silence on Shocking Claims of Divorcétante's Decade-Long Love Affair

See the cheating photos that ended their marriage

I take the phone and scroll through pictures of Linc and me—kissing on the grand staircase here, in the rain outside the dating mixer, at Whisk & Whistle, and on the observation deck at Amicalola Falls.

A gasp pushes past my lips. "What the hell…"

As I zoom in, though, I notice the photo credit beneath each image. Benson Marks. My mind wades through a sea of names, trying to place it. Then it hits me.

The PI.

Cornelia hired the same one I hired to follow Julian. I didn't imagine seeing someone outside Madison Manor the night Linc and I kissed on the stairs. I'm the one Benson was following—at the mixer, at brunch with Zeek…

I was right.

A manic energy floods through me as I meet Vincent's stare. Concern and pity are etched into the shadows and lines of his face. I'm waiting for him, for anyone, to tell me this is a nightmare and now I can wake up.

But no one does.

(470) 555-3269

Chapter Twenty

The Partnership

Lincoln

"WAIT FOR ME!" I RUN after Ebony, a mix of desperate fury and fear pumping through my veins. I catch up to her halfway down Madison Manor's footpath, barefoot with her heels clutched in one hand. I pull her into me, hugging her to my chest. "Please, look at me, baby. I tried to tell you about Hillary. You've got to believe me."

"I know you did," she says, voice clipped. She shakes her head, as if physically trying to dislodge the thoughts swirling in her mind. "I'm not mad at *you*. I'm just…angry. Disappointed. Tired of watching everyone move the chess pieces around me, right in front of my face."

"Baby, I'm so sorry," I whisper, my heart aching for her.

"Goddammit!" She squeezes her eyes shut. "I knew—*knew in my gut*—that Cornelia was plotting. Then Julian shows up, like I owe him something. And yes, I guess I wish you'd made me listen about Hillary. I'm so freaking pissed off at *her*…" Her voice breaks, and she screams her release.

In one fell swoop, she was betrayed by Cornelia, Julian, and Hillary, who was once one of her closest friends, and I know it stings.

With the pad of my thumb, I swipe away the tears spilling from her beautiful hazel eyes. "It's okay to be mad at her. You've got every right. I'm here to listen, vent with you, give you advice—whatever you need."

As Ebony trembles against me, though, I sense this isn't just about Hillary and Julian's affair. It's the blog pictures and that rage-bait headline, too. The confirmation of all the levers she *knew* Cornelia was pulling behind the scenes.

"Open your eyes, baby. Look at me." She's in my arms, but distance is wedged between us. I can't stand here, helpless, doing nothing. "What did you say to me when we were in Dawsonville, hmm?"

"Linc, I might just need some space to think—"

"About what?" The words rush out, urgent and drenched with every emotion and insecurity I feel right now. "Honestly, fuck Julian, and fuck Hillary, too, if she can do that to you and still bring herself around like nothing. And Cornelia sets off a smear campaign, and what? We lose? No, I just got you back." A humorless laugh huffs out of me. "This is our alternate timeline. *We* get to choose this version of us."

Ebony drops her forehead to my chest, her whole body sagging and weighed down.

Anger and anxiety flare in my gut. "You know what you said to me in Dawsonville, Ebony? You said we can't let her win, right?" I swallow back the emotion thickening in my throat, making it hard to breathe. My lungs constrict. My heart wrenches. Every inch of my skin pulses with the fear of losing Ebony again, as if it's urging me to say something, *anything* to convince her we belong together. That I'm enough. Together, we're enough.

But I don't rush her.

I shake my head, still lost in my thoughts, a mix of powerlessness and anxiety swirling in my gut. The weight of it, the ache—it steals my wind. Rather than intrude on her moment, and even though I'm losing the battle with temptation, I let her feel everything coursing through her. I let my patience gnaw at me.

"Yeah." She bites her lip softly. "I said it."

I breathe.

"Mm-hmm. She could smear your name, you said." I take a small breath. "But she couldn't take me away from you again."

Her lips quiver.

"And what did I say?" I ask. "Please remember, baby."

A somber smile slowly curves her lips. She rests her warm hand on mine. "That you were mine if I wanted you."

I lower my gaze to our hands, nodding.

A warm breeze sweeps over us, gently tousling her hair and carrying the scent of fresh grass and magnolias.

"That's right." A rush of relief floods through me, and I choose my next words carefully. "I meant every word. I'll always want you, Ebony. As long as I live. I would never lie or hurt you. And I'm damn sure not letting Cornelia Livingston take you away from me either. I *need* you." My voice thunders, tense and tortured to my own ears.

Her hands slip around my waist, and I lower my forehead to hers, gently resting my fingertips on her face as I hold her gaze, letting the intensity of the moment overwhelm me. Fire singes the corners of my eyes. "I *need* you, baby," I whisper, again with every ounce of desperation coursing through me.

Tenderly, I kiss her lips, taking my time, sinking into the familiar warmth and wetness of her mouth, connecting us in a way words never could.

She exhales, and it feels like coming home as she drags her tongue over my lips, teasing and tasting. I deepen the kiss, loving the way her eyes glaze over with lust, and the tiny, insatiable moans that seep out of her. Her needy hands set free on my body are like fire, igniting my skin through the thin fabric of my shirt, welding the tiny, cracked pieces of my heart.

My entire body vibrates to our rhythm.

"My question for you, baby, before you get me too excited out here"—I chuckle, sinking into the lightness—"is what are we going to do about it, huh?" I whisper against her soft mouth. "Are we just going to continue allowing this vindictive woman write *our* narrative, painting us as villains?"

"Or…?" she asks, the first flickers of hope radiating from her hazel irises.

"Okay, hear me out." I tilt my head, my eyebrows raised. "We let her go low, and instead of us going lower—"

"We take it to hell?" Ebony giggles.

Tipping my head to either side, I say, "Trust me, after her weak-ass son tried to come at me sideways back there, I'm more than tempted. He quickly found out, but that's beside the point. No, what I'm saying is—we get *Chronicle*…" I cock my head slightly, willing her to catch my drift.

A real, unguarded smile spreads across Ebony's face, the kind that makes my heart full. It's a "let's make them play" sort of smile that reaches right into my chest and squeezes.

Yes!

This is what I love so much about this woman. Our connection isn't just deep because of our roots. It's more. She can look at me, and immediately it's clear we're communicating on another plane. We bring out the best in each other.

It's the slight dip of her chin, and the widened eyes, as she subliminally absorbs my entire plan.

"You know what she did wrong, don't you?" I straighten, my shoulders back, my throat bared, absolutely no bull.

Ebony nods, slowly, as if she's attuned to my every whim. "Yup. It seems she started with the wrong partner…"

A laugh, straight from the gut, tumbles out of me, loosening the tension further.

I take a deep breath, staring at Ebony, overwhelmed by how much I love her. "Exactly. You always start with the right partner. That's what I'm doing."

So, no, we're definitely not taking the high road either, trying to beat Cornelia at her own game. If there's one thing we know about calling a spade a spade, it's not a trick-taking recreational activity. It's absolutely *not* a game. We're taking books and names.

Because that's what we do.

As we give the metaphorical deck a long, overcomplicated shuffle, we take inventory of our hand—Julian's multiple documented infidelities, including Hillary and Nora, that we know of, Ebony's *Divorcétante Chronicles* platform, and both of our businesses. Most importantly, our "big joker," the president of the National Association of Spades Activities.

Then we make a careful cut and deal the cards. We're playing big joker, little joker, ace. All cards on the table first wins. Sandbagging and trash talking allowed.

Our bid is based on a single goal—force Cornelia to play her cards.

After I scoop my barefoot sweetheart into my arms, I walk away from Madison Manor toward my truck. Setting her on the hood, I gently place her heels on her small feet, fastening the straps one at a time. Then Ebony takes out her phone, swipes away the endless stream of notifications, and, like she's summoning strength from some unknown depth, positions me against the door of the car and stands in front of me. With her back pressed to my chest, phone aimed selfie-mode at us, the PopShot app counts down the live.

"Hey, divas… By now, I'm sure you've seen the pictures, blogs, articles. The endless comments attempting to smear my name. *Our* names…"

She breaks off, looking past the mounting viewer count, the tiny bursts of animated hearts and flowers, and the tapestry of thousands of comments climbing the page.

But I'm reading and loving their support for this woman who needs to know the world isn't against her or us.

I'm seated.

Told y'all she wouldn't leave us hanging. She's standing ten toes down.

Oh, shoot, he is foinnnnnnnn. My man, my man, my man.

I would pause, peace, power all day…

"And I'm here to tell you that she got one thing right. Love. I'm in love with this man."

Softly, I kiss the crown of her head.

"And yes, it's been over ten years that we've been friends. But in my heart, I believe I might've chosen him for myself if not for a few women, whose guidance and opinions I valued, telling me otherwise.

"When I said 'she got one thing right,' I was talking about one woman in particular who'll do anything in her power to see me flounder. Her influence is indeed powerful."

The comments take a sharp left turn.

Say less. We already know it's Cornelia Livingston.

Has that woman ever considered shutting tfu?

I haven't believed anything she's said.

We CLOCKED it

Exposed

PopShot, do your thing.

"Make no mistake, I wasn't the faithless one in my marriage. Period. Those pictures you're seeing? They're from the past couple months, since the end of June, when I've dared to find love—*accept* love—in my life from a man who has given it so freely without condition. So, yes, I'm in love with Lincoln Bridges."

Ebony lets out a sigh of relief that quickly turns into a giggle.

"Trust me, y'all, when I tell you saying those words to you is an act of resistance. Lord knows she wants to ruin both of us. She'd love nothing more than to see us and our businesses snuffed out for our ever daring not to listen to her.

"She was hoping this smear campaign would do the trick. But last I checked, our businesses are our own, and my divorce has been final for over a year, which means I'm a single woman, free to love whomever I choose. And I choose Lincoln Bridges."

Cornelia Livingston turns out to be a master manipulator just like her son. I'm so glad that this woman has the smarts to protect herself.

That family is a joke.

Love wins!

This woman is unbelievable!! I'm glad you've found love.

She's the type to remind you that you don't belong if you don't bow down.

Lawyer up. Then let that man love you hard and fast, right in her face.

I'm over the Livingston hype. Vile, lying individuals.

What's her deal???

"But that's not all."

Ebony's smile is almost sinister, and I love it.

"There's a good reason behind this campaign, though. She's got ulterior motives, secrets she wants to keep buried…"

The comments fly by so fast they're almost a blur.

"Which I'll be posting about soon. So, I hope you'll join me, because I'm bringing receipts.

"But for now, I'm going to leave you with two diabolical crumbs. Check the photo credits, and a Luxe Lady wasn't the only woman who wrecked my home."

Ebony lifts an eyebrow then winks.

"Pause, peace, power. Love, your divorcétante!"

Heat singes my skin as she tucks her phone away and twists in my arms and kisses me.

"Not going to lie. That felt really good."

"Yeah?" I smile, brushing soft pecks over her lips.

She nods, deepening the kiss right out here in broad daylight for God and Ellswood to see. "Now, take me on a *long* lunch."

Over the next few weeks, we move on autopilot, gathering the necessary research, establishing the house rules. Our first course of action is a purposely vague post, stating to *stay tuned for my side* on her *Divorcétante Chronicles* page, meant to keep the buzz alive and build more anticipation.

We keep our heads low, talking to no one outside of our families, *confirmed* friends, and the crew. There are no calls, no texts, no emails—and no podcast, televised, phone, blog, vlog, or stitched online interviews.

Not yet.

By day, we work diligently, finalizing the restoration at Madison Manor and setting the stage for the Winston-Livingston wedding events (Hailey and Donovan have officially banned Cornelia from the premises). By night, we sneak kisses under the grand ballroom's chandelier. Or we're at Ebony's condo or my house, making love, watching horror movies—she's got to practice her scream-queen techniques—listening to music, cooking elaborate meals, and playing Spades.

We're biding our time, waiting for Cornelia to make her move.

Then I run into an old buddy from the city council, who, via the grapevine, heard from a friend of a friend from the mayor's office that Cornelia was seen down at the county clerk's office. That's when Ebony and I decide to do some digging, fact checking. And suddenly, we aren't just waiting anymore.

We're ready to watch her renege.

You're invited
to our
Wedding Day

Chapter Twenty-One

Books and Names

Ebony

"OH MY GOD, THIS FEELS like déjà vu…" Priscilla spins slowly inside the grand ballroom, her brown eyes saucer-wide, shaking her head. "I mean, I get that you need to confront her—what she did was foul as hell—but are you really sure this is the best move? Couldn't you wait until the shower's over and corner her on the way out?"

Whitney and I exchange a brief glance.

"No," we say in unison.

We're absolutely on the same page.

First, I've given Hillary ample opportunities to reach out to me. And second, this is a three-birds-one-stone situation. Face Hillary, call Cornelia's bluff, and figure out if Hailey will fire me out of sibling loyalty. At the end of the day, I need to know where my business stands, and they need to understand that I'm not an easy target.

Period.

Although, to acknowledge Priscilla's point, my plan—*if* I can even call it that—isn't exactly ideal. Nor professional, per se. Cornering this woman at her sister's bridal shower, that *I* planned, isn't how I envisioned this going. I can't very well walk out there, clear my throat, and interrupt the "What's in my phone?" game.

What would I even say?

"Sorry, just checking on the shower. More tea? Hey, drama-magnet friend Renee, did Hillary by chance mention she's a two-faced, conniving homewrecker? No? Well, you'll love Cornelia, but be careful—she'll fabricate an entire cheating scandal out of thin air to tear you down. Anyway, enjoy your brunch. Hope we're still good to go, Hailey…"

Uh, no.

Damn, this is bad.

Then again, should I care about interrupting this event if I might get fired anyway? I'm done sitting back and waiting.

"In the words of the great divatante, Whitney Graves…" I plant my hands on Priscilla's slender shoulders and project to the echoes of this magical, gloriously spotlit ballroom. "I'm not letting these bougie, low-vibrational folks define nor destroy my happiness another day.'"

My girls erupt into howls and cackles.

"But do y'all *hear* me?" Whitney presses, too serious. "The way we apparently need to say it a little louder for the duplicitous folks in the back…" She stretches her arms wide, eyes locked on the double doors leading out to the terrace where Hailey's bridal shower is happening. Then she switches into full preach mode, delivering a one-size-fits-two sermon, undoubtedly aimed at Hillary just as much as it is at Cornelia. "Louder for those who think what's done in the dark won't come to the light."

Priscilla nods, fidgeting with the hem of her chic layered ruffle number—they're dressed for the occasion. "Yeah, you're right, I guess."

The thing is, after I told them about Linc seeing Hillary with Julian years ago, Priscilla and Whitney nearly lost it. Tatiana and

Chanel were ready to book flights home. They were furious, too. Being with Julian wasn't only betraying me; it was a betrayal of everything our friendship stood for. When we first formed the divatantes, we made a pact through thick and thin, sickness and health, come shitty men or matchmaking mamas, we'd always support one another.

Hillary broke that promise.

So, yeah, losing her as a friend only compounded the pain of losing my marriage. Our bond was a constant in my life, and without her, everything has felt off balance. We're missing a piece of us. Luckily, Priscilla, Whitney, Tatiana, Chanel, and I remind each other daily how fortunate we are to have this friendship. This *family*.

But what Hillary did…

A betrayal of this magnitude can't go unchecked. Might as well have two showdowns at the once, right?

After all, isn't that what bridal showers are for? Spending quality time with your closest family and friends before the big day?

With my hand on the door handle, I meet Priscilla and Whitney's stares, giving them one last chance to talk me out of this. I smooth my hands over my tailored, blush-pink silk chiffon dress paired with nude heels.

I'm protecting my reputation, integrity, and professionalism.

Well, two out of three isn't bad.

"Okay, so I'm doing this."

On a deep breath, I exit onto the terrace, forcing a huge, too-perfect smile as I casually make my way over to the buffet table. I take a quick inventory of the food and libations—the jasmine-infused mimosas, pre-portioned French toast dippers, and the salmon eggs Benedict platters, which are already looking a little picked over. All the while, I'm listening hard, trying to catch where the guests are on the agenda, and positioning myself just right to get the best view of the table.

We've transformed this outdoor space into a chic garden gathering straight out of a magazine. There's a sprawling thirty-two-seat table nestled between the gardens, with a perfect blend of rustic charm and black-tie elegance. It's modern, glamorous. The tablescape itself screams contemporary luxury—string lights suspended above, crisp white linens, taper candles, gold-rimmed glassware, floral-printed plates, and fresh blooms spilling from long-stem vases. And, of course, no upscale bridal shower is complete without those little towers of bite-sized cucumber sandwiches and flaky scones. Oh, and the simmering drama from the women in floor-length frocks, just waiting to boil over.

"Own a dog or own a cat…" Hillary and Hailey's mom, Mrs. Winston, calls out, her voice carrying all the way from the garden.

Ah, they're playing Would She Rather. So, they've already finished What's in Your Purse and moved on to the second game.

Yes!

That means we're officially done with mimosas and mingling. Hillary's already made her maid-of-honor welcome speech, so I turn back to the buffet table. Judging by the empty photo station and the state of the buffet, brunch and photos with the bride are over too.

Even better, the only thing left on the agenda that Hailey and I put together is refilling mimosas before the cake cutting and gift opening.

Perfect.

"Okay, Ebony…you've got to do this," I whisper to myself, trying to hype myself up. I still have no idea how I'm going to start this conversation, and now here I am, exposed, in the name of… what? Setting boundaries? Prioritizing joy? Taking away Cornelia's power to define my worth? "Good Lord, Savannah, you've got me over here ruminating in motivational phrases."

My skin prickles with anticipation, and my breath quickens. Except, as I let my focus drift back to the gardens, here comes Cornelia, stalking straight toward me.

On cue, I refocus my energy, dialing in on the goal—one-third of it, anyway.

I'm here to confront Cornelia. But I'm also going to speak to Hillary and check in with Hailey, so for now, my ex-monster-in-law has my full attention.

My heart races, but I steady myself.

"It's a lovely affair," she says, though there's nothing breezy about it. In fact, her usual smarmy tone is in full force. Not a smile in sight, just those disdainful eyes, currently cutting through me like a thousand blaring judgments.

You don't belong here anymore, they say. So typical. So clichéd. *Crawl back into your hole.*

But they don't work the way they used to.

I steady my gaze, matching her energy. Lifting my chin, stone-faced, I straighten. "Yes, just as the bride envisioned."

Play your card, Cornelia.

And then she does.

"It's truly unfortunate that the planner has chosen to drag herself, and this entire event"—she waves an indignant hand in this air—"into such unnecessary drama."

A small, disbelieving giggle escapes me. "Oh, I dragged myself? That's rich, coming from you."

"And here, when I hired you, I expected the professionalism and exquisite taste that you so often boast about." She snickers, sarcasm dripping from her precision-lined pink lips. "Now you're embroiled in scandal with such childish theatrics."

And that does it. "Do you really think I don't know you hired Benson Marks to track my every move?" I scoff, fury searing far deeper than the surface of my skin.

Cornelia gasps, falsely outraged. "Well, I never—"

"Oh, *please*." I hold my palm out to her, urging her to stop. *These are theatrics, if ever I've seen them.* "I know you're trying to ruin me, but guess what? You *clearly* think of me as easy target, a pawn in your little game, but I'm not. Not anymore. So you should be aware that I'm not going to just sit here and take it. I will fight back."

Her whole expression smooths, her eyes narrowing to slits.

"Is that what you call your sad little confessionals on the Internet? You're making a spectacle of yourself," she spits out, showing her hand.

"Does that really burn you up, Cornelia? Hmm?" Laughter bubbles at the back of my throat, but I manage to lower my voice, searching her eyes as I ask, "What bothers you more? That I've got the audacity to face the world and still pick myself up? Or that I'm not just making it, I'm *thriving* without your 'perfect' son, who, lo and behold, turned out to be an absolute disappointment and a waste of space?"

"Don't you dare say another—"

An utterly sinister smile curves my lips. "You know it just as well as I do. He's lost his job, and he's constantly texting me, begging me to take him back. And now, to top it off, he's got a child on the way with a Luxe Lady." This time, I can't hold back my laughter. I'm outright cackling in this woman's face, and it feels damn good. "You're about to be a Luxe Livingston grandma. You must be so proud—"

"That's enough!" she interrupts, her tone jagged and sharp.

She means it to be a quiet whisper of a warning, but her hard voice lands with a crash, garnering the attention of the entire garden party.

"*Oops.* We wouldn't want anyone to hear, would we?" I smile, feeling diabolically satisfied. "Then again, everyone knows *I* wasn't the one caught with my pants around my ankles."

She drags in a long breath, fidgeting with her hands.

I shrug, loving every moment of her discomfort. "I don't know, Cornelia, maybe it's not about me living my best life in my townhouse with my beautiful Lexus and Ebony Grace Events thriving—despite your weak attempts to sabotage me—while I plan your son's wedding. Which is just diabolical." I jerk up my eyebrows. "No, *maybe* it's that I'm not your little puppet, or that I'm not staying in a 'woman's place.' Isn't that what you said to me once? I think you thought I'd give up on love and waste away without the Livingstons. And shocker, here I'm gloriously in love…"

Hey, sometimes the ex-wife takes a wedding-planning gig and falls in love with the venue preservationist.

A cloud passes over the sun and Cornelia's whole face darkens, the shadows around her eyes deepening until she looks on the outside like the monster I know she is within.

Good God.

Then, just as I planned, with enough trash talking, she reacts.

"You're right, I hired Benson Marks. He did such a great job for you, after all." She runs her velvety fingers through her silvery-gray bouffant, looking genuinely vexed, as if her underhanded move is the same as my daring to hire a PI to confirm my suspicions of my husband doing dirt.

Yeah, okay…

Her voice is low, her self-satisfied little grin glowing with superiority as she inches closer to me. "Did *you* think I'd sit back and let you ruin my son's life? My good name?" She swallows, her smile taut. "I had you watched, even way back in college. I knew the Bridges boy couldn't stay away. He comes from weak stock."

And there it is.

She still thinks she's got the *winning hand.*

For a moment, I let those words sink in. *Weak stock.* My head is scrambled with disbelief. In so many words, she's just admitted everything Linc's parents told him was true.

It's the little joker.

I have to bite my tongue to keep from smiling. Instead, I take the bait between my teeth, contorting my face in false horror. Really, I should be a contender for an Oscar, for the role I'm playing.

"What?" I manage, shaking my head.

If I could cry on cue, it would be over for her.

"Yes, Ebony Grace, I paid a young kid to keep tabs on you then." She lifts her chin as she whispers, "I won't be blindsided. Ever. Of course I knew. That's why I ensured Julian proposed the instant you returned to Ellswood."

"You're crazy…" I stumble, making my hands tremble. A little too much, though, so I have to reel in the dramatics a bit.

Movement in my periphery snags my attention. Just off her shoulder, I see Hailey and Hillary talking with jerky hand gestures before Hillary turns and starts walking swiftly in our direction.

All over again, it's the switch-up.

Except this time, there's no fire igniting in my chest, searing through my veins. I can breathe just fine because the spotlight is on them. A few dozen pairs of eyes are directed their way, and I'm the one holding the APPLAUD NOW cards.

And then I catch Cornelia's expression.

That sneer.

"Maybe I'm a little crazy…" She giggles, and as wild as it is, she waves her hands in the air, like she's relieved to finally admit it. "Every mother is, in one way or the other. But also, once you've been in this town long enough, that'll happen."

I nod, biding my time until Hillary is within earshot, taking in the dark, desperate brown eyes attached to the woman who betrayed me to bed my husband. Her tall, lean frame in a lavender satin dress with lace trim. I barely even recognize her.

There's no Black Girl Magic and nineteen years of friendship bonding us. She isn't my ride-or-die, who knew the dark places I went after the divorce, whose hugs and laughter were like a balm to my heart. No, my ventricle and vessel feels like it's weighed down with a ton of bricks, and I hate that I want her to feel even a fraction of my pain.

How could she do this to me?

I'm confronting the truth. Proving that even in the face of betrayal and sabotage, I'm still standing.

I lean into Savannah's advice, willing it to calm me down. I halfway expect an angry hiccup to spill out of me. The thing is, though, I'm not so much mad anymore as I am confused and disheartened. Still angry. Disappointed that our relationship has come down to this.

"What are you going to do, Cornelia?" I jut my chin slightly. "Make him marry Nora just because she's pregnant—"

"Yes!" Her voice cracks into the air. "He made his bed, and now he'll have to lie in it. Unless, of course, you want him back,"

My mouth falls open.

Is she fucking kidding?

I've finally unraveled myself from the Livingstons. I remember who I was before Julian, who I want to be now. And she thinks I'd take him back?

"What the hell? No!" I cringe. "Just in case you don't know, Nora isn't the only woman your son made his bed with. What are you going to do about them, huh? What about Hillary?"

"Trash!" Cornelia spits out, like even the mere suggestion leaves a rancid aftertaste in her mouth. "I took her out, just like I'm going to do with you."

Hillary gasps, hurt and humiliation glistening in her eyes.

"You uppity b—" Mrs. Winston's verbal lashing is drowned out by an angry gust of wind swirling over the courtyard.

Cornelia turns, registering the audience before spinning back to me, her face red with rage. "You're fired!" she snaps.

A collective gasp echoes from here to the gardens, so loud it's almost a physical blow.

For a second, the air shifts, crackling like a live wire.

"Well, what took you so long?" I blurt out. "Wasn't this always your plan?"

"Enough!" Hailey yells from clear across the path, her arm reached out like a safety bar, holding her mother at bay, and all I can do is laugh.

Part of me *knew* it would come to this. Deep down, in my bones, I sensed Cornelia only hired me to enjoy the satisfaction of firing me later. And what's more, she gets to do it with an audience.

Lovely.

Hailey, with her mother hot on her heels, is steaming mad as she makes the trek over, wringing her hands, her fiery eyes fixed on us. "What in the actual *hell* is wrong with you?"

I block out all the faces, all the noise, and pull in a deep breath, bracing myself. Then I release it, along with all the tangled emotions, prepared to explain myself, but then I realize that Hailey isn't looking at me.

No one is.

They're all staring at Cornelia Eunice Sterling Livingston.

"What? You think because I'm marrying your son, because you're helping to pay for the wedding, that it gives you the right to disrespect my family and belittle my sister?" Hailey looks so beautiful in a soft blush-pink satin dress with her dark curls pinned up in a loose chignon, her brown eyes blinking back tears. "News flash, it doesn't."

Hillary's unwavering gaze locks on to mine.

Cornelia still hasn't said a word.

"And yes, Hillary is wrong." Hailey turns her attention to her sister, whose green eyes are rimmed with tears, too. "You are. There's no other way to put it, and honestly, I'm sad I had to learn that you slept with Julian at my *bridal shower*," she says, glaring at Cornelia.

"Oh, shucks! Are you really surprised?" Cornelia looks at the group with a pompous air of vindication, as if anyone shocked is simply disillusioned. "First she betrays her best friend to try to land Julian, now her sister is marrying Donovan… She wants that adoration, the clout of being married to a Livingston—"

"Wow!" Hailey and I say in unison.

"Don't flatter yourself." Hailey's bright brown eyes lock on to Cornelia. "My *sister* may be self-centered, disloyal—"

Hillary scoffs. "Thanks so much."

"Before you say a word to excuse yourself, you are. Otherwise, you wouldn't have slept with a married man. Period." Hailey shrugs, cutting straight to the bone. "Especially considering that man was your best friend's husband. A friend who's been nothing but loyal and supportive of you—*and* me." She tosses me a quick glance. "By the way, you're not fired. And I don't agree with Hillary's actions, but I'm not going to disown her for them either."

My mind snags on that word.

Disown.

A million scenarios run through my mind as to how one of my closest friends could do this me. But I realize…I don't give a damn anymore.

There's no reason that'd make it okay.

"I am," I say, straight-faced, not even bothering to hide my ambivalence. "Disowning her, I mean."

Finally, after months of dodging me, ignoring my calls, and only sending that weak text reply, Hillary steps closer. "I wasn't trying to hurt you, Ebony." *Well, in that case...* "I know I've broken your trust..." She hesitates, like she's struggling to find the right words, before settling on, "I'm so sorry."

And it still isn't enough.

With a decisive nod, I turn toward the door to the ballroom, ready to leave. I did what I came here to do. I confronted Cornelia, faced Hillary, and got fired—then that firing got rescinded. But otherwise? I'm free. "I'll see you at the rehearsal dinner, Hailey."

I turn the knob and leave, an immediate rush of joyous anticipation flooding through me at my knowing Linc and I have the big joker, and Cornelia won't win.

You're invited
to our
Wedding Day

(470) 555-3269

Chapter Twenty-Two

Watchers and Players

Lincoln

NEVER HAVE I SEEN A crew pack up faster than the Monday my team gets the news that the restoration has passed inspection. The rest of the morning it's all hooting, hollering, and grab-assing as we lock up the last of our equipment. Not because the job is done. No, not my guys. Believe it or not, after the "Bridges vs. Livingston Knockout," as it's now been coined, they're all excited about *The Morning Tea* replay watch party I'm hosting at my house tonight.

As far as I know, none of them are outright fans of Azalea and Yvette. But it's today's special guest they're particularly interested in.

None other than the little joker herself.

A laugh bubbles up in the back of my throat, and I try, I do, but I can't keep it in.

I drop the shovel I've been using to fill up my outdoor rolling cooler cart with ice, folding my body over my backyard bar. I'm gasping for air and letting it hold me upright.

"This is about to be so good," I say to Ebony between laughing tremors.

"I *know*." She starts giggling, too. "Every time I think about her uppity, high-saddity ass on that hideous fur sofa, her mouth turned up, silently picking their outfits apart…"

We both laugh.

That's right. After her son's infamous beatdown and Ebony baiting her at the bridal shower, Cornelia Livingston somehow came up with the brilliant idea to appear on the show that she's infamous for calling "unwatchable, low-class television." And to do what? Shame me for defending myself against her son's attack? One-up Ebony for dragging the truth out of her?

I still can't believe she admitted to hiring the same private investigator that Ebony used to track Julian to follow her.

Oof, wild.

And that's not even the half of it. This shameless woman told almost three dozen women—*with phones in hand*—that not only has she been having Ebony followed for a solid decade, but she forced Julian to propose to Ebony to keep her away from me, *and* she's going to take Nora out like trash the way she did Hillary Winston.

Like, what?

Diabolical!

And then. *And then…* she boldly announced she's now forcing Julian to marry Nora Whitfield.

Talk about one too many mimosas.

"Damn, what I wouldn't have given to be there, listening to this woman stand ten toes down. The sheer audacity…" I shake my head, borderline impressed and wholly amused. "How can she not see what's coming?"

Ebony stops dead in her tracks, half a dozen water bottles lodged underneath her arm, and looks at me with one of those stares of solidarity.

Part of me is fully invested in this conversation. I'm also a little lost in the moment, too. We're hosting a party together. Albeit it's to watch televised history in the making. But still, I could get used to this—us. We. Twenty-four seven Ebony and Linc.

"I mean…walked right into the trap. About to be sitting on camera, alongside KTLE *News Now*'s own Nora Whitfield." Ebony taps her fingers to her head and explodes them. "The way I feel like this is about to be a real theater buyout to watch a feature film."

"Might as well be," I say, scanning the yard.

It's a little after six now. For the last hour, Ebony and I have unloaded the truck, set up the old-fashioned popcorn machine, and gathered extra loungers, blankets, and even my beanbags. They're all facing my patio, where there's a half wall housing a motorized TV lift with a 132-inch television for cinematic occasions of this magnitude.

It's definitely an occasion.

We've got a fully stocked bar and concession stand, and the grill is smoking up a skewered feast.

All day, everyone—the crew, us, my guys, Ebony's divas—has stayed off social media and vowed not to watch the show to avoid any spoilers. So I know the anticipation is at peak levels. And they'll all be piling in here any minute now.

Or thirty minutes late, judging by the currently ringing doorbell.

"Ooh, I'll get it." Ebony jumps up from the beanbag where we've been lazily taking advantage of the extra alone time. Then she halts, mid-stride. "Wait, do you mind? I mean, this is your house, and—"

"Not at all. I love sharing this space with you."

"Aw, baby…" She walks slowly back to me, face contorted into a mushy, swoony look of love as she drops to her knees in front of me. "I'm going to need you to say that to me again tonight when everyone goes home," she says, suggestively, pressing soft kisses on my lips.

Then the doorbell rings again, and she jolts to her feet, rushing to greet our guests.

A minute later, the noise level goes up about ten decibels.

"Look at your old, sorry, *tired* ass," Josiah says, at the same time he steps out onto the patio.

I make a big production of craning my neck to look past him. "No Jade?"

"Oh, you got jokes?" He chuckles, his thick, dark eyebrows raised to his hairline. "I could say something about you finally coming up for air now that you're with your girl, but…"

"He's in *love*," he and Dom sing, teasingly.

I bark out a laugh. "How long have y'all been waiting to say that? Tell the truth."

Neither says a word, though, because Ebony walks out, double-fisting bottles of champagne, her divatantes—Whitney and Priscilla—plus, Manny, Vincent, and the entire crew following behind her.

"Damn right, *we're* in *love*." She flits pointed stares between Dom and Siah. "But is that why you came here tonight? Or are you ready for prime-time television at its finest?"

Collective cheers fall over the group, and they start pumping their fists and chanting, "*Bridges! Bridges!*"

"Now…" She pauses to meet each of their stares. "Tonight, we're not just watchers. Yes, my baby and I are going to feed and liquor you up in celebration. But we're also participating."

A few dozen looks of confusion land on me before Ebony explains with precise detail. As soon as everyone makes their plates, grabs a beverage of choice, and finds a seat on a chair, lounger, beanbag, or even a blanket on the grass, they'll receive a game card.

Yes, my baby made a Fantasy Foolishness Bingo Sheet.

For anyone looking to join in on a bit of friendly competition, there's a chance to profit off their predictions for how this appearance will unfold. Among some of my favorite options: Cornelia insulting Linc and/or Ebony; Azalea and Yvette gaslighting Nora with "old" or "OG" *Luxe Ladies* references; a fight breaking out; Cornelia announcing on air that Julian and Nora are getting married (and it's the first Nora's hearing about it); fainting; a dramatic walk-off; and, of course, for the truly, unthinkably outlandish, there's a wild-'n'-free space.

"The rules are the same as regular bingo," Ebony continues. "The first person to get a confirmed bingo with five in a row—diagonally, vertically, or horizontally—wins some seriously coveted prizes. Trust me, you'll want to win."

With that, everyone scatters, hurriedly piling their plates with skewered surf 'n' turf and vibrant, colorful veggies. It's pure chaos. Some grab beers and wine, while some stock up on popcorn and candy. And yes, someone might've slipped two bags of watermelon Sour Patch Kids in Ebony's pockets.

I come up behind Ebony and lean in close, whispering in her ear, "Guilty."

She bursts into a fit of giggles. "What? They're my favorite."

"I know," I say, pressing a kiss along the soft curve of her neck. "That's why I bought extra. Because I love you."

"Okay, get a room!" Whitney calls out from her cushy beanbag, snuggled underneath a thin blanket, smiling from ear to ear. "Are you all seeing this mushy, syrupy sweetness? Cute but gross."

Ebony and I deflate into each other, laughing as we earn a round of applause from a yard full of people, all thrilled to see us so happy together and loving each other so deeply after so long.

Soon, with everyone seated and Foolishness sheets passed out, I stand at the edge of the patio. "Before we get started, I just want to take a few minutes to say what a true privilege it's been working with you on this monumental journey, restoring and preserving Madison Manor, this vital part of Ellswood's history…" I pause, the TV lift remote in hand, shutting off the patio lights and taking in the sight of the warm moonlight cast over my friends and crew. I try to focus on their familiar, smiling faces around me, but my attention keeps drifting back to Ebony, overwhelming love for her prickling at me.

"*Aw*, now here we go…" Vincent groans loudly, clearly already clocking the way I'm staring at her.

A sharp laugh escapes me. "What? I can't celebrate the work we've done *and* the love of my life?"

Laughter ripples through the group.

Vincent waves me off. "We didn't wait all day to see this for you to be out here giving love monologues," he complains, shaking his head. "You should know we're fresh out of patience."

"You've got this, man!" Dom yells, still cackling.

"On the real, though, I know everyone's anxious to watch the show, and you don't want to listen to me rambling on." I straighten, pride swelling in my chest. "The long and short of it is, we're down to the eleventh hour with only the indoor garden to finish before we start up our next job, converting the historic Everwood school." This earns me a raucous round of applause. "But you all should be very proud that, with the work on Madison Manor, we've officially solidified our contributions to a cornerstone of Ellswood's rich heritage, *and* I may or may not be a believer in the magic of that grand ballroom…" Emotion catches in my throat, stealing my words. I manage a small smile.

Ebony rushes to my side, kissing me sweetly.

Our small crowd erupts in applause.

Half of me knows it's time to wrap up my speech and press play, but this feels like a full-circle moment.

Josiah loudly clears his throat. "*Wrapitup!*" He does a terrible job of masking his cough, sending laughter dancing over the impatient group.

"Okay, okay. To *wrap it up…*" I chuckle. "Thank you, and without further ado, I give you…Cornelia Livingston and *The Morning Tea*."

I point the remote, my heart full as the television rises from the wall, the screen lighting up.

Then Ebony, using my iPad, presses play on the YouTube video.

Azalea and Yvette, the co-hosts of *The Morning Tea*, face the camera.

"Can y'all believe it?" Azalea crosses her long legs, leaning toward the edge of her seat in a navy suit. "We've got Cornelia Livingston with us today!"

The camera pans to the crowd applauding. There's nothing wild or raucous about this welcome, and it's clear they're all waiting for the scandal to unfold.

"I don't know if they're ready," Yvette says, waving her *The Morning Tea* cue cards, prompting louder cheers this time. "And Nora Whitfield, the OG Luxe Lady, will be here."

The noise level explodes, both on- and off-screen.

"Oop! Gaslighting 101!" Priscilla calls, already marking her sheet. "OG Luxe Lady, check!"

After about five minutes of ads and a monologue about the upcoming season of *Luxe Ladies*, Cornelia walks out in sensible black heels and a stiff-looking black dress adorned with gold-threaded flowers. Her gray hair, as expected, is styled in a severe updo, fit for a principal handing out demerits.

"Thank you for having me." Cornelia looks like she might hurt herself trying to smile. If I'm judging by the pageant wave alone, it's clear she's uncomfortable.

Right on her heels, Nora walks out, heading straight for the audience. She shakes hands and hugs people before she even acknowledges Azalea and Yvette. "Yes, it's so nice to be here with my favorite local morning show hosts," she says, the subtext thick with animosity, especially after they've practically called her old.

All in all, though, things start off pretty tame.

The co-hosts congratulate Cornelia on Hailey and Donovan's wedding next week, commenting how honored she must be to have her son and soon-to-be daughter-in-law hosting the first event in the newly restored Madison Manor. Then, in true gossip-seeking form, Yvette adds, "And the first event planned by your ex-daughter-in-law—the viral sensation, the divorcétante—in over a year since her untimely divorce from Julian." She's got the decency to look contrite, but it's below the belt. Even for a duo who built their fame on scandal and salacious tea.

Yet everyone in the yard is loving every bit.

"That's right! Dig, Yvette!" Whitney yells at the screen. "Earn your ratings!"

On screen, Cornelia laughs, but it's clear she's unamused. "Yes, especially in light of her recent brushes with the paparazzi unearthing all those unseemly photos with the man overseeing the restoration."

The shame.

Now I'm rooting for Yvette. "Yeah, keep digging, Yvette! Get in there, Azalea!"

My guys are in stitches.

I'm taking it all in stride, though. Cornelia's got her just desserts coming.

"Yes, Lincoln Bridges," Azalea interjects, prompting everyone to look at me. To which I take a well-deserved bow.

She's saying something about Bridges Heritage Conservation and Ellswood's familial roots, and I missed the first part of the sentence, but I turn back in time to catch Cornelia pursing her lips.

Undoubtedly, she's hating giving me even a moment of exposure.

"It was a clear mistake on my part, hiring either of them, given how unprofessional they are. Who knows what unsavory acts they've committed on the premises? Honestly, it's a disgrace to the other event planners I interviewed, who would've done a far superior job, and to the city of Ellswood."

"I'm on the board," Manny says, triumphantly, shoving half a skewer into his mouth. "Got my money on either a fight or fainting spell up next," he adds, just as Cornelia uncrosses and recrosses her legs.

Looking straight into the camera, she tips up her chin. "I can assure you, we definitely won't be using Ebony Grace Events for the next one."

An audible gasp ricochets through the audience.

But Yvette is already tugging on the loose thread. "Next wedding?"

Cornelia gives a single, decisive nod.

"Wait for it!" Vincent is up on his feet, hands out, warning everyone to stay silent. "Is this it?"

One of my crew mumbles, "At this rate, I'm going to be bingo-ing in no time," and then gets immediately shushed by Vincent.

The air crackles with electricity.

"That's correct." Cornelia blinks repeatedly, but I'm sure every single pair of eyes watching is focused on the tightness in Nora's expression, screaming *what are you about to do* as Cornelia fixes her lips and says, "Julian and Nora will be wed next summer."

Oh shit.

Everyone goes wild, Vincent running laps around the yard, the audience in an excited uproar, and Nora Whitfield—OG Luxe Lady with an expensive bun in the oven—is shaken with tears.

I scrub a hand over my face, resting my palm over my mouth. "Wow."

"I called it." Ebony nudges my shoulder with hers, still shaking her head. "She literally admitted it to me at the bridal shower. The woman truly knows no limits to her dirty, underhanded work."

Priscilla is gobsmacked. "I cannot believe she just did that."

Azalea and Yvette share a loaded glance.

"Oh, *wow!*" Azalea is reading the distress all over Nora's face. And still, she grins like the dang Cheshire cat. "Look at us getting the freshly brewed tea this morning."

"And there's more," Ebony says at the same time as Cornelia on the screen, smiling smugly, before Cornelia announces that she's recently requested for the mayor—an old friend of hers—to initiate a petition to change the city's name from Ellswood to Livingston.

Suddenly, all the blaring noises, the shouting about wild-'n'-free spaces, and the audience booing her—they fade into silence, leaving me numb.

This isn't new information. I've got friends on city council and in the mayor's office. But hearing her say it so nonchalantly, that she'd erase my family's history based on a completely fabricated smear campaign because of a grudge...

Jesus.

I'm dumbfounded, even *knowing* it won't pan out. Still, it's the cue that we weren't one hundred percent sure she'd deliver.

Ebony slips her hand in mine and squeezes, grounding me in the moment, reassuring me that we're doing the right thing.

"Interesting." Yvette tilts her head, her eyes lowered like she's still turning the information over in her mind. She asks more questions about the petition, specifically Cornelia's reasons for the proposed change when Ellswood has such a long history that's so important to this community.

Leave it Cornelia to be cavalier. "Why would you want to live in Ellswood when you could thrive in Livingston? Doesn't it have such a lovely ring to it?"

The co-hosts lean in closer with that casual, knowing air, as if it's just them and the audience—conveniently forgetting the millions watching from home.

"This is it," Ebony says, bracing. "It's the switch-up. Tea will be spilled. Expeditiously."

"Cornelia Sterling Livingston…" Yvette dips her chin, her dark brown eyes narrowed. "Now, I know you're here celebrating the upcoming nuptials of your sons, but *my dear*," she says, far too familiar, "can we dig a little deeper for a few seconds?"

"She said that to me," Ebony whispers. "This is where Cornelia could change her fate. It's a small, seemingly insignificant choice, and she can say no."

But she doesn't.

Perhaps too proud to admit she isn't untouchable, Cornelia gives a small laugh. Hand to heart, like she's summoning every minuscule ounce of grace, she smiles for the audience. "Of course!"

Of course.

Yvette claps and squeals, and if I wasn't paying close attention, I might've missed Azalea giving a quick nod. It couldn't be clearer that she's signaling to go in for the coup de grâce.

"Are there any *other* reasons you'd want to replace the name Ellswood?"

Cornelia's got to know what's coming.

She gives a nervous laugh, and for a second, I think Manny might be onto something with his faint-or-fight predictions.

But then Yvette tag-teams with Azalea, dragging Cornelia, willingly, into a public scandal. "Tell us about your relationship with Theodore Bridges."

She gasps, and I'm pretty sure it's the first time I've seen Cornelia Livingston's expression resemble anything close to human.

Outright indignant, she insists, "There is no such relationship—"

"But there was," Yvette presses, really digging her heels in. "Once upon a time, before either of you were married, he was your Zion & Zara cotillion escort, wasn't he?"

Cornelia tries to recover, tossing a shaky laugh to the audience because she knows this is the end, the way she knew she shouldn't have agreed to be on this "unwatchable, low-class television" show.

Right about now, I'm guessing the words *oh, shit* are going through her head, because this is not just trending gossip. Turns out, along with scandalous, salacious details about the Ellswood's elite, Yvette and Azalea are more than titillating daytime TV hosts and fame-seeking former *Luxe Ladies of Ellswood.*

They did the research and checked the sources. Twice.

Cornelia inhales deeply, then locks eyes with Yvette. "What has that got to do with anything? It's ancient history." She flashes a small smile, glancing at Nora, who looks like she's counting the minutes until this nightmare is over. Then to Azalea, who doesn't give her any reprieve.

"Because we've got sources claiming your parents were discussing marriage"—Azalea clears her throat—"before he dumped you for Carlotta Bridges, formerly Carlotta Ellswood."

Damn.

"Isn't that the real reason, as the president of Zion & Zara, that you rejected Lincoln Bridges from membership? Why you're holding a grudge against the Bridges family, and why now you're seeking to remove Carlotta's family name from the city that her ancestors built?"

The audience is already a chaotic mess with applause.

"She's going to faint!" Whitney tosses off her blanket, waving her Foolishness sheet in the air.

As if determined to regain control before she completely loses her mind, Cornelia twists dramatically on the over-the-top faux-fur sofa, pressing an unsteady hand to her chest. "Who put you up to this? Please tell me you can do better than using disreputable sources. It's clearly fake news."

She claps, awkwardly at first, trying to summon enthusiasm from the audience before sitting up straighter, eyes laser-focused on the co-hosts.

"All of it, fake," she says.

"And she's doubling down." Ebony's tone is infused with disbelief.

Cornelia's full pink lips curl into a thin, placating smile. Then she shifts her gaze to the audience, her expression begging for sympathy. *You're going to sit there and allow them to harass me like this?* it says. *I'm an esteemed guest...*

A collective laugh echoes through the studio, and none of us feel the least bit sorry. So, the poor, diabolical grudge holder is in the hot seat. And?

Give up.

"No one is buying the victim routine," I call out to the screen.

"So, you're denying it?" Yvette asks.

Cornelia nods. "Wholeheartedly."

Azalea's face hardens, her eyes narrowed with that challenging *bet, we'll see how long the lie stands* look. Then she turns to the audience.

"Oh, *friends...*" She grins, practically bursting at the seams. "We've got a special treat for you today. Joining us remotely from their Ellswood home, we have Cornelia's high school crush and nemesis."

Cornelia face flushes, her eyes wide with panic. "This is ridiculous."

"Though they're not here with us in the studio, we're excited to bring them into your living rooms via the magic of technology. Please give a warm welcome to Theodore and Carlotta Bridges!"

As my parents appear on half the screen, Cornelia presses her fingertips to her lips, utterly blindsided.

"We'll get to the bottom of this today." Yvette smirks.

A restless, low murmur stirs through the studio.

Then Mom looks into the camera and says, "The Ellswood name should be protected at all costs."

"This is a joke!" Cornelia scoffs, fire blazing in her murky brown eyes. "You stole him from me, Carlotta, and you know it!"

The instant the words leave her mouth, Ebony gasps. "You see? Look at Azalea. It's that *you heard it here first* look."

At least honesty's got merit.

And still, Cornelia keeps unraveling, accusing me of trying to repeat history, stealing Ebony from her son before she pushes to her feet, and then, in a flurry of fire and fury, she hauls off and slaps Yvette, sending her flying back onto the sofa.

"Oh, shoot!" I press a fist to my mouth.

A collective wave of gasps washes over the world.

"I can't believe she just did that." Ebony blinks slowly, obviously as shocked as I am.

"Don't you dare bring me onto this show, attempting to sully my good name." Cornelia's fuming, her eyes darting this way and that, seemingly very aware of the security guards that we're seeing glimpses of on the sides of the screen, waiting for her. No doubt the host will press charges. "And since she thinks she's so far beyond the Livingstons when her life—her *business*—has gone up in flames, ask Ebony Grace, your so-called *divorcétante*, why hasn't she changed her last name?"

"Oop!" Whitney cringes on Ebony's behalf.

But, as an ad cuts into the truly frightening close-up of Cornelia Livingston daring either of these women to try her and quickly find out, I give her question real consideration.

It's been more than a year.

Why *hasn't* Ebony changed her name?

Honestly, it could be for any number of reasons. She could've kept it for business reasons, bills, or maybe it's just too much of a hassle. She was still open to dating again—she could've been taking *extra* time to avoid the redundant step of changing it back to her maiden name only to fall in love and have to do it twice. I don't know. How *would* I know?

But I can't ignore it.

Whether it's some prehistoric, territorial caveman stuff or not, there's a part of me that hates another man's name on the woman I love.

Which, truly, is just some chauvinistic bullshit.

The woman has barely decided to entertain *more* with me. Who am I to make demands about her surname because I, selfishly, don't like it? This isn't some old-fashioned social norms about labels and claiming ownership. She has agency.

But even putting aside feminism, why should I give a damn if she changes her name or not?

Ebony removes her hand from mine, gliding her fingers around my waist, snuggling into me with a soft moan, calling my bluff.

"Tired?" I kiss the crown of her head, rubbing soothing circles over her back.

She buries her face in my chest. "Would it be rude if we told everyone they don't have to go home but they've got to get the hell out of here because I want to fuck you right now?"

"Is that so?" I ask, instantly aroused. Except my head hasn't caught up with my hard-on. I'm still stuck on "we."

Again, it's bull…

Somewhere deep down, though, I just keeping thinking how honored I'd be for her to adopt a piece of my heritage. How much I want Ebony and I to be a family and share a future together.

Undeniably, I want everything with her.

"What if we give them another half an hour, then I suddenly feel inspired to give a speech about exactly how much I love you?"

"Oh, you've got yourself a deal," she purrs, letting her needy hands loose underneath the hem of my shirt, her fingertips blazing a trail of fire over my bare skin. "And I'll just get started on the PDA…"

We've been through a lot, faced down Cornelia's whole plan to tear us apart. Now, looking at where we are, the lengths we're willing to go to in order to be alone, it's clear how amazing we are together.

I see it, plain as day.

So even though I don't want to rush Ebony into anything prematurely, I can't sit still, either. Somehow, despite everything she already endured in her last relationship, I've got to figure out how to prove to her that this time, it's worth giving this version of us—and maybe even marriage—a shot.

You're invited
to our
Wedding Day

(470) 555-3269

Chapter Twenty-Three

Building Bridges

Ebony

"WHAT DID I JUST CATCH you doing in here?" Hailey stabs a finger into the air, her eyes wide, mouth hanging open in disbelief.

I freeze, slamming my iPad against my chest because…what even *am* I doing? And more importantly, how much did she see?

"Okay, yeah, I just… I came inside for a minute to make sure that…" I swallow hard, working on the lie. "Wait, what are *you* doing inside? Shouldn't you be with the guests in the courtyard or getting your mind right to walk down the aisle tomorrow?"

Hailey wags that finger, wordlessly telling me to try harder—and also reminding me that shouldn't the wedding planner be out there, communicating with the bridal party to ensure everyone knows their roles and places?

And I absolutely *should've* been out there…

In all honesty, I came inside for a better Wi-Fi signal when I got an email notification from a new client. Despite Cornelia's outlandish efforts to sabotage my business, a high-profile bride-to-be wants me to plan her wedding. It was such a *yay, me* moment, and I was eager to sign my half of the contract and send it back quickly.

Except when I signed my first and middle names, I hesitated.

I kept thinking about the watch party, about Cornelia's comment about my still carrying the Livingston name. Everyone in the backyard was laughing and mingling, refilling drinks and plates, still trying to find out if anyone had gotten a bingo. Then the ads ended, the show came back on, and my pulse spiked. As the camera panned over the studio—the guest sofa noticeably missing the Livingston matriarch—I stood there, holding Linc's hand as he told me, for the millionth time, that he loved me. But all I could think was, *Why* haven't *I changed my name?*

I can't think of one good reason.

Am I still holding on to the past? Why didn't I go back to my maiden name right after our split, when I'd been a King for so much longer? Even in business, I left Livingston off *Ebony Grace Events*.

So, before Hailey snuck inside, there I was, in the magical grand ballroom of Madison Manor, staring at half my signature, my Apple Pencil hovering above the screen, trying to figure out what it would feel like with Linc's name attached to mine.

Big mistake.

Huge.

I toggled over to my drawing pad app, just to see. And Lord, did I fake around and find out.

Ebony Grace Bridges.

It was so simple and easy. The sweeping B felt natural, complementary. All those soft, flowing curves, rounded letters rising and dipping with an elegant flourish, then ending with an effortless tail, before I placed the simple dot above the i. *Honeyyyy…*

It was sexy, imagining being Linc's wife. Imagining him *calling* me his wife. *Chile...* The way heat blazed down my spine and time seemed to speed up.

Except it really did.

I blink and there's Hailey—pointing and laughing at me scribbling my name with a guy's last name five dozen times.

She clears her throat, clearly still waiting for me to explain why I'm in here and not outside, moving the wedding party around like pawns on a chessboard and orchestrating her ceremony processional.

Humiliation burns hot on my skin.

"It's the, um, vendors." I snap my fingers like I just remembered this important fact. "For tomorrow morning. They need access to the grand ballroom *early*, you know, to set up—"

"The forty huge round tables?" She fans out her arms. "These here, that are already dressed in pristine white linens with gorgeous china plates and spotless silverware, and are only missing the flowers? Is that what they need to do?" Hailey giggles.

Yeah, still needs work.

It's obvious the grand ballroom has been prepared since yesterday. The crystal chandelier is a magical, sparkling beacon of hope and true love glittering over an elegant wonderland. Delicate fairy lights are strung around pillars. It's romantic and whimsical, and proof that I've absolutely outdone myself.

Clearly, proof that I'm a whole-ass liar about why I'm still inside.

"Well, the rehearsal is scheduled to start in a few minutes, so..." I suck in a sharp breath. "You should get back out to your guests."

A smile teeters on Hailey's lips. "Funny, because that's exactly why I came in here looking for you. And what did I find you doing, Eh-bo-nyyyy?" She draws out my name, each syllable dripping with accusation.

"I was jotting down notes." I rush to correct the story she's cooked up in her head—though, to be fair, she might be right.

"*Mm, mm, mm…*" The shame. Hailey plants her fists on her hips, chin tilted down with amused disappointment. "Ebony Grace Livingston—or should I say, Ebony Grace—was that *Bridges* I saw you doodling at the end of your name?"

Shit.

Yes. "No!"

She's already rushing me, yanking me into a full-body hug. "Friend, no one has to know," she whispers in my ear. "Girl, don't be ashamed. You're in love and radiating a fierce energy."

"Absolutely not." I try to break free, but she tightens her hold.

"I freaking love this for you!" A quiet scream squeaks out of her. "Honestly, this whole transformation you're undergoing… The hair, the clothes, the divorcétante looking luscious and landing legends."

"Legends?" I repeat on a half laugh.

Hailey gives me a double snap. "*Oop*, and we can't forget, leveling Livingstons."

A deep sigh spills out of me.

"No, for real, *for real*, Ebs." She blows out a breath, kisses her fingers, and presses her thumb and forefinger together, giving me the universal "chef's kiss" symbol. "You are straight up my *hero*. I want to be you when I grow up. And I probably shouldn't say this, seeing how she's about to be my mother-in-law, but the way you handed Cornelia her ass at the shower, then she had the audacity to take herself onto the ever-loving *Morning Tea*…"

See, resistance? Futile.

"*Ugh*, fine." I throw up my hands. "Yes, I was doodling my name with Lincoln Bridges's. There, now you know."

She finally releases me from her iron grip, stepping back to give herself a round of applause. "Ooh, I'm so happy for you, Ebs!"

Yay, more squeals. Love that for my ears.

"We're *not* engaged. I was just…trying his name on for size." I laugh. "But thanks. Now, is there any way you can just *pretend* that you weren't being nosy as hell, lurking around in my business when you should've been outside rehearsing for your grand wedding tomorrow?" I flash a small sorry-not-sorry smile.

Of course, my annoying little sister from another mister is having none of it.

"*Sooooo*, speaking of weddings…" She unleashes her spirit fingers at me, doing a goofy, shimmying happy dance. "Maybe there'll be more wedding bells ringing in the near future? *Hmm, hmm, hmm?*"

Because time is ticking and we need to get outside to the courtyard—and the last thing I need is Hailey slipping and telling her big-mouthed friend Renee that I'm in love—I march toward her, quiet and determined.

"Hailey, sweetie. Honey. Sugar." I force a tight smile, deepening my stare. "I'm going to hold your hand when I say this to you. Lincoln Bridges and I *just* started dating. I've been planning weddings forever, and only a fool would rush into marriage just because everything feels right, and they've known the guy forever. And I'm *definitely* not that kind of fool."

She nods slowly, biting her lip as if to stifle a laugh. "You? No, you're *definitely* not that kind of fool. Where would anyone get an idea like that?"

I'm *not* that fool…am I?

All my insecurities claw to the surface of my mind. What if all this doodling is actually just repressed teenage infatuation from being love-starved? And for that matter, at this big age, am I just scared of being alone? Is this my last shot? What if I end up hurt again? What if I lose myself in Linc the way I did in Julian?

What happens to the divorcétante? Do I become the remarriedétante? Whatever the hell that is. It doesn't even have a cool ring to it.

Worse, what if marriage isn't something Linc wants?

Lord, Jesus, I'm a cautionary tale.

Pause, peace, power.

Hailey's shoulders tremble, and it's almost painful to watch her trying to hold in her laughter.

For a moment, I stare at her deadpan, mentally rummaging through my own words, playing Whac-A-Mole with my insecurities. Everything does feel right with Linc, and I've known him forever. Isn't that the *only* reason to rush in?

Playfully, I roll my eyes at her. "*Ugh*, just let it out."

And let it out Hailey Winston does.

The cackling is downright insulting—and hilariously contagious. For what feels like an entire minute, we're bent over, laughing so hard we can barely breathe.

"*Girrrrl…*" Hailey's holding her chest. "If you could see yourself doing mental gymnastics."

I'm cry-laughing. "Shut up! I'm scared."

"It's love between grown adults, not a horror movie," she says, and I literally cannot breathe, thinking about Linc calling me a scream queen. "Girl, no need to check under the bed. You're not in danger."

Of course, humor turns out to be the gateway to gabbing, because once I start telling her about Linc and me, she can't shut me up. We talk about everything. The love stuff, yes. But the part I haven't told anyone about is the nerves. I'm freaking petrified of the magnitude of my feelings.

"How can I feel *everything* when it's barely been a few months?" I throw up my hands, shaking my head in disbelief. "None of it makes sense. And now he's been acting all nervous, and I'm scared of even wanting more. You know, it's not like the last go 'round worked out so well."

Loudly, she sucks her teeth. "Why are you acting like this is some one-night stand and he's your new boo? It's been a few months, yes, but it was over a decade of being with sorry-ass Julian when you should've been with Linc."

Well, when you put it that way…

The door to the main hall cracks open, and Hailey and I freeze.

"What are you doing here, Nora?" Hailey asks, coolly, her posture going rigid.

That's right. I'm not asleep or being punked.

Nora Whitfield steps into the ballroom cautiously, her stance hesitant, striking green eyes wide with nervousness, and I *wish* I had it in me to be mad.

But I can't even hold myself together.

A hysterical laugh stirs in my belly and explodes into the air. "Are you serious right now? You detonate my marriage, get knocked up by my ex-husband, and sic your #TeamNora fandom on me, and *you're* tiptoeing in here? Oh, you are a piece of *work*, honey."

"Ebony, I… I need to tell you the truth."

I'm breathless all over again, gasping for air because…is she for real? "Listen, save yourself the trouble. I've moved on and I'm living my best life."

The funniest part is, I thought when we finally ran into each other, I'd be overcome with hurt or surprised. At the very least, fall into a fit of angry hiccupping spasms. But no. I'm calm. Almost scarily so.

Nora nods repeatedly. "I know you are, and I'm so happy for you."

But she doesn't leave. Instead, she stands on the edge of the ballroom, her face twisted with…is it fear or indecision? I don't know. So I feel like I need to put her out of her misery.

"Again," I say, slower because it doesn't seem to be clicking, "I'm good." I shrug, confused. "Listen, if this is part of some *Luxe Ladies* twelve-step program, and you need to acknowledge the harm you've caused, or make amends, or whatever—"

"No, it's just… I need to tell you the truth." She takes a deep breath and steps farther into the room. Her fingers nervously twirl her purse strap as if she's unsure where to start, but she needs to get something off her chest.

Hailey sighs and taps her diamond-encrusted wedding heel impatiently on the wooden floor, and I fear if I don't save her from getting worked up on my behalf, the practice I-dos with Donovan may be a little too close to a seasoned marriage.

Without even looking at my watch, I flash Nora a deadpan look. "You've got three minutes," I say.

She wastes no time.

"Okay, so when I met Julian, it was at that fundraiser two years ago. The Luxe Ladies introduced us, saying we were supposed to do a segment together about news anchors in Ellswood," she starts, then goes on telling me the producers told her that Julian was legally separated from me, that we'd filed a separate maintenance motion.

"What?" I shoot her sharp, assessing look. "And you believed him?"

Hailey's eyes narrow slightly.

"They showed me the document." Nora's voice shakes, but her gaze doesn't waver. "It wasn't until later that I learned it'd been rejected by the court. I had no idea about his gambling problem—"

Gambling problem?

"Wait." I slice my hands through the air, then squeeze my eyes closed, taking a moment before I open them again. I glance at Hailey. "Can you—"

"Already on it," she says, furiously tapping away on her phone, pulling up her browser to fact-check.

Over her shoulder, I follow along as she pulls up Georgia's Superior Court website. After she searches Julian's and my name together, there on the screen are two records. The separate maintenance filing and the rejection, dated two years ago.

Neither of which I knew about.

Wow, okaaay.

"Oh my goodness…" Hailey, clearly on the same page as me, toggles over to the filing requirements.

As the list populates, I skim over *Georgia residents*, *evidence of a valid marriage*, and *no divorce pending*, straight to the part where Julian was supposed to arrange for me to be personally served with the petition.

"Those damn messy producers…" Hailey continues reading. "They sniffed out trouble in paradise and pounced for a chance at scandalous TV."

Lord, tell me it wasn't you, Zeek…

My gaze snaps to Nora. "So, the producers knew about this?"

She nods, her long, dark waves spilling over her slender shoulders. "Yeah, they knew about his gambling and his 'marital problems.' So, you see, I swear, I didn't know. And by the time I found out, I was horrified but I—I was already…falling for him." She looks down, guilt written all over her face.

"So, he needed money, and they were making him, what, your love interest or something?" I ask.

"Yeah."

The mere thought of caring about Julian and Nora feels like a distant memory.

I chew the inside of my cheek, utterly indifferent, detaching from this chapter of my life—from being a Livingston.

"I know I can't undo any of it, but I'm really sorry," Nora says, her voice small. "I just thought you should know I never wanted to hurt you, and it's over anyway. He told me back in May he'd be getting his finances together with the insurance money from the Ellswood Mill fire, but after that stunt Cornelia pulled on *The Morning Tea*, announcing our engagement…how he treated you and Hillary… I don't want my baby to be part of that family."

"Interesting." Hailey blinks way too many times to be natural.

Part of me is wondering if she's also on the same wavelength, tracking dates. It's awfully fortunate to know in May that you're coming into a windfall of insurance money for a fire that didn't happen until June thirteenth.

She thinks she's so far beyond the Livingstons when her life—her business—has gone up in flames…

"Indeed," I add, buzzing with pure, cold satisfaction.

Nora stares at me with her bright, pleading eyes, and I sense what she wants. She's apologized. She's explained. She's trying to make things right.

While apologies mean nothing to me at this juncture, I respect the effort.

"Nora, you didn't break up my family. Julian did," I say. "He's the one who lied, he's the one who cheated, and he's the one who dragged you into all this…the lies, the mess. Not you. So I'm not angry at you. I just don't care anymore."

"I…I understand," Nora says, her voice light. "Thanks for hearing me out."

She smiles and, without another word, turns away from Hailey and me. She doesn't look back. She walks toward the main door to slip out of the manor as quietly as she came.

"Uh…" Hailey's eyes go saucer-wide. "So, now you're definitely my role model, because the way I would have thrown hands—"

"*Hailey!*" I laugh so hard, letting the moment of clarity and peace wash over me. It's like I'm lighter, somehow. Unburdened, as I glance at my friend, this gorgeous bride-to-be.

Mrs. Winston peeks her head inside the terrace door and clears her throat as if she's unsure what she just stumbled into. "Sorry to interrupt—just wanted to check in. Pastor needs to use the restroom and is wondering how much longer before the rehearsal starts."

I toss Hailey a *let's do this* look. "What do you think? You ready to go get these practice 'I dos' underway?"

A few minutes later, we finally make it out to the terrace and into the courtyard, where rows of guest chairs line a long aisle leading to the wedding arch. Tomorrow, it'll be draped in flowers, a stunning focal point for the ceremony.

It takes a few minutes to get the pastor and wedding party, including all my exes—ex-husband, unhinged ex-mother-in-law, ex-best friend—settled and in place. Once everything's organized, though, I give a few last-minute instructions about guest seating arrangements and confirm Nelly and Hillary have the rings, and we're off.

Hailey's a mess of tears, staring at Donovan like it's the real thing—which usually would make me say, *Chill, save it for tomorrow.*

Oddly, I love every minute of it.

We practice the processional a good handful of times, making sure the bridal party order and timing is on point. There's a whole lot of "who stands where," listening for the beat, and watching the couple approach the altar. Hailey and her stepdad are adorable, borderline skipping down the aisle.

Luckily, Donovan and his best man, Nelly, have had some practice before—thanks to my last wedding. They take their places, and boom, we're ready for action.

My favorite part of the day? Listening to Hailey and Donovan saying their "improv vows." Straight-faced, he promises not to steal the covers, not to get mad when she puts her cold feet on him, and to resist the urge to eat Doritos in quiet movie theaters. So cute. And accurate. He'll be there to laugh first whenever she falls, though, before he'll help her up. After my own heart, Hailey promises, with actual tears in her eyes, to use his razor on her legs, hijack his comfort sweatshirts, and scream in terror when encountering creepy crawlers.

And it might just be all this love and laughter in the air, but when my watch vibrates with a text notification, my heart flips as I see Linc's name.

Lincoln

> Hey, love, just wanted to check in and see what you're craving for dinner tonight.
> Let me know and I'll make it happen.

Love.

I'm breathless and missing him all over again, my mind stuck in that never-ending, swoopy B for *Bridges.*

Ebony Grace Bridges.

The spell doesn't break until the pastor declares, "You may kiss the bride."

Time snaps back with a thunderous rush, the atmosphere charged like a lightning strike, jolting me out of my stupor in time to see Donovan getting really serious about the task at hand.

"I do," he says on a low growl before he cradles Hailey's face in his hands, kissing her with his entire body. And I mean all six-foot-infinity of him.

Lord, it's a real, full-tongue, not-safe-for-wedding-guest-eyes, whimper-and-slow-whine fest, requiring me to intervene to get us to the recessional.

Thank goodness the flower girl and ring bearer aren't here.

I don't think there's a cool collar among us. Which is why I tap out a quick reply to Linc.

Ebony

> I'm craving you, my love. I'm leaving in ten. Be ready, because I'm starving.

A small, mischievous laugh bubbles up inside me, and I feel flirty and fizzy, like I'm a bottle of champagne about to pop. Thankfully, *finally*, the caterer gives me the nod, saving us all by the bell.

"Dinner is served fireside in the patio hearth room," I announce to the guests.

Relief rushes through me as I fan a clammy palm out and let the couple lead the way toward the warm, inviting space. It's dancing with the incandescent glow of string lights and the soft, flickering embers of the fire. The rich scent of burning wood and savory, sizzling steak fills the air, mingling with earthy, sweet seasonal vegetables. Jazz plays below the easy din of conversation and merriment.

Once everyone is settled, technically, my job here is done. They'll eat, laugh, and toast with the bride and groom. Between the catering staff and the manor servers, everyone will be fine.

But as laughter ripples across the long table and the caterer hands me her tablet, requesting for me to sign her service and gratuity acknowledgment forms, my chest tightens all over again.

I look at the thin signature line sprawled across the bottom of the page, and my hand stalls. It's almost like my hand, of its own autonomy, refuses to write that name. Legally, I'm still a Livingston, but the surname no longer fits the person I've become. I cannot tie myself back to a life I've already outgrown.

I swallow, glancing up at this family I used to quietly be a part of. I'm reminded how I put decorum and etiquette first. I put *his* family dynasty before me and mine.

He had ten years to change—for better or worse.

But so did I.

No more clinging to the shadows of a past I've left behind. No more attaching myself to a family that tried to erase me.

The funny thing is, as I sign my first and middle name, stalling again, my guards are up. Not from anyone in particular but from setting firm boundaries. For the first time in the longest time, it's about my intuition, a quietly undeniable sense of self.

So, as I set my emotions aside and sign a hard period in place of a last name, I inform the caterer, "I've recently shortened my signature," and hand back her tablet feeling a renewed sense of clarity, knowing exactly what I want.

You're invited
to our
Wedding Day

You're invited
to our
Wedding Day

Chapter Twenty-Four

Bells and Belles

Ebony

FIVE RED LIGHTS.

That was how many it took before I started paying attention to my mood on the drive back to Linc's house. Now, maybe it was just my philosophizing and projecting into the universe, but this overwhelming sense of calm hit me. Like, *Stop, Ebony! Pause for a minute, revel in this peace, and step into your power. Even if it's for only the thirty seconds—or two excruciatingly long minutes, if you catch the light off Peach Vine Avenue and Peach Vine Road. Just breathe a sigh of relief. I know what the hell I want, and this job will be over tomorrow.*

In my mind, that's cause to celebrate.

So that's what I do.

At the next yellow light, I slow at the intersection, skipping right over my Calming Water Sounds playlist. Instead, I crank up the volume on Melanin Magic and roll down all the windows, letting the sweet September Georgia air rush into my car. And as I gaze at the bursts of orange and purple smudged across the sky, I yell out, *"One more day!"*

One more day until the wedding events are over.

One more day until I finally escape all the exes—ex-monster-in-law, ex-husband, ex-best-friend—in exchange for more o-o-*ooooohs*.

One more day until I'll finally get to just *be* with Linc, free to plan a future together.

A chill skitters across my skin, and I suck in a breath, my mind racing as the light changes and I speed through the intersection. Again, I think about closing this chapter and stepping into something new with Linc—how celebrating together is the perfect way to honor this shift.

That's all I can think of as I burst through the door and rush to Linc, finding him at the stove in a white T-shirt and gray sweatpants, cooking for me. A vase of red dahlias sits on the island, a "Congratulations" balloon tied to it. I can't get my heels and coat off fast enough. I make a beeline for him and take a running leap into his arms, and he catches me.

"Hi," I say.

Amusement crinkles in his stormy gray eyes as I wrap my legs around his waist, linking ankles behind his back, my hands on his neck.

His are roaming all over my skin. "Welcome home."

His gaze drops to my mouth, and I can't hold back another second.

Kissing him feels like breathing.

I inhale, filling my lungs with his comforting, familiar scent—zesty, fresh soap, sweet air, and home. I hold it, letting my body absorb him before exhaling. All the tension in me melts away into his solid chest.

For a moment, we're still, letting our bodies reset. Then we fall into our rhythm. We're a mess of ragged breaths and jerky movements, knocking into cabinets as he fumbles to turn off the fire before we burn the house down.

"You weren't kidding about starving, huh?" In one solid swipe, he clears space on the island, lifting me up onto the cool, smooth surface. "Is this a thing? Like, do rehearsal dinners usually make you—"

"Ravenous? Excited? *Horny?*"

Linc chuckles. "Wow, all of that?"

"*Mm-hmm.* Oh, *yeah*," I say, laughing into the kiss. "Nothing like processional music on repeat and knowing that in less than twenty-four hours, this project will be complete. So hot!"

Linc glides his hands up my calves, slowing along my inner thighs until his fingers reach the thin fabric of my panties, and my entire body pulses with need.

For a beat, he pulls back, searching my eyes, the anticipation beyond intense.

"So, we're celebrating?" His voice drops, turning hard and tortured as he slips two fingers inside my panties, no doubt finding me wet and slick with heat. "Oh, dear *God...*"

"Mm-hmm. If you want to," I say, slipping my hands underneath his shirt, physically overwhelmed by how badly I need to feel him moving inside me. "Hard and fast, no holding back..."

He shifts his gaze to mine, and heat swarms my body. "Yeah?"

I nod so many times, I feel like I'm glitching. My heart jackhammers against my ribs, my hips grind against him of their own accord, and it's so surreal—almost like an out-of-body-experience.

"Baby, I wanted to *last* tonight." Linc grabs my hips roughly, stilling them in place, but it only turns me on more. His huge hand unyielding, his fingers flex into my aching skin, taking control of me. It feels so amazing.

I close my eyes, my lips parted, arching into his hand until I feel like I might come undone, and *ohhhhh...*

"Please," I whisper. *I don't want to think.* I don't say that part aloud. I keep it locked in my head with all the other things I'm dying to say to him but haven't found the words for. "Sorry, wait…"

Linc stops and slowly pulls back, searching my eyes, so sweet and amazing—which only makes me want to cry more.

Lately, being this close to Linc does this to me.

One minute, I'm having fun, teasing, kissing, and pondering how I can inject orgasmic fireworks into our celebration. The next, my emotions intrude on the moment, their mere arrival disrupting the flow. And suddenly, there's an awkward silence and forced small talk, making everything uncomfortable.

Just because I finally know what *I* want, there's no guarantee that Linc wants the same thing. Not by a long shot.

And what if those red lights weren't telling me to pause and celebrate? What if they were signs to stop with all this romanticizing and carrying on because I'm not a teenager, and this isn't a fairytale?

So I keep the words buried inside, and smile, letting my hands say what my mouth can't—yet.

"Baby, is there anything you want to tell me?" Linc asks. "Did something happen today?"

I want to tell him that this isn't just love for me. I'm deeply *in* love, and all I think about is spending my life with him, in his house or my condo, or traveling the world together. I don't care—as long as forever starts now.

But I can't say any of that yet and risk what we've just started building together.

So, instead, I say again, "Please… I'm ready now," letting it spill out on a whimper, begging Linc to help me stay in this moment with him.

As if he's somehow able to understand what I need based on that simple phrase, Linc drags my panties down, letting them fall to the floor. He kisses me with all the hunger I feel. Then he skates his lips over my chin, lower to my neck, and behind my ear, lingering on the sensitive skin, relishing in my tiny moans. As he curves a hand to my ass, scooting me to the edge of the counter with his other hand, he tugs at his sweatpants, already hard, palming himself shaft to tip.

A thrill shoots through me, my body aching for him.

His voice is low and husky in my ear as he whispers, "Let me celebrate you." He begs me to tell him what I need, and I can't catch my breath.

Warmth blooms in my belly. Then he's settling between my thighs, pressing his dick into me, slowly gliding deeper until the friction is so delicious, it steals his breath, too.

"Fuck." He closes his eyes, gritting his teeth as if against the mind-numbing sensation. And I relish his holding me like this for a while, his face buried in my neck, his warm breaths lulling our tangled bodies into submission.

A vibrating sensation zips through me, sending pleasure sizzling down my spine. I'm breathless and panting. And then I let lust take over.

It surges deep, consuming me as I lift my hips, urging him deeper still. Then he slides his strong hands under my knees, opening my legs wider, his long strokes driving deeper, and it's exactly what I want.

His mouth on me.

His hands on me.

His dick filling me completely until I fall apart.

Nothing about the way we make love is sweet or tentative. It's rough and passionate, like he needs me to feel all the longing bottled up in his chest.

I lie back on my elbows, arching into his thrusts until my hips buck, pleasure coiling tighter. My sex clenches around him, my body unraveling in a mess of ragged moans and short-circuited nerve endings.

And still he thrusts again, over and over, drawing out my orgasm until his body turns taut and trembling, and he shudders over me. We stay like this for a moment, clinging to each other, my pussy contracting around his pulsing dick, every fiery ember of waning friction lulling our bodies from the edge.

"Baby, you all right?" He chuckles, spent and smiling against my stomach, still catching his breath.

"Mm-hmm."

Linc's head pops up, and for a moment he studies my face, searching my eyes. Then, without a word, he gathers me up in his arms and carries me to his bed.

He lies down beside me, silent, just staring, waiting. Without words, he's saying, *As long as it takes…*

"Okay, fine. I'll tell you." I take a deep breath, steadying my nerves to pour my heart out to Lincoln Bridges. "But first, I need you to promise that you'll respect my request."

"Anything," he says, tenderly, and I almost backpedal.

"Let's just say that finalizing the wedding isn't the only thing I'm celebrating," I start off vaguely. "I finally know what I want—and it's you."

Linc opens his mouth to speak, but I press a finger to his lips, silently telling him I need to get this out uninterrupted.

He kisses my fingertip, then props his head on his elbow, giving me his full attention.

"And not to just *be* with you, Linc," I continue, diving into the deep end. "I've been thinking a lot about my last name, and, uh, I sort of tried yours on for size."

His handsome face lights up, and it's the most adorable thing in the world when he clutches his chest.

Be still, my heart…

"I'm not done," I chastise him, playfully.

Linc pantomimes locking his lips and throwing away the key, and it must be killing him not to be able to pester me for the results of the name fitting. It's no wonder I'm traipsing around here all with my libido all hot and cold, *Night of the Living Sour Patch Kids* on him.

Pause, peace, power.

I only torture him for a few more seconds before I put him out of his misery. "It fits. So, surprise!" I throw up a pair of extra-jittery spirit fingers. "I want to be your wife, Lincoln Bridges. That's my big secret I've been keeping."

My heart is a *Jumanji* drum pounding deep and loud, summoning the magic and danger of the game.

Cutely, he tries to unzip his lips, but I halt him again.

"Almost," I say, pressing a chaste kiss on his mouth. "Just a couple more points. First, I'm fully aware of how unhinged I must sound, talking about rings and marriage when I've only been out of my last one for a year. But…I don't need another decade to know I want to spend forever with you, because you're the person who makes my ordinary moments feel extraordinary."

He deflates onto his pillow with a soft groan, like this censorship is utter torment, and I can't suppress my laugh.

"So, second, if by chance your heart is on the same page, I want to share my life with you in a way that turns every day into something worth remembering. *And…*"

Linc jolts upright, arms folded, giving me a *seriously?* look.

I'm dying at the dramatics.

"*Finally,*" I say, dragging out the word, then quirk a shaky smile, "I want to thank you for listening so patiently. Without further ado, my request is that you *do not respond* right now out of impulse, but instead, only after you've given it some real thought."

Because I can't look at him without dying a slow, tortured death from wondering what he's thinking, I turn out the lights—still starving, but unable to eat a thing, because who can eat with my whole future at stake?

The next morning, my faith in the Lord is reaffirmed. Not only is the weather app reporting a warm September wedding day with sweet magnolia blossom breezes like I promised Hailey, but my baby is still fast asleep when I leave his house before daybreak. I'm still terrified what he'll say after mulling over my bombshell of a strange proposal—or plea for him to hurry up and make me his wife, depending on how you look at it.

Either way, I figure it's out of my hands now.

I've shown all my cards, and now Lincoln Bridges must decide how he wants to play it. Meanwhile, I'm out, set to ensure the wedding of the century goes off without a hitch.

At home, I quickly brew a cup of coffee, shower, and dress in my Carolina Herrera floral embroidered cap-sleeve midi-dress with red bow-knot stilettos, simple diamonds, and an evening beat on the face. Then I dash out to Madison Manor armed with my Ever After Essentials Kit tucked under my arm.

The ceremony isn't until five thirty this evening—however, within twenty minutes of my eight a.m. arrival, the place is buzzing. Florists are installing gorgeous, fragrant white rose and red zinnia arrangements in towering vases in the alcoves and the grand ballroom. It's loud and chaotic with the sound system and microphones being tested, but the decorations are brimming with exquisite style. Both the photographer and videographer are setting up their lighting and equipment for the sunset photo, so I dip into the kitchen, where the caterers are hard at work, preparing a culinary experience.

"…and you've got the labels for the food options?" I ask, my attention flickering between the chef and the menu. I've made sure the catering staff knows the menu and serving schedule, but we've got to have clearly marked plates for our guests with allergies.

"We've prepared, stored, and labeled them separately," the chef says, calmly.

For too long, I study her even expression before a small smile tugs at my lips. "Let's see, it's almost eleven. The bridal breakfast—"

"Is on its way up now." She blinks slowly, and I can take the hint.

"Yes, of course." I nod a few times. "Thank you so much. Everything looks exquisite."

She thanks me, giving me a look that screams, *Duh! Now get out of my kitchen, trying to micromanage me and my team*, before I leave her to her it.

The thing is, I've still got a dull ache throbbing over my skin.

I plan quintessential, exclusive affairs—premier events geared toward refinement and ultimate glamour. I'm great at my job. But the one thing I can always count on is something going wrong. It's the only guarantee, and I've made a career of handling snags before they become tears. That's what sets me apart.

However, I can't do that if I don't know what the problem is.

So, after I confirm all the vendors have arrived on schedule, I run around checking in with the manor staff, tending to last-minute details.

It's no surprise with all the family drama surrounding the Livingstons—and the sister of the bride—that there are no cancellations. The final guest count is intact, including the who's who of the Ellswood elite. And likely, Luxe Ladies from other regions. Yet there are also no news vans or press helicopters hovering overhead…

My chest tightens as I take my time, completing my indoor walkthrough, dissecting every speck of dust and misplaced flower petal. I take shallow breaths, inspecting with an eagle eye any slippery surfaces, checking the restrooms, flushing the toilets, making sure the ramp I had added at the entrance is wheelchair friendly.

Honestly, I must look like a deranged drill sergeant skulking about the premises, and still, everything is going smoothly. But...*too* smoothly?

In the back of my mind, I just know Cornelia and—hopefully, no longer—Nora's fandom would love nothing more than for something to go terribly wrong at this event so they could blame it on me and Linc. Who still hasn't called or texted me.

"Breathe, Ebony." *He's giving it real thought, like you asked. And besides—he's not going to propose over text message.*

Part of me—the clearly dramatic half—was low-key hoping he wouldn't wait more than an hour. That he'd wake me up in the middle of the night and profess his undying love with a glorious, delicate, and classic diamond ring. *"I'd love nothing more than if you'd be Mrs. Ebony Grace Bridges."*

But that didn't happen, and it likely won't, because the man honors his promises.

For now, all I can do is get over it, unearth this wedding's problem lying in wait, and solve it.

Only then will I get to face reality.

So I quickly glance at the intimate courtyard where the ceremony will be taking place. Unsurprisingly, the floral arch is secured and breathtaking, the guest book is in position, and the gift table and programs look magnificent.

Perfect.

As determined as I am to find that snafu, though, I've got to admit I'm pleased that everything looks amazing, so I snap a few photos for *The Divorcétante Chronicles*—which I'm keeping just as it is, because people need to know it's never too late to start again— then run upstairs to the bridal suite.

Bracing myself for rage-fueled hair pulling and tiny, empty alcohol bottles scattered across the floor, I announce myself.

"Knock, knock. Wedding planner extraordinaire, at your service!" Gingerly, I crack the door, peeking inside.

Shockingly, there's no hitch in sight. Hailey and her bridesmaids are in blush-pink satin robes with giant rollers in their hair, cheerily stuffing their faces with croissants and fruit and sipping brightly garnished mimosas like wedding royalty.

"*Ahh*, Ebs!" she shrieks, rushing me and pulling me into a hug. "Today's the big day! I'm so freaking excited!"

"Oh my God, you're going to be the most beautiful bride." I squeeze her tight, genuinely grateful to be here in this moment to ensure her day is as amazing as she is.

But as I glance past her shoulder, I make eye contact with Hillary, and there's the hitch. *She's* what's going to go wrong today.

And yet this woman I've known half my life, who betrayed me so deeply… I don't feel the urge to spew venom at her or call her out of my name. Really, I just feel sorry for her.

She quirks a small, sheepish smile at me. "Thank you for making my sister's wedding a dream come to life."

Everything in me wishes I could forgive her. Just say, "*We don't have to be as close as we used to be,*" and move past the betrayal.

But as she walks over to greet me, I can't even make myself say, "*You're welcome.*" Instead, I say the only words that ever made it onto the page in my journal. "I can't forgive you…however, I can be cordial for the sake of your sister's wedding."

It's the best I can do.

Take it or leave it.

Thankfully, she takes it, and together with the rest of the bridesmaids, we support her sister. She's fed well with a full spread of fruit, meats, and breads, and sitting in the makeup chair.

With the same iron will, I leave to check on the groom and his men.

Again, I'm utterly surprised when I'm met with the same grace and respect from my teary-eyed ex-husband, who apologizes for everything he put me through and thanks me profusely.

Honestly, the date on the invitations could be misprinted and a tsunami could crash through the grand ballroom and I would be more prepared.

When I leave that room, I have to lean against the wall the to hold myself upright because… "What the hell is happening?"

More importantly, what is wrong with this picture?

It's like the universe woke up and decided to rectify all the wrongs in my life.

Soon, the sun is low in the soft, dusky blue sky, and as Hailey appears at the end of the aisle in a delicate lace Armani Privé wedding gown with thin, graceful straps, its sheer fabric whispering timeless elegance, my heart yearns for this romance again. The love shining in Donovan's glassy eyes as she strides toward him on the arm of her father. The heartfelt promises and the intimacy of trust and deep love as they exchange vows, and Donovan lifts her veil to seal it with a—far too X-rated, in my opinion—kiss. But all the same, I want it.

It's the gift that keeps on giving, and I can't contain my laughter.

Now, I'm holding my heart and gasping for air, barely able to stand upright as I swipe away my tears. "Cheers to the happy couple!"

"Get a room!" someone yells, sending laughter rippling through the rows of guests.

"Now you're stuck with him," says another.

Still another calls out, "Let's get this party started," lifting the energy higher.

As the couple jumps the broom and the recessional starts, I know, deep down, I've got to get it right this time. I want to feel that profound connection, commitment, and devotion with Linc—whenever he's ready.

"Please enjoy," I say, leading the guests around to the reception hall for cocktail hour. Then I walk around for bit, observing them enjoying spirits and oysters before I sneak away.

The sunset photos with the family and bridal party look like something out of an upscale magazine feature highlighting the Black upper echelon of society. The welcome toasts are warm and lighthearted, filled with joyful stories of togetherness and beautiful reflections of the love Hailey and Donovan share. By the time we raise our glasses to toast, the tone is set for a joyful—and wildly hilarious—celebration.

All my expectations for a bougie, elitist, and quiet dinner with tasteful dancing go right out the window. Between the groomsmen doing a full-out choreographed pop-and-lock dance, and the bridesmaids peeling off their shoes and half their dresses for a super-risqué lap-dance routine on the groomsmen in the middle of the wooden dance floor, I can't believe this is the magic of the grand balloon chandelier. But who knows, maybe the Ellswood elite has grown more progressive.

"What in the world?" I say, laughing.

Well, maybe we wouldn't say they've progressed *that* far.

Meanwhile, the Livingston brothers are all smiles now, defying the matriarch.

Quickly, I run over to the deejay and request a few playlist changes leading up to the cake cutting. He's bent over in stitches. "I've got you. Don't worry."

But I do.

Even though the night is winding down, I'm still looking out for the hitch, the thing that could ruin it all, and silently praying that with any luck, the more conservative guests will start to filter out before the sparkler send-off.

Hopefully.

Except when I glance over at Cornelia, dressed in all black—in protest of the way she's been treated by "this new generation," as I heard her say to one of her snooty Zion & Zara board members—she beelines straight for me, her precision-arched eyebrows shooting up to the edges of her neatly coiffed, curler-set gray hair.

"Bring it on," I say under my breath just before she reaches me. "Cornelia—"

"You think you've won?" she scoffs, teeth clenched. "Watch me make your life hell if you don't—"

"Don't what, Cornelia?" I cut her off, standing firm. Then, for optics, I fake a loud, exaggerated laugh, before I lean in, wrapping my arm around her, my mouth mere centimeters from her ear. "Listen closely. I know how much you love to make threats," I whisper as she struggles against my hold, but I don't let go. "Everyone saw the *slap heard 'round the world* on *The Morning Tea*. And believe me, most of Ellswood is tired of you trying to rewrite this city's history. You've publicly slandered the divorcétante's character—and, well, I could sue for defamation and libel, couldn't I?" I pause, letting the weight of my words sink in. "Or I wonder how people would react if they knew your involvement in conspiracy to commit arson and insurance fraud?"

I release her, letting out another cheery laugh. "Oh, thank you, Cornelia, for that little reminder. Everything's turned out so lovely, hasn't it?" Then I lock eyes with her. "Stay away from Linc and me. Stay away from our businesses. And stay the hell away from our families."

She mutters something I can't quite make out.

"And please, do let me know if you need any tips on rebranding," I say as I walk away, hiding in the corner for the best vantage point to suss out trouble, but then my phone vibrates from the outside pocket of my Ever After Essentials Kit. When I pull it out and look at the new message, my heart rams against my chest.

I'm done thinking.

Then the tiny ellipses pop onto the screen, and I can't breathe.

"Hey!" Hailey startles me when I look up and discover her directly in my face. "Do you think you can help me with something in the foyer? Someone said there's something wrong with the door…" She shrugs, like it's no big deal.

And to her, it probably isn't. How could she know that my heart is playing a snare drum in my ears because the love of my life is being terrifyingly vague right now?

Still, I say, "Sure," because first things first, right? I'm a professional.

We move at a brisk pace, weaving through the guests, out through the double doors to the reception hall, and into the foyer, where…

"Linc?"

Moisture gathers in my mouth.

I study his handsome features, a ghost of a smile playing on his lips, his easy charm as his gaze sweeps appraisingly over me. He's standing in the doorway in a sharp, sleek black tuxedo looking like a devastatingly handsome prince.

My prince.

His Adam's apple bobs, and he traces his tongue over his lower lip.

For a moment, I allow myself to feel the electricity buzzing over my skin. To believe he's here because we want the same thing. But only for a moment.

Then I glance back at Hailey, whose eyes are shining with tears.

"I owed you, and I always repay my debts." She slips away, back to her happily-ever-after, and I take a deep breath.

(410) 555-3269

Chapter Twenty-Five

Magic

Lincoln

AFTER HAILEY LEAVES US IN the foyer, Ebony doesn't move toward me. She stands there, facing me, her feet rooted to the stark white marble floor, her chest rising and falling with each shallow breath. She's waiting, tear-filled eyes fixed on me, as if she's expecting an explanation for my text and wondering why I'm here. I see it in her eyes, though—she's in her head, too afraid to draw conclusions on her own.

She told me she wants to be my wife, then asked me not to respond immediately, to give it some thought.

As if I ever needed time.

"You're staring," I say, taking a step toward her. "Are you surprised I'm here?"

A disbelieving laugh slips out of her, and she shrugs as if to say, *Is this what we're doing? Playing a guessing game? Put me out of my misery.*

"I'm assuming you're Hailey's guest," she says softly but impatiently. "You said that you were done thinking…"

"Mm-hmm. Hailey thought I should come get my woman."

Ebony watches me, her bright hazel eyes searching mine as I take another step closer. "She said that?"

"Hey, that woman can be *very* convincing. When I told her I was respecting your request to give it time, she flat-out told me that no woman *really* wants a man to take his time." I chuckle. "She said no matter what advice I got from my guys, it was a test that I was clearly failing if I'd waited more than five seconds."

She laughs through her tears, throwing her head back and smiling to the sky. "Aw, what am I going to do with that woman?"

With long strides, I close the distance between us and cradle the soft curves of Ebony's face.

"I'd say you should probably thank her," I murmur, "the way I did, for helping me get out of my own way. For helping me understand what really matters."

I lower my mouth to hers, but she pulls back, eyes wide.

"You still didn't answer my question. What does 'I'm done thinking' mean, Linc? Can we talk about—"

Her words dissolve on my lips as I kiss her quiet, the weight of her questions fading into the background. Everything falls away as she teases her tongue into my mouth, the kiss quickly growing urgent, her fingers flexing and pulsing over my chest. And in this moment, it's just the two of us, our hearts beating in rhythm, our breaths mingling.

God, I want to tell her, to explain everything, but I can't. Not yet. It's not time.

A few seconds pass before I break the kiss, lingering for a moment, our foreheads pressed together, letting the warmth of her skin against mine anchor me. "Baby, I only gave you time because that's what you asked for. And I might've gotten some bad intel from

Dom and Josiah, but the point is, I respected your request, and I *will* give you my answer—but I've got one of my own."

She closes her eyes, shaking her head. "I should've known you'd find a way to flip this around."

"Not flip it around," I correct her. "It's just a small request. A teeny-tiny favor." I pause for effect, savoring this moment, needing to watch her beautiful face react. "Dance with me first?"

In my head, it sounded smooth, *GQ*—nothing like a brotha laying his heart bare and asking his woman to dance. Right?

Wrong.

Ebony blinks repeatedly. "You want to *dance?*"

"I do. So is that a yes or a no?"

Her lips part as if she wants to protest, but then she seems to think better of it. Instead, she laughs an infectious laugh that I feel all over my skin.

"Uh, okay." I offer my hand to her. "I'm dead serious."

"I *know.*" She tilts her head, arching an eyebrow. Then she snorts. "Lincoln Bridges, I know a lot can change over the years, and far be it from me to judge, but last I checked, the only dance you knew was the Electric Slide."

A laugh rises from deep in my chest. "Oh, *wow.* Okay." My cheeks heat as I stumble back, arms stretched wide. In so many words, I'm saying, *What you see is what you get. This is what you'll be signing up for.*

"Oh my God, put your arms down." She's beaming.

"What?"

"Please don't be one of those guys who throws his arms out like he's greeting his imaginary audience." She tries to pull my arms to my sides, but I wrap them around her instead, pulling her flush to me, smiling into another kiss.

My body hums with anticipation.

But then the deejay slows the music, calling out for "the lovebirds."

"That's us," I say.

"No, it's for the bride and groom," Ebony protests.

But I assure her, after pressing one more kiss to her lips, "Baby, no. Trust me," before I take her hand in mine, guiding her to the grand ballroom, through the crowd, undeterred in my mission.

An ease settles in my limbs as I twirl the love of my life in my arms beneath the soft, glittering lights of the crystal chandelier.

It's not about the familiar faces of Ellswood scattered around us, their eyes trained on us, the low hum of their whispers floating on a cloud of a thousand judgments of Ebony and me.

No, it's so much more.

"Look at me, baby," I say, blocking out all the faces, all the noise, as I pull in a deep breath. "It's just you and me, okay? No one else matters."

She nods solemnly.

And with Maxwell's smooth falsetto crooning "Whenever Wherever Whatever" in the background, I nudge up her chin and ask, "Would it be okay if I told you a story?"

With her permission, I tell her about the reading I've been doing—the tale of Amara and Elijah, who, amidst dust and dreams, built Madison Manor. Her, with the vision and grand design to fill the walls with life, and him, with the rough hands and heart to tirelessly work until he saw her dream through.

"Under the glow of candlelight, they laid every brick with care, built every room with their growing love."

Ebony gives me her rapt attention, her focus entirely on me as we sway to the tender ballad.

"As the final touches were added, there was only the grand crystal chandelier, a family heirloom, made in the likeness of the Baccarat chandeliers Amara's grandmother had told her stories of."

"Oh my goodness." Ebony's mouth is on the wood-slatted floor, her eyes saucer-wide. "No!"

I give a single nod. "Mm-hmm."

"I've never heard this part of the legend. Go on."

"Elijah pulled Amara close…" I tilt my head, squeezing Ebony to me. "They danced, slow and easy, beneath its warm, sparkling light. Their laughter filled the air as the manor seemed to breathe with them, sighing with the love they'd built."

She swallows hard, still shaking her head. "I love this so much."

"Legend has it, anyone who dances beneath that crystal chandelier"—at the same time, we both look up, then deflate into laughter—"with their true love will be bound together forever, hearts as one, love eternal. But…"

A gasp pushes past Ebony's lips. "But?"

"Okay, hear me out, because I've got a theory." I tip my head to either side. "So, couples were coming to Madison Manor, scrambling to get under the chandelier with their boyfriends, new boos, situationships, whatever."

Ebony winds her hand in circles, signaling for me to wrap up the editorializing.

"My point is, two people Electric Slide and share a peck under this chandelier thinking they'll find the same magic that Amara and Elijah found, right?"

"Mm-hmm." She rolls her eyes playfully.

"Well, I feel like they've forgotten the most important part." I shrug, hoping it's obvious to my baby, too. "They *built* this place. There was construction going on—by candlelight, no less. They made this place their own, shedding blood, tears, and sweat inside these walls."

The music slows.

I see the exact moment the dots start connecting.

"Like us," Ebony says, piecing it all together.

"Yes!" I throw my head back, blowing out a breath, vindicated. "Baby, *yes*. We didn't just set foot into this manor, dance a stilted two-step, kiss for five seconds, and keep it moving. We *re*built this place to welcome others. You filled it with life."

She reaches back, removing my hand from her waist to place it over her heart. "These rough hands worked to bring my vision to life."

I nod repeatedly, overcome with joy.

My baby gets it.

"Madison Manor was Elijah's gift to Amara." I brush a chaste kiss over Ebony's lips. "I mean, they did it all together, but *he* worked like crazy to give her the dream. So…"

"So…" Ebony prompts me, her eyes narrowed.

And that's when I realize the music… Yeah, it's not slow for the lovebirds.

Chancing a glance around the ballroom, I notice almost everyone is surrounding the stunning, six-tiered, semi-sculptural buttercream wonder. *Almost* everyone.

"Um, baby?"

Ebony's brow crinkles. Then she slowly follows my line of vision to a fuming, diabolical lady in black and her disgraced son.

"Oh, don't worry about her," Ebony says, then laughs. "She won't be bothering us anymore."

"She won't?"

The funny thing is, I was so focused on my plan when I led her into the ballroom that I didn't even notice Cornelia and Julian. Or Nelly, holding them back. I didn't actually see *who* was looking at us. I just figured all eyes would be on us because…well, because I'm the man who's stepping into the groom's brother's shoes.

Also, Ebony's scheduled *Divorcétante* post, calling on all Julian's mistresses to come forward and join a support group, *might* have gone live during the ceremony.

But now, it might be best to just dash.

I grab her hand, taking advantage of the cake-cutting distraction, and pull her out of the ballroom. We race down the hall, and I'm so eager to reach the indoor garden just ahead.

"Lord, I swear Cornelia's eyes were about to shoot laser beams, the way she was glaring at us." She's breathless and beautiful, still giggling. "So, what's the plan? I've got to stick around until the sparkler send-off, but we can definitely hide out in here."

"It's a good thing Cornelia doesn't know we've discussed teaming up for a sweepstakes for 'one lucky support group member'..." I chuckle and wince. A wedding planned by Ebony Grace Events and hosted at my next restoration property being the prize?

I'm already dreaming of the cease-and-desist notices clogging up my inbox.

Ebony's still catching her breath in the corner of the room, poking around at a small hanging ficus. "She'd have an entire conniption," she says, absently.

But soon, the humor fades.

When I don't say anything for a beat, she shoots me a sidelong glance as if it's just occurred to her that our presence in this garden isn't exactly accidental.

This isn't just a garden. Really, it's more of an overzealous potting room, with lots of garden tools, water cans, and bags of rich soil used to prepare plants for the conservatory. The shelves are lined with an array of terracotta and ceramic pots. There's a long, weathered wooden table with, overwhelmingly, lots of potted flowers blooming in vibrant colors at varying stages of growth.

Mostly, I love the soft, natural moonlight streaming through the windows overhead, and the air, thick with an earthy-fresh, floral scent.

But also, it's quiet in here.

"To answer your question…" I say, choosing the rest of my words carefully.

Ebony tosses me a glance, all the way in, as she hovers by a terracotta pot, sniffing the pink flowers spilling over. "Yeah?"

"When I said I was done thinking, I meant, of course"—I lean against the door to the conservatory, making sure I've got her attention—"that my heart is on the same page, Ebony. I've never needed time to know I want to spend my life with you. Every minute of the last ten years we've spent apart felt like I was living my life on pause."

This gets her attention.

She straightens, turning all the way around to face me.

"I want to be with you, to share every day, every moment, writing our legend. And I'll work like crazy to give you the dream, Ebony."

Reaching back, I open the conservatory door for her and step aside for her to enter.

Light pierces through the glass walls and in between the lush greenery and bright, fragrant flowers spilling from every corner. Twinkling fairy lights add a little whimsy, but it's the focal point, anchoring it all together at the center of the room, that delivers the magic.

"Linc, I can't believe you built me a waterfall," Ebony says, her voice thick with emotion.

I step behind her, slipping my arm around her waist, holding her close. Together, we stand mesmerized by the sparkling water tumbling down the textured stone wall, its cascade framed by a blanket of lush foliage and bright blossoms.

We're captivated by the rhythm of the water, neither of us speaking. Her breath is steady, but I sense her curiosity growing.

"You know, I wasn't even supposed to be tutoring history that day," I say, my mind traveling back like I never left. "My friend had a wedding to attend out of town that week, so I said I'd cover him. It wasn't a big deal. Just an everyday choice that felt inconsequential at the time."

She rests her head on my shoulder, listening.

"It wasn't until I walked into the library, and there was the new girl, that I knew that choice had changed the course of my life." Tears singe the corners of my eyes. "Because with a single look, she stole my breath. I'm pretty sure I fell in love with you that day."

"Oh, Linc."

I kiss the crown of her head. "But, oh, the eldest son of Ellswood's beloved late mayor and the Zion & Zara chapter president spotted her first. And he was tall, athletic, handsome—the quintessential small-town prince. So I waited as you held hands and wore his letterman jacket in the hall."

She swallows, shaking her head. "I didn't know."

"And as he escorted you to cotillion, call me crazy, but I was still holding out hope. I even knew that your mothers had marriage designs, plotting behind the scenes. As hard as I tried, I couldn't ignore the way I felt about you when I saw you the night we shared in college. And now, here we are."

"Finally."

"Like water, we found a way," I say.

I flex my fingers, restless, still working up the nerve, my heart racing as I step back. I'm moving on autopilot, the question I've dreamed of asking her repeating in my head, and I'm helpless to the desperate urge to get down on one knee, to make this moment perfect.

And then she turns.

Tears glisten in her eyes when I kneel before her, holding the sparkling two-carat, precision-cut symbol of my promise, capturing the light.

"Ebony Grace," I say, my voice steady, "if you're at all still interested in a clean, decent-smelling, gray-eyed Spades champ—cute, consistent, and committed—I'd love nothing more in this world than if you'd be my wife. Will you marry me?"

"Yes!" Ebony laughs through her tears, and I rise to my feet, overjoyed, kissing her with every fiber of my being. She smiles against my lips. "You make everything feel like magic, Lincoln Bridges."

"And you're the reality I've been waiting for. I don't want to miss a single moment of us. Not now, not—"

Outside, a loud succession of pops steal our attention.

We glance up through the glass ceiling as fireworks explode across the dark sky in brilliant bursts of red, white, and gold. They flicker against the windows, casting dazzling reflections across the room, followed by the glow of sparklers twinkling in the distance.

As I slide the ring onto Ebony's finger and scoop her up into my arms, twirling her around, her laughter mingling with the crackle of fireworks, it's as if the entire world is celebrating us, one magical, sparkling moment at a time.

Beneath the fireworks' shimmering glow, our hearts are beating in unison, filled with the same magic, knowing ours is the kind of love that lasts forever.

You're invited
to our
Wedding Day

You're invited
to our
Wedding Day

Acknowledgements

Writing a book this grand was both an incredible opportunity and an amazing escape into a new world. It's filled with twists and turns, flawed but beautiful characters, fashion, messy, immersive love and so much delightful drama that I crafted with you in mind.

To the readers, reviewers, social media fam, and booklovers who've been with me through friendship contracts, love and games, and have become part of my Sister Circle. Thank you for picking up this book. Whether you laughed, cried, or threw the book because your flabbers were thoroughly ghasted at the lifestyles of the flawed and fabulous… I'm grateful for the time you spent with my words. Thank you for your unwavering support, encouragement, and enthusiasm for the whirlwind journeys I get to take with each new book. Your kind words, beautiful posts, and excited DMs are the fuel that carry me through every late night, hair-pulling moment of doubt.

An arms-wide-open thank you to Keisha, Toya, Tianna, Lauren, and everyone with Honey Blossom Press for the honor of helping launch this new chapter in publishing. Thank you for making this story shine and amplifying my voice. It has truly been an unforgettable journey and I'm excited to bring more Divatante joy to shelves.

To my Wordmakers (Tasha L. Harrison, Gabrielle Brown, Karmen Lee, Raeshawn, Meka James), Plot Twisters (Margo Hendricks, Kelly Cain, Monique Fisher), BWP, and Denise N. Wheatley, thank you for your friendship, plotting sessions, Zoom meetings, and for cheering me to the finish line. I'm lucky to have you. I'm learning to prioritize ruthlessly and decline compassionately.

To my Fam Bam, Daniel Heintzelman and my girls. Thank you for believing in me and supporting me. Knowing you're proud of me means so much more than you'll ever know. I love you.

And finally, Mommy and Daddy, your presence in my life is a gift I'll never take for granted. Thank you for loving me and lifting me up.

Discussion Questions

1. What surprised you most about *The Divorcétante*?

2. Which scene has stayed with you the most?

3. Would you fall for Ebony or Linc?

4. Strong friendships play an important role in both Ebony's and Linc's lives. What was your favorite moment that highlighted those connections?

5. How does the title work in relation to its contents? If you could give the book a new title, what would it be?

6. Was it the scandal, the romance, or the steamy scenes that surprised you most about *The Divorcétante*?

7. Which character's motives caught you off guard the most?

8. The media plays a major role in Ellswood. Between the news headlines, *The Morning Tea*, *Luxe Ladies of Ellswood*, text messages, and *The Divorcétante Chronicles*, which would you want more of, and why?

9. If you were to re-read this book, what details do you think would stand out the second time around?

10. What do you imagine happens to Linc and Ebony after the final chapter?

11. Which Divatante would you love to see take center stage in a future book?